The Voice of the World

Tome I

The Awakening Arc

A.J. Forster

ISBN: 978-1-7391557-4-2

ORSCHAL DOMINION
CYTHEA
THUNDREEN
THOUSAND ISLES
SHAHLEIS
KHEDA ISHAN
ZAKOET

Bhakto River
Kamol River
Ghultahir Forest
Damchoe Mountains
Tsundue Forest
Rapton Gulf
Chokphel Island
Tenzen Plain
Nyandak River
Location names scribed by
Cythean cartographer Sedilia Gessler.
Original names provided by
Orschallian cartographer
Largacreth Cevalit.

Table of Contents

Dear savant

I wish you finish this book

Before the book finishes you.

Vincentas

Chapter I

"Is it me, or is this thing starting to smell?" Fleur complained. They carried the chained coffin under ashen light, after disembarking from Konniak's commercial airdock.

"Implausible. Thurible dispels all odours." Arno, the Chanter, led them on. Faunish hooves clopped on wet stone, dull-brass thurible smoked by his side. It was only a matter of time before Fleur pulled Arno into another verbal confrontation.

"Doubt it priest. You carry this thing, and you'll smell what I'm smelling." Fleur, the Combatant, murmured. Amalgamation of neglected architecture, cracked cobble and rusting, corrugated iron, overshadowed their ascension to Upper District. Deserted streets a destitute companion for a quiet journey, except Fleur's words and pounding, heavy boots echoed with each laborious step.

"You smell what you want to smell, Combatant." Arno replied. The Chanter did not like being called priest, even though he served the Continental Church and its military wing. Terraced houses grew narrower, darkness created that undesirable affect in Konniak's honeycombed city. Black iron wrought Gaslamps, cast vague yellow putrid orbs, its artificial glow nothing but hinderance through hissing steam and eternal night.

"Smell what I want to smell? Want to smell beer, bath, maybe a man." Fleur sang.

"I want to smell quietness." Vincentas's rasping voice echoed within Konniak's walled, corroded terraces and forgotten alley's, carrying his voice with a magnified power. The dull quietness broken by metallic, piping hiss.

Footsteps haunted their walk. Windows closed with suddenness, denizens in rags drew their shawls, shaking hands on bowlers tipped a salute in their direction. The desired effect of an Inquisitorial retinue walking through a close-minded community.

A loud toll knelled through the corrosive air. Vincentas looked up, hoping to see the Inquirer Hall. In any other city, at any other night-time, it would have been normal to see the moon, but there was no moon. No moon could be seen in Konniak, even in Upper District.

"Lucky. Not far now." Fleur broke the silence between deep, long breaths. Vincentas admitted he was not getting any younger, carrying the coffin made him feel his fifty-six years in all their strained agony.

"Keep moving. Don't stop." He instructed and his retinue obeyed.

Second toll hummed through his core. A call to pray for the Continental Church, a call most habitants of Konniak would never hear. A call he never answered.

Rounding a street corner, a gated fence speared their path. Motley group of people queued, their impatience a rhythm of feet tapping the road. Whispers grew, turned heads followed, murmurs churned to gasps.

"Bless you, sir." One voice called out.

"Death to the unbeliever."

"Praise the Inquisition." A shaking voice prayed. Shouts filled with fear than adulation, Vincentas expected it more than Konniak's unclean stench.

The mob parted, yielding the Inquisitorial retinue a wide berth, as if they had the plague. The denizens queued for a slithering chance at work or to move between districts, waiting for candlemarks, even days, to pass between gated sections.

"Should carry one of these around more often." Fleur laughed, patting the wooden coffin.

The coffin contained a dead Mystic. Pursued, hunted and killed by the Inquisitorial retinue. She was no older than Fleur, hiding outside Drachenbar, posing as a crofter. The battle, which he could not remember, ended seven days ago and she was starting to smell.

"Inquisitorial retinue coming through." Barked a disgruntled Arbiter of the Law. Clothed in thick pauldrons they looked wider than any man, their desired intension. Fenced gates screamed open, and they passed through the opened gateway.

"Thank you, big boys. Ooh a girl too." Cooed Fleur, as usual. She only flirted to rile Arno, toyed with his stringent sense of morality. Vincentas allowed it, she was a Combatant after all and one of the best. It never affected her combat ability.

"Close the gates." The Arbiter ordered, after the retinue passed. The Arbiter's grim jawline and scowling lips caught Vincentas's eyes, their remaining features lost behind low, black sallet helm. Image was power, for

Arbiter and Inquisitor. The less human they appeared, the easier their job, to civilian and Mystic alike. The tattooed "I" covering his nose gained an irritating itch.

He looked up, murky light paved their way. An orb of paleness, flared and ebbed, lay held in blackened, rising fingers. The Inquirer Hall. Shadowed spires, angular spiked spirals and extended metallic arms grew from the body of the building, like branches from a decaying tree.

"At last, back we are." Guttural tone of Dehqan cursed. He did not blame the Sabanese Combatant, it was not his religion to fight for.

"Drop this dead weight off then straight to Gin Alley." Fleur licked her lips.

"Stick around, retinue." Vincentas piped up, taking deep breaths while ascending granite steps to a levelled, flat area before the rising Inquirer Hall, darkness eclipsed them under the shade of the Inquisition Headquarters.

The plaza threatened to drown them in isolation and insignificance. If it contained a full congregation, it would take a day to cross. During the Purifier Rebellion, and the Unification War, people flocked for eternal redemption, obtain a slither of hope or bestowed a patronage by the Continental Church.

Now it was a void.

"Quieter here than the Interrogator." Fleur mumbled. Interrogator Reticence walked behind him holding the back of the coffin parallel with Dehqan. Faint sighs of old vestments signalled the giant remained. He was always silent, unlike those he worked on. Interrogator's take vows of silence, Vincentas had not even heard Reticence speak since the torturer joined him six years ago. His previous torturer, Miseres, overwhelmed by an Afflicted.

"Not long now." He urged through gritted teeth. The quicker they offloaded the coffin, the better for his aching arm and burning legs.

"Should use cart. Cart bear weight." Dehqan complained.

"Cart wouldn't have made it through here. Would have to wait till morning, with this stinking thing." Vincentas replied, not looking over his shoulder.

"See? Even your old pal agrees this thing stinks." Fleur chimed in, talking to Arno's back. The Faun did not reply. They arrived before dusk at the airdock. Red sun died in the west. It would be the last time he would see natural light for some time, but a minor inconvenience. Even in the Upper Reaches, with the pampered perfumed echelons of Konniak, sunlight a rarity wealth could not afford.

As they approached the Inquirer Hall, its black building drank bright light from standing braziers and distant looming Gaslamps. Dense as factory smog, the glass orb of the observatory shone within the talons of the structure's spires, stonework clasped the ball of glass as sure as a hand would grip a fortune crystal for the ignorant.

"Mystic for the morticians." Arno declared, stepping aside as a group of attendants neared, their heavy, rushed steps rustling in his ears. They were eager, spoke of their naivety and youth.

"Greetings Inquisitor, welcome back and a glorious slaying for the Inquisition." A rotund man bundled forward. Round in his robes, a red tabard stretched neck to naval, on most it hung loosely, showing poverty through hunger.

"Lower." Vincentas breathed. The four lowered the coffin until it thudded on the concrete. Hollow, wooden sound knocked twice, signalling the body's stillness. Four attendants, robed in blue cassock, black cowl and wearing the red interlocked "C" on their back and breast, picked up the coffin and headed towards the Inquirer Hall.

"Sign here, please." Cleric handed Vincentas a scroll tied to hardened wood for legible signatures. A burning candle attached to the board, in a dirtied glass, shone little light. He watched the coffin carried away, with as much trouble and complaining his own retinue made.

A hand circled the obsidian hilt of his rapier, expecting the coffin would move, break apart, and the Mystic would fight one last time. Vincentas's warped vision did not turn into reality. The grim procession carried the coffin within the Inquirer Hall.

"Inquisitor?" A squeak from the clerk. He sighed it and turned back to his comrades.

"Have three days leave. Meet here on the fourth morn." Looking at each of his retinue. Fleur, Arno, masked Reticence and Dehqan. They went their separate ways. Arno, as usual, waited.

"Inquisitor, you have not signed with your surname." Stammered the clerk, who grew silent under the Inquisitor's gaze.

"I never do." The Inquisitor broke his stare before the boy shattered. Heading for the Inquirer Hall, smoking incense, sweet and pungent, lingered as he walked, knowing Arno followed. He stopped, cursing under his breath. Turning around, he looked at the boy carrying his haversack, who he accosted at the dock. Age showing itself.

"For your service to the Inquisition." Vincentas took his haversack, no older than eight. Dirt smeared a gaunt face. Rummaging through the coin satchel at his belted waist, he produced a coin and handed it to the boy, whose eyes widened, blue stars flashing and daring not to blink.

"Thank you, my lord, my sir." The boy took the hexagonal coin, a Hex, or six-pence, worth more than a week's salary in the lowest of Konniak's districts. Grasping the coin and bowing, the boy sprinted into dawn's redness.

"Twice generosity has afflicted you." Arno mused.

"The retinue served well hunting the Mystic, the boy served by carrying my haversack. We must always pay servitude." Vincentas turned and headed back to the Inquirer Hall.

He climbed the dais steps; isolating footsteps shadowed his own during the ascension. Several doors, the extent of their height, came to the first overlooking balcony, remained open. Precious light escaped ajar doors, spilling golden contents.

Removing his cockel hat, the first visible symbol of being an Inquisitor, Vincentas entered the Inquirer Hall, already hearing the numbing chatter and buzzing conversation. Already he was eager to leave. Removing his greatcoat, he proceeded into the building of his profession.

To call the Inquirer Hall a building was blatant injustice and borderline heresy. The darkness outside merged with industrial, bleak surroundings of Konniak's high-rise dwellings tricked the eye. Robed clerks, cockel-hat wearing Inquisitors, thurible holding Chanters, grim faced, multi-weapon carrying Combatants huddled in their retinues. Their numbers small and lost within the vastness they occupied.

Vincentas headed towards the ledger. Each Mystic kill had to be recorded for official reasons. It stopped rogue Inquisitors slaying who they wanted for profiteering, which was not uncommon during strife, warfare and before the formation of the Inspectors, an independent body who monitored the Inquisition.

His curiosity and concern led him left, away from the ledger, laying ahead with no queue, an old man sat beside the plinth containing the opened book. Eyes stayed clear of the glassy reflective walls he walked between, which rippled with a sea of letters carved and inked onto polished metal.

Ignoring the wall of letters which grew to words, words to countless lists, a countless list of dead, heroic Inquisitors and valiant servants of the Continental Church. An aisle of dull iron gleaming under candlelight. Even the floor, echoing with his harsh boots, glazed with a reflective sheen.

"Unlikely will he be listed." Arno insisted, but Vincentas had to check. A scribe, doubled over with chisel and ink-well in hand, stencilled another name onto the list at the far end of the aisle. The latest casualty against the unknown. A warrior lost against the Mystic menace. An endless war.

Ignoring Arno, he headed towards the scribe. Two candles lay perched on a black iron stand, aiding with minimal light for his morbid duty. Vincentas read those above the scribe. *Toran Inquisitor, HighSun season. Found north Cythea. Modares Combatant, HighSun season. Found north*

Cythea. Amalindis Interrogator, HighSun season. Found north Cythea. They were recent, the iron fillings hanging off their carved letters. 1872 lay above them. This year. Their last year.

Vincentas held his breath as the scribe stood up, groaning on aging knees. He could sympathise. The scribe moved aside, leaving his candlelight to shine on the recently carved name in the ironwork. *Bekir Combatant.*

"He still lives." Arno's voice echoed in the iron aisle. Vincentas turned, looking at his Faun Chanter. Brown eyes sunk deep within a shrivelled face. Leather worn skin as creased as a dying leaf.

"An absent name does not mean life." He replied. They found bodies of Inquisitors weeks after a Mystic encounter. It would have been closure for Athgeric's disappearance.

"We'll pen our hunt, then rest old friend." He placed a hand on Arno's bony shoulder. Vincentas removed the hand and walked away, leaving the dead as they were alone, remembered only on iron and in silence.

Footfalls reverberated on stone flooring, as they walked to the ledger, Arno and his thurible welcomed company. He stood before the raised plinth, looking down at the opened book.

Inquisitor Cinzia kills Mystic, outside Riemkeler, the 14th day of LeafFall season. The last entry. Thirteen days ago.

"Inquisitor name?" A robed scribe stood behind the plinth, raised and looking down. She was young, too young to be associated with the Inquisition. Under dying candlelight, Vincentas could see ignorance within the starlight eyes of the bewildered youth.

"Vincentas. Inquisitor Vincentas." He dipped the used, smooth quill into the last vestiges of the ink well.

"One moment, sir." Ruffling clothes signalled the scribes' departure. He catalogued the Mystic slaying. Knuckles ached by tracing letters; words struggled to form in joined cursive. Finishing his name and title, he looked at his hand, frozen in agony. Thumb did not move as commanded, fingers stiffened against his will.

"How many days into LeafFall?" He rasped, switching much needed attention away from failing ailments.

"27th LeafFall day. Incorrect, according to Segeric Calendar or the Guilliel Almanac." Arno stated in his stoic manner, as usual.

"27th would do. Old friend." Vincentas's hand moved to his will, bound by thoughts to continue writing. Frustration melted away.

"Penny for troubles. Penny. Penny." Croaked the sitting man beside the plinth. The sitter's smell made his head turn. He smelt like a corpse. Even the aromatic thurible did not dispel the man's stench.

"No penny on me, old man." Vincentas continued writing. Paying no heed to people who wanted things was a sure way to be rid of them. It was the Cythean way.

"Penny for troubles. For a dying Inquisitor." The man's debilitating voice made him grip the quill tighter.

"Death comes to us all." He continued writing, the quill pressing hard into the thin, yellow paper threaten to carve into the ledger.

"You. You. Penny for troubles." A bandaged hand shook in his periphery. The ragged, pungent man looked up. One beady black eye glared, the other hidden behind brown stained bandages. Crusting puss formed yellow tears down ruined, unwashed liver-spotted face. The very visage of death stared back, along with unescapable age.

"For your troubles." Vincentas rasped. His free hand reached up to small caches strapped diagonally across his chest. Retrieving one wooden bolt for his handbow, he dropped the ammunition in the decrepit lap.

"Take that. Load it. And remove yourself from your troubles." The Inquisitor never broke eye contact with the shaking man, as he looked at the handbow bolt, picking it up a hand with missing fingers and peered back, the wanton need of desperation vanished from the remaining eye replaced with a hate he only knew too well.

"You. You." The man whimpered. His words lost in dying sobs. Vincentas had no time for it. This was not the profession that saw retirement, old Inquisitors a rarity, broken Inquisitors a blight.

"Greetings Inquisitor Vincentas." A deep, resonating voice shook his guts while writing the entry for the Mystic kill.

He turned, a broad-shouldered Chaplin, naturally wider than any Arbiter he had seen before, stood in front of him. The two subordinates flanking the Chaplin looked like children in comparison, but they were at least Fleur's height.

"Chaplin." He nodded, returning the quill to the inkwell and leaving the spluttering, pungent man to his ruin.

"Blessed are vigilant, strong ignited in fire of prayers." The Chaplin enunciated each syllable in his thick tone. There was no time for prayers, church, or faith. He lost that on joining the Inquisition.

"Prayers give strength to sword and my will." His reply measured, but courteous. The Chaplin could have been an Interrogator, his stature alone would make anyone confess.

"Entrants available, Inquisitor. Guardianship they need. Your will, testing." The Chaplin turned and walked away, his flanked Clerics beside him. Entrants. New Initiate's to the Inquisition, unbloodied, untested. Vincentas had no time for hangers on, he needed to find Athgeric the closet thing he had to a friend since joining the Inquisition, except for Arno, who had been there since the harsh beginning.

"Haven't had an Entrant since Adaline." He remembered. Four years ago, she was young, but not naïve. From the streets like Fleur, but without the violence and gang affiliation. Adaline was an Inspector, as far as he knew. She had the appetite for it, always asking wrong questions.

"You're getting old." It was blunt, but true. He turned to see Arno, the Faun shimmered, shrouded by his smoking thurible. His words cut deeper than any repeater bolt.

"Old yes, but don't need someone young to teach." There was no time for it, Athgeric was out there, alone.

"Did Hadramiel complain about you, I wonder?" The Faun questioned. Vincentas swallowed a would-be outburst. His old mentor, who killed himself. He never knew if he was a burden to his old mentor, the aging Hadramiel. Full of anger when joining the Inquisition, questions filled him. They shed fewer answers. His guiding mentor the calm in the storm.

"Entrants, Inquisitor Vincentas." The Chaplin announced. Passing the broad-shouldered giant of a man to see three people within an alcove of the library. Candles were scarce, but yellow light illuminated their features. Even the floor lay swallowed by darkness.

"Entrants. All three?" Vincentas asked.

"Yes, all three Inquisitor." The Chaplin bowed and departed without a sound other than his hushing vestments.

"They are young." Too young, he noticed. An orange haired youth read a book by poor light candles. Bifocals took up half his face. The only girl sat cross-armed opposite the reader, looking as unimpressed as he felt. The last stood behind the reader, biting his nails.

"We were young once." Arno reminded him.

"We were young, but not this young." He left Arno and walked towards the three waiting Entrants. On seeing him approach, they moved to form a line. The reader fumbled with his glasses, leaving his book open on the table. Vincentas stood before them, eyeing one at a time. Robed in the Cleric uniform, washed and clean.

"Name." Vincentas asked the girl.

"Luciana." She replied, tilting her head up further. Brown eyes sparkled, a hidden drive to prove herself. Like so many others who had failed during their life.

"Karomeier, sir. Inquisitor." The bright fiery-haired male spoke, his eyes widened on saying Inquisitor, wanting to brown nose authority.

"Alleck. Sir." Alleck did not know whether to salute, keep eye contact or say more. His mouth twitched on the verge of spewing nonsense. He stopped himself.

"Why have you joined the Inquisition?" The Inquisitor within him asked, keeping arms locked behind his back.

"Hunt the Mystic." Luciana announced.

"Keep the faith in Cythea." Karomeier stammered.

"To help." Alleck's eyes widened momentarily before his head lowered.

"It doesn't matter why you joined. You're here now and you've got options. Serve or die." Vincentas explained. "Causality is your friend. Your life is now not your own."

A Savant, grey-haired with skin of curdled milk, approached, carrying the safe box of Mystic sightings. Retrieving his Inquisitor key from around his neck, he unlocked the box.

They kept possible Mystic sightings in a box once collected by the Inquisitorial retinue, superstitious individuals and weary theocrats.

"To prove that causality is indeed your friend." He gestured to Alleck. The youth stepped forward. Fingers twitched above the mound of scrolls. He picked the first one and looked for answers.

Vincentas shook his head. "You chose it."

Alleck broke the wax seal, unfurling the scroll in clumsy hands.

"Lower Konniak. Sighting of Mystic activity. Near free standing water pump forty-seven." Alleck read it out like it was his death sentence.

"Four days' time, we head for the Undercity. Prepare yourself Entrants of the Inquisition." Vincentas smiled.

Cass

Chapter I

With a disgruntled bleat, the sheared sheep bundled out of her grasp. It was the twentieth sheep that day. Cass's strained, numbing legs stretched out, joints ached around tight kneecaps, an irritable price sitting for monotonous chores. Better than mines, cleaner than factories and safer than warehouses.

Would have been perfect cutting corn in adjacent, golden fields beyond green, rolling hills, sowing crops during LeafFall season, the ground easier to toil. Natural heat for it. Idyllic stillness with lack of winds beneath an azure sky. Wheat was a precious bargain, too. Ripe corn made for valuable trade in cellblocks.

"Another for shearing." A tender, sweet voice spoke up above the demure bleating. Cass looked up, seeing Stell lead another sour cream-coloured sheep.

"You're on a roll today, Stell." She pointed out, holding onto the steady, docile sheep. Nostrils twitched with dampness and a humidity of uncleanliness. The drawback of shearing, she would be nose-blind in a few days.

"Well, they're a simple bunch to herd, like men. Find what they want and they'll come calling." Stell shrugged with a hint of a smile, creasing the branded pair of lips burnt onto her right cheek; the mark of her crime: illegal prostitution.

Cass placed a hand on the sheep's flank, her left hand holding the shears. She started cutting, steel scythed through thick, dirtied coat of the calmed animal. Incarcerated years had perfected the skill, a skill nobody would hire her after being released. The branded mark of theft on her cheek cemented status with prejudice. She gripped tighter, thin legs stomped on moist ground.

Four years had passed on Ralake Island, the main penal colony of Cythean justice. Cass sheared sheep for textile factories throughout Cythea, mainly for the clogged, fuming city of Konniak. Other times, she cut corn to grind into flour, ready for the burning ovens and cluttered, stuffy bakeries.

A soldier could wear the wool she sheared, or a pauper cleaning the streets, or a maid cleaning wool of their masters. Bakers baking flour, she grounded. The rich eating bread she helped create. Those only having the luxury of crusty bread wafting down into the Undercity of Konniak. Her daughter, abandoned, in the dark dwellings of the Underbelly of Konniak. Lilly could be starving. She probably was starving, because Cass remained in prison, not being a proper mother.

Snapping crack whipped in her ear. She jerked. The sheep bolted. Stinging pain flashed across her back. Jumping forward, teeth gritted, she faced the grinning Overseer, retracting the whip around his bicep. Cass panted and crouched. Sweat bleed into the strike, she felt it now, burning, stinging, throbbing.

"Warning for you, Brand." sneered the Overseer. "Next time you stop working, it'll be across your face." He sauntered away; a low, reverberating laugh shadowed him. Thundering on the ground told of fleeing sheep.

She knew the Overseers liked to use the whip; she had the marks to prove it. Better in LeafFall season than HighSun. Sweat on open wounds brought delirium and a grim chance of fever. The shears gripped in her hand spoke of vengeance. They could do the job. It would bring momentary respite, but the repeater-carrying guard in the tower would be watching.

The pen had been closed while the whip struck, making some sheep scatter in the enclosure. Her half-cut job stood near the locked gate, its wool trailing down one side as if peeling. Holding the shears tighter, Cass walked over to the sheep. Other inmates gathered their bolted sheep's, they exchanged some words, but nothing meaningful.

In silence except for metallic clicking, Cass sheared the half-cut sheep and a further three without faulting. The pile of wool grew, looking like a damp smelling cloud. Lavison, an inmate serving a Bit for theft, pushed the wheelbarrow of collected wool. She scratched her arms at any opportunity, not from the itchiness of the wool, but the withdrawals of Sniff.

Two long, drawn out horn blows signalled break. Cass sighed and her shoulders sagged, whip wounds singed as a reminder. She could wait until dusk and see Jolam in the cell, but she owned the Faun too many favours.

A granite sky threatened rain, an ebbing red disk burned like a candle, counting down until day's end, growing shorter with each passing glance. Green grass and hills smothered the land. Cass watched as prisoners headed towards the black, metallic, abandoned factory for rationed meals. Her stomach growled at the thought of food.

"I'll bet you five silver Dragets it's mutton today?" Stell whispered at her side, linking an arm through Cass's tight posture. Four years on the penal colony and she still felt uncomfortable when someone came close, bracing herself for defence.

"You don't even have Dragets on you." She glanced at Stell. The illegal prostitute shrugged.

"Not on me, no, but I can get some." A mouth full of envious teeth smiled in reply, a rarity in the prisons. Cass closed her lips, knowing the gaps of hers would be prominent.

"I'll take your bet then." She resigned. Stell only arrived last season. Fresh and serving a Bit, a short term of four years. Plenty of time to gain bitterness. Cass had four years left to go. Her daughter would be fourteen on leaving Ralake.

"Five Dragets heading my way." Stell hugged her arm and leaned in, head resting on Cass's shoulder. She flinched, expecting a hug to apply pressure on the whip mark. Unaware, the innocent girl still hugged the arm. They walked like an aristocratic couple towards the factory, a dull, bricked building with funnels breaking through a slate roof in a multitude of intervals.

Wide, opened gates could allow an airship to fly through, but a daredevil pilot would only try an audacious move like that. Merrick could try it. She shook her head, dismissing him from her mind. In the distance, white specks of prisoners entered the yawning mouth of the factory.

"How many sheepies did you skin today, brunette?" A woman jogged up to Cass. She shrugged at the unwanted attention of the social pariah heading towards her.

"Hey Raven, how's it going?" Stell piped up. A nickname not for Karwen's black hair, sleeked back and off her sloping forehead, but a slur. An insult Karwen has not picked up. Raven, an inmate slang for craven, a con who slept with guards for an easier time, making her an untouchable among inmates.

"Not right, having us cut corn in this due can smell them. What is it, HighSun? Or nearly SnowFall?" Karwen peeled off her thick, leather gloves and slapped them together, pale, milky eyes flashing to Stell, eyeing up the youth like a snake stalking a weasel.

"Prison doesn't award you with time, you should know that by now." Cass replied. Her shoulders tensed.

"HighSun, SnowFall, Leaf Growing. Seasons, days, night, dusk, it doesn't matter. What matters is food." Stell grumbled. She agreed. They skirted through the growing mass of prisoners, female prisoners, she noted. Men were segregated after dawn to toil in the mines, active refineries, or the quarries, but sometimes females worked there, too. Coolness washed over her as she stepped under the shade of the refinery, blocked out sunrays with its metallic hand rising higher into the sky than the burning, blood sun.

Cass came to the refinery edge; a handful of others were looking at the crowd. She waved on seeing Valda.

Valda raised her right fist. They picked up their pace and joined Valda's group.

"Feeding time again." She clasped sweaty hands in greeting. The woman shook her hand with a firm grip.

"Got any Faunleaf, got the lash." Cass whispered.

"See me before dusk." Valda nodded. It would cost her, but needed, the stinging grew across her back. She turned, watching labourers form a semi-circle around the disappeared tables of food. Prisoners parted, carrying what they could.

"I think it's mutton today." Stell whispered.

"It's always mutton. Have you seen any other animal in this damned place? If they served anything other than mutton I'd be concerned." Karwen interjected.

Chatting broke around them. Streams of light revealed dust hovering in the air. Prisoner's mere ants in the colony. Everything dwarfed the people. Cass looked up to see the wrought iron gangways patrolled by armed wardens, the real muscle of the prison.

"Thinning out on the left side." One of Valda's group said.

"Let's go." She brought her eyes back to the lessening mob and headed towards the left. Ralake Prison had gangs. You walked alone, you died alone. There are survivors or the dead. That was it. Cass had her group; Valda, their leader. She stayed and followed and lived; it was simple. A cold shudder rippled across her back. She had done things in prison, never to repeat. Lilly would never experience it.

She came closer to the feeding tables, sweating stench replaced by steaming bowls of something overcooked. Prisoners shouted; arms waved in the air like long grass of a Cythean plain. Tattered, muck-stained bodies milled around.

Bodies swarmed around her, vision limited, nose invaded by labour and putrid stenches. Breaking free of the turmoil, Cass reached the tables, breathing without stifled odours. Feet scrapped the floor; voices broke out in a dimmed tone. She looked to her left and right and found herself alone. Holding her bowl in steady hands, she turned around and straightened her back. A shiver clawed down her spine.

The woman before her stood, stoic and unreadable. Blackened brand M for murder covered a right, hard cheekbone. Eyes bore into Cass, and she felt it. She did not want to break the locked stare, allowing silence to grow within self-inflicted prison.

"Move." The woman rasped in a voice harsher than pickaxe biting stone. Her cracked, scarred lips snarled. Taze the murderer. The gang leader, the leader of The Sweet Sisters.

"No." She heard herself saying. Eyes shot wide. Eager mouth opened to swallow the sound, but too late. A hushed silence fell around her. Clenched fists of Taze lowered, they hung like the loose, long-black braid of hair on her right temple, which fell to her strong, bare muscled shoulders.

"You're brave, for a thief." Taze stalked forward. Tanned features spoke of how long she had been here, but her skin was not leathery, worn out or tired. It was fresh, alert, and predatory.

"Or foolish, it explains why I was caught." Cass spoke, surprised that her voice remained steady, but her knees shook. Loose grey, patched rags obscured the shaking. Faded fabric grew itchy with pulsing sweat.

Taze laughed a guttural laugh.

"Here, I insist on saying no before." She held out the bowl of steaming food. There was more steam than food, grey in its watery texture, a little meat, more bowl than cabbage. It smelt of seaweed with a vinegar twinge.

Taze placed a hand on the bowl, Cass fell under the shadow of the murderer, broader than herself and taller. Her features darker in their confined, shared space.

"Your name, convict?" The gang leader asked. Her hands remained steady as Taze took the bowl. Knees trembled. She wanted to brush the sweat from her brow but dared not make sudden movements.

"Cass." she replied, her neck straightened.

A smile carved onto the hardened face, filling her vision.

"I'll remember you, Cass the convict." Taze turned and left. A sigh escaped her body, pushed from deep within a quivering stomach. Prisoners parted before the singular gang leader. Stell came up to Cass and clasped her on the shoulder.

"Thought you were in a wheelie for sure, or worse."

"No idea what came over, stupid, stupid." She closed her eyes. Four years in Ralake, keeping head down with four years to go, made no enemies and survived the eagerness of men.

"Come on, foolish thief, let's get dinner." Stell nudged her and handed her a bowl, this one smelling just as bad. The bowl cold within her grasp. Water sloshed at the sides. She looked at the shaking bowl, wishing her fingers would get a grip.

"Mmm." Sighed Stell and slapped her lips together. "Grey water, rotten cabbage, and some overcooked mutton, for the hundredth time, always get better. Might find a surprise today." She feigned skipping away but kept pace.

The food smelt awful, not as bad as army rations. Cass sunk her thoughts on the army. It's where it all went wrong, or right, in its own twisted way. What a fool to stand up to Taze like that. She did not know where the thought came from and did not want it to surface again. Lilly remained further away than roasted meat, brown, crusty bread, carrot soup and parsley. She hoped Lilly was eating better than her.

She crouched down. Stell sat beside her cross-legged and already wolfing food down. Cass tipped, one-handed, the bowl to her lips and drank the thin liquid. She closed her eyes and imagined honey, mushroom soup, broth, or even wet grass compared to what she was tasting. She sighed on finishing the liquids. Now it was the cabbage and meat.

"Eyes down, eyes down." Hurried voices whispered and spat down their group. Cass kept her eyes down, knowing an Overseer was on the prowl. No point in giving them the satisfaction of using the whip, or worse.

"You, thief." A solitary voice barked. It echoed in the refinery. Clattering of bowls ceased. Her head craned up; eyes trailed upwards. An Overseer, the same one that whipped her, stood half-grinning.

"Take the wool outside to the warehouse."

There was no point arguing. She clenched her fist around soggy meat in the bowl and stood up. It slipped between oily, sweating fingers. Sighs and long, drawn out breaths rippled around her, the sign of relief at not being chosen.

Before leaving the cool, shadowed refinery, she stuffed the mutton into her mouth and chewed on it for nourishment. Teeth ground into the rough, rubbery meat. It would be enough to see her till next feeding. It felt cooked. Her stomach gurgled.

The nearest wheelbarrow stood waiting. Wool lay piled on top of it, threatening to spill. Nearby two legs and an arm lay over the rim of a second wheelbarrow, no boots clothed grey feet. Flies gathered, darting on the leg, then flashed away. The price of overworking. The dead were nobodies. Cass would not mourn. Lilly needs her. She needs to survive this.

Grasping the handles of the rusting wheelbarrow, she pushed the barrow to the warehouse beside the refinery. Wooden gates lay open, stacked crates formed by towers of wool. It hummed with sheep, nostrils trickled of a coarseness nothing could clean.

Cass winced, back stinging from the whiplash. She needed Valda's Faunleaf. Sweat itched at her forehead. She rubbed her head with the back of her forearm, palms were greasy with mutton and a brass coloured from the wheelbarrow.

She turned to leave and stopped. A man stood before her, smiling. He rubbed his fist with his left hand. The dull shine of a shank drew her attention. Cass backed away. He walked forward.

"I'll give you a chance to talk." His drawling Undercity accent prickled her hairs to stand. Dust pasted tight breeches and bare, muscled chest. A quarry worker.

"You're a strapping man, there, I talked." She kept backing away, knowing the crates would greet her back soon. Eyes glanced to the sides, looking for something to defend with.

"About the loot." The man laughed. "Where is it, Cass?" It hit her harder than a punch to the stomach. The loot, she did not steal it, but guilty of association and convicted. Lilly was a baby when she last stole for a criminal Undergang, now she wanted nothing more to do with the criminals of Konniak.

"You can tell Vansic I don't have it and never did." She replied. Her back braced against solid crates, pressure on the whiplash forced a wince.

"Vansic Lo says you'll talk, you'll talk alright." The shank lowered. He approached, closing the distance. Her hand clasped some wool and pulled it free, falling to her side.

"I never stole from Vansic Lo." She swung the wool pelt at him.

The man blocked the swinging wool twice and three times. Goading her and waving the shank. She matched his stance; the wool hanging low, growing heavy. She let go.

A hand outstretched for her throat. She parried, swinging her arms out. The shank flashed forward. Stumbling, her hand grasped his fist, forcing it down. Barrelling into her, his tobacco laden, rotten breath on her ear, his muscled body pressing against her. She bit down on to his collarbone. A pungent growl replied. Something hard hit her stomach. Blood-tasting air exploded from her gagging mouth.

Cass hit the ground, blinding pain swept down her back. She rolled. The man scrambled onto her, pinning an arm above her head. His face nearing hers. Legs tussling, parting hers with trembling brutality. She gritted her teeth, groaning to ply him away. A saliva spluttering laugh bellowed over her face.

"I'm not gonna kill you. I need to know where the loot is." He grinned. "But I'll visit you. Every. Single.

Day." She felt her hand slipping around the shaking fist holding the shank. It neared her. Cold steel pressed into her cheek.

Her leg struggled and slipped between his. Digging nails into clasped wrist above her head, Cass kneed him in the groin. Stale breath burst out of him, his weight eased off. The shank dropped. Her loose hand hammered down on his broad, broken nose. She hit again, striking through burning pain in her hand.

He rolled, howling, holding his face with bloodied fingers. Cass gasped, rolling away. The steel wrapped in yarn lay in arm's reach. Snatching the shank, she pounced on top of him and hammed down. Blood spurted across his arm. He roared. Arms flailed above him, swiping at her.

Cass hacked.

She growled and shouted, cried and screamed, driving the shank down time and time again. His arms failed to defend himself. A wild lunge stabbed his neck. Pulling the slippery blade from the gurgling, red flowing throat, she drove the shank down.

Her fist smashed into his face. She pulled on the shank. It snapped.

The yarn thick with congealed blood stuck to her hands, his left eye shivered with steel. He twitched, shaking. Blood welled across deep wounds. Red tears broke across a quivering face and flooded a spasming head. She pushed off him and staggered back. The attacker jerked. A convulsing hand clasped his gurgling throat. Feet kicked sporadically at the ground.

Cass dropped the sleek yarn. Hands rubbed together, slapping on her breeches. Her shirt, tattered, splashed red. Tears welled in her eyes. She turned and emptied her stomach on the ground, retching hard. Vansic Lo, the crime lord. It would not be long till he raised his foul head again. The past long buried returned with a vengeance.

He knew her location. They would come again. Her stomach sunk further with a realising thought. Lilly. They could use Lilly. If they found her.

"Got to escape." Cass whispered. Clutching her stomach through tattered, makeshift blouse. "Got to escape."

Vincentas

Chapter II

"No light lives. Darkness only." Dehqan verbalised his own thoughts.

For two days, Vincentas and his retinue descended into the Undercity of Konniak. It could have been longer. Reek of money had long transpired. No Arbiters of the Law marshalled order down here, their weapons always drawn.

Blackened vents expunged smoking steam; water pipes drip a cheap consolation for rain. Disgruntled shouts erupted at every shadowy turn, and industrial stench spoke of unseen arduous labour.

His world nothing more than buildings. Shacks extended on ruins of the ancient city, criss-crossing planks joining onto the jig-saw puzzle of overgrown, soot-stained dwellings of the impoverished. Dirtied windows exhumed a toxic yellow, unnatural light. Echoing footfalls rattled above, below and to the side, bringing rapture of complaints.

"Into the very mouth of hell, we go." Arno Ferde lamented. The Chanter kept his smoking thurible by his robed side, thin incense dissipated in Konniak's womb. Even holiness vanquished here.

Deeper they descended, fewer people they encountered. Many scattered on witnessing the passing troupe of the Inquisition, his tattooed face and the markings of his kills had this desired effect.

A broad roof, rusting with iron, ended the turbulent staircase walk. Raising his black wrought iron lamp, yellow rays of light lanced forward, cutting across the makeshift walkway to illuminate the path ahead. One, two, maybe three people scuttled off, their feet sending waves of noise ricocheting back to where the Inquisitor stood.

Fleur Lantine stalked forward, fanning the right side of Vincentas. Her raised repeater-bolter, preferred to her automatic composite bow, aimed towards the steady light and the creeping shadows beyond. Every Inquisitor had the right to recruit a Combatant; a warrior who guarded the Inquisitor and protected them on their duty, Vincentas knew none better than Fleur.

"They're already done here." She lowered her repeater, hands never leaving the stock and trigger. Brass half-mask obscuring the right side of her face swallowed light, her golden hair a subdued amber in the city's blackness.

Two pale feet caught fading light. Another unnamed casualty to the Undercity of Konniak.

"Oh, my." A gasp forced Vincentas turn. Karomeier's shaking hand covered his mouth. He paled. Putrid yellow cast by the Gaslamp could not give him colour.

"No shoes. Why?" Luciana asked.

"Worth more than life." The Inquisitor's voice echoed. "A nameless corpse. Three, maybe two perpetrators. Your role, Entrants? Seek the murderers?" He rounded on the two Entrants, Karomeier floundered, Luciana's brows knitted together. They were not quick to think.

"Continue looking for the Mystic." A youthful voice chirped. Vincentas raised the handheld lamp, showering Alleck in light.

"Fleur, carry on." He turned his back on the Entrants.

Fleur stalked ahead, admiring swiftness of her bolter, quicker than a blinking eye. Chanter Arno mumbled as he passed the stripped deceased. Vincentas knew Combatant Dehqan would keep the rearguard alongside the silent Interrogator, their own footwear sending ripples and vibrations through corrugated iron roof. The three Entrants huddled behind, their breaths growing more than the surrounding darkness.

"It shouldn't be too far." Vincentas growled, keeping his lantern at arm's length. The ache growing burdensome again, but it was no coffin at least. Leaking pipes and the stench of raw sewage led to the source of another free-standing pipe.

Rounding a corner, a line of dwellers grew through thin smog. Dishevelled, tattered clothing clad them all. The stench curled lips to snarl. Impatience twitched along the line, eager for unclean nourishment of water.

Two small children operated the hand pump, creaking as it rose and fell, dribbles of yellow liquid spluttered from the half-cut pipe, red with rust. A waiting bucket caught spitting water. Welded iron underneath a lamppost read in crude, large, drawn numbers "47."

"Next." A large man, wearing a lopsided top-hat, shoved a kneeling woman aside. She clawed the bucket to her before she fell. Feeding the bucket under her loose clothing, giving the appearance of being pregnant, and waddled off. Would make her less of a target.

Vincentas walked towards the man guarding the pipe, his scowling face retracted into fleshy bewilderment, and removed his hat. The cockel Inquisitor hat Vincentas wore drew this reaction, still a surprise to see how fabric could sow fear.

"Mi'lord, want water?" Chins rippled as the man spoke.

The queue parted, mumbles, and low chatter filtered along the line. The children kept their labour with the hand pump, in case they lost pressure, losing what fickle water could be harvested.

"Looking for peculiar activities, seen anything around water pump forty-seven?" The Inquisitor raised his voice, while standing before the stocky man. He looked up, hating that he had to. The man stood on a crate, giving him added height and visibility. A long-handled axe lay posed for defence or street justice. Two scrawny men lurked nearby, rat-faced and local. Sign of the pox lay on gaunt cheeks, cut and scarred.

"I do not know, mi'lord." Chapped lips wobbled; eyes watered. "Stop gawking, you Bog-trotting rats. Anywhere curious? Or I'll tan your hide." The man threatened, shaking his fist to the weasel faced backup. One replied in a string of words in the Bogside dialect. Vincentas could not understand it. The other shrugged.

"Down there, Garlock." One boy pointed while jumping up and down with the water pipe. "Near Bessie's Brothel, the Free Food place, ma' says not to go."

"Good lad, Mo, good lad. You can have a Hex for it." The man ruffled straw-coloured dirty hair of Mo. He pointed to his left. Vincentas noticed the steady hand. Shaking hands being a visible cue for cannibalism, commonplace in the Undercity of Konniak.

"Less than a Candlemark. If I be lying, come back and I'll send tens of hundreds to look for it." Garlock spoke, voice cracking in eagerness to appease the Inquisition, like everyone else.

Vincentas looked to where he pointed, towards what resembled a narrow street with several working Gaslamps bleeding light onto dark, high-bricked world.

He knew the man was a vagrant, making a living by conning the poor in the poorest areas. Charging them for water, which was free, but making a tariff. The law did not extend its iron grip this far down in Konniak. No reason to start a fight with a petty Undergang. Priority of finding the Mystic took precedence over bringing would-be civilisation into the depths of the old city.

Walking over disjointed, cobbled pathways, sleek with residue. He looked down, an oily black, putrid liquid trickled between stones, overriding stench told his senses it was not water.

"This should be it." Fleur injected.

Two swinging Gaslamps scattered yellow light across the front of a timbered shack. White cloth not aged with the Undercity stood out. "Free Food" lay carved on the fabric in fancy cursive writing of cobalt and amber. The door lay ajar, the lock smashed.

Vincentas pushing aside his brown, muddy duster and retrieved his loaded handbow. Fleur's repeater locked behind him. Interrogator's rapier sighed on being unsheathed. He nodded to Dehqan. The Sabanese duellist stayed on guard, the Entrants stayed with Dehqan and retrieving what constituted as weaponry for their meagre price. His aging heart quickened; heat bubbled along his neck. Dimming the heavy Gaslamp in his aching arm, he stepped inside.

Emptied boxes and smashed debris littered a dark corridor, leading to a staircase eclipsed in shadow. Unseen water dripped into a pool, its sustained drip matching his heartbeat. Suffocating moistness clogged his throat. He suppressed a cough, burying it within his gut. Dampness crawled over his skin.

Fleur flanked him, inching into the building. A soft sob entered his hearing. Floorboards creaked under the Combatant's footsteps, rounding a corner before backtracking.

"Clear." She shouldered the repeater, keeping her finger on the trigger.

Vincentas turned to face Arno, the smoking thurible hanging by his robed side. "Check-up stairs. Bring the Entrants. Go with him." He issued this to the Interrogator.

The cream-robed Interrogator, iron chains rattling and resonating off each other, followed Arno. Vincentas followed in Fleur's awake, heavy boots creaking on dilapidated floorboards.

Subdued light fell across a huddled figure.

A woman crouched on her knees, buried in the room's corner. Sobbing. Her shoulders racked with uncontrollable emotion. Clothing ripped; signs of struggle littered the flooring. Gaslamp illuminated pale hands with red knuckles.

There was no need for consoling. She had enough of men for one day. Yellow light pooled over two bodies. Their smell hit him stronger than a gut punch. Stripped of boots and clothing, wore nothing but wounds. One a man, clearly not from the Undercity. The second a woman, whose red hair mimicked embers of dying fire.

"Robbers. Rapists. Madmen." She listed. He turned to see her look up with purple, swollen eyes. Hands pulled at torn, stained blouse clothing her shoulders, trying to hide her modesty.

She buried her head into bare, bleeding knees. Blonde hair flooding across flesh. Hands combing through tattered locks, keeping herself hidden. Horrid reality of the Undercity of Konniak visited this woman. He was not here to teach harsh truths, but to find the Mystic if there was one. Vincentas did not wish to disturb her more with questions and accusations.

Vincentas faced Fleur, while she planted a boot on the chest of the dead man. She surveyed the bodies, looking for a cause of death and suspicious activities. He should do the same. The Combatant had less in common with the female victim than Vincentas had.

"Retinue outside. Fleur takes rear." The Inquisitor instructed and holstered his handbow, drawing his duster closer around him. He could not help the woman any longer. They were too late.

He removed the cockel hat, thinning hair plastered a balding scalp. Lesser men bought perfumed wigs. Vincentas had no time for it. Arno stood beyond the doorway, before the ascending staircase to the first level of the structure. Gaslamp in his hand expelled light. Water dripped into an unseen pool.

"Hear that?" Arno whispered. The Inquisitor stopped walking. Smoke wafted, sickly sweet and dispelling decay of the bodies. The woman's meek sobs became quieter. Fleur ceased her movements.

Cold water licked his chin.

Vincentas's hand snapped for his handbow. Gloved hand rubbed his stubbled face. Slow, monotonous dripping of water echoed up the stairs. Arno's Gaslamp cast a glow on the first steps of the decrepit ascent. Plaster veins broke across the wall. Faint droplets of water hung in the air and twirled, reflecting murky yellow light.

"Water, water drips down." Arno stated. He raised his Gaslamp. Light broke into the darkness, bathing stairs in colour of the sun. Vincentas's eyes tracked the light as it whipped shadows away illuminating the staircase and the landing where the stairs levelled.

"Nature twists before the Mystic." Arno whispered, citing the Inquisitor manual of Mystic Hunting.

A water droplet hovered before Vincentas's vision. It circled, twisted and broke apart. Bubbles of residue, crystal clear, swirled together and rippled on congealing. He outstretched his arm; water collided upwards with his hand, blocking its ascension.

His eyes looked up, tracking another droplet of water floating upwards. The droplet dripped into a pool floating below the ceiling. It rippled. Wavy shadows broke, oily and opaque.

A half smile pulled at tight skin, hand pushed back the duster, fingers sliding around the Inquisitorial sword in its sheath. Two days not wasted.

"Fleur, guard the entrance with Dehqan. Interrogator waits on the stairs. Lead the wounded woman outside and wait for my signal." Vincentas ordered, keeping his eyes on the pool, shivering above him, defying gravity.

"The Entrants?" Arno asked.

"Time to initiate them." The Inquisitor replied, watching the anomaly continue. Water rose and dripped into the pool. Consistent, like a heartbeat, regular and methodical. The drip echoed throughout the house. Soft gasps whispered prayers and mild curses forced his gaze to break and face the Entrants. He forgot how young they were. They looked like a child seeing a predator.

"Two things can kill a Mystic." Eyes ripped from the ceiling and faced him. "This." Vincentas tapped the obsidian hilt of his sword.

"And this." He pointed at his skull. "Do not think. That is their weapon. You think we die."

Vincentas ascended the stairs. Wall scabs peeled, footsteps creaked with every step, and shuffling boots signalled his retinue preparation. Dampness wrinkled his nose.

On the landing he looked up, staring into a floating pool. Murmur from a nearby tavern filtered into the room. *That must be Bessie's Brothel, best not tell Fleur about it.* A stiff chill scythed across his neck. Three doors stood before him on the landing, two were open, leading to dusty, smelling rooms.

The third door was closed and chained.

With measured steps and controlled breaths, the Inquisitor moved towards the padlocked door. The key lay in the lock. Turning the key, a sharp click loosened chains, Vincentas pulled the chains free, each link grating off the handle they wrapped around. He gave the

Entrants one knowing look. Their faces bright in the Gaslamp. Their eyes unblinking. Shadows flickered behind them, shivering as they did.

Placing his hand on the door, he pushed it open.

She sat upright on a bed.

Black, straight, wet hair obscured her face. *Stop that*, he told himself, *stop thinking*. Vincentas's eyes flashed around the room. Unlit candles, a wooden pulpit at the side of the bed, crimson symbols carved into the wall behind the sitting girl, running like blood from a fresh wound. Stench of beeswax lingered through the putrid, bloody smell. Flies buzzed, nicking exposed skin. An unbearable need to itch scuttled across burning skin and sweating neck.

"There are one hundred and eighty-three people in that tavern. Their thoughts are terrible." She spoke in a multitude of echoing voices. One distinctly Kheda Ishan, the guttural, thick toned accent eclipsed the others, but she had the skin tone of a Cythean.

"Large groups are harder to stand, yes?" Vincentas asked, standing three feet before the girl. Hair sleek through saturation. Thin linen on the brink of transparency with the deluge of water.

The door behind slammed shut. The Entrants gasped; quivering mouths rapped prayers.

"Stop thinking." Vincentas growled. Knuckles tightened around the Gaslamp handle.

"Just kill it. Kill *him*." Karomeier shrieked. Luciana circled the bed, head shaking side to side. She backed away until hitting a bordered-up window. Alleck made no sound.

"Be quiet." The Inquisitor snapped, keeping eyes on the apparition. Pulsating Entrant nerves shredding through the room. Licks of static and coarse sparks burst intimately.

"Thoughts are wonderful," the girl giggled, but her voice was that of a boy. "The tavern was fun, but this is perfect." A sultry, oozing voice pulsed, a voice older than her form.

"What is your name?" Vincentas placed the Gaslamp onto the floor, while feeding a hand into his duster, fingers inching for the handbow.

"I have many," her head tilted up. "And none of them want to talk with you." Rattling of chains a chorus to her contained movements. Eyes flashed to the bed. Skeletal, thin legs of the girl, bones protruding through flesh, held in iron bonds chaffing red skin raw.

"I didn't mean to. I didn't mean to." Karomeier cried. Vincentas glanced at the Entrant, breaking his gaze from the Mystic. Karomeier's handbow levelled into his own mouth.

"Stop thinking, damn you." The Inquisitor turned. Thudding twang echoed around the room. The Mystic girl smiled with black, cracked lips stretching gaunt face beyond possibility. A heavy thud collapsed onto the floor.

"My name is Arno, it is a pleasure to meet you." He kept his gaze on the dripping wet, ebony hair of the girl.

"These meat vessels have no sense. Their aqua vitae contains more aliments than most apothecaries. Their weakness will be their downfall." A man's hissing voice slipped from the body of the upright girl; chains rattled with sporadic movement. Her head turned, facing the barred window nailed shut, planks of wood crossing its frame.

A shriek startled Vincentas. Snapping wood ripped through his hearing. He turned. Luciana tore wooden planks free off the window, bloodied hands, splinters cutting her arms to shreds, and dived out of the window. Head smashing through dust-stained glass.

"All Mystics have weaknesses." The Inquisitor faced the bed. One silent Entrant remained. His sweating, gloved hands closed around the handbow. Blood and flesh fell into her dripping lap. Hair melted down a flat face. Rising infested stench threatened to empty his guts.

He stared at the festooned eyes looking at him constituting the girl's ruined face.

"Flesh is weak, Inquisitor." A voice whispered in Vincentas's mind, its sinewy fingers stroking within. Flesh prickled with coldness; hairs stood on end. A bone breaking snap echoed in the room. Her exposed scalp, festered and wriggling, consumed his sight.

"But the mind is stronger," she levitated. Arms fell limp, legs dangling, broken neck exposed bloodied bones. "You think that artificial design in your grasp will change the inevitable outcome of this meeting?" Her voice sneered.

"Haven't thought that far ahead." Vincentas retrieved the handbow and laid it by his side.

"Mortals don't." A man regarded. He turned seeing a man, bleeding with a head wound, standing before the boarded-up windows. The apparition looked at Vincentas with hollow eyes.

"But we do." A girl giggled, clutching a wooden toy to her chest. Wearing a faded nightgown. Standing by the bed, a double of the floating, limp ascending body without ruination.

"And we would like you to join us." A sultry voice oozed into his ears. Soft, pale knuckles caressed his chest and rubbed down. A veil faced woman stood at his flank, her arm and chest encroached on his own, leg curled up his back. Her bare body stitched together with crude wire.

"Your true colours revealed." Vincentas lowered his head, eyes peering up at the girl hanging below the ceiling, held in dangling animation by the chains at her feet. She hung like the dead justice of a town Arbiter. Water dripped onto the bed; repetitive beating tapped onto the soiled mattress.

"And what colourful form are we?" Three voices spoke.

"Temptress." The Inquisitor hissed as he turned to face the woman, her leg and arm exploring his body, her ice touch leaving visible, shaking breaths. Behind the translucent veil a grinning face, too big for her mouth, scarred her face.

"I'm sorry, mother, sorry. I couldn't." Alleck's voice cracked through the Inquisitor's distorted hearing.

"We are more than searchers of lust, Arno, or should I call you Vincentas." The swooning woman by his side whispered. She smelt of hanging meat, a fresh kill. Buzzing flies twitched skin, wanting to scratch at the sound in his head.

"You're right," Vincentas nodded, perfume igniting nostrils. "You're an apparition, not searchers of lust." He turned his head to see nothing beside him.

"How wrong you are, Vinny." A shiver rippled down his spine. The same voice rising memories of a tortured past to the clear present. A voice that broke him. A voice he condemned to fires of purification.

"This is no concern of yours." Vincentas brought himself to face the only presence in the room. Eyes closed, lips tasted of frost, but his arms burned with heat. Shaking, uncontrollable and ready to unleash.

"Battling within yourself again, Vinny, it's all you ever do. It's all you ever did." Her words melted into his mind; the letters caressed his temples, massaging themselves against the very being of himself.

Blocky, cumbersome wood tapped his cranium. It rested. Steel tip dug into bare flesh.

"You will never win." Vincentas smiled. Eyes peeled back.

"Think what you will, Vinny. Time will decay this world, just like us, legion, decaying you and your kin." She floated where the chained girl was. Auburn tussled hair. Jade dress hanging off her pale shoulder. Opal eyes flooded with light.

"Before time decays completely, I'll be there." Vincentas levelled the handbow at the apparition of his past and fired.

Cass

Chapter II

"I need to escape. There is no other way." She signed. They used Hand-Code, devised in prisons for secret communications at night. Any guards who caught prisoners using Hand-Code would remove the left hand of any prisoner, but that did not concern Cass.

"They may not send another." Jolam, Cass's cellmate for four years, replied. The Faun lay on his side, opposite their small, mesh-fenced cage they shared.

"He won't stop. He thinks I stole the loot." Her bicep ached. Under moon rays they signed since sundown. She wanted to sit up, easier to move, but it would draw attention above and below. Clustered snoring broke above and to the sides. All around them, the world slept. Prisoners in their hundreds smelt like a herd of animals.

"There must be a way to get the information to him. You didn't steal it?" Jolam mimed. His dirty musk overpowering, light broke between the Fauns muscled arms.

"News has spread too quickly. His contacts will find out before I can get the word out." Nothing escaped notice in Ralake. It happened two days ago. The rumour mill spread gang retaliation the main talking point; guard brutality another, while others said he was a Short-Eye convict, a man who liked the company of children, who got his just deserts.

"Eyes down." Jolam snapped with his hands. Cass laid on the thin mattress and shut her eyes. Tawny mattress made her already aching spine tingle.

Low chatter grew closer. Boots walking on solid concrete approached. Occasional squelch in mud echoed in the conversation. Common for guards to walk the cages; seeking to vent out frustrations on unsuspecting inmates.

"Couldn't believe it though, hasn't been a murder in here this year." A voice hissed.

"That you know of." A snaking second voice chimed in.

"Can't wait for leave…" the first voice added, sounding younger, naïve, vulnerable.

"Quiet." snapped the second. "Don't talk around here, all connected on the Out." He was not wrong. Voices trailed away, highlighted by retreating footsteps. Cass opened her eyes, Jolam's were still closed. She looked up, the meshed fence above close enough to touch, and the mattress pressing into it housed another inmate, their back an arm's length away. Only the fence separated them. Privacy vanished the moment branded conviction scarred the face.

She looked at Jolam, hearing the mattress creak under the Faun's movements. "That was close." He mimed.

"Too close." She nodded and held her hand up, showing the "alright" sign of gratitude.

"So, how do you escape without causing a full-scale riot?" The Faun asked.

Cass shrugged. Her eyes narrowed at the slight twinge on her back. She rolled her shoulder, rubbing the knot of muscle against the thin, soiled, unwashed mattress.

"How's the back?" The Faun asked, his eyes brightened in the darkness. The Faunleaf Valda provided too few to aid, but Jolam worked his alchemy skills on the limited leaf. Without his work, she knew the night would be long and full of tears and weeping blood. Instead, the wound healed, minor stings returned along with infrequent pain.

"Good." Cass smiled. "I owe you one."

"You owe me more than one." Jolam's smile mimicked the moon slicing above.

"I owe you nothing." She mimed, finding a grin forming on her face.

"You're right. I saw you naked earlier." The Faun made gestures Cass grew accustomed to for years. Four years and never changed. Wardens thought it humorous to house a female with a convicted rapist. They did not know Jolam was not the criminal they thought he was.

Cass extended her fist and raised her middle finger. The Faun bowed, despite laying on the mattress.

"I need to think about escaping, not you and your stares." She mimed.

"Sorry." Jolam signed, his smile fading. "You need to keep a clear head, think straight. It'll get you back to Lilly safe and sound. Not in a wheelie, or box."

Cass reached out and linked her fingers between the Faun's calloused hands. They had watched each other's backs since their first night. He could be trusted; he was the only man she could trust.

"Despite thinking with your other head, you're a good person." She replied, wishing to say it out loud. Darkness swirled in her vision, blurring. Rubbing moisture out of her eyes, she swallowed a tremble in her throat. Lilly, all about her. Returning to her, she had to be calm and focused.

"You're a good person too but remind me never to cross you when you have a shank." Jolam replied. He retreated his arms to cover his mouth, his body shook, a creasing smile broke across his wrinkled, bearded face.

"Only if you threaten my daughter." Cass replied and pointed at Jolam.

"Deal." Mimed the Faun, grinning. "So, I can stare at you all I want, and you won't shank me?" He extended a hand to shake on the agreement.

"You. Already. Do." Her signs harsh and waved away the outstretched, furry hand. The Faun stifled a yawn, exertion louder than he wished. He stayed awake to listen to her. Jolam had worked well on treating her back from the Overseer's lash. He had done more in one night than anyone had done for her in years.

"You need sleep, we both do." She signed, her hands stuttered with her own yawn, hands reacted to cover her mouth.

"I agree with that." Jolam replied. "Goodnight, Cassy."

"Night Jolly." She laid down, stretching herself on the croaking mattress, mesh fencing below crinkled in her movements. Her cellmate already snored, a nasally ingestion of air followed by a whistle that mimicked a boiling pot.

Cass's eyes closed, seeing her daughter cry on the mattress beside her. It smelt of roasting bread fresh. A smell as foreign to her daughter than a coal-coloured Kheda Ishan man. Warm, dough humid air coy with its unattainable taste.

Vibrating shakes snapped eyes open. Blinding light flooded vision. Sweet smelling bread replaced with the overriding odour of bodies. A cough wracked her parched throat and aching body. Residue soaked her back, the Faunleaf numbed the sting.

Her hand fed through short hair, shaved to the sides, making it an easier burden to bear with the raw, uncontrollable humidity dawn brought and lack of washing. Cass peeled the new sleeveless work shirt off her body and dropped it against the dangled clothing at the foot of the mattress. She laced up boots. A chorus of chattering inmates hummed in her skull.

Croaking laughter, mumbles of conversation, spitting and robust shouting echoed around. Nothing new seeing naked occupants housed in cages around her, men and women both. Jolam lay sprawled out, an arm length away, snoring and body exposed for the red blood, sun-drenched morning. She shook her head, always a heavy sleeper, an envious trait.

"You look how I feel, Cass." A tired voice wheezed behind. She turned, rubbing grime and moisture off face and neck, avoiding eyes as much as she dared.

"Must feel haggard then." She gave Rosemia a smile. An older face stared through the mesh fence. Round eyes peered back, sucken in taunt skin.

"Maybe the shanked man had it lucky." Rosemia spoke between interspersing coughs. Retched blood spotted the inmate's hand. She wiped it on her thigh.

"Maybe." Cass replied. He died painfully. The shank in the eye, the twitching body. Sliced neck. Gurgling sounded like a flooded drain clearing.

Cass pulled on her blouse, a stolen one. After killing Vansic Lo's man, she had to change. Tattered clothes showed sign of a fight with red splashed over clothes. Linen breathed easier against her skin. The front laced shut, ideal for the ending LeafFall season.

A shrill horn blew. Jolam jerked awake, kicking the fence with his hoof. He groaned, a hand covering his eyes. A smile pulled at Cass's lips. At least his hoof was not caught this time.

"No. No." He groaned.

"I know, next time I'll not talk all night." She flexed her toes, which became visible through the left boot.

"Bah, sleep, who needs it." Jolam flapped his arm. "I missed you getting changed."

"There'll always be another day." Cass sighed, shrugging.

Grinding steel on fence signalled the bar sliding free across the cages, sparks flew. Cage doors opened, those incarcerated below and above exited their cramp, fenced cells.

Cass pushed the cage door down, held onto the handrail and climbed down, making sure nobody descended above. Touching the ground, she waited for Jolam. A sigh escaped her when she stretched. Cages made little room for moving. Mesh fences gave the impression of open space, but always an illusion of false hope.

Jolam's hooves clopped in the waiting mud. Together they walked with the mumbling mob as they headed to the closest warehouse for morning meal. Cass looked up. Prisoners converged towards the metal maw of the depilated iron refinery, one of many that doubled for feeding halls in the morning and at dusk. Running parallel to the cages, both structures made an alley of bodies, dwarfing their ever-growing number of prisoners climbing down the cages.

Inmates gathered, thousands of them, streaming from cages to her left, to meld with the flooding tide of hungry people. Heat prickled skin. Sweat and grease forced bile to rise in Cass's stomach. She spat out phlegm bubbling in her throat, making sure not to spit on a convict. Prisoners shouted, arms waved in the air like long grass of a Cythean plain. Black, soot-stained bodies; dust covered torsos; flour pasted hair, they were all unwashed and stood with their backs to Cass. Even on turning it was indistinguishable who was male and female, everyone an inmate.

Dried, cold oats stuck to the wooden bowl. A chunk of old bread, black burnt, lay dumped in the oat-water. No point in using an unwashed spoon, easier to use hands. Cass sat within the pandemonium of conversation. She kept the bowl in her hand. The table always knocked with people vacating seats.

"Probably a gang killing. Taze and her gang want to take over the block." Valda mused. She studied her group, bare elbows on the table propping up her chin.

Valda remained much in the dark as anyone. Her emerald eyes surveying each of them.

"Heard he was a Short-Eye, touched up one of the kids here." Elin leaned in. Cass's back tensed. Her head lowered, she ate quietly, wishing to disappear, but it would never work.

Thoughts of escape held her mind. Could pose as a guard, but the possibility of attaining guard's clothes would mean killing one, or least rendering one unconscious. Airships came to Ralake heading for Cythea three times a season. Taking wool, flour, metal and stone back to Cythea, or shipped further abroad. Stowaway was realistic. She had to gain a guard's trust. It would take time, time she did not have.

"You're hacking it like a butcher." A stony rasp ceased her planning. Daylight's sun pulsed down, squinting eyes.

"We don't need more mutton for the damn kitchens." Taze's face scarred into a smile. She held her own sheep held in one steady, muscle-bulging hand around its throat. Its beady eyes shivered as it stood half sheared.

Cass looked at her own sheep. Tuffs of wool clung to its body, ragged bits littered the ground, patches lay uncut. She had made a hash-job of the shearing. Rubbing sweat off her forehead, she applied shears to the sheep, cutting softly down its flank. A murmuring bleat left its lowered, steady head.

"I was talking to you." Taze spoke. Cass's back prickled with standing hairs. Lowering the shears, not wanting to look aggressive, she turned and peered up at the sitting stoic murderer.

"I got whipped for less." She tilted her head back.

"I killed for less." Taze replied, holding her gaze with black, unreflective eyes. The murderer dismissed her with a shrug and returned to shear.

A coldness crept down her back. No wind stirred, and the sun blazed overhead, its heat mild compared to flaring brightness. Constant cutting of shears, echoing bleats, they magnified to a claustrophobic level. The world Cass could not escape from despite the stretching horizon and open skies above.

"You heard about that killing?" The iron rasp broke their growing silence. "Cass." She drawled over the word. Fingers clenched the shears tighter in her slippery, shaking hands.

"Yes." She replied and looked at the murderer. The thousand-yard stare of the woman working beside her buried deeper than any blade.

"He was shanked so good. Cut, ear to ear." The murderer drew her shears across her broad, muscled neck. Cass returned to shearing. The more she cut, the more it would drown out her thumping heartbeat.

"Wasn't gang related. I'd have known first." Taze's rasp sharper than her blade. She turned facing the smiling murderer, twisted grimace distorted tattoos across high cheeks, morphing around the pitch-coloured branded "M" burnt on tanned skin.

"Might have been a Short-Eye. Got his just deserts, less of them around the better." Cass tripped over her words. She looked around, no Overseer anywhere to be seen. Whenever needed, they were never there.

"Fewer." Taze spoke, enunciating each syllable.

She looked at the murderer. Short, trimmed black hair crowned an angular, powerful head. A solitary braid of hair hung on the right side of her face. The blackened brand of her victim, 'Wilmar', scarred her forehead as a tight frown knitted together.

"You went into that warehouse." Taze smiled. "You didn't come back to the refinery." She leaned back, leisurely. Her broad, muscular bare shoulders glistening with labour. Long legs stretched out, leaving go of the sheared sheep, and darted away.

Trickling heat flushed down her back, coldness washed away. Tension flexed Cass's muscles, tightening the hold of the shears. Dryness invaded her parched mouth. She coughed and licked her chapping lips, looking at Taze. Vansic could buy her.

A single horn blew. Cass sighed and dipped her head, dropping the shears. The sheep bolted, sheared of wool. The potential mutton would be free for the time being. Casting a glance at the sky, keeping Taze in her periphery, the sun had not reached its highest point. It was not a sign for food, but something else.

"Not dinner. What is it?" Someone called, sounding like an angry Overseer.

She looked at Taze, who stood up and dropped her shears. The murderer cracked her knuckles, one at a time and stalking off, with a slowness that mimicked leisurely walks only bureaucrats took.

"A meeting, heard anything?" Stell jogged to catch her. She flexed her sticky fingers and looked at them as sunlight broke before the shadow, drowning skin in yellow rays. They did not look like her hands or felt like them.

"Haven't heard a thing." Cass replied. They journeyed to the raised platform for gathered meetings. An amalgamation of corn cutters, sheep shearers and flour makers mustered together. People chatted to her side, coming closer, encroaching on personal space. Her shoulders tensed, hairs bristled, fists clenched.

Silence swept through the gathering, her head raised daring to look up, the gantry glowing silver in the sun. Red uniforms stood along the platform. Cythean soldiers.

"War has come." A voice shouted; its strained tone sounded thin. It must have come been the central figure, the one in black with the distinctive white helmet, or was it a powered wig, the wealthy status of Cythea. She bit her lip and snorted. He was a thousand leagues from home, but Cythea never left him.

"All abled bodies will serve in the penal core of the Cythean army, for an immediate termination of sentence." Cass thought she heard. Isolated laughs and rumbled ruckus of noise sporadically rose around her.

"For Cythea." An inmate shouted, heads veered to the left, her eyes followed, and laughter erupted. Her eyes turned to the gangway. The iron walkway circled most of the prison complex. The figure in black reached near a Cythean soldier. Alarming shouts rang at the front. The tone panic ridden. Harsh whistling broke through the air. Cass ducked. The whistle of a repeater being fired.

"Silence." The speaker shouted. Huddled voices mumbled as she faced the gangway, moving right, staying clear of the left. Everyone moved from the left. Where the repeater bolts must have fired at.

"Immediate termination of your sentence will be carried out after two seasons of service. In Orschal." The speaker shouted.

A light wind blew through short hair, caressing her scalp. Two seasons of service, or another four years here, allowing another chance for Vansic to strike again.

Longer from Lilly. Cass knew Cythean government and bureaucrats would not keep their word, but it was the chance to escape back to Konniak, to Lilly.

"Sign up before nightfall. We head off in the morning. Who's with me?" The speaker shouted. A deafening shout erupted around her, drowning out the racing heartbeat thundering in her ears. She flinched and rocked on hard, aching heels.

Cass's mind swam. Break free of prison chains, get into the army and escape into Orschal and get back to Cythea. A fresh smile formed on her face. It would take two seasons and the rest, but it was not four years. She could survive, she could fight, her life in the army before prison taught her resolution.

Cass raised her fist, mimicking the others in the crowd, but did not cheer. She needed the energy to plan, to think, and to escape.

Vincentas

Chapter III

She knitted continuously. Needles clicked like beetles crawling over gravel. Click, click, click. Buried into Vincentas's skull, deeper than a maggot entering a wound. A gulp swallowed his words. He could only say one thing.

"Evalyn." He sighed.

The knitting stopped. Wind ceased. Opal eyes that always melted him looked up.

A convulsion rocked the ground. Deafening gust of air blasting him backwards with a force he could not stop. Corn skinned his face as he skidded to a halt. Black, monolithically rock exploded upwards, rising higher and higher, breaking through gathered clouds. Debris of the house lay scattered around him: wooden panels; shining glass; a smouldering knitting needle. His roar of defiance dwarfed by the rush of sound and the surging rock piercing the heavens.

Vincentas broke through the surface, escaping the towering monolith and a haunting reflection of his wife. An explosion of colour settled with a dim ebbing yellow, fighting against eclipsing black. A singular hand-held Gaslamp, crowned in smoky glass, burned on a bedside cabinet. Something smashed to his right. He jumped in damp sheets, pulling moist linen against his body. Grogginess forced eyes to close, and a tightness burned down his neck.

"Easy, easy." A woman's voice soothed his temples, while a wet cloth dabbed a sweating forehead, skirting around sticky temples. A sigh escaped parched lips; tension held his body in place.

"Where am I?" Vincentas demanded, his throat cracked. Chapped, rough lips brushed together as he spoke. Swallowing hot air, heavy eyes peeled open.

"Dunright Hospital." The woman's voice replied. Cooling cloth dabbed at sticking brows, tracing around his face. Soothing and perfect.

The asylum, the insane asylum. He faced a wall, shadows twitched across black crumbling mortar pockmarked with tuffs of moss. Markings scratched across its surface; talons flickered from Gaslamp's projection.

He turned to see the caring woman. A long, hooked mask faced him. No wonder patients departed their sanity when wardens looked like human crows. He could see nothing humane about her, not even her eyes lost behind black, opaque lenses. The nurse moved back when he recoiled. Dark crimson skirts rustled. Her shadow spread, congealing with ebony talons of the rooms shade.

"How long have I been here?" He gripped moist linen sheets of his bed, trying in vain to sit up. The woman flinched; her pitch-coloured blouse tensed as she moved to the ajar door of his enclosure.

"How long?" Vincentas rasped, it echoed like a lunatic. Already at the door, hand posed to close it behind her. Her red asylum skirt casting shadows that strangled the corner of the room.

"I'm an Inquisitor. I demand to know." He mustered strength to project his voice.

She turned in hesitation. Hooked mask peering back, dim yellow light caught her triangular face. The nurse slipped out, her deep sighs filled the void she left behind. The iron door closed. Bolts slammed; locks turned. His chest tightened with meagre, thin air.

He collapsed onto the rock-hard bed. Iron hinges groaned with ill-care. Stomach growled, hunger gnawed, his guts pulling at aching muscles. He had no luxury or time for food. He had to leave.

The Inquisitor searched around, making a conscious effort not to look at the walls. Already one scratched comment on the dilapidated brick work caught his gaze, crawling deep within. All in block capitals. Carved like a vicious Angrim had done it. AM I NOT IN HELL? It read. A laugh cried out behind the wall.

He turned his back on wriggling words caught by treacherous light. Weary eyes latched onto a pair of wings. Majestic, dominant, supreme and etched on the wall with more than chalk, looked like the veins of the wall. An effigy of the nurse, no doubt.

Superstitious nonsense was not his style. He believed what he saw. Philosophers and mimics talked about a mythological race of winged people living in the clouds.

They were stories to keep children indoors at night in rustic farmsteads, or to amuse youngsters dreaming of being an adventurer to find one in an airship.

They glorified mythologies and stories when history contained vacancies. Winged people never existed. There were no winged people. Mystics were real. They were the only demon that had come true from stories he read in his youth growing up, those and the bestial Primals.

Spare clothing lay ready: a simple buttoned shirt, cream breeches of Cythean design, and boots of worn leather. They looked clean; room smelt distinctively unclean. Sweat lingered in the air, more overriding than green veins of moss creeping up stygian corners of his cell.

Vincentas shuffled to sit up, bed creaked with every wiry hinge as he changed into the waiting attire, each layer recovering his weary muscles. The mattress, how he slept on it, defied logic.

Unseen bolts grated, and a multitude of clicks unlocked the door. His eyes averted to its opening, followed by hollowed boots stepping into the room. His jaw tightened. A cockel hat silhouette fell upon him. This was his chance to talk sense into insanity.

Inquisitor Constance Kal'zager entered the room.

"Inquisitor Vincentas, I am glad you are ready. Come, you are leaving." Constance turned, not waiting for a reply. He followed her, walking clumsily in boots without laces. They prohibited laces in the asylum in case of suicide.

"Good to see you, Inquisitor, I can assure you of my sanity." Vincentas spoke, while they walked down echoing corridors of the wards. Isolated Gaslamps shone brittle light throughout the long, black-stone ward, fighting against lashing shadows eager to claim the world.

"You have loyal friends Vincentas and in these times those are more precious than hard truths." Her calming voice matched her unreadable, cold features.

"How long have I been inside this mindless prison?" He kept his voice low, knowing two wardens shadowed their footsteps fewer than five paces behind.

"You can ask Arno when we leave." Cloud-grey eyes framed in wrinkled pale-skin creased in hardship. Her jaw tightened. She wanted to say something else. He knew her too well.

Two larger Wardens braced themselves on a closed door, ready to enter. Concealed occupant cawed repeatedly. As one, the wardens opened the door on the unsuspecting troublemaker. Rough shouts erupted as hinges groaned. A naked man with wild grey hair broke free.

"Coming, coming! The Birdmen are coming." His arms flapped in a gratuitous symbol of a bird.

Two wardens descended on the man. A baton sent a dull crack echoing down his spine. The insane man collapsed on hard stone. Boots unleashed savage fury. Vincentas watched as unrestrained brutality rendered the man unconscious. Picking up one leg each, the wardens dragged the bloodied man back into his cell.

"That's one way to silence someone." Constance whispered. Her gloved hand squeezed his forearm. Vincentas slapped the image of himself entering Dunright Hospital as wild and uncontrollable as the beaten man. He had to know. Not turning back or looking at the smear of shining crimson tracing the man's returning to his cell, he followed Constance down the corridor on his way to freedom.

Rounding a corner, his shoulders slackened on seeing barred gates and an exit. He could have run, like a mother reuniting with her lost daughter. He snorted at the thought of rampant emotion, sending a phlegmy spit ringing throughout the shadow drenched, damp hall.

"Have to sign out before you leave." Constance pointed to the left. A desk hid within the natural stone crevasse which grew into view. He picked up the pace on seeing a ledger. A bifocal wearing clerk stared up at him, lost behind the barricade.

"Inquisitor Vincentas." Constance stood beside him, speaking to the clerk. She rang her long fingers together, pale gloved hands moving like a northern spider.

Scraping the wooden chair back, sending brows to crease, the hunchbacked clerk stood and turned to investigate the multitude of pigeon-holes that honeycombed the wall behind him. Fleeting fingers rapped on wooden holes; inaudible mutters spluttered.

"LeafFall. No wonder." The wizened clerk explained to nobody but himself. Pulling out a roll of paper, sealed by crimson wax, he snapped it open, unfurling documents in gnarled hands.

"I'll sign." Constance placed her hand on the desk, her right hand picking up the lead pencil attached to the threadbare string. She was eager to be out of here, nobody could blame her.

A crow-masked warden, wearing a stark white shirt, breeches and gloves, twirled a set of keys as he walked towards the last vestige of freedom. While Constance signed the release, the warden unlocked the barred door and pulled it open, grating across the floor in a steel shriek.

Not forgetting his manners, Vincentas waited for Constance to finish. Soon the Inquisitor placed the pencil down and turned to leave but waited for Constance to vacate first. The grinding scrape of iron on stone clawed his ears as the fence closed between him and the wards. A deep sigh escaped his lungs.

"Don't stop, we must keep moving." Constance strode ahead, striding into greying horizon of metallic buildings and an off-coloured sky for LeafFall. Coldness nipped an exposed neck. He turned up the flimsy collar and fed arms into each other. Even at his age, he should not be feeling the icy nip of a freezing temperatures.

"My retinue. My things." Vincentas inquired, looking at the older Inquisitor, who looked as gaunt and frail as his muscles.

"Patiently waiting for you." She kept it brief. Her jaw tightened; eyes stared ahead. He remained as much in the dark in the hospital as outside of it.

He surveyed the grounds of Dunright Hospital. Gowned patients in black-strapped harnesses walked in front of their crow-faced wardens. Idle whimpers, mewling's that mimicked stray cats, one or two cawed like a crow. Others stood, isolated and forgotten. Men, women, old and young, as dishevelled and drained as his aching legs and stiff joints.

"Metal. Metal." One called out.

"They fly, fly, flying high." A woman shrieked, before being bundled away. A curtesy blow across the face silenced them.

Victims of Mysticism ended up in Dunright. Fragmented people that could not be pulled back where the Mystic had dangled them over the precipice of sanity. Vincentas had no time for it. He remained who he was in the mind, memories fogged but not torturous.

"Do you hear the voices too?" A man's face blurred his vision, a voice starting with a throaty growl before shouting. Neck red with veins, eyes bulged to the point of bursting. Yanked back, the patient collapsed onto the gravelled path and pulled by its warden. He gargled against the leash, hands clawing to break free from suffocation.

"We have admitted more within the last season than any time in recorded history." Constance spoke beside him as he watched the raging man gagged and hooded.

"Did I…" His stomach gained weight. An unsettled gurgling that he could not digest filtered throughout his weary body.

"No, you did not come in like that. If you had done, you'd not be walking out." A gloved hand, resilient, gripped his shoulder. Footsteps ground on gravel. A hush of stones trampled underfoot signalled her departure.

Blackened sky scarred by industrial might grew above the granite hospital grounds. Stonework blocked ominous clouds, barbed spires lanced between steaming pillars of acrid smoke and billowing ashen smog. Even the hospital, when Vincentas turned to see its welcoming disappearance, shrank into pillared obscurity within the bowels of mountainous buildings and iron-crafted dwellings.

"Any news since I was in there." He pulled what feeble clothing he had around himself, anything to stop encroaching chill biting at exposed, wafer-thin skin.

"I'll let your retinue indulge you." Constance replied, sounding rehearsed.

"There's something you are not telling me. I must know." His head dipped, avoiding a brief swipe of icy wind. Too cold for LeafFall, even in its latter stages. Confinement affecting his years in Dunright Hospital.

"I'm not here as a pawn of causality, but to free you from ignorance." She stopped walking. Vincentas stood and watched her. Greying hair that matched weathered skyline. Wrinkles beyond counting spoke of experience. Her eyes held a spark but hidden around withered corners.

"Causality is our friend. We are all part of its game." He remembered his words to the Entrants. Students of wishful thinking. They were young, everyone was young once. Coldness scythed into aching, tired limbs.

"However, you wish to see it," Constance waved, her Inquisitorial tattooed "I" twitching with thin, hairless brows knitted together, the tallied Mystics kills on her cheeks broken in wrinkles. "You are better out here fighting than stuck in there rotting."

"Glad we agree with that." Vincentas nodded, his way of thanking Constance. She would know.

"Your retinue, I presume." Her eyes glanced beyond black iron-wrought gates that connected to a black fence ringing a sparse excuse for a garden in the hospital grounds. Fleur's golden hair stuck out more than her bronze half-mask. Two haversacks lay at her feet. Dehqan stood nearby with his slouched hat.

The Inquisitor narrowed eyes on the third member, bald as an egg and pale skin, hands locked within robes two sizes too big for him, bifocals wired around a gaunt face: Alleck the Entrant. No Arno or Reticence. A pained feeling ignited within his stomach. No Chanter, his old friend since the beginning.

"Only half." He answered. Black gates opened with the aid of four wardens, sending hairs to stand on end under steels shriek.

Fleur entered the compound carrying his own haversack and a bundle of clothes. Greatcoat, green and fading. Black boots and other attire belonging to him. Dehqan carried his obsidian scabbard.

"You look like shit." Fleur stated.

"Always appreciate the honesty, Fleur." He took his coat and clothed himself, needing a respite against the biting cold. Vincentas nodded to them both, before facing Constance flanked by her own retinue, including an Interrogator. Four Combatants hung back, repeaters drawn and primed to fire. A savant in crimson stood near, quill and board in hand.

"Inquisitor Vincentas." Constance used her voice, projecting over a frosty wind. He stepped forward, eye to eye with the Inquisitor, her head up, chin pointing his way.

"Inquisitor Vincentas, I discharge you from the Inquisitorial Service. Return to the Inquirer Hall three days hence, to relinquish your malachite sword. In the name of the High Inquisitor Maximus Kael, sentence has passed." Constance spoke like a true Inquisitor, with authority, gravitas and unwavering power in her conviction.

"What… is this a joke?" Fleur stammered. No wonder Arno and Reticence were absent. Someone informed them, since they were part of the Inquisitorial service; Combatants were not and served the Inquisitor. A deepening entered his guts and settled. Hearing blurred. His heartbeat a murmur within the maelstrom of a racing mind.

Constance stepped forward. Eyes searched, reading his own. A thousand and one thoughts flooded through his mind, opening the gates of emotions swirling within.

"Stay in Konniak. Wander the viewing balconies." He read her silent lips.

"Thank you." He replied.

Stepping back, Inquisitor Constance gave the one-handed Continental Church salute and left with her retinue.

"Well. That was worse than a hangover." Fleur spat, tying her flowing hair into a ponytail snaking down her back onto the black butterfly-style dress-coat hugging her athletic, statuesque frame.

"Can't be serious? Finished, are you?" Dehqan moved forward, sheathing his handbows.

"Stay in Konniak, all three of you. This hasn't finished. Being an Inquisitor only ends in death." Vincentas belted the scabbard around his waist, feeling like himself for the first time since waking in Dunright Hospital.

Cass

Chapter III

Humidity of contained populace. Putrid boiling wax. The stench of home, the fragrance of uncertainty. Cass looked up with a shudder, rusting red glow of corrugated iron infested her vision. The forsaken sun cracked through the furnace of Konniak and its interlocking houses. With a gulp, she faced the one-tier shack that had been her residence for six years before her incarceration.

A shake rattled her arm. Numbing mind whispered spitting, doubtful words. Children laughed their feet jolted down iron gangways, broken vents hissed, unseen people lost in the city maze shouted with echoing voices. Cass found more space in prison than in society.

Shouldering her light haversack, she walked forward and read the slate of names, which revealed who lived in the house. *Cassidy, Daralis and Lillian.* A slow breath escaped her. The knocker on the door more coal coloured than bronze and rough to her calloused fingers.

It hammered three times. She winced. They were heavy, forceful knocks.

No response welcomed Cass. Her racing heartbeat, mechanical hum of pipes and hidden voices of Konniak filled her senses. Placing a shaking hand on the door, she pushed, and it opened inwards on creaking, dilapidated hinges. She would fix the door; she had many things to fix.

Gaslamps burned a venomous yellow in two corners, shadows stretched across low-roofed enclosure. The sparse room containing items and furniture strung throughout the room obscured the floor. Dust dulled the vision as a flickering light fell upon it. Thunderous footsteps signalled a gantry on the single tiered shack. Cass's eyes averted to the ceiling, where a swinging unused Gaslamp shook.

A heavy tightness clutched her beating chest. This was not the house that she was taken away from four years ago.

Smashed glass forced Cass to spin around. Someone stood shrouded in shadow, a silhouetted stretching to Cass's feet. A girl. Her child. An abandoned daughter. Unrecognisable in the darkened room.

"Lilly." She whispered, the word caught in her throat.

"Wake up, mom." Her daughter's voice rippled through her mind, shaking her to the core.

"Wake up, Cass." A gruff shout echoed in her ear.

She jerked and slipped; legs flailed until slamming still on a sleek surface. Cass held onto hanging hemp rope for security. Yellow vomit rolling under her feet, rippling with vibration along metallic, bolted floor.

"No idea how you could sleep through something like this, it's a talent." Jolam laughed, his arm around her waist. Engines roared through her head. The world blurred, shaking up and down, teeth chattered, threatening to snap in her skull.

"You can stop holding me now." Cass half-turned and beckoned over her shoulder.

"Pity." Winked Jolam. An inmate on the other side of the narrow landship vomited. Bile splattered the prisoner in front and greased the bronze decking of the transport.

Cass had been in a landship before, in same conditions. During The Purifier Rebellion heading north to Riemkeler, a stronghold for zealot Purifiers fighting for independence, the first time she had been in one. Tossed around like racks of lamb on skewers. A bitter war, a long campaign. Only two seasons to survive in this war and she would be home.

"Easy, easy, Cass?" Jolam's gloved hand cupped her side, steadying her.

"You always have my back?" Cass shouted.

"It's the second-best part about you." The Faun laughed. She did not take the bait. Better than the alternative. Another four years in Ralake, or a stint in war. She could stay alive. That was down to her. Cythea would have to keep its bureaucratic word to release the prisoners afterwards.

Shaking vision caught Stell nearby, her face a pale shade like the moon in SnowFall. The illegal prostitute only had a few years left, fair and had teeth. No need for her to be wasted in war for a chance of freedom.

The landship skidded. She crashed into the broad body before her. A black braid of hair whipped close as the brooding face of Taze half turned, surveying Cass with disinterest. Whooshing air and churning cogs gave way to mechanised hiss and grating of gears. The landship slid to a slowing stop.

"'Bout time." Someone spat.

"Least that's over. Hooves were killing me." Jolam patted her on the back. Wars were usually not so lucky. The group in the transport coughed and groaned, skidding on sleek surface of the landship.

Grinding cogs and chains rotated, front part of the landship lowered like a brass arm dragged down. Inmates filed out. Only one direction Cass could go, for now, and that was forward. She had to survive for Lilly.

The world came to a steady focus. Cass looked up at Orschallian granite skies, grey with brewing thunder clouds. It would have been clearer if smog had not smudged the sky in coal's industrial belching.

"Blessed Tree Father, is it always this cold in Orschal?" Jolam wrapped his tattered greatcoat around him. Cass fed her hands deep into pockets. She was not lucky enough to have a belt. Disadvantage of the Penal Legion: second-hand gear.

Jolam was right, she observed. It was cold, even for Orschal, famous for its snow, grey winds, sleet and ice sheets. She had lived through 1869's bad SnowFall season, even had to bunk with Jolam. Her last time with male company.

Frost hacked against Cass's face, tasting like cold steel. She knew it took some time to travel from Ralake to Orschal, another continent on another map, but that did not concern her. Narrowed eyes cast a glance at spreading grey clouds, a web of thunder boiled within ashen skies.

Cass jolted to the side, pushed out of the way by Cythean troopers streaming past. Cream pith helmets glistened with frost; panting mouths steamed, rising in their industrious march. Speckled flags hung in the dying breeze, trumpets blew, and coarse voices barked. Pale sun faded as foreign birds flew overhead, their six wings beating madly in their retreat, heading west. Heading away from where the army marched.

"Not what I expected at all." Stell grasped Cass's arm and linked them together.

They stood, huddled. Low skies shed fleeting snow. Already the surface of the earth peppered white, dying yellowed grass among the victims of SnowFall season. Cass looked up, tightening her grip on Stell. LeafFall season must have been short.

"Penal Legion, follow me." She tensed and faced east, in the army's direction. Her breath steamed, drawing the greatcoat closer. Stell shivered in their embrace, the youthful look of innocent greying on her inmate's skin.

Pale, high-cheeked boned men and women wearing pitch-coloured uniforms, lined in rich purple, filed back. Elaborate bows strung over their backs. Spiked black helmets crowned their heads looking like thorns. Beside them, in armour that appeared to be made of glass and in the fashion of mosaic tiles, another troupe of soldiers marched west away from the crimson and cream current of the Cythean army.

"Orschallian elite, pulled back." Cass heard a Cythean trooper trotting beside her, talking with a colleague.

"If the elite are leaving, the battle must be done. Can taste freedom already." Jolam grinned. Snow crested his curly, chestnut-coloured hair.

"You don't waste your best in a meat grinder." She recalled from a previous life in the Cythean army. Grunts went in first, weakening the enemy, then the best mopped up, the same in life as it is in the army. She tightened her grip on Stell and held her closer.

"Penal Legion. Pike and carry!" Barked a commanding voice. Cythean soldiers, beige pith helmets and carrying bolt-repeaters, formed a three-ranked line. Typical Cythean formation, relying on discipline, bolt-repeaters and overwhelming firepower. Nothing pretty, but efficient. A hundred years ago they wore scarlet coats and black breeches, now they wore khaki greatcoats for weather and fur-lined boots for hard, foreign terrain. Experience taught them practicality and versatility for battle.

Pikes, eight-foot spears, were held in carrying crates. Two inmates handed them to an approaching prisoner. Cass led Stell forward. Jeers and shouts rained down on the inmates. An Arbiter of the Law waved his iron cudgel, directing the prisoners, his grim, lantern shaped jaw the only vestige of humanity.

"Hold it against your chest, wrap your arm around it for support." She guided Stell.

"It's too big." Stell whimpered.

"That's what she said." Jolam sang.

"Not now." Cass snapped. Beads of sweat tickled down her face, itching cold skin. Silence grew between them as Jolam flared in redness. He trotted away with his pike. Mumbling.

"Make a soldier out of you yet, thief." Taze rasped.

Cass headed to the front, the Arbiter's cloaked form facing them. She passed Jolam crouched beside him.

"Time and place, Jol, not now. Sorry." Cass laid out her pike. No point in holding it now, only when it mattered.

"Prepare pikes and die for Cythea." The Arbiter shouted. He marched down the ranks, looking broader than an aurochs. His crimson cloak skirting the mud churning ground, heavy and thick.

"I want a repeater." An inmate demanded, four places down.

"Eyes down." Cass warned Stell. The iron cudgel drove down on the inmate. A splitting crack felled the protester. He got his freedom at the price of his life. He got off lightly. Arbiters were renowned for their brutality of keeping their victims alive longer.

"Get the pike ready." Cass encouraged Stell. Snows fell, peppering a chestnut brown muddy field. She gripped the pike in steady, gloved hands, placing the shaft against her foot in the earth's sludge. Soon it would be hard with frost and ungainly.

"Against your foot, like this." she instructed.

"She's crow food, Cass the thief." A rasping voice breathed in her flank. She gritted her teeth. A shiver coursed down her spine, from the voice not the swirling snows or the threat of frost crackling in the air. Cass turned, seeing Taze kneeling beside her, pike raised.

"Repeaters, lock and load." The orders shouted down the line. Taze winked at Cass.

Grumbles echoed along the lines, tips and shafts of the spear line wavered as she glanced past Taze, pike points stretched until disappearing into a descending mist. Belly somersaulted with fluttering butterflies. She gripped the pike tighter.

A bestial howl echoed in the distance. Wind died. A coolness shadowed above. Nature cowered under the roar. Coldness touched Cass's heart, a different cold. Leather boots creaked, wooden repeaters shuffled and steady breaths turned to shaking pants.

"It would have made a great oil painting, an artist like Shintani and Freath could capture this day and save if for an eternity." A whimsical voice lamented behind Cass. *Shintani be damned so long as they could live this day to see the end.*

Convulsions rippled along the ground. Pike trembled against her boot. She gripped it tighter. It was a herd of animals; it had to be, a thunderous pounding of hooves fleeing across wintry plains. Cass dared not blink. Pikes along the lines fell, twanging off the ground.

"Steady pikes!" The Arbiter blasted.

Through low-lying mist, they thundered. Grey and black, brown and red. Primals descended on the thin Cythean line. Cass's eyes blinked at the mass of animals baring down on them, some on all fours, others limbered on two gangly legs. Simian featured with horns, open maws, a tinkering of metal glittered among the horde, carrying scattered remnants of their defeated foes. Always the noise. Howls and roars, deep and stomach shattering, a resonating baritone with the intensity of a furnace. Her stomach could have turned inside out had she eaten this morning.

"Repeaters fire." A commanding voice ordered.

A multitude of deafening whirs echoed in response. Cass's head lowered. Stell cried out beside her.

"Stay still, don't move." She shouted. Someone laughed beside her.

Primals dropped and rolled, skidding in the slick snow, but more leapt over the mounting dead and kept coming with a ferocious, booming determination. They stood, waving their claws, hammering talons on chests while throwing things at the line. A blood strewn pith helmet landed in front of Cass.

The beasts stopped. Gave a last howl and leapt backwards, ploughing into their own ranks, running from the Cythean line. "Cease fire." A relieved voice shouted down the line.

Jubilation rang out, laughing and shouting of hysteria. Cass dropped her pike and hugged Stell. The young woman racked with sobs.

"First wave over, but you must be ready. Pick up your pike, come on." She rubbed the shaking back of Stell. Cass knew Stell only signed up because of her. She would see them both survive.

"I can taste freedom already!" Cheered Jolam. She elevated her pike, digging it into the ground, gripping it tighter, knowing its secure balance would take her home, give her a chance to see her daughter.

"Ah, see that convict, we didn't even need you." A Cythean shouted.

"Ready weapons." Cass shouted. Silence descended on the ranks.

"Who are you to give orders, criminal!" A chorus of voices rebuked.

"Damn Brand telling us what to do."

"They were testing for weaknesses." Cass snapped, half turning back to face her accusers. Two Cythean soldiers stared at her. Repeaters clicked on being reloaded. Taze balanced her pike, levelling it with strong rigidity. Her lips pursed, ready to speak.

"But… they're animals." A voice called out.

"No," Cass sighed. She turned her back to the Cythean's. Purple veins grew and flared in the clouds, wind picked up. Her eyebrows knitted together. "They're worse."

"Here they come." The warning called down the ranks. Hysterical laughter and celebration ceased in a heartbeat. Breaths caught in the tightness of mouths. An edge of unnatural light grew in the fleeting ambience of the sky. Something was different.

The ground shook. Tremors paled compared to the first charge. Thunderous rumble that continued to pulsate and grow powerful and constant. No howling, screeching or roaring. Silence broken with the vibrations through tight leather boots.

With a frightening speed, they descended upon the Cythean line. A rippling splinter of a sound echoed overhead, followed by air piercing cries. Arrows thudded into the ground, dropping and catapulting the closest Primals. The heavy repeaters could only do so much.

Primals parted. Massed in groups, they barrelled towards the line. Bolts killed them, arrows rained death, and they still advanced with a hunger and malice in their maws. Cass circled her numbing fingers around the pike's heavy shaft. Arm burned. Limbs ached. Cacophony around her continued to ring and thunder. An ear-splitting screech and a careen of noise sounding like metal grinding off metal waved through the air. Her eyes narrowed, the sound penetrated her skull, rattling eyes in their sockets.

The Primals flanked her periphery, the sound obvious enough. They hit and swamped the Cythean lines. Cartridges of repeaters clattered to the ground.

Roaring grew and barrelled around her. The fog thickened, moving with the Primals, shielding them.

"Stell, at my side. Jolam, come close." Cass shouted, her throat burning raw and strained.

A blood-soaked Primal leapt forward. Stell shrieked. She levelled the pike at the beast. The pike bent, snapping. The beast crashed to the ground, thrashing. Her arms tingled, holding the broken shaft of the pike.

"Hold on." Cass discarded the broken pike and wrapped her body over Stell, holding her pike. Another Primal, ravenous, leaner, leapt forward, skidding past its fallen kin, twitching like the man in the warehouse.

Whirring whistles zipped overhead. Bolts pierced the charging animal. One, two, four, six. It would not stop leaping, becoming more aggressive with each shaft shot at it. Cass gritted her teeth and lunged with the pike. It lanced wide of the beast, unbalancing it. A crossing pike flashed. Primals face exploded, its maw severed and fell to the ground. The killing pike yanked backwards.

"You owe me." Taze shouted.

"Get behind me. Behind me." She roared, voice cracking. Stell scuttled and latched around her, the girl's face buried into her back. Jolam came to her side, pike in front. Taze knelt beside her. Cass's world shrank as she realised the Cythean line had become a disjointed circle, before her Primals and nothing else.

"Repeaters are empty." A shrill cry caused a chill to steel her arms. Primals ripped into people, cries of desperation echoed through the suffocating fog.

The beasts lurched from the fog, black shapes on all fours, then walking upright. One Primal carried a blood-splattered, broken pith helmet. It crunched under its four-legged walk. It bore into her mind. Meat and flesh smeared the ground as it lumbered forward. Bile bubbled in her throat. She would get back to Lilly. Cass gripped the pike.

They stopped.

Primal eyes widened, and their simian heads averted to the darkening sky. In a shrill shriek, they bolted away, tripping over each other in their wake. Cass sagged, Stell's weight pressed on her back.

"We, did it?" Jolam hesitated. "Did we?"

The world turned obsidian as silence descended. The pike slipped free of aching limbs as Cass stood, aiding Stell to rise. Everyone looked to the skies. Nobody moved in her periphery. People muttered. Fog rolled back. Purple light filled the world, forcing Cass to shield her eyes. Squinting through the cracks of her fingers, hairs stood on end along her arm. The sun was not there.

A void opened in absence of natural light, only purple bathed the world. Clouds departed. *Something* moved. It rotated; a ball of whiteness halved with a slit. Entirety of the sky split. Cass's skin jolted at the eruption of noise around her, but she kept staring, gripping Stell, who quivered in her arms, to reassure her, even though it was more for herself. Those that dared to move ran, others rooted to Orschal's frosting ground.

"It's an eye." Cass breathed.

She blinked, trying to ignore the truth of her own realisation, but the slit moved, peered, and changed into its searching mass.

The world washed in redness. A redness matching a raging furnace. Cass heard stories of dust-storms that blow through Kheda Ishan and how it turns the world red, like a veil of blood, a fog of fire. This was no burning fog or veil, but crimson light had washed the earth.

"Mom?" Lilly's voice asked. Cass lowered her head. She shook it from side to side. A girl stood before her. She could be Lilly. She had her father's eyes and her hair.

"Mom, I'm scared." Lilly's voice cracked. Small mouth trembling, eyes wide. She stepped forward.

"No, please." The child's shaking arms reached out. Cass stopped, paralysed at the sight of her daughter denying her closeness.

"Sorry. I didn't mean this." Restless arms lowered by her side, fingers twitched. Feet pivoted in sleek mud, half ready to run.

"You must go." Lilly covered her mouth with her hand, tears streaming down her angelic face. Brown hair tangled and unkept, exactly how she likes it.

"No," Cass shouted, her vision blurry with emotion. "I'll never leave you again, I promise."

A roar thundered behind Lilly. A clawed hand burst from her green dress, outstretched and tattered in black, bloodied flesh. The child's face contorted with death, but eyes glared with disappointment.

"NO!" Cass shouted, running forward and hammered her fists onto the Primal hand.

Lilly fragmented. Breaking apart into dust, she drifted like a thousand decaying leaves ascending to the heavens, swirling with snow. She collapsed to her knees, sinking into muddied ground. Gloved hands curling in vain to catch the ashes of her daughter.

"Lilly." She panted. Tears stung her cheeks, burning cold from relentless, biting Orschallian frost.

An eclipse shadowed overhead. She looked up through blurring eyes and glanced at retreating metal slither into thunderous clouds, violet light faded into granite, wintry skies. She shook her head, tear-soaked eyes playing tricks, making her see an iron moon shift behind rolling thunder.

Her head sank. Arms dropped. The world outside Cass's mind exploded into a hurricane of erupting madness. Her world shrank to gloved hands gathering fallen snow.

Vincentas

Chapter IV

Through crimson, burning mist of industrial smoky breath, Vincentas's eyes lit up with the entrapping of Konniak. Black religious spires, furious belching vents and jets of flame, a red scene played beneath a bleeding sky. Constant grinding of a city at work filtered into his ears, reverberating down his arms. Released from one self-isolating prison into another cage of endless pathways, unnamed faces, continuous buildings, and screams of mechanisation. A dizzying spectacle with no direction or natural purpose.

Maze of structures grew, melding into one cathedral of habitation and labour. Communion of endless unfamiliarity; always heading to toiling chores. Dense congregation, a multitude of people, prone to stab and rob than say good morning and tilt a top hat.

"Read all about it. Cythean troops in Orschal fighting Primals." A boy news-crier shouted headlines, trying to entice the marketers and buyers to purchase the paper.

Even in the merchant's ward, where most viewing balconies were located, SnowFall sky remained distant as Athgeric, muddled with bleakness of the present. It should have been snowing, but affluency stop natures showing. A patter of rain, barely noticeable, added a sheen to the murky world, highlighting its grim glory.

Vincentas flicked his collar up as he drew his faded greatcoat around himself. He should be cold, but there was no coldness in Konniak. Nothing natural lived here.

Buzz of chattering forced the Inquisitor to turn, to check voices were not his imagining, it would not be the first time since leaving Dunright Hospital. Nearby stalls opened, denizens milling around, maids carrying heavy buckets supported on tired shoulders. Coal-faced boys ran with a circular wooden hoop. Annoying laughter, the putrid stench of perfume. Eyes narrowed at their collective throng.

Raised shouts and shrill gasps forced Vincentas's glance. Two men in top hats knocked over. People screamed. Many parted. Hand gripped the obsidian hilt. The malachite blade could harm others, but he would rather use it on the Mystic. Wild grey hair caught his vision. He looked more Primal than human. Turning around, he kept looking at the encircled crowd. Blue, crazed eyes lost in a mass of tangled, ashen locks.

"It's not real, none of it. I can't be real." He barked and giggled at his nonsense. Leaping between his gathered audience, they naturally backed away like he had the plague, tripping over themselves. A woman screamed, forcing Vincentas to pick his ear. A man wearing a crimson waistcoat hacked with his cane.

"Get back, you Bogsider!" The man lunged.

"They rule, they rule. Birdmen rule." He flapped bare, bony arms, cawing as he circled. His audience chuckled in sparse relief; the mob parted, knowing he was more harm to himself than to them. Others held firm, captivated by the maddening individual. Someone threw a rotten turnip, which splattered over his naked, scarred body.

Stopping mid-flow on his prancing, he faced Vincentas. One foot aloft, his arms half raised as if being crucified. Silence grew, whispers increased. They were looking at him. Noticing the "I" tattooed over his nose, the tallied tattooed count on his cheeks and the cockel hat of Inquisitorial authority; how a brand and cloth can change people's demeanours in seconds. The crowd were puppets following their puppet master and his crazy sideshow.

"They are here. Here. Here." He shouted, collapsing to scabbed knees. Two Arbiters of the Law ascended on the scene. They descended on the man. One clubbed him on the head. Boots unleashed savage street-justice. A stray, sharp clap saluted the Arbiters and their brutal sentence. Another joined. Every Cythean city has one thing in common: no-nonsense Arbiters.

Vincentas's time in the asylum laid witness to not so dissimilar ravings. Mad rantings of birdmen. A snort of remembrance emptied throat of industrial bile. The asylums perfect for them, but not for him. He turned his back on hearing the man dragged away and vowed it would never happen to him. He would sooner use the handbow on himself.

"That's one way to make someone silent." A female voice purred, mimicking his own thoughts. His periphery vision blurred, a scent of lavender tickled nostrils, flaring his past to life.

"Who would believe him anyway with that look?" The woman beside him continued. She could have been in his head. Vincentas had to agree. A fashionable haircut, sharp tailored suit, a top-hat and a walking cane would make the man more presentable. Nobody in Konniak would listen to anyone unless they looked like high society.

"Why are you so quiet? I am talking to you." Her voice hardened. He turned, brows knitted together. Her plain face, unmarked by soot, lay level with his own. Brown hair drawn back formed a chignon held at her scalp. Precision and delicate care had gone into her appearance.

"Prostitution is illegal unless you have a permit." The Inquisitor stated, he had no patience for a lady of pleasure. He had no time for ladies, the only women he knew were in the Inquisition. Or his dead wife.

"If I was that sort, I would not be talking to you." She tried to pat him on the chest with a red, leather-gloved hand. He parred it away with a harsh slap. Fingers clenched into balled fists, creaking leathers spoke of her own hands shadowing his stance.

"That eager to have your crinkled chin broken, old man?" Narrowed, pencilled eyebrows revealed nothing as the woman stepped back.

"I'm not the one backing away." Vincentas snarled. Dry skin bled sweat, itching at his fading hairline.

"I should have introduced myself sooner, than to experiment with an Inquisitor. But your friend told me so much I had to do my own investigating." She smiled, a glimmer ignited brown eyes.

"Only the blind or foolish would not see I am an Inquisitor." He stepped forward. The woman braced himself on the railing, separating her from certain death by a thousand feet.

"There are many Inquisitors. But only one Vincentas, friend to Athgeric." The woman nodded, almost a bow, her unwavering eyes never breaking the gaze they shared. Black velvet boots crowned long legs, a close fitted emerald jacket revealed bulges to her left and right side, holstered handbows. Moving with a lethality that spoke of a murderous profession, she drew her red gloved hands together, knitting them as one.

"You're a Combatant." The Inquisitor smiled.

The woman mocked a salute. Her left hand entering her tailored jacket, fingers clasping an object within. This must have been Constance's message about the viewing balconies.

"You're a smart one. This is from my former employer." She threw a red rectangular object at him. Vincentas fumbled to catch it. He studied the tattered book, eyes widening upon noticing Athgeric's diary in his grasp.

"He wouldn't part with this willingly." Eyes tracked up to the smiling woman.

"Only if it meant you finding out. Doing what you do best, investigating." She revealed nothing. Not a trace of sweat lined her unblemished, pale face. Brown eyes vacant, reflecting himself and the metal enclosure of Konniak.

Twitching fingers opened the small red book. First page contained his own cursive High Cythean lettering.

When the night is at its darkest, the dawn will be the brightest.

Vin.

He could have written it yesterday, if not for the yellowed pages and stained, dog-eared curls. Undeniable, Athgeric's notebook.

"How did you get this?" Vincentas knew his friend was dead. He had to be. Nothing would separate him from the logging notebook he kept.

"My Inquisitor said for you check the last dated entry before he dismissed me. Inquisitor Constance found me later. She told me how to find you." He strained to hear her words through the rising hum of the city. News-crier continued; cranes winched their swinging cargo higher. Paper flicked as he opened the diary. Towards the end, his fingers ceased the book's movements. Dry skin tightened at the ruffled pages.

Date scratched out multiple times, threatening to tear the page apart.

… *Day of LeafFall. Check the morgue.*

A finger traced over the scratchings. LeafFall. Check the morgue. The Mystic bodies.

"You saw him last?" A gulp reverberated down his throat.

"Before he vanished without a trace, he let go of his retinue, even dropping the boring Chanter." She backed away, linking gloved hands together.

"How did you come into possession of this?" Vincentas levelled his eyes at the Combatant.

"Not a good listener, are you, for an Inquisitor." Her hands raised. "Alright, I'll say again. Athgeric gave me it, told me to find you."

"Good day to you, Combatant." Snapping the book closed, he pocketed the diary and headed for Inquisitorial Ward.

"Wherever you go, I follow." The woman spoke at his side, as he navigated between milling groups, ponderous walkers and sweaty labourers moving goods. Allure of her perfume dissipated among the festering sweat and oily combustion.

"You've served your Inquisitor well, now you are dismissed, unless Constance has need of you." Vincentas retorted.

He spun without realising it, misty world a blur of molten red and faded ebony before staring at the woman levelled with himself.

"You are without a Combatant." A grasp tightened on his inescapable wrist. A determination flared within opal eyes. Athgeric picked them well. Inquisitor Hadramel's influence always lasting.

"We are not going anywhere with us holding hands, Combatant." A smile curled at his lips. Faint, cold rain patted his face, flickering at the heavy greatcoat bound over his shoulders. The vice grip loosened.

For the worst part of two candlemarks, Vincentas manoeuvred through intersecting structures of Konniak. Crossing into wards with a mere glance, bypassing columns of habitants and workers.

Industrial might give way to devout iconography. Spires that cleaved a black landscape with impunity and raw technological marvel heralded the proximity of the morgue within the bowls of the Inquisitorial Hall.

"Pray for the faithful departed. Their souls know peace. Their bodies free of anguish." A strong, toned voice barked at a crowd of kneeling citizens. Black mitre lined in red, three tassels hung bearing the years of office. A Bishop of the Continental Church.

"Ahem." A shrill voice cried.

"Praise our saviours." An enthusiastic woman cried out before collapsing onto cold, black concrete.

"Parents of soldiers sent to die in Orschal." The Combatant snorted, shaking her head. The Inquisitor studied the woman, as she placed a tricorn hat over her fashionable, tidied hair.

"You're like Fleur." He mused.

"Mhm?" The Combatant questioned.

Vincentas waved it off. "What's your name, anyway?"

"Violet." She kept a good pace without breaking sweat. Coldness ached his bones, itchy beads of perspiration clawed his face. Age cursed him. Never an alignment before was ever a concern.

Inquirer Hall lay in several sections, a maze of growing spires, blackened corridors, lightless halls and web coated ceilings. A novice could be lost within the city-sized ward and never find the beginning. A decrepit adumbration of its former self.

A skull-vibrating strike echoed like a thunderclap, signalling another candlemark had passed. Coldness crept over him, under black-taloned shadows of enormous towers, ensnaring himself and Violet. The plaza, enough to fit fifty dwellings or more, drowned under theocratic power.

"I have a day." Vincentas spoke, remembering Constance's words. An Inspector would investigate if Constance had recorded the sentence. No Inquisitorial office, no malachite sword and no power to find Athgeric. No means to pay retribution for the past.

"Hope you know where we are going." Violet mumbled, as he headed towards one of many several doors lining black pillared walls.

Gaslamps lay hooked, ready for taking. Dust hugged the brass contraption, their light limited until cleaned by rough sleeves on smooth bell-shaped glass. A good shake revealed the well-stocked oil.

In silence, the Inquisitor lead Violet through blackened corridors. Echoing footsteps their constant companion, shadowing click of heels and rising heartbeats. Isolation accompanied a long journey, bypassing an odd savant, lost in a book, an acolyte praying to a standing statue or a warden scholar carrying tomes.

A familiar scent of primrose and lavender disappeared. Hanging dampness violated nostrils. Violet coughed, her sleeve covering nose and mouth, eyes and eyebrows twitched against old stenches. Rats scurried along moss growing corners, fleeing under revealing light. Two red fading doors lay ahead.

"Use these." Vincentas encouraged, outstretching the Gaslamp towards a rack of scientific cylinders containing amber liquid.

"Blocks the scents." He dabbed two fingers into one cylinder and rubbed his taunt skin with the liquid beneath his nostrils. Never enough, but every little helps in the morgue.

Without waiting for Violet, he killed the Gaslamp light and entered the red doors.

Coldness hit him first. Shivering, gloved fingers pulled his greatcoat closer. The stench came second. Lingering in nostril and throat, an odour both pungent and sweet, incense and rot. Even the alchemy mixtures dabbed across the nose could not withstand nature's putrid decay.

Humming a childish nursery tune, an Orderly bent over examining a grey-skinned corpse on the verge of bloating. Unmoving legs, still features, bare limbs and shoulders. Another Mystic brought in by a successful Inquisitor.

"Greetings, Orderly." Vincentas strengthened his voice and stepped forward, boots echoing on stone, slippery surface of the morgue.

"Oh my, I never." The Orderly straightened. Turning around, he removed spectacled eyepiece. A whole plethora of glass monocles lay attached to the device fitting perfectly around his bald cranium.

"An Inquisitor. Good show, good show sir." He spoke, while peeling off elbow-length gloves, a slipping sound emitted after removing the gloves sent shivers down the Inquisitor's spine. He strode to Vincentas, oblivious to the crimson splashes marking his apron, shirt and dirtied trousers.

"Love your work. All for the greater good. A good Mystic is a dead one." The Orderly laughed in short, dry heaves. Ice eyes sparkled with life. A mouth smiled with too many teeth. Smoky vapours left his mouth on every word spoken.

"I need your assistance; my name is Inquisitor Vincentas." The Inquisitor tilted his head up.

"Vincentas." The Orderly placed crimson, withered hands on his face, cupping them together beneath a hooked nose.

"Yes. Yes." A gnarled finger waved. Burgundy stained valleys of wrinkles after removing his hands from his face.

He shuffled off with purpose, muttering "Vincentas" over and over. Hands skittered over scrolls, knocking aside leaflets and opened books. Operating tools, grimy and unwashed, rattled on the cold floor after pushing them out of the way.

"He left something. An Inquisitor. Good man he was, good man." He watched the Orderly. Vincentas patted the diary near his chest, reassuring that the diary was in his possession. He turned, noticing Violet had not joined him. Most never had the stomach for the morgues.

"Ah ha! Here." Holding up an envelope in two hands, the hunchbacked man hooted. The Orderly hobbled to him, a fixed grin rested over pale, withered face. This job suited him perfectly.

Taking the envelope, he opened it and removed the faded parchment. In steady hands, he unfolded the paper and read the scribbled note.

Check the recent Mystic bodies. Athgeric.

"I order you to reveal the last body Inquisitor Athgeric and Inquisitor Vincentas brought in." He pocketed the paper.

Like a man possessed, the Orderly pulled creaking winches, spun grinding cogs and pivoted levers that needed his entire body weight to move. One hand remained on the obsidian hilt, as Vincentas watched iron square doors, lining the wall, numbering in their thousands, light up with flaring Gaslamps.

Mechanical contraptions came to a grinding halt as two tables lowered before him. Bodies lay beneath white shrouds, their distinctive shape smoking in coldness. Both lay beside each other in death, laid on the operation tables the Orderly winched together.

"Last two Mystics brought in by Inquisitor Athgeric and Inquisitor Vincentas." Wheezed the morgue attendant, gesturing to the bodies.

Despite their deaths two seasons ago, no pungent smell grated his nostrils. Standing beside the corpses, the Inquisitor removed the white shroud covering them to reveal two girls, barely out of their teens.

"Ooh. Twins." Hissed the old man, leering over the bodies. They *looked* like twins. They could have been twins. Black hair, exact height. Two identical moles on their neck. Even the liver-coloured birthmark above their naval was exact. As if a mirror lay between them, casting a reflection on the parallel operating table.

A shiver rippled down his spine, igniting his hands to flex. Fingers fixed around the obsidian hilt. Dared not to blink. A coldness grasped him not caused by freezing mechanisations to keep the bodies preserved. An inevitable icy touch clawed his body.

Vincentas circled the joined tables, boots clicking off hard, wet stone. He studied the Mystic he killed. Her illusions killed Karomeier and Luciana. She nearly ended his own life. He still had no recollection of her demise. Arno must have been behind it; the Chanter had saved him so many times the Faun should be the Inquisitor.

"What's this?" He pointed. Black angular marks lay on their skin etched over the taunt bicep. It tracked down their body, ending at the hip.

"I see, I see." The Orderly slipped on his gloves and pressed the skin. Bifocals extended on his nose, several lenses protruded, almost touching the dead body.

"Markings. But, significantly different." He piped up. Glee rippled through a nasal voice.

"Tattoos?" Vincentas asked. Cult markings, Mystics had them to identify each other without expressing who they were.

"Better." His gloved fingers stroked the markings, taking measured precaution and nerve to place the dead body's arm beside the resting Mystic. "It's skin."

His eyebrows knitted together. Mystic rituals. Athgeric knew, and only he would know. Looking at the note in his shaking hand, he turned it upside down.

Writing rippled against the note, ignited under soft light from Gaslamps.

Hairs stood on end, cursing himself for not seeing it before. His hand could not stop shaking. A single word scrawled in haste.

Riemkeler.

"Thank you, Orderly." Vincentas headed for the exit, thankful to be done with the dead.

Opening the doors, he stared eye to eye with Arno. He stopped, pocketing the note near the diary. Boots slapped on sleek marble. No sign of Violet, not even her perfumes.

"Add creeping up on people to your list of expertise." The Inquisitor half smiled.

"Implausible. You were concentrating inwardly to not observe your surroundings." The Chanter countered in his stoic manner.

"Right again, old friend." Vincentas nodded. The Chanter clothed himself for travels, a haversack strapped to his robed body, hood raised, bracing for rough weather.

"Where do we head next?" The Faun tilted his head up, light catching his eye.

"Riemkeler."

Cass

Chapter IV

"Sentence." A multitude of voices hissed. Brittle paper crackled. Shuffling chains bound Cass to stand before the judge, towering over her. The solitary word penetrated deeper than any infliction of pain.

Judge's hood fell back. The blindfolded adjudicator, a mockery that justice is blind, peered down at her with a thin-lipped smile.

"Seven years' manual labour, Ralake Island." Cass did not react to the iron cudgel hammering on the unseen gong that reverberated. She could not show her daughter weakness and did not react to the growing sickness and heaviness swelling her stomach, churning it like papers ruffling at her feet. She could not show her daughter how it affected every muscle in her body.

"No!" a girl's voice cried out in desperation. Snapping out of helplessness, her daughter, tears streaming down an innocent face, held by an Arbiter of the Law.

"Lilly, it'll be alright, I promise." Cass choked on her empty reply.

Her daughter struggled with the Arbiter, rolling her shoulders. She tried to reach her daughter, but iron chains denied her, chafing skin raw.

"Lilly, I'll be home soon, I promise." She wanted to say.

"Mom, no. Mom." Lilly screamed, while carried away.

"Leave her alone." Cass raged, blinded by tears, blurring her vision. She saw her mother, slumped over the bench, a bottle of liquor swimming in the sea of scrolls.

She screamed as her daughter, mother, and the court disappeared in streaks of light. She slammed onto a hard surface; the wind knocked out of her and locked into place.

"Well, what we got here?" A slathering voice declared.

Cass smelt him. A nose broken too many times blurred her vision, thick lips cut and grazed, eyes too far apart. A brute of a male face leered down.

"Ralake Prison, you're heading, poppet. Who is gonna hear your squeal or believe you?" He grinned with more gum than teeth. Rough hands fondled her. She twisted in limited capacity to free herself from unwanted, prying hands.

"Feisty, that'll be burnt out of you." He laughed.

A poker, smoking and hissing, raised before her sight, redness burned with a fierce tenacity. Temples bled sweat. She did not blink. She stared, shivering.

"Smile pretty, you're now branded." The poker lowered. She screamed.

Cass rushed from the vision.

Arms flailed in all directions, fighting to push away the man with the poker that faded into nothing but grey mist. Snow swirled. Coldness scythed into her mouth, choking her with frosty tendrils snaking around a dry throat with an icy grip.

"Lilly." Her steam words left a coughing mouth. She brushed snow from wet legs and stood up. Two eyes stared up at her. She staggered back, boots slipping as she fell backwards. Kicking herself away, she stopped and looked at the Primal half buried beneath falling snow, dead and blue.

"Jolam. Stell." Cass looked in vain, hoping the words would summon them. Fog lingered, sleet fell, black shades of the dead lay still on the ground, nature's burial mound of snow lay over them. She was alone. Her breath, her freezing company. Turning up her collar, the fabric nipped at her neck. Cass touched precariously at her cheek; the rough outline of the brand remained.

Crossing her arms, she placed hands under armpits for warmth and narrowed her eyes, trying to see through thick, congealed fog. Nothing moved. Nothing breathed. The wind silent as snow fell from an unseen sky.

Cass looked up. Nothing but wintry clouds.

She closed her eyes, trying to steady her breathing. Beating heart pulsating down her stomach. Eyes snapped open. Crying, a low desperate cry. A groan, a shrill shriek, a manic laugh, and a rampaging roar joined the chorus of growing noise.

Cass crouched low, ready to sprint, but nobody was there. Conversations blurred, children merrily laughed, and a distanced couple bickered. Wherever she turned to look, she heard the chatter of society and civilisation.

"My mind, is all." She mumbled.

Crouching down, she dug at the snow, revealing yellow grass beneath. Orschallian grass of the Sabinate region. The battle. Vaulting to her feet, she looked again at the sky. The eye had gone, purple and nausea inducing colours had vanished, replaced with a drab granite curtaining the world. A perfect SnowFall day, ideal for a painter.

Pulling her greatcoat tighter, she walked on. Others must be here. Hunching her shoulders, crunch of the snow beneath her hard-booted feet rippled up her spine, wind picked up, and the chatter continued. She shook her head to clear them away.

Her foot kicked something hard. A black shadow lay sprawled across the ground, too long to be human. Smelt like wet dog. Primal. Cass covered her mouth to stop the steam of her breath. It lay still, too still. She approached the lying shadow and inspected the carcass. Lacerations scarred its neck and face, no bolt protruded lined head, back or arms. Its claws flaky with dried black blood.

"It killed itself." Cass whispered, thinking back to the battle, the panic of the Primals as they bolted away, the madness that followed. Her daughter. Her eyes widened as she remembered seeing Lilly here, in the Sabinate Lands. She turned and peered, head moving to search the battlefield. More shadows broke through the veil of fog, snow shrouded black distant statues of the fallen.

Her daughter could not be here, but in Cythea. Cass covered her mouth as she walked on, bypassing the dead, the mutilated, the forgotten of war. Cythean, Primal and Orschallian littered snow-covered ground. Convict, beast, citizen, man or woman, they all lay frozen as they died.

Ignoring as best she could the blackened, rotting faces of the fallen, in fear she could see Jolam, or even her daughter, Cass stalked on.

Movement ahead made her stop. A distant figure knelt beside someone. They rocked back and forth, too gentle and lithe to be Primal. She sighed.

"Hello." Her breaking voice called out. "What's going on here? Where's the rest of the army?"

They wore a greatcoat of the Penal Legion. Beige breeches saturated in mud. A bare foot blackening with frostbite.

"Penal Legion? Me too, it's Cass…" She ceased walking.

The Penal soldier violently moved back and forth, mumbling incoherently, unseen hands moving against the unseen body of the dead Cythean as they crouched over.

War could affect the mind; asylums were common for wounded and the returned of war. Asylums for the Mystic. She backed away, keeping eyes on the rabid Penal soldier.

She knew the hair, black and sleek backed. Pointed straight ears. Karwen.

A snap echoed in her ears. Sound of dry bark rendered in half by a Bulkett, shook Cass through her core. Karwen rose, fog blurring vision as the convict compatriot turned, but she saw nothing beyond a shadowed form.

"Cass, is that you?" A voice, not Karwen's, asked. The shadow shuffled forward, arms limp. A purple glow emitted from its face.

She stepped back. "I'm here, Karwen. Have you seen Jolam?" Her arm trembled.

"Cass." Karwen's pained voice shouted.

"Run, Cass. Run." sneered a teasing, male voice.

It broke through the mist, shadow taking a knowing form.

Cass stared at the purple glowing eyes of Karwen and the blood-soaked open mouth. A contrast to the ghostly pale of her skin. Her hard, high cheekbones drawn and thin.

"Run!" Karwen shouted, raising her arms and lurched forwards. A slewed, mangled head fell from her grasp.

She turned and bolted. Heart racing louder than the flood of thoughts and voices. Her arms slapped over cold ears, blocking in vain against constant chatter grinding her skull. She ran, disjointedly, with her hands shielding ears.

Cass stopped running, taking deep, stomach heaving breaths, stench of decay filled her empty belly. A Cythean stared up lying dead before her, she spat up bile. Thin snow highlighted the bolt-repeater beside the fallen. She snatched the weapon. Loud groans and stomps of pursuit increased; the thing neared.

Karwen stumbled forward. Arms outstretched, head flung back, purple eyes flashing at Cass, searching, pursuing. She fumbled with the repeater as she knelt, the same design they used during the Purifier Rebellion. The voices, shouts, conversations, and laughter built and overpowered her beating heart. The thing growled and lurched forward.

Cass held the repeater under arm. Stinging sweat bled down her face, burning eyes. Twitching, icy fingers squeezed the trigger, the repeater clicked. No bolt fired.

Eyes widened. Karwen lunged. She screamed and closed her eyes rapidly, clicking the trigger.

Hiss of the bolts expelled from the repeater. Cass opened her eyes. The thing staggered back, three bolts covered Karwen's chest. Purples eyes dimmed. It collapsed, like a drag doll, her life strings cut.

Cass scrambled to her feet and inched forward; shaking hands grasped the repeater. She stood over Karwen, mouth agape. Purple glowing eyes returned to her distant black ones. Drawn skin melded into fuller, perky cheeks. Natural colour returned to the dead convict. Blood seeped from mortal wounds.

The repeater grew heavy in her trembling hands and slipped, clattering to the ground. Legs buckled beneath her and she fell to the hard earth; shoulders racked with sobs. Her hands rubbing away warm tears. Curling fingers into fists, she beat the snow twice and stood up. She looked down at Karwen, laying on the snows of a foreign land. Like so many others.

"Cass. Cass." She turned, hearing real voices compared to the multitude of haunting chatter and their ghostly conversations, which had ceased.

Rubbing away tear stains, she pulled at her greatcoat. She dared to hope on recognising the voice but could not see the Faun through the grey mist.

"I'm here. Over here." She shouted, after clearing her throat with a cough and spit.

Three black shadows travelled through the mist, becoming clearer as they approached. Tension left her shoulders. A deep sigh escaped a tired throat. Jolam. The Faun carried a repeater, two bandoliers crossed his chest which was clothed in a thicker, black duster coat of

Orschallian design. He carried a large haversack on two straps.

"Glad to see you, Cassy." Jolam approached and was about to embrace her. Hesitation stopped. He saw the corpse nearby. "By my manhood, Karwen. Pity."

"Always you even in this hell." She punched Jolam's arm. "How did you find me?"

"Cass." Stell's youthful voice chimed. The young girl flung herself forward and hugged her. She stumbled, surprised by the force of the illegal prostitute and her strength in the embrace. Warm, needy. She hugged back, tightening around Stell's back.

"Heard you shouting, well, didn't know it was you," Jolam replied between breaths. "Glad it is though."

"Guess Cass is now a killer, as well as a thief." A rasping voice commented. Breaking her hold of Stell, Taze circled on Jolam's left. The murderer removed an Arbiters sallet from her head. A repeater hanging at her side. She moved with an elegance of a rapier, despite her size and breadth.

"She was different, crazed." Cass replied. Too quick of a reply. Jolam crouched down to inspect Karwen.

"Poor shame, pretty lass." The Faun lamented.

The branded "M" on Taze's face twitched with her scowl, the scarred "WILMAR" on the murderer's forehead creased under frowning.

"In madness, we can all justify murder." The convicted murderer whispered, head cocked to the side.

Cass's fingers clenched, her eyes fixed on the branded murderer. "Karwen wasn't herself, she…"

"Had purple eyes." Jolam muttered.

"Yes." She gasped, studying the Faun, who stood there, eyes glassy.

"Cass, what's going on?" Stell asked, her hand squeezing her own. Only now realising the warmth within her calloused hands.

"We're going to get out of here, trust me." Cass squeezed Stell's hands. The girl smiled, the only warmth she felt seen since leaving Ralake.

"Where's the army?" She faced the Faun.

Jolam shrugged. "It was, it was. Chaos." His eyes blinked. Eyes furrowed in brows.

"Your human-fantasising Faun friend here is lost for words of the brutality we have witnessed." Taze explained while unpacking a plain tin and shovelling the dried beef in her mouth.

"Primals?" Cass asked.

Taze shook her head, held up her hand, and chewed the food. On finishing the mouthful, she licked her lips and smiled. "Worse." Head averted to the ashen sky and lowered her eyes to face Cass. The shuddering of coldness creeping down her unescapable.

"We need to get moving." Cass broke her gaze and clasped a hand on Jolam's shoulder. "Need to get moving, Jol, come on."

"This place, Cassy." The Faun whispered, his head turning and shaking, "It's nothing short of hell."

"Come on, Faun, let's leave this place." She offered.

"You'll need this, Cassy," Jolam said. He removed his haversack and unclasped the buckles, pulled out a rolled up Orschallian coat, a double of his own. "Better than the flimsy Cythean makes, better for colder weather."

"Thanks Jol, you always have my back." She removed her own greatcoat and dumped it on the ground. Cass fed her arms into the black Orschallian coat. Its length reached her calves. Warmth hugged her.

She buttoned the coat up, the size not meant for her, but the shoulder width fit well.

"Best back to look at, eh?" Jolam managed a half smile and shouldered his haversack.

"Where next lovers?" Taze rasped, resting the repeater against her hip, the barrel pointing upwards.

"The army lines. They'll know what to do." Cass suggested, putting distance between herself and this place, the first and only thing on her mind. Chance to escape would be the front lines, any chance to get back to Lilly lay in the army.

"And where do you suggest that is? Can you see through fog?" The murderer waved the repeater either side of her.

"No, but the land might help us." She pointed towards the fog that shrouded them. "We fought downhill, so going uphill will take us back to the owls."

"I like that idea." Jolam agreed, looking to where she pointed.

Cass picked up the repeater that killed Karwen, dusting off fresh, melting snow and checked the mechanism. Next time it would fire when needed. Lowering her head, she closed her eyes.

Killed Karwen, the man in the warehouse, before that in the Purifier Rebellion, but today she killed a convict that seemed afflicted by Mysticism. She had seen Mysticism before, purple eyes never fading until death.

In madness, we can all justify murder. Time to put madness in the past and reach the future of sanity.

"Come on, let's go." Cass turned, taking Stell's hand in hers.

Under granite, unchanging sky, they crossed the foul-smelling battlefield. Taze leading the way, which came second nature to her. Cass fought against gnawing hunger at her belly as she held up the rear. Stell stuck close.

Through low-lying fog, bodies lay frozen on the ground. More were human. Bloating. Black hands and missing noses. Stench like raw venison, upper-cutting punch of an odour left in Cass's nostrils and stayed there. No amount of gawking reduced its sick inducing taste.

Checking the dead, they looted corpses, necessity lead them as the dead do not need trinkets, food, coinage. The sound of silence deafening but compared to the unseen conversations from distant, whispering voices a relief. Cass deliberately placed her footfalls louder than necessary, so she could hear something or anything. Better than eclipsing silence. Dead silence.

"No birds." She commented.

"Huh?" Jolam grunted, eyes peeling around him.

"No carrion, or crows. No vultures. Nothing eating the bodies. No scavengers. It's not right." She thought aloud, keeping eyes on the unchanging sky, half expecting red light to wash the world in blood

Taze stopped and raised a clenched fist. Trouble.

Cass lowered, pulling down Stell. Jolam crouched, the Faun found it easier; she found it difficult with the longer coat. They came to Taze's side, who looked straight ahead. Fog peeled away, a scattering of violet hues dowsed the mist in murky colours. Unmistakable black shadows lay ahead.

Shapes crouched, kneeling. Animalistic grunts caused hairs to stand on end. They were no Primal grunts. Sets of purple lights shimmered in the distance on each silhouette. Just like Karwen. One shadow barked, another roared. Cass raised her repeater in shaking hands.

"Go around?" She whispered, arcing her left arm in circular motions. "Best avoid, could be more."

"I agree with the thief." The murderer added, winking at Cass. Taze skirted to the left, crouching low. Cass led Stell, who kept her eyes down and mumbled, flinching at any sound. A shrill shriek blasted through the snowy world. She snatched her hand over Stell's shaking mouth.

"Shh, it's going to be fine, trust me." She eyed the direction the cry erupted. Fog threatened to part at any moment, thinning as they wandered up the natural slope. Snow crystallised on the ground, sparkling like a sea of eyes. Remembering the eye that obscured the sky on the battlefield, Cass looked up. Clouds did not resemble a metal moon. Sky turned darker, it threatened night.

Something grasped her leg. She snapped her head down, seeing a bloodied, shaking hand hold her leg. Heartbeat flooded her mouth. Stell's muffled scream moaned into her gloved hand.

"Help me." A face streaked with mud whispered, tears watered blue eyes. "Help me, please."

Jolam levelled his repeater, Taze sauntered back. Trembling fingers let go of Cass, the figure outstretched their hands in a sign of surrender. She backed away, taking deep, methodical breaths as she looked over the lying man. Clothed in regular Cythean army attire, a conscript. No older than mid-twenties.

"We need to get moving." Taze turned.

"Can I come with you? Please?" The soldier pleaded, his voice breaking.

"Quiet, they'll hear." Jolam replied in swift spitting words.

Cass looked at the soldier, who looked between herself and Jolam. She nodded her head in response, her heartbeat steadying. She caught up with the murderer.

"He'll slow us down." Chuckled Taze as she approached, Stell stayed close, hugging into her body. Bodies on the ground thinned, the main battlefield long gone.

"We need everyone." She glanced over her shoulder. The following soldier had nothing but his beige, mud-stained uniform, broken pith helmet held limply in his hand, his face twitched side to side. "Everyone." Cass whispered.

The murderer muffled a dry laugh. "Convicts, conscripts and even Fauns."

Jolam tapped her on the shoulder and pointed to the ground. Parallel grooves churned up mud, partially filled by light snow. Long and rectangular, side by side.

"Owl tracks." She sighed. The transport landships were nowhere in sight. They were close. The smell of combustion lingered in the stygian air. Fog thinned.

"We must be near the supply wagons, let's keep moving." Insisted Taze. The group picked up the pace, disregarding their flanks and rears, but focused on heading away as quick as they dared.

"Down." Shouted Jolam. Cass jumped to the ground, dragging Stell with her. A heavy beating of wings flew overhead, followed by a whoosh of wind battering over them. She strained to look up under the downpour of the forceful wind, a large, shadowed bird disappeared into the mist.

Taze laughed and clapped slowly, looking at Jolam.

"It was heading for us." The Faun stammered, "It was huge."

"Too small to be a Roc." Cass interjected, looking at wide brown eyes.

"So much for the lack of carrion and crows." Taze teased. The gleam in the murderer's eyes reflected. *That was no crow or carrion.* She pushed herself up, pulling Stell to her feet.

"Look." The soldier pointed with an outstretched, shaking hand.

Looming outlines of transportation devices broke through the swirling haze. Some smoked, others lay on their sides. Snow buried their wheels. Mist grew thinner. Bronzed husks glinted.

"No luck using these." Taze dismissed the machines, climbing the brass chassis to inspect the closest transport.

The Faun scratched his chin. "Where's the army?"

"Ask the boy, Captain Hidden will know." Taze shouldered her repeater, looking at the soldier, who stood arms crossed and head lowered. He blinked, mouth opened to speak but swallowed his words and remained silent.

"He's like us, doesn't know what's going on." Cass moved between the transports, the stench of fuming coals and copper more accepting than decay of men and the debris of battle.

"Then what's the plan? No army, crazed people and a foreign country. I'd rather be back on Ralake." Taze laughed and kicked an abandoned box.

"We head west, back to Orschallian territory, away from the Sabinate Lands." Cass suggested.

"They'll kill us for desertion." The soldier spoke out, stepping forward, but as soon as Taze clasped eyes on him, he quietened and looked away.

"We're not deserting, not yet." Cass smiled at the soldier and winked. No army, no one to report too on a foreign continent with SnowFall season growing stronger. A chance to escape back to Lilly brightened in her mind as the world drew close on a dying day.

Vincentas

Chapter V

Blinding light curtained a silent world. Shadowed hands raised, blocking a constant barrage of golden rays. Blurring colour bled between fingers, but no heat scorched the shielding palm. A multitude of blues formed a pure sky. It could have passed for a Freath's masterpiece. A distant, yellow sun crowned an azure canvas.

Noise drowned him. Brass trumpets blasted, windy pipes blew, a familiar resonating pierce of a Hardanger's harmony crawled down his spine. Hooting of elated cries rang as a chorus for the instrumental play. Laughter punctuated loudest; celebration swam in lapping waves. Colourful streamers and flapping bunting waved.

Nothing could prepare him for succulent, tempting aroma of spitted sausages. Sizzling over roasting coals, a smoky finger curled into approachable nostrils - his stomach surrendered.

Vincentas inhaled the celebratory atmosphere. Vibrancy a foreign emotion since joining the Inquisition. Ravishing hunger gave way for a yearning of colourful country, an indifference stirred within, allowing a hand to reach out and touch soft air. Everything was different to suffocating Konniak; an industrial, sweating city.

This was life.

Children's laughter peeled to his right. He turned seeing a puppet-show. They re-enacted the tale of *Aristeo and the Roc*, along with all the quips and songs. He knew the fairy-tale, a northern tale for northern children. Only those north of Volkar River would understand it. He would sit near the back, not wanting to be suffocated with the weight of bodies around him craning necks to see wooden, jarring performers wave and jerk about.

A man lifted weights to test strength, admired by clusters of women chittering in hushed voices behind embroidered fans. A Kheda Ishan woman read palms, but all coming away with the pungent smell of Molskae as the fake seer anointed them.

A lady in an emerald dress brushed past, her bodice drawing more than a few unwanted eyes. He shook his head, alluring of false, wanton promises, a weapon not wounded by, not since his wife's passing. Two gentlemen in powdered wigs cleaned monocles and rapped their canes on cobbled streets as they passed.

"Decadence of body does not bring salvation to the soul." A clear, damning voice tore through the cacophony of celebration. Vincentas turned, catching sight of a solitary figure. Ebony and crimson vestments of the Continental Church hung from the speakers' lithe frame. Red leather-backed Book of Atonement lanced into the bright air, held aloft by a saluting arm. His brows knitted together, he only wanted one chance to clasp sight with the unseen eyes of the cleric.

He scanned for distinctive landmarks. A blue and gold ornery stood on the horizon, its dome circled in cogs, gears and mechanical tracks. Astronomical apparatus hung on the side of buildings, yellow stoned structures enclosed the festival, jagged spires and winged motifs cloistered tiled, symmetrical roofs. Two towers stood beside the ornery, noticeable any side of the city.

A prominent symbol of the city state Vincentas had seen only last year; he stayed to recover and studied, considered by Arno. Wide eyes searched for anything to discredit the idea sinking into his mind. It could be nothing but a vivid dream, or he had wandered into the realm of another's mind, or Mystic's had painted this trap for his ignorance to fall in.

Stiff, chilly breeze curled at his bare neck. A sign swung near the banners, made of oak, prized lumber of the region. His eyes widened. *Riemkeler's Market Feast.* Unblinking, he looked down at the cursive High Cythean lettering to see the date, sending a chill to course down his spine.

1872. This year. An event already transpired.

Vincentas held his breath. An eager finger jabbed into his ear, wriggling around to clear his hearing clogged by a heartbeat muffled within his ears.

Sounds of the city vanished. No rhythmic music, no peals of laughter, no tormenting preacher. Even the wind made no sigh. Bunting lay fixed, curled and unmoving.

A reveller hung in mid-air, falling back off a bench, tankards brown ale suspended in air, a foaming waterfall of murky mud-coloured alcohol caught in stillness. Faces contorted in speech, mouths ajar with laughter. None of them gave sound.

They froze. Everybody. Black birds lay in the blue skies, stuck in perpetual moment. Vincentas blinked, rubbed his hands. He clapped. An icy touch crawled down his back. No sound ruptured from connecting hands. Palms damp with sweat rubbed against each other, he fumbled to clap again.

Something breathed at his neck.

A cawed breath, drawn and broken, ignited his skin to leap. Something burnt, charred to the point of unbearable stench, circled behind him.

Softness combed through fading hair. Crackling noises like split wood followed the violation of his head. Shaking knees paralysed him. The same stench on his inauguration, the one odour he could never clean since widowed. All too familiar, all too real.

"Relax. Relax." croaked a woman's voice, spliced with cracks of whimpering.

Vincentas burst into colour. Groaning wood jerked clammy fingers to clutch linen. Something rolled beneath; a metallic object rocked into an unseen cupboard. A door knocked on a wardrobe in his periphery. Dampness soiled his nostrils.

"Awake at last then." Arno's unwavering voice alighted his sense to a singular focus. The Chanter simply dressed in extra layers. He stood at the foot of the bed; arms folded into long, warm sleeves. Coldness pinched his toes, Vincentas relaxed and sank into the uncomfortable bed, softer than the asylum.

"Can't believe how cold it is." Wisps of breath visualised his words. Eyebrows knitted together. Nothing showed where cold conjured. No draft behind

Arno, who stood looking at him. The Faun seemed to move but made no gesture to steady himself. Vision swam with motion.

"Plausible." Arno whispered. "It is the airship, rough going."

Nausea pulled eyes to close, to aid against rockiness building in swaying guts. He hated airship travel but understood its necessity to reach Riemkeler.

"Cold. Very cold." Vincentas commented, directing thoughts to the goose-pimples prickling clammy skin underneath the weight of the bedsheets.

"Must be my Faunness. Cannot make out the cold." Arno lamented. Hooves clicked on wooden flooring. "But it is SnowFall, so it must be cold. The rotation of the world and the unmoving sun demands it." His words easing the brewing headache behind the Inquisitor's eyes.

"What do you remember?" The Chanter enquired; hooves ceased their movements.

Vincentas's eyes opened. Brown oak arches like a ribcage spanned the ceiling. His damp nostrils smelt burnt hair, decayed flesh. Nothing could shake off remembrance.

"Fleur drank with the new apprentice. That foul cook served steaming lumps of grey meat." Dry, cracking voice sounded distant to his own ears, his voice not his own.

"I meant, what do you remember of the dream?" Arno asked, knowing eyes surveyed him.

"Nothing." Vincentas rubbed his temples.

"You are a poor liar." He looked up on hearing the growl in Arno's voice. The Chanter's head shook slowly, brown unblinking eyes held his gaze.

"A festival. They attacked it. Nothing really." His stomach growled in reply on mentioning food, his head swam with a nausea that threatened to engulf his throat and project its feelings.

"Strange. Unlike you to be so reclusive." Arno's head tilted. "Stranger still, you have had no nightmares for four years."

Vincentas snorted. "Keeping count? Primals draw the conclusion of fear within me." He wrung hands together, skin like paper. Age catching up in a remorseless march.

"Plausible." Summarised the Chanter, snaking arms from captive sleeves. "Some fear, to bring on screaming." Arno's voice sounded sincere, but the Inquisitor did not rise for the courteous bait.

"It was just a dream. Nothing more." He dismissed, fixing gaze with the serene Faun. Beads of sweat clawed down his itching face.

"Dreaming is far from nothing, Inquisitor." The Chanter warned. His voice had that lecturer's edge, Hadramiel's teaching in full swing. Vincentas heard it before.

"A dream is a dream. Nothing to it." He snapped at the cold air; his breathing prominent with each sign.

"Mystics are powerful, Inquisitor. Dreams are their gate. A dream is their weapon. A dream can be our undoing." Cold words crawled down his spine with an icier touch than the frosty, nipping air in the cabin.

"Leave me, Chanter." He finished. Vincentas remained silent, watching Arno as he turned without his customary bow and headed towards the door, hooves clopping, echoing his own heartbeat.

"One more thing." The Faun raised his head, drawing his long coat around him and raising the dirtied collar. "You were not the only one screaming tonight."

The Faun opened the door. Swinging with violent ferocity, dragging Arno with it. He turned his head as wind blasted into the room. Eyes closed, a shielding arm raised in vain, hoping to endure the onslaught. The door rattled shut, an uneasy, broken silence descended in the cabin as wind snuffed to a whimper.

Vincentas's sigh caused limbs to sag. His first breath since Arno left. Dehqan would wait. Once the Sabanese had a task, he would not stop until finished. Dishonourable to keep him waiting. He could not stay in the cabin during the trip, even if his nauseating stomach protested.

He changed, finding it easier to sit down and force limbs into clothing. Feeding arms into his faded greatcoat, he opened the door and met, head down, blustery weather. Sleet whipped his face, lashing his retreating hair. No need for the cockel hat right now.

"'Bout time you showed yourself." A punch knocked his arm, a bruise would form when before it would not. Cursed age than the mocking punch. Fleur's bronzed half-mask blocked grey, windswept skies. She smiled as far as he could tell.

"Thought I'd rest longer." The deck of the airship stretched out to the fog bank. Wooden poles holding propellers faded to dark shadows, blurred in wintry blizzard. Vincentas only glimpsed silhouettes of the propellers. Their spinning strained over howling gusts. So long as they kept spinning, he did not mind their noise.

"Aye, rest. You did it." Fleur laughed. Distant crew members milled around the port-side. A tall crewman dragged an arbalest bolt towards the mast that contained the crows-nest. Biting cold gnawed at exposed cheeks. He rubbed them with his gloved hands.

"How's the new one?" He asked. A minor conversation hid his observation of the deck and the human cargo.

"That fella. He's got stamina." Fleur nudged him, not where she landed the punch. Felt like a dead arm, muscles numbed.

"He is an Entrant, don't ignite his mind." Vincentas looked at his Combatant. She crossed her arms, hands clasping elbows. Strands of blonde hair whipped before her face underneath a raised grey shawl.

"Aww. But he's so young." Teeth flashed brightly underneath the polished bronze mask. "We were playing cards, and it got down to strip version of it, men, can't seem to handle it then. But *him*."

"Cut to the point. Your drawling is rocking my head more than this floating death trap." Vincentas groaned.

"Well, he was winning. I lost my jacket, leather cuirass and the bodice. But his investigating eyes were not on my eyes, or his own cards, for at least a candlemark. So, I tapped him on the cheek, went out like a light and put him to bed." Her hands re-enacted the night, gratuitously making images only a blind person would miss.

"Striking an Entrant of the Inquisitorial Order is a death sentence." He met her playful gaze with his returning, hardened eyes, which died abruptly.

"You're losing your edge, old man." Fleur leaned in, her aroma of stale beer and two days of unwashed sweat uppercut his nostrils.

"Anything else you want to report on." Hands fed into pockets, drawing the surrounding coat in vain, shielding against icy wind and whipping frost-tasting rain.

"Ah, don't give me that look. Don't worry yourself, I didn't take advantage of him, I've got some class." Fleur mocked a surrender with raised hands.

"Sleep well during this?" Vincentas cocked his head to the wintry weather, more so than the airship and its turbulent voyage. *You were not the only one screaming tonight.*

"Slept like the dead." One brow drew close behind the mask, her thinking face. "But the new kid, he didn't sleep well."

"Sick from the journey?" He tried to sound sincere through a grating, dry voice.

"No. Not sick. Not even from the amount he drank. He was screaming something wild. Nearly knocked me out of the hammock." Fleur smiled. Arno was right. Vincentas made a mental note to investigate Alleck's nightmare later.

"Thank you, Fleur. Be ready for the airdock." He nodded, Fleur mocked a salute.

Her eyebrows wiggled, and she nudged him. "Get some more meat on you and you'd have more chance than the Entrant." She sniped before leaving.

"I'll not pass on the extra slice of aurochs then." The Inquisitor smiled and Fleur winked. She wandered off, keeping her hands in her jacket pocket.

Vincentas surveyed the deck. The odd crewman glanced his way, then turned back to complete chores. Passengers who roamed the deck, suitably dressed, gave him a wide berth. A stray wolf-whistle headed for Fleur but shot down with a hand gesture. She had the knack of having a reputation spread quickly.

A solitary female figure stood on the starboard side. Her black dovetail coat looked as drab and unrecognisable like the thousand others in circulation. Her silhouette, unrecognisable, but keen instinct, told him it was Violet. His headache swept to the side, becoming a mild nuisance.

Drifting eyes caught the unmistakable slouch-hat of Sabanese design. Through mist, Dehqan stood stark as a burning visage. Yellow glowing light cast over Vincentas as he approached the Sabanese man. The effective Combatant, his duel wielding handbows on each hip, studied his miniature orrery and posed sextant, how he read those in this weather was beyond his Inquisitorial skills.

"Least someone's working. Even I'm slacking." The Inquisitor grunted his appreciation. Snow frosted cold nostrils, dampening anything he tried to smell. Pungent coal and moist wood all over his nose digested. He longed for sizzling meats or even a thick porridge.

"Must be captivating. Don't know how you read it in this weather." Placing gloved hands on the nearest rail. Nothing revealed itself. No discerning, jagged mountain peaks. No green, stretching forest. A mist blanket clouded their travels.

No reply from Dehqan. Vincentas turned to see the Sabanese man looking at him, sextant in hands. The slouched hat flapping in the wind. Wrinkled features hard.

"What's troubling you?" He inquired, keeping his voice as low as possible.

"Missing days." The words colder than biting wind.

"Are you sure?" Keeping his head low, he moved closer to Dehqan, not wanting their secret conversation to be captured by an eager wind.

"Can be no other way." Vincentas's eyes caught the sextant shaking in the Combatant's grasp. He never shook. Steady Sabanese, a trait known throughout the world. A frosty hand touched a nerve at his spine. Tension gripped a tired body.

A smoky haze signalled his words. "How many days?"

"Forty-nine." Vincentas heard but could not believe. Dehqan nodded, lowering his brass implements. The Inquisitor searched the wrinkled, stern face, seeing if this was dry humour of his land or a hidden joke waiting for a punchline that would never come.

"More could be, fifty-six, or sixty-three." The Combatant added. His grey, drooping moustache twitched as he spoke. There had to be something missing. Images of the asylum raced back. Crazed denizens of padded cells screaming. Safer in free ignorance than carrying knowledge. *More had committed than ever before.* Constance's words echoed in his mind.

Penetrating yellow light glossed through Vincentas's vision, bathing a grey world a hued amber where shafts of indiscriminate colour fell. Raising a hand to obscure invading strobes of light, he turned to view the direction of the hull, seeing light burn from magnified glass. They were searching. A guttural horn blew above. The crow's nest signalling for a nearby airdock. Unseen Riemkeler drawing near.

"Get the others. Say nothing to them about this." The Inquisitor looked over the raised bow. His vision could not contain the entire granite mist wall circling the airship.

Riemkeler held the answers, and Athgeric will still be alive. Without reason, a hand reached for his sword. Fingers curled around smooth obsidian pommel. He would need it soon enough. Dehqan must be wrong about the missing days.

A convulsion launched Vincentas forward.

Wood exploded. People screamed. Metal groaned under pressure. Splinters spat and nicked skin. Flaying hands tried to grab something, anything. Thousand thoughts blitzed through his mind.

He rolled, the world nothing but wood; faint snow and a shrouding fog. Drawn fabric tugged him back, choking him. He clawed and kicked wildly. The brow looked eaten. Crushed and pushed against the deck. Feet flew up, a sense of weightlessness overcame him. Bile erupted, hung in cold air until splattering on soiled breeches.

"Arm on railing!" Dehqan's voice roared in his ears. The resilient Combatant grappled with his own arms, wrapping them around a durable railing. Coldness of the brass hardened on his arm. Railing rattled with his contained grasp. Slouch hat flew upwards, taking off like a brown heron. Boards, planks and lumber catapulted towards a disappearing grey cloud.

Gravity won.

Vincentas gritted his teeth and closed his eyes to the rushing wind sucking into his ears. The entire world sunk down with a gale-force scream and splintering timbers.

Cass

Chapter V

Ashen, serpentine bank of fog never lifted. It swirled, thick and oozing, across the world. Black, formless silhouettes lay beyond. Rusting iron gangways of Konniak rattled. Banging footsteps echoed. No burning wax, no shouts of vendors and troubled individuals. No sickly stench of oils or pungent grease of turning cogs, or smell of unclean water pipes disused for seasons. Only the fog, only her footsteps.

Things moved. They strode in shadow. Lumbering monstrous beings on six or eight legs, towering over shacks and iron works of Konniak's Undercity. A roar of steel, a rush of gravity. Buildings fell. Fallen debris whipped past her. Black Orschallian coat snapping at raw calves. She turned as dust blasted through the fog, showering her hunched body, forcing eyes to close. A raised hand defied the onslaught of collapsed wreckage.

Cass strained for signs or significant markers of importance. She ran down iron gangways, thundering steps vibrated in ears. A linked chain fence brought her to a skidding stop. She tripped and stumbled. Structures razed around her in a cacophony of screaming metal crashing down.

Konniak was falling.

Outstretched arms collided with chain fence; fingers stung. She cursed. Tired throat burned and sweat scarred her brow, threaten to burst down her face. Sinking weight in her gut as heavy as her legs. Ringing footsteps rang ahead. She looked up. Footsteps continued nearing. Her mouth dropped as a Purifier emerged. They were not alone.

Masked in tall, white hoods, slashed in deep, black blood, a figure came towards the linked fence. It hacked at the fence, metallic screech shivered through her spine. Other Purifiers, blood stained and sleek in grease, stumbled to the barrier, the thin barrier that separated herself from them. She backed away, looked down through the grated iron gangway. Eyes stared back.

A hand turned her around. She jumped screaming into a Purifier hood, leering at her. The person ripped their cowl off. Her heart sank, lips trembled.

Cass saw herself. The name "LILLY" branded on her forehead. "M" burnt on the right cheek.

"How could you!" The branded Cass shouted.

Eyes burst open. Coldness smacking ribs, cutting deep into raging lungs fighting for air. She rubbed sweat and grim off her head and pulled the black coat around her to keep warm. Sitting up, she buried herself in the coat.

"Trouble sleeping?" A female voice questioned. Cass looked up, dull senses igniting, waking fully into the real world. Sabanese fragrance of dampness, dead trees and serene stillness added to the darkness of night. More comforting than fog, but further away from Lilly.

Taze sat with her long legs parted before a slow burning fire. She twirled the long, single obsidian braid. Branded "M" flared a furnace red.

"You can say that." No point denying it. She could have been thrashing around, shouting. Cold sweat stuck to her back, pinning loose shirt and breeches to skin.

"You didn't attract any unwanted attention, so I'll forgive you." Taze half smiled. They had been in the forests for three days since leaving the battlefield. Luckily, they did not encounter animals like the famous Orschallian Snow Lynx, Mountain Troll, woolly Sabre Bear. Not even a bird. There was only one bird, the giant winged one, that flew over the battlefield.

"Women are trouble sleepers, men though." The murderer's voice pulled Cass from her mind, who jerked her head to Jolam snoring and the soldier cradled on the ground. "They are simple creatures, sleep anywhere."

"How's she sleeping then?" She cracked a smile, her chapped lips cursed her for smiling. Stell lay curled up, like a baby, before the fire.

"She's a girl, not a woman." Taze spat, who stared at Stell. The murderer's fists clenched.

Jolam was a gardener by profession, nothing simple about him, unlike his admiration for the female figure, human female figure, not Faun-kin. Merrick. He was the past, a past that promised to be more and he came into her mind starker than her need for Lilly.

"Speaking of men, what's the boy's name?" The murderer asked. Cass abandoned gnawing deep memories. A brief chill shuddered down her spine. Taze's legs cracked before the hissing fire, then crossed them with an agility a circus performer could only manage.

"He's called Lucijan." She replied. Taze had not spoken to anyone since they left the battlefield. Cass knew to be careful with her and did not trust her here. This was the wilderness, and they needed each other. Food became scarce. They had a haversack, each of which grew lighter by the day. A look of anxiousness and unease twitched on Lucijan's face when they looted the equipment.

"Stupid name, I can't pronounce that. I'll call him Lucky J." She let go of her braid and stretched her arms, cat like, above her head, arching her back.

"Where now?" Taze inquired. Not bothering to look at Cass as she rolled her shoulders.

"Find a town for supplies, keep heading south and get to Cythea." She had to return to Lilly, been a season or two since the attack on Ralake and news would have reached Vansic Lo. Her eyebrows knitted together. She could not remember the time passed between leaving Ralake to the battle, as if it were a blur. She shook her head.

"Sounds like a plan." A mocked salute headed her way.

"Do you have an idea?" She asked, feeding arms under her a bigger Orschallian coat, better suited than Cythean ones. She caught a whiff of her own scent, her nose creased.

"Head to the Thousand Isles. Or make a living out here." Taze outstretched her arms. "Lots of opportunity."

Cass played along with it. "What would we do?"

Taze's dark eyes smouldered. "We?" She rasped.

Head tilted up. Sharp features flared in low light cast by the fire, high-angled cheek bones cut hard as granite. She raised a finger and placed it on her branded cheek and tapped the "M".

"I'm kidding. I've got a few ways of making a living." Keeping eyes on Cass.

"I'd rather get the hell out of here and never see Orschal again." Shoulders rolled, trying to fuel warmth throughout her body. Dawn's red light broke through bare branches and thinning clouds. Snow, white and dull, lay still across the earth, blanketing trees and covered roots.

Taze rattled a tin in her hand. "You hungry?"

"I'm starving." She entered Ralake, famished. Her army days remained the last time she ate a truly nourishing meal. It's why she stole, to feed herself and her starving daughter, a daughter she let down and must return too.

"Here, it's the last." Taze tossed a clear tin. She fumbled, catching it, cold in her hands. Cass stared at the tin containing the last of their food.

Clanging of metal cut through the forest. The murderer kicked out the low, hissing fire. She looked around. Ringing circled at all angles. Could be deserters, or another Orschallian patrol which they hid from only yesterday. Taze grasped her repeater, Cass grasped her own and stood up, placing the stolen Cythean pith helmet on her head and upturned the collar of the Orschallian coat.

Low, strong animalistic bleating followed. An aurochs, a docile farm animal of the Sabinate region. She inched towards thinning tree line near a path they camped beside.

A small wagon, pulled by a single, large aurochs, trundled over dirtied, snow-sleek path. Wagon took up the breadth of the churned-earth track, trinkets jangled louder. A solitary driver held leather reins as the shabby aurochs pulled the tented cart. A click reverberated side her, a repeater being armed.

"No," her hand covered the muzzle of Taze's repeater, who eyed the wagon, brows narrowed. "We need the driver alive."

"Why?" Taze growled. Waves of steaming air exhaled like a rapid dog eyeing prey.

"Five Cythean soldiers commandeer a rustic wagon with no local driver? Looks like theft, or worse." Cass let go of the repeater. "Let me go down, talk to the driver. You can come as backup."

"Let's go then, before the wagon disappears." The murderer replied without blinking. An icy hand crawled down her spine, not caused by SnowFalls climate. They made their way through the forest, crunching over laying snow towards the unsuspected wagon.

Emerging from the tree line, Cass stood before the aurochs, which grunted to a stop. Heartbeat pounded faster; repeater raised at the driver. Wheels creaked to a halt. Sabanese features widened, arms shot into the air. Wind picked up, rippling tight covers of the wagon. Sunrays broke behind the cart, crowning it in red flames.

"Caravan, yours, free." Driver repeated in a chattering voice, he spoken in a broken dialect.

"No." She replied. The driver ceased talking, controlling smoky breaths. She lowered her repeater. "Town, people, food." She shouldered the repeater. The Sabanese man pointed beyond Cass and Taze. His arm shook.

"Take you. Town."

"Take us all." She ordered. "Wake up Lucijan and Jolam. Get them here quickly." She whispered to Taze.

"You don't trust me here, do you convict?" Taze rasped, her repeater trained on the driver.

"I do trust you, but we need him to be at ease." Cass stepped forward, leaving the murderer behind. On approaching the wagon, a dark-haired girl, no older than nine, peaked between the closed wagon. He smuggled her to his side, eyes on Cass. Her heart sank, a lump grew in her throat. Complying to protect the girl, anything a parent would. She bypassed the unwashed, foul-smelling aurochs and mounted the wagon to sit beside the driver.

"We won't harm you, I promise." Trying to look at the nine-year-old girl. Young, just like Lilly. Lost in Sabanese clothing. Ragged furs, woollen, roughly sewn garments. Her delicate face, with narrow, horizontal brown eyes, lost in the fur-trimmed hood, peered at Cass. Mouth ajar.

"What's the idea of this like?" Jolam yawned, rubbing his eyes.

"Get in lazybones, we're out of food and need to find a town." Cass waved him over. Lucijan, Stell and Taze followed.

She sat beside the driver, to reassure him, her Cythean patterned repeater covered by the haversack beside her boots. She would not need it, and he would not risk the safety of the girl. Cass regretted sitting at the front. The aurochs reeked, passing gas as frequently and as deadly as Jolam during the night. The Sabanese wagon owner passed her a strip of cloth. She took it and tied it around her mouth. They soaked it in local herbs that left a bitter taste. Better than the aurochs.

The wagon rumbled, jolted and rocked along snow covered pathway. Red flares of light gave way to stronger orange glows, fading out to yellow showers scything through decaying trees. They headed west, judging by the sun. Cythean pith helmet served well to guard low, bright beams of radiance.

Trees thinned to the sides; snow faded on the cracked earth. An occasional gnarled, black root poked upwards, and abandoned, rock-made walls of a pathway appeared as snows shrank further in their travels.

"Need to drain myself." Grumbled Jolam. Cass shook her head.

"You looking at me?" Taze's voice teased. She emphasised every word.

"No… no, would never." Lucijan quickly replied.

"Would never look at me? Why?" Taze's voice hardened, the "why" she shouted. The driver and girl flinched. Even the aurochs lowered its fur covered head.

Lucijan stammered. "I mean… I would, not now."

Low, crackling laughter broke out from the murderer. Cass let go of her repeater.

"Men." She sneered. "So easily controlled, aren't they, Stell?"

"Um, sure." The girl piped up in her reply.

"Sabinate?" Cass faced the man holding the reins. He stared at the road.

"Yes." He rasped. Sabanese were known for guttural voices, their throat singing an amusement in Cythean cities if they travelled that far or were lucky enough to escape under Orschallian Enclave control.

"Battle. Primals. Survivors?" She asked. Making the journey easier to speak and not dwell on her own thoughts, creeping back into her feigning mind.

"Gulneh. Battle." He faced her with narrowed eyes. Thin, black eyebrows added to his raised, shrugged shoulders. He encouraged the aurochs with a tsk of his tongue and ruffled reins.

"Gulneh? What Gulneh?" She pressed.

Little girl's face appeared, who pulled a beastly face and raised her gloved hands to make talons. "Gulneh." Cass whispered. Girl nodded, dropping her posture.

Different name for the same creature, a creature nothing more than a plague. He did not know of the battle with the Primals. Cass turned to see the others. They were quieter now, eyes cast low, heads turned from one another.

She ate from the Sabanese stores in his wagon. Crackling of some animal, not pig, a delicacy that nearly took her teeth out. Turnips, boiled leeks, roasted potatoes and parsnips. Everything coated in an ebony herb. It made the food look burnt. Jolam knew the herb and its name, but it was unpronounceable. Feeding brought smiles and even a laugh.

Dusk bled on the horizon, when they stopped. Cass jumped down, stretching her legs. She walked to a low man-made wall. Her mind roared like waves, salt stench lingered in her nostrils, a relief from the aurochs odour. Distant horizon rippled, making two of them come together.

"The Great Green." Jolam voiced beside her. "Emerald Sea, must be Orschals southern coast." The sea, another barrier to home, a hurdle to clear to reach Lilly.

"Look. Lights." The Faun pointed, his hand grasped her shoulder. She looked, lights clustered together forming a horseshoe of ebbing glows, unnatural to be lowered stars. Cass gulped. Civilisation. Four years in solitude with her own code, own rules. Now a distinct set of rules to play, a different mask to wear, but always judged on the burnt brand.

"It may have an airdock, or a passage to the Thousand Isles." Jolam's elated voice lifted her dampened thoughts. She forced a smile.

"Can smell freedom already." Cass spoke. They branded thousands in Konniak, thousands hardly worked and lived in lower, gutter-filled reaches. She hoped Orschallian lands did not know the meaning behind it.

"Freedom smells of salt?" Taze rasped aloud. Her skin crawled. The murderer snuck up on them without making a sound, booted feet deathly silent on the sharp, thinning snow.

"You won't reach home without rest." She turned and left, walking back to the wagon where the Sabanese man and Lucijan unloaded blankets and furs. She headed back to help.

Warmth tingled toes and gave life to flexing fingers, curtesy of a crackling fire. Her shoulders eased back, sighing in comfort. A peculiar feeling. Her eyes moved to the tree line, expecting the worst, but never coming true. There was a stillness that kept Cass sharp.

"You reckon we'll walk right in and jump on a ship bound for home?" Taze's voice cut through the quiet. Flames crackled. The Sabanese man, named Grodol, made the fire. If a rustic was confident enough to make fire in the open, then it was good enough for Cass.

"Nothing is ever easy." She rubbed her hands under the fur cloak provided by Grodol. He gave them clothing in the Sabanese style, fur brimmed hoods sewn on woollen coats. Ushanka hats that smelt of a dead animal, but nothing could not falter its comfort and added warmth. He even had valenki boots, doe skin and supple. They would not fit into the tight-fitted constraints of Cythean society, but they were warm, comfortable and alive.

Cass peered at her hands, calloused whiteness moulded to palms, worn knuckles and fingers. Worker's hands. She cupped them together with relative ease, feeling rough as a sailor. Merrick's hands would be like this now. She knew he owned a ship.

A cawing echoed through the darkness. She tilted her head up. Hand reached for the Cythean repeater.

"If a bird startles you, how did you survive Ralake?" Taze laughed.

"By being on edge, expect the worst." Cass replied. Grodol and the girl slept together. The Sabanese wrapped in embrace beneath their own fur-lined blanket of patches.

"You think he's a Short-eye?" Taze's voice piped up.

"No." He could not be. They looked alike. The age difference wide between them brought some doubt.

"Must be brave, or foolish, taking a wagon and a girl to a village. He must be running." Taze continued. Aurochs stamped hooves into snow, shaking wide, horned head pulling at the tethered roped. It was pulling away, its black mass visibly wrestling with bonds that kept it trapped.

"Wagon is for selling goods, takes the girl to protect her since she can't be alone." Cass replied, turning to face Taze, who sat cross-legged on the other side of the fire. Her face hidden in depths of the Sabanese cloak.

Steaming breath, calm and repetitive, left her shadow casting hood.

"What goods? The wagon's empty." The murderer tilted her head. Redness flared along chiselled features, black eyes smouldered. Cawing echoed again, shaking hands clenched the repeater.

"Why are you concerned about him?" She asked. Eyes averted to still trees and creeping darkness.

Taze's face split into a smile. "Expect the worst."

A screech split Cass's hearing in half.

She collapsed backwards. Force of air knocking her down, ripping icy breath out of aching lungs. Swirling aurora borealis above, stirred with colour. Blacked wings scythed emerald in half, a sharp beak blurred above, too black to be shadow, too stark to be night. Her leg snatched by grasping talons. Cass clawed at the ground, while dragged and lifted from the earth.

A second screech erupted. She gritted her teeth and slapped her hands over ears. She fell. Snow and solid, welcoming earth punched into ribs and legs. Involuntarily, Cass turned over onto her back. Jolam's face lowered to hers.

"Stay still. Stay still." His muffled voice broke through clasping hands over ears. He laid across her, pinning her down.

"Get off, off!" Cass raged and pushed, kneeing Jolam. Eyes searching for the repeater.

Jolam rolled off. Whistles of repeater bolts scythed through frosty night air. Taze fired wildly. Lucijan loaded his own weapon, kneeling beside her. She looked for Grodol and the girl. She had to help.

Cass scrambled to a crouch. Repeater lay in the snow. Her eyes darted to where Taze fired.

Stell writhed in the air, blonde hair waving against blackness that was not night or shadow, but something, something with wings beating as powerful as an airship's engine.

It vaulted up. Stell vanishing. Her scream lingering in the downpour of beating wings.

Cass ran and skidded, snatching the repeater and aimed into the sky. There was nothing but blurring aurora borealis. Stillness returned. The aurochs groaned and huffed.

"Stell." Cass whispered. Icy breath leaving her shaking mouth. She wiped frosting tears from blurring eyes, fearing her vision would fail. The heavy repeater shook in her hands. Light snow fell.

Stell's shriek faded into eternal night.

Vincentas

Chapter VI

A blackened face screamed silently. Charred skin breaking with wild excursion. Vincentas drowned under heated breaths whipping into thinning hair. Woman's bleeding mouth exploded in gargled, tortured cries. He could only remain silent.

Her opal eyes bright and feverish within the ebony face.

Solitary, penetrative whistle echoed, gnawing into his skull, ringing every muscle in his face. Burnt, familiar skeletal face shook. Whistling grew to blowing winds, churning to gusts of violent torrents and howling hurricanes viewed only in the Thousand Isles.

"Easy. Easy." A voice pulsed into his ears, reassuring and claim. Vincentas felt numb below the waist. He tried to sit up. Paper-thin, parched lips muttered a guttural groan.

"Whatever you do, don't be sick. I can't handle sick." Laughed, a close voice. He recognised its demure tone anywhere. A bronzed half-mask came into focus.

"Fleur." Vincentas coughed. Icy wind sunk into his stomach. Shivers trembled up aching ribs, curling through taunt and battered muscle. Silently he prayed to an unknowing, unresponsive God that he was not broken. His first prayer in decades.

"Right here, Vin." Something callous rubbed sweating forehead. The stench of aging leather lingered in his nostrils.

"Not going to be sick. I promise." He spluttered. Turning his head away when something sickly sweet pressed under his nose. It followed him. Rough fabric crowning a sweating forehead. A hand kept him rigid and still. Solidified Fawnleaf made that aroma, his dull senses pulling together.

"Easy, easy. Faunleaf. You can thank Arno later." Fleur's voice drifted away. Red veins lit up before him, crossing green vines. Bruising purples merged with the beating pulse of crimson lines flaring like blood. Faunleaf's fragrance faded. Fleur's voice diminished. The tight hold of his forehead eased.

Crackling fire spat. Warmth comforted limbs. He dared not move in case he could not, numbness laid on still legs. Age reinforced caution. Heavy eyes peeled open and filled with Fleur, glowing under veins of fire. Mask removed, a rarity. She picked at the straps muttering under her breath. Gloved fingers brushed back blonde, tatty locks from a disgruntled face, combing behind her ear, not before witnessing the branded mark, black like cinders by a raging fire. It marked her face with a convictional "M". M for murder.

"Are you admiring again, or lost for words?" Fleur chuckled as she fixed the bronze mask in place, covering the brand on her cheek. No wonder she wore it. War wounds admired, but convicted sentences brought prejudice, even in the company of an Inquisitor.

"More the latter, but if it please you, the former." Vincentas replied. His words drew a racking cough, ribs spoke of a sting penetrated by tired lungs.

"You're supposed to be an Inquisitor, not a gigolo wannabe." Fleur laughed. She brushed her knees and made to stand, grunting as she stood.

"Where are we? And… am I?" The Inquisitor asked. She strode over and crouched, in creaking leathers, beside him. Her eye through the mask surveyed him. Warm hand cupped his neck, her strength the same rough, callous grasp that pinned down his forehead during his grogginess.

"Outside what used to be Riemkeler, we think. And you didn't ask how I was? Tut, tut, I'm hurt." Fleur lightly punched Vincentas on the arm. Outside, what used to be Riemkeler. He should have felt something for that remark. What used to be Riemkeler. A shiver rattled down his spine.

Fleur eased him up. The Inquisitor groaned, using tired elbows as leverage. No crushing pains in chest, breathing steady. Still some sting near the ribs, but that would be age.

"You're doing good, Vincentas." Fleur patted his back, forcing a wince. Eyes focused on crackling, warm fire, illuminating the cavern he occupied which smelt of damp wood and coal. Looking around, moving his legs measuredly in case of damage. He wiggled toes and sighed.

"Inside the Sojourn, or what's left of her." Fleur answered his mind's questions about their surroundings. It was not a cavern at all, that much was clear with awakened senses. Carpets hung like folded tapestry, swinging like the dead on a hangman's noose. Rendered cupboards bathed in shadow feigned movement. Only Fleur moved towards the fire and a satchel beside it.

"Get that down, ya. They'll be back soon and tell you of what they've found." Fleur tossed a tinned ration. She tore open her own, scooping up food with fingers. He thought of Violet. The crew. The others. Vincentas opened the tin and thoughts of survivors melted, igniting his stomach with life. Fingers sleek with juices from contents of the tin.

Ration tin contained a meat substance that looked like charcoaled porridge, smelt like burnt horse, but Vincentas's guts gurgled. A parched mouth salivated like it was a meal prepared in Cythean luxurious kitchens in Upper Quarter. He devoured the food, compared to some he had tasted worse.

Fleur belched. A cough made The Inquisitor turn. Several people lay sprawled around him, illuminated by dim small fires. Only their movements told him they were alive. Stench of old rags, unwashed hair and soiled blankets flared within his nostrils. Violet or anyone else not among them.

"Most of these are the crew. All retinue is good. Speak of evil and they shall appear." Fleur's voice echoed behind him. Vincentas stood up, allowing the blanket to fall. He winced; pained belly protested on standing.

"Inquisitor. Most grateful am I see to you conscious." Arno greeted him, ignoring Fleur and bowrf. A sombre smile could not help but break his stoic face and nodded his thanks. Dehqan flanked Arno along with the new Entrant Alleck. Ugly bruises shadowed beneath haggard eyes. He knew their pain, tender and battered.

"Your report?" Vincentas moved forward, closing distance between them. He noticed they were all dressed for SnowFall Season; extra furs and layers clothed them. Even Arno wore a longer coat that obscured hooved legs.

"We must be outside Riemkeler, but an entrance into the city… implausible." Arno shook his head.

"The city is barred?" He pressed, surveying them one at a time. Alleck portrayed more emotion, to be expected. He knew little of the Entrant, but knew enough: he originated from Riemkeler and would be resourceful.

"Entrant." Vincentas snapped, using an Inquisitorial voice. Alleck's head bolted up, quivering eyes alert. "We need to enter the city, show us."

"I can't." His words were as weak as his face; softening beneath harsh rays of a hanging Gaslamp.

"Inquisitor, you must come and investigate. It is something I have never seen." The Chanter lamented, keeping his eyes on Alleck, the weak link within the retinue. He did not have to be a Mystic to understand the fragility of the boy.

"Fleur, gather supplies." The Inquisitor instructed, tending to his own baggage and haversack. The obsidian pommel lay beneath a fur rug, tugging free the sheathed weapon as he holstered the malachite sword to his waist. He would need it.

"Your injuries…" Arno's voice broke through his mind, sure and precise, like a surgical blade. Cutting deep.

"… Will heal in time. Time, we do not have." Vincentas did not face Arno, knowing his eyes would betray him.

"I am sure they will, with rest, Inquisitor." Faun's words caused heat racing through his mouth, threatening to spew a barking retort. Vincentas added further layers to his already clothed frame, feeling confined and stiff in his movements, aching, aged limbs cried for a moment's peace.

"I will rest when I am dead." The Inquisitor fastened the holster of a handbow bought by Fleur on their departure from Konniak, with shaking, numbing hands.

"There is something afoot, Inquisitor. The city. There's something." He turned, unspoken words silenced Arno. The Inquisitor had to look away from the Chanter's eyes as they revealed a raw emotion he had not seen in his old friend in decades.

"We must investigate something that is strange. Whether batted, bruised or on the brink of death. We are the sword against the Mystic."

A rustle of voices grew at the yawning stygian entrance of their makeshift shelter. He strode forward, keeping eyes tight in a fixed, narrow frown. All he could muster to stop wincing at every step.

"And what are we to do? Wait here and die from a Primal attack?" A raised voice argued, agreeing chorus chimed in.

"What is the meaning of this?" Vincentas inquired, remnants of the crew and passengers, who could walk, forming a semi-circle before Fleur, Alleck, Reticence and Dehqan.

"You going into Riemkeler? We're going too." The captain of the Sojourn stepped forward. Still blessed with youth, tired eyes caught hold of an old light in teal-coloured pupils.

"My retinue would think that unwise, I would agree. This is a course the Inquisition must take first, to protect the people from unknown dangers." Vincentas kept an unblinking gaze on the captain while surveying the throng of people. They outnumbered his retinue but were unarmed. Most were passengers that the strong would sway.

"The only danger out there is cold and snow. Riemkeler offers shelter, not for us but for them too." He gestured to the groaning wounded. He would have been a pleasant addition to the Inquisition. Others added in grunts of approval. No sign of Violet.

He stepped forward. "It is for that reason the Inquisition must go first. We will investigate to find a safe passage, then summon you to Riemkeler. Gather your possessions, tend to the wounded and await my signal." A cheer rang up. The mob dispersed for their desperate tasks. The captain stood alone. Vincentas made to leave. A hand stopped him.

"Keep to your word." The captain spoke, close enough for his fragrance of oils and labour to invade nostrils, bristled stubble greyed an angular chin. The Inquisitor gave a knowing look at the hand on his arm. The captain released, taking a small step back and keeping his eyes fixed.

"If not for our situation, the cold would be the last thing to kill you." Vincentas's words came to him easier than breathing.

"I need your word. You'll send someone back." Unrelating, the captain continued. He had to be admired. He cared unless another motive pushed him onward.

"Don't take his word, take mine." A woman's sultry voice piped in. Clad in thick furs, moving with a lethal edge, Violet moved forward, repeater held in crossed hands.

"Begging your pardon, you are a passenger and I don't know you." The captain nodded to Violet.

Twirling the repeater round, it clicked with the promise of firing. She stabbed the muzzle at the captain's chest, jabbed him again until he broke gaze with the Inquisitor.

"So, a passenger can't be trusted? So eager to save others, but not willing to trust others to help him?" Violet tutted and shook her head, withdrawing the repeater within a blink of an eye.

"Begging your pardon, but you could be killed out there." He retorted through gritted teeth.

"Could have dropped you before you blew a kiss. Can drop Primals at two-hundred yards, while they're leaping around." She smiled. Two crew members of The Sojourn flanked their captain.

"Any problems." A large man rasped.

"No, Kimmel. Keep helping the people." The captain replied while surveying Violet. "On your word then, miss."

She mocked a bow and turned to leave. Vincentas followed her, reaching the hull of the ship acting as the shelters makeshift front.

"Thought you might be dead." He whispered, standing still beside her.

"Takes more than a downed airship to stop me, Inquisitor." The Combatant replied.

"Dehqan should lead the way, we'll follow." Arno insisted.

The Sabanese man stalked forward, leaving shadow stretched habitation into a maw of darkness. Only handheld Gaslamps, tied to his waist, gave colour in the curtain of night.

Fleur nudged Vincentas and winked at him through her bronzed mask. The silent Interrogator followed Dehqan. He turned back. Crew and passengers milled together, gathering what equipment they could. Alleck hung back. Weakness drowned his face.

Vincentas faced the eternal night and swirling flakes of snow. Frost nipped exposed ears, cheeks and eyes. Raising the collar of his greatcoat, he stepped from the security of the Sojourn.

He turned back after walking a hundred yards. Red glowing silhouette of the upside-down ship ebbed on the white sea of lying snow, like smouldering coal within a dying furnace. Vincentas shook his head. How he survived the crashing ship only the gods knew. An icy shiver stroked around his temples, thinking about what could have caused the ship to crash.

SnowFall Season shrouded vision to a harsh blizzard. Judging by steps taken, he assumed they had travelled for a candlemark. Frost gripped bones, icy, cruel hands yanked at bruised flesh and prodded aching limbs.

"Cold enough to lose toes." Fleur laughed at his side; her cheerful laugh snuffed by callous wind.

Two short waves of a Gaslamp signalled ahead. Group fanned out, heading towards Dehqan. Vincentas looked down at the uneven ground. Snow, thick and rough, formed a crude blanket covering any morsel of grass. Whiteness buried his feet, a freezing touch circled aching knees.

"Look." Fleur jerked her head.

Crunching snow trudged under determined feet. He reached Dehqan, holding a Gaslamp before blackened shapes which looked impossibly darker compared to the surrounding sky. Dampness curdled in cold nostrils.

Reaching out with a gloved hand, he gripped the nearby blackened object. It snapped in his hand, weakness more than strength breaking the burnt thing. Holding up the Gaslamp, light poured, revealing a wagon. Spokes half-buried under snow.

"No Primal attack." Fleur observed. Winds picked up, pushing against him to turn back and walk away. Eyes tracked the shifting faint light, he covered his mouth expecting a smell. Half buried in snow, skin bloated and grey, three people sat against the wagon. Childs eyes locked on Vincentas, glassy and doll like, reflective and shining.

"Dressed for LeafFall." Fleur stated, brushing away plastered snow and sticking jewels of frost to skin and clothing.

"Burnt the wagon to keep warm. Stayed near it as it went down." Vincentas rationalised. Near Riemkeler and resorted to this. Dressed for LeafFall, they must have been here all this time, waiting outside the city. Unnatural coldness fed into his guts, a feeling he could not melt away.

"Back there two more." Dehqan came forward.

"Another one over there." Violet pointed.

"Riemkeler must be close." He insisted and headed into darkness where Gaslamps pushed light into blackness. The world swallowed within the mouth of shadow. Isolation a growing emptiness that extended beyond his reckoning.

He looked around in desperation to seek surroundings in a snow filled void. Skin crawled, his throat tightened. Creeping into his frantic vision, distorted colours blurring in an endless horizon. A wall of mottled purple took shape, blurred beyond constant, still blackness.

It should have torn a gust of wind into his skull and not a sigh eased from the glowing, ominous phenomenon. Sickly flowing liquids ebbed and melded back into circling tendrils of an impassable barrier. Moving without a sound, it oozed like lava rippling in a disjointed current, causing his stomach to quiver with each shifting, coloured distortion. Vincentas turned his back on the coloured anomaly, illuminated with a magenta hue.

"You… seen anything like this before?" Dehqan questioned. The Sabanese Combatant had served five noble years and had not experienced the worst of Inquisition findings and justice, but even this paled in comparison. Lavender glaring mists rolled right, a fogged curtain unfurling. Beyond, a blackened mountain stood idle through the violet-coloured, transparent shade.

"Riemkeler?" Arno's doubt gave voice to Vincentas's thoughts. He looked at the Faun.

"This was here before?" He asked, facing the Chanter. Their faces transfixed on the unknown.

"It shrouds the city. Covers it entirely." Fleur spoke, steam masked words. He wondered if the airship had crashed into this, but his mind failed him. He gritted his teeth.

"It's open, we go." The Inquisitor commanded, walking towards the ebony silhouette, which should be the city's walls.

Arno placed a firm hand on his shoulder. "It's never opened before. Not for two days."

"Then we must take this opportunity." The Inquisitor strode on, quivering fingers slipped to a familiar obsidian hilt.

Between parted veils of lavender obscurity, glimpses of people's faces faded within swirling mists. Several moans and grunts filtered through shallow wind. Lack of light playing tricks, distant wind howling. He shook his head, averting gaze from the bypassing lavender swirl.

One of Riemkeler's gatehouses lay open. Dirtied and moss covered, untouched by snow or corrupted by season. Uncleanliness retaking man's structure. They entered the gatehouse, echoing footfalls rang metallic as they walked on. Water droplets patted his cockel hat. He unfastened the greatcoat as heat flushed flesh.

The Inquisitor turned back, purple tendrils linked, surging into each other like interlocked lovers of a thousand lavender bodies. A gulp coursed down his throat that did not stifle a flapping stomach. The Sojourn crew and passengers would receive no help. Athgeric would be in the city and the unknown lay in Riemkeler.

Cass

Chapter VI

Cass could not recall folding blankets. She could not remember arguing with Grodol about taking them further. Only when Taze raised a loaded repeater at the native Sabanese girl, sense dawned on the group and she could not find the memory of consuming food under red morning glow, but only that her stomach did not protest. She found it easy to close her burdensome eyes, but it was Lilly, not Stell, that the winged creature took screaming into the night.

Cass did not close her eyes again.

Wooden thatched rooftops blazed under a crimson horizon, glittering before a sparkling, shivering sea, as the wagon trundled towards the coastline village. Citizens milled, black dots on a snowy canvas. Houses breathed; grey steam vented in post-morning hue. A large stone structure lay to their right, like a ribcage of a stone beast fallen on its front. The carcass building grew among western peaks and cliffs.

Her nostrils flared under pines aroma and decaying trees. Winters scarf hung around tree necks thawing on jowls of nature's sentinels. The girl sniffled. The bravest to show emotion and the only one being true to themselves. Cass knew the girl did not grieve for Stell. Those sniffles were uncertainty caused by a parent. She brought Grodol into this. They could have made it to the village on foot in three days, at least.

"Next time I see you, Stell, I owe you five Dragets." She mumbled. "I'll eat double the mutton for you, too." She curled up her collar and cupped her nose and mouth in gloved, warm hands and blew, showing a facade of keeping warm, in truth she hid the tremble of quivering lips.

Jagged cliffs, straight and sharp, lined western route. A multitude of towering peaks continued into the distance, snow-capped saws facing upwards ready to half teal-coloured sky shining in waves of jade. The fishing village grew, stench of decaying pine wafted away, replaced with pungent dampness of salt, fish and ocean spray.

Cass rubbed her cheeks. Time to see if it was worth the price of Stell. No visible airdock, so no airship would be nearby. No ships in the seas with over three sails or two masts meant limited transportation. She sighed. It was a fishing village, and she hated fish.

"Mmm." Jolam murmured. "Roasted shrimp. Haddock pie. Eel soup. Shark fin broth."

"Faun leg." Taze rasped.

"That's cruel." Jolam breathed, she heard him, not loud enough for Taze.

"No flags or banners. Who owns this place?" Lucijan asked. Cass noticed it too. Defensive walls nothing more than piled snow. A few sharpened stakes lay pointed, jutting randomly along natural defence. Wagon tires slipped and squelched; the aurochs rocked as it milled forward.

Cass had no time for politics, but knew the Sabinate region lay under the tight leash of Orschal dominion. Sabanese people were not free. If she knew anything about oppression, it was a coiled spring ready to break free. They had to keep a low profile.

Wagon rolled between the village's earthwork defence. She trusted Grodol as he navigated through narrow dirtied pathways. People's faces peered behind raised, fur-lined hoods. No shock, anger or resentment, but a quiet study, a stare-down to see who would blink first. She ignored them.

Triangular roofs reached snow covered ground, frost crowned longhouses with fanged icicles. Animal motifs coated buildings as roofs curved outwards. They looked bird like. A shiver reverted down her spine. Stell, taken in the night, came to her waking vision. No numbers on doors, or door handles. No windows. Cass remembered lights on the ridge last night, but no evidence of fires remained.

Grodol steered the wagon towards a paddock. Slowing down, she observed other wagons. Grodol waved his hand, as if to shoo a fly or a pest from his possessions.

"Dismount." Cass looked at the others.

She kept the repeater underneath her cloak and furs. A hand grasped its wooden stock. No need to cause panic if they saw the repeater, steady with the shoulder strap. The others had their own repeater and, equally concealed, Taze had two since she had Stell's.

"He helped us, we must give him something." Cass spoke, looking at Grodol several paces away, talking to a native of the village.

"We have given him something," Taze replied, her hood high enough to cover her forehead, obscuring the name of her victim. "His life." The murderer finished. Cass looked at Lucijan and Jolam, both shrugged. She shook her head.

"Outsiders, outsiders." A broken-accented voice chimed up. She turned; the others squelched in mud. Jolam cursed, finding it difficult with hooved legs to stay still long enough.

A black-haired man with a broad smile approached. His teeth spoke of wealth, clothes reeked of trading. He padded over the mud, not seeming to care for his long, crimson cloak lined in a fine fur to trail behind him. His eyes hardened.

"Cythean. Yes, yes. Not a trader. No, no." He greeted and nodded to each of them. His glinting eyes lingered on their brands. The man's smile faded.

"Not trader. Lost." Cass replied.

The man laughed. "Very lost. Wrong land."

She tried to force a laugh. It sounded like a gargled cough.

The man, who looked Sabanese, but with Orschallian features, leaned closer. His perfumes of bitter cheroots and spiced drink started a numbing ache behind her eyes.

"Lost. Like the others. You like others. Soldiers?" He whispered.

Cass stepped back. Others. Other Cytheans that made it from the battle. Back to self-indentured service. Further away from Lilly. Her heart sank.

"He said others." Jolam whispered. She turned her back on the trader.

"So much for heading back to freedom." Taze added.

"I didn't see any transports on the way here. Might be less than us." Cass looked at Jolam.

"Fewer." She thought Taze whispered. The murderer's head lowered.

"Might be deserters like us. Could help us." Lucijan interjected.

"You'd like that, wouldn't you? Be among your own. There is no *us*, Lucky J." Taze's voice rasped so deeply it sounded like phlegm choked her words.

Cass shivered caused by coldness not of nature's weather. Her eyes looked westwards. The others talked. Icy wind stirred. Faintness of the aurora borealis added a shimmer of green to the snow-capped cliffs above the ribcage-bone structure. Stone steps lined an ascending route.

A group of people descended lead the way by one in cream breeches and beige chest.

Battlefield lay in silent ruins, Stell taken. Vast seas separated herself and Cythea, now news of Cythean soldiers. They would have to fight again, be further from Lilly, further from home.

There was only one thing to do…

Cass saw her.

Raven haired, sleeked back behind pointed ears. Hawkish, distinctive face. Raven her nickname and not because of her hair. But she was *dead*, killed by *her* own hands. She cannot be alive. She barged through Jolam and Taze's conversation. Her hands shook. Breathing picked up with echoing heartbeat. Shadows grew and stretched, blotting the churned earth in murky, ashen shadows.

"Karwen." Cass gasped. Silence hushed the world, tides lapping at the coast ceased their hissing spray.

The group descending the stone steps from the cadaver building halted. She stood at their front, wearing Cythean army Penal Legion uniform. Alive. She was alive.

Her pale face unreadable. Stoicism masked features. Cass stepped forward, pulling her feet from sinking mud with relative ease. A female Faun, holding a staff and clothed in feathers of a black Orschallian bird, walked beside the convict. Curled horns, crowned in ebony hair, twisted in knots.

"Cass." Karwen broke into a grin and walked forward. She stopped walking after Cass shot up her hand, her other slipped to the concealed repeater. It stopped smiling.

"Cass it's me. Karwen." The thing laughed.

"No. You." Cass stammered. The repeater bolts were deep. Colour left her. She lay on the ground, unmoving, in the snow, silently surrounded by the dead. Here she stood, alive. *Alive.*

"I'm glad you all got away, the battlefield…" Karwen continued towards them, her pace slowed.

"Back off." Taze's shout jerked Cass out of her skin. Shouts, screams and gasps of alert crashed around her. Taze stepped forward, repeater held ready to fire, steady stock against her strong shoulder, barrel aimed at the alive convict who stood with her hands held up. The group who accompanied Karwen did not move. They stood in cloaked serenity, clothes ruffled with the chilling breeze.

"Taze, not the time." She whispered under her breath.

"Peace." The female Faun spoke in an accent not recognisable. She glided forward, despite walking in mud. She moved as elegantly as a deer, dark feathered dress giving her a weightless appearance, tall and languid for a Faun.

"Peace sisters, trouble not ourselves, of greater things come." Her staff lowered; a laughing skull mounted the stave. A human skull. Cass gulped. The others behind her moved, flanking Karwen.

"Stop right there." Taze's voice could have commanded the wind to stop. She held her breath. "I've got thirty little friends in this repeater, all are quicker than you lot."

"She's feisty." Jolam breathed. Cass could have hit him.

"Save your little friends, Cythean, need them soon you will." The Faun leaned back her head, looking down her nose to Taze.

"I killed you." Cass spoke, her voice cracking. Hands shaking. "Karwen *I* killed you."

"I saw the body. Dead. Finished." Taze barked. The repeater visibly shook in her grasp. Weapon rattled.

"We'll head to Cythea, forget this." She faced the murderer, whose lips frothed, parting with rapid breathing. Steam exhumed between trembling lips quicker than the world darkening around. Her features hardened. It was a miracle her skin did not break.

"Forget this?" Taze half laughed. "Can't forget this. I saw the body. Dead people stay dead, Cass. That, there. That is not Karwen." She could not deny it.

"Taze." Cass placed a firm hand on a strong bicep, hard with muscle, despite the layers. She knew Taze could shrug her off at any moment. Nothing would stop her. "We need you."

The murderer turned. Bloodshot eyes peered back. Cass had seen the look before, the man who wanted information for Vansic Lo. The possessed look of fighting for life, ready to claim others for their own survival. She had shown it before, plenty of times.

Cass squeezed the arm with a tenderness. "We'll find out who she is. I promise you. But this, this isn't how we do it. We'll get out, I promise." Mustering all the calmness she could. She had not used this on anyone since her daughter could do "things" and pushed the worrying thought into her gut, stomach grumbled on failed digestion.

"Cass." Jolam's voice blurred in her hearing, piercing the bubble of her thoughts, and Taze's breathing which steadied, along with her grip on the muscled arm.

"Get back to Cythea, we'll go together." Words steamed. Her grip eased on the arm.

"Cassidy." Jolam's quivering tone forced her unblinking gaze away.

The Faun stood four feet away, cloaked in night. Whites of his eyes shaking, curling hair shrouded under blue shadows. She turned, Karwen and her group too far to be seen. It was quiet, too quiet. Taze cursed.

"Can't be night?" The murderer asked.

Cass faced Taze.

Features instantly illuminated in purple.

Light spread throughout the village. Hues of exotic violet, sickly pink, pulsing lavender filled the world. Nothing the colour as it should be. Cass's breathing increased. She tracked her head up, hoping not to see the eye again that covered the battlefields sky. Sweat itched skin, eyes strained against the need to blink. She could not look away.

"Like the battlefield." Lucijan gasped.

Smoke grew above. Swirling opaque mists blotted the sky. Thickening in mauve richness. Sweat of foundries clogged her nostrils, irons odour clung around her throat squeezing cold air down a tightening mouth.

A high-pitched scream jolted Cass. She tore her eyes away staring at the rolling fog bank. A woman grappled a man, trying to push him off her. Shouts erupted, another tussle broke out.

"Get back." Jolam squealed. She turned. A villager stumbled towards them, feet dragging in the mud, head flung back. He twisted, spasmed. One hand shot up and hit his face, clawing at his throat and collar. The other hand, twitching, lurched forward, extending limbs towards the Faun.

His eyes. Bright, burning purple. Karwen's on the battlefield.

Whistling sliced through the air. Three bolts thudded into the man's body. One in the throat, one in an eye socket, the other through his ribs. No gargling panic for mercy, no screams of hysteria. No raging torments of revenge. He stumbled silently and splattered in the mud. Lying dead.

"Nice one, Lucky J." Taze rasped. Cass turned, Lucijan stood with his repeater raised, chin quivering, eyes wide and unblinking.

"There." She pointed at the stone, ascending steps. "Get away from this place. Let's move."

She leapt through the mud, gritting teeth, forcing herself onwards. Shouts of panic flooded ears, dense violet mists descended, veiling her vision. Whistling repeaters signalled someone firing.

Lucijan struggled as he pulled on his leg. His face contorted in effort. Cass hooked her arm around his shoulder and pulled. He gripped her back.

"Leave me here." He groaned through gritted teeth.

"Don't be stupid, we're all getting out of this." Cass grunted. Lucijan's foot squelched free. He continued climbing up the embankment. She stopped, turning back. The mist faded, thinning in parts. Rooftops became visible, shapes moved in the distance. Others came towards her, their eyes petrified and not glowing. Cass's repeater raised as they surged forward, climbing over the mud.

Grodol, the girl.

She searched. Eyes wide and not blinking. The girl too similar to Lilly, too young to be alone. Too young to be abandoned and afraid. Too young to be let down. She stopped a fleeing villager, their face streaked with tears. It was not Grodol. A lonely child stumbled and crawled up into the mud. She bent down, pulling them to their feet. A boy. She cursed, her eyes blurring.

A child's scream. A girl's scream ripped through her heart.

Cass snapped round, watching a child carried in the distance. She surged forward, repeater raised. She squinted. It had to be them. A figure descended on the child. Another came to their flank, eyes burning with lilac light.

"No." she screamed. It tore out of her, ripping her lungs in half. She fired the repeater. One shadow with pink eyes twisted and flung back, Cass slowed on aiming at the second threat. It clawed at the man carrying the girl. She fired the repeater. Her finger stayed on the trigger till the whistling ceased and her finger ran with numbness.

Shouldering the repeater. Heat flared on her skin as she neared the man carrying the child.

"Grodol?" Cass gasped. The man stopped. Old face peered beneath a raised hood. Greying, drooping moustache. Wrinkled but alert eyes looked at her. The girl, drenched in tears, stopped sniffling.

"Up. Stairs. go." She pointed.

"Cass, where the hell are you?" Jolam's voice called out.

"On point. Heading to stairs." She shouted, voice cracking as she moved.

"Mom." Cass heard. Heart stopping.

It could not be. It should not be. She stopped. Squelching mud of Grodol's feet slapped her hearing, her heart quickening with a deep thud. She had to see. There was no other choice. Turning around, she shook her head as a girl stood before her.

"Mom." It sounded like a young Lilly. The sweet, innocent voice of her daughter before Ralake. The voice of doubt and question, the voice of disappointment.

Blackness shifted beyond magenta mists. Her eyes shot up, tracking the lumbering mass. One pillar of darkness, stark and bold, lost within the fading fog. Cass's neck burnt with aching as she tilted her head, witnessing the height of a towering, unknown shape lost in purple light.

"Come on, come on." Jolam's voice blurted in her ear.

She jolted, Jolam yanking her arm. She turned to see Lilly disappear. Just like the battlefield.

Rolling thunder grumbled. No lightning followed. A suction of sound chorused the unnatural world. It repeated, grunting, groaning gale echoed by the distant inhale of noise. Like breathing, it *was* breathing.

Her periphery blanked in obsidian gloom. Mud splattered them. An invisible force of wind blasted their flanks. Trembling ground forced them to keel over, Jolam and Cass holding onto each other.

"The stairs." They both shouted.

Quick as the churned SnowFall earth allowed, she scrambled over slippery terrain. Shadow doused them. Coldness engulfed tired lungs. A strong wind scythed through clothing. Howling winds rumbled, like hot iron grating down an anvil.

Clawing up the stone stairs, not turning back, she did not want to know what was behind, only focused on ascending to the granite ribcage structure. The building, where Karwen would be. Her eyes narrowed, shielding them from the burning purple glare of the sky.

The incline forced Cass to stop. She fell to her knees, panting. A cough spluttered in her throat, the stench of steel hacked out of her. Arms trembled, threatening to give way. Other pleas voiced those unseen around her. Clopping hooves resonated on the steps. Humidity bubbled on her back, sticking to shoulders and itching down her spine. She gritted her teeth.

"What the..." Jolam wheezed. Pushing herself up, she turned, standing next to the Faun.

More black pillars extended, leaving lavender boiling sky and struck the ground through the mist. They moved interchangeably, like ant legs. Cass shook her head, watching them vault with a swiftness and come down again. Whatever attached them, controlling them, moving them, she could not see.

"The stone building. Let's go." Jolam breathed. Cass tore free from witnessing the unknown but could not believe. Magenta light ebbed, deepening. Thunderous rumble echoed above. No sun. No sky. The world a violet mist, it mimicked the battlefield with a precision only she knew too well, her only thought as she ascended, arm linked with the Faun.

Vincentas

Chapter VII

Silhouette blackness gave way to definitive structures. Granite walls with scaling, blood-veined moss; a yawning mouth made of an inescapable void flanked by wooden gates three times taller than Reticence. It should have been a welcoming sight as opened gates of Riemkeler came into view. Absent guards ate into uncertainty.

Despite blanketing the world in a curtain of deep, sickening lavender mist, the air moist in the mouth, they did not need a gasmask. New prototypes stunk worse than Bogside in Konniak. Wood groaned on metal. The airship struck something filtered into the Inquisitor's mind. He looked up, airship did not crash into the walls, they flew too high for a wall collision. His heart slowed on the realisation that the airship may have struck something else. The airdock.

"Entrant. Hurry." Cawed Vincentas. He needed to focus, since Alleck was returning to his hometown.

Mystics would sense his weakness, his birthplace, and twist imagery for their benefit. The Entrant trotted, who had stopped around the Inquisitors Gaslamp. Sleek cobbles ignited under amber light, as his approaching, echoing footfalls ceased.

"Whatever we find in here, know that you are doing the Inquisitions work." He spoke, eyeing them one at a time.

"Stick together as we enter the city. Remember, clear your minds, don't think of anything." Vincentas kept his gaze fixed on the Entrant. He could be the death of them. The boy's shaking eyes matched his gaze without blinking.

"Let's move." Holding the Gaslamp higher, scattering taloned shadows away. Artificial light could not dispel eternal darkness filling an endless tunnel of the gatehouse.

Taking one last, longing look at the snaking purple veil shrouding the city, Vincentas turned and walked into the gatehouse. His emptying mind, his only companion, swiftly joined with solitary, steady breaths.

Heat bubbled around his neck on entering the yawning maw. Sweat drenched arms. He stopped, a pounding headache brewed within, like a hammer trying to break out of captivity. Turning around, Fleur's Gaslamp caught his eye, the combatant's blonde hair stark in the shadows.

He lifted the Gaslamp, held high as far as a shaking, tired hand could reach. Hammering footfalls continued, the headache thudding with the surrounding cacophony. They stood in silence. He raised a leg and stomped down, brutally. Metallic pounding reverberated up his leg, echoed louder in the long, darkened tunnel.

"Peculiar." Arno announced. Three times, the blackness echoed the Chanters' observation.

"Mystic." Vincentas's word hissed around him.

"On the contrary. It's as real as it can be." Arno stepped forward, hooves clopping in unison, sharp like needles clicking together. "A new defence. To deter attackers, unhinge them."

"It's doing a good job." Fleur spat, a wet slap echoed.

Vincentas narrowed his eyes. They stood alone in twisting shadows. The gatehouse width drowned in ebony, not even the Gaslamp's they carried, fanned out in formation, found an end. He tried to focus on specific items: Arno's blue long coat; Fleur's gleaming brass mask; Violet's repeater.

Darkness consumed them. Humidity grew, sweat bled across forehead and in-vain wiped it away as another streak of dampness broke through thinning hairline. Unbuttoning his coat the sensible solution.

"Must keep moving." Dehqan voiced. The Sabanese man moved on, bypassing Vincentas. The Combatant eyes snapping left and right.

Hammering continued as they walked, grating inside his mind, clawing at a vein attempt of escape. Radiant glow ahead signalled their end. Pace quickened, not only himself. Light grew brighter, the exit yawned wider, freedom inched closer.

Within a heartbeat, blinding strobes of violet colour forced eyes to close. Vincentas squinted. Sickening glow burned within the rims of closed eyes. He opened them, sensing the light had eased or feeling the courage that he could stand the glare, but the colour retracted to a softer purple hue.

Black, silent buildings clotted an unmoving horizon of a town submerged in bruising colour of swirling pinks and vague lavenders. Structures looked intact, no other colour illuminated Riemkeler. He looked up, expecting snow to fall from the snaking cloud obscured sky. Nature not acting in accordance with the time of year.

No sound stirred within strained ears, except his own quickening heartbeat. He finished unbuttoning his coat. Moisture stuck clothing to skin, stiff shoulders sleek in wetness.

"Fleur on point." The Inquisitor's command broke surrounding silence. Fleur moved ahead, her repeater locked. She moved with a predatory grace.

"Very peculiar." Arno whispered. The Faun stood beside him, his words carried and echoed, sounding nothing like the Chanter. Sounded feminine, then childish. Edged in hysteria, then in malice.

"Mystic." Alleck spoke. Vincentas faced the Entrant. Too far back to be heard, but he spoke with a closeness to a whisper.

"Keep your thoughts to yourself. Silent as we head into the city and everyone clear your minds." Vincentas's fingers circled the sword hilt. The Inquisitor extinguished his Gaslamp, attaching it to his belt. His free hand removed a handbow. If Athgeric was alive, he would be in the Inquirer Hall. Each city state on the continent of Cythea contained an Inquisitorial headquarters.

He followed Fleur, who melded into shadows, disappearing at will and re-emerging moments later, bronze mask a midnight-blue under magenta ambience. Interrogator Reticence's robes skirted over cobbled stones; he blurred under glowing purple. Dehqan, his two handbows ready, head barely moved, shoulders hunched ready to fire.

Boots clicked over uneven cobbles. Vincentas remembered when he was last in the bustling city, a living contrast to its current state. The similarity to the dream on the Sojourn sent a cold ripple down his back that he could not shake off. Carts would trundle over uneven stones. Children slipped when it froze. There was no ice here, no snows, despite SnowFall season. If you were lucky, they could find a coin between the cracks.

There were no carts now. No people. No luck.

"To where do we head?" Arno spoke beside him, thurible alight, sickly incense smoking.

"Must get to the Inquirers Hall, we'll learn more among our own." No sign of life in the city, which should teem with peddling sellers, children heading home and students preparing to leave for the SnowFall semester.

"Implausible." The Chanter retorted. He looked at his old friend, surveying the Faun for a hint of joke or amusement, but he knew better with years of friendship.

"Then where would you go?" The Inquisitor asked.

Arno stopped, Vincentas ceased. The Chanter looked past his friend's eye contact and raised a slow, methodical hand to point towards the horizon.

A smile formed across his face. "There." He articulated. The Inquisitor turned, following Arno's stare. Familiar, recognisable dome crowned the distance. Visible in all sectors and districts, a beacon of intelligence, wonder, astrological and intrigue. The fabled Academy of Riemkeler.

"The academy. Why?" He kept looking at the beacon of intelligence. He swore it was more distant and central. Violet skies playing tricks of the mind. Its glass orrery, large, building-sized cogs, mechanisations mimicking a beetle scaling purple dome doused in nauseating lavender, discoloured under the putrid, wound coloured sky.

"Centre of the city. People would go there in times of trouble. Enormous crowds." Arno listed all plausible reasons to head there. It would attract all reasons for a Mystic.

Vincentas continued gazing at the abnormal surroundings. He faced Arno, whose features shimmered a purply blue. Sweat glistened across the Faun's bearded face.

His hand vaulted up. They ceased together as one. He strained hearing in hope. Desperation grew within, blocking ecliptic silence with thoughts. Breaths circled in and out of his aching, tired body.

"What is it?" Arno asked. Vincentas cut the air with his hand. The Inquisitor looked at the assembled retinue. Dehqan and Fleur, weapons drawn and crouched, preparing for the worst. Alleck stood beside Reticence, dwarfed by the Interrogator in height and stature. Violet remained dignified and calm, hands snaked to holstered handbows.

"Can you hear that?" Vincentas spoke into the silent void, broken as soon as his lips parted.

"Implausible. I can't hear anything." Arno replied, thick eyebrows knitting together.

"Down. To the walls." Fleur hissed. He scrambled to the nearest wall, flinging himself against the shadow. A heavy beat thumped overhead, air rushed down. He looked up. Blackness blocked ambient lilac hues. A second heavy force of wind beat against him. Lavender light returned.

"A Roc?" Dehqan guessed.

"Too small for a Roc, but that's one gigantic bird." Fleur replied.

A hand squeezed his shoulder. He followed Arno's fixed wide eyes. Alleck stood, shaking, hand outstretched, mumbling inaudibly. The Inquisitor leered, stretching out of the shadow. Pale silhouette of a man stood before Alleck, flickering and fading. Something hung above the indefinite shape. Cross-legged and staring at the enraptured Entrant, who only had eyes for the silhouette.

Running straight at the Entrant, he levelled the handbow at the apparition and fired.

It faded. The Entrant turned. Emotional conflict ruptured his thin face, streaked in fresh tears.

"Stop thinking. Just stop." Vincentas raged in Alleck's face. The Inquisitor shook the boy. Boots skidding on sleek cobbles to keep balance, but in vain, he collapsed on Riemkeler's abandoned streets. A mechanised click reverberated in his ears.

"You're going to put us all in danger." He explained. In a steady hand, levelled the handbow at the collapsed, quivering Entrant of his charge.

"Old friend, it's not him." The voice of Arno added. A dark hand smothered the muzzle.

"Don't come between an Inquisitor and justice, Chanter." Vincentas spat, eyes on Alleck, who lay crumpled on cold, wet cobbles, hands covering his shaking head.

"Look around you, implore reason. You think he could do this?" Arno tilted his head at the sobbing boy. His throat sucked in hot air. He was summoning the apparition. Alleck had to be. He was talking to it.

"You saw him, moving away, seeing something that wasn't there." The Inquisitor rasped, voice growling until he barked the last word. Many he had seen succumb to apparitions, the desires they create and illusions they offer. All lies.

"A Mystic alters his vision, opening his eyes to torment." Arno counted. Vincentas turned on his loyal Chanter, keeping handbow lowered on his target.

"You're defending him?" His own voice breaking.

"We must protect the innocent." Arno retorted, retrieving his hand off the handbow.

"You two want to keep it down, you're attracting others to your party." Fleur hissed, breaking into the conversation. Vincentas cursed himself for his outburst, holstering the handbow. Alleck's sobs leaking into his unwarranted hearing.

"Well, this is new." Arno breathed. The Inquisitor's eyes blurred as he looked, searching. Pounding heart beating within, threatening to render from his body. Eyes flashed upwards. Exhumed breaths smoked on rooftops. Several more gathered. Ebony shapes scattered on black buildings.

They growled.

Sharp clicks tapped bare slate. They crouched. Others moved on all fours with a bestial crawl. Some stood. Shadowed things stark against purple light of Riemkeler's ominous horizon.

"Primals." Fleur hissed, her repeater tracking over blurring shapes. "And they're everywhere."

"On the rooftop, only." Vincentas spoke, observing with unblinking, tracking eyes. He cursed age, not seeing beyond his means. Hate boiled within, strengthening arms and legs. Primals. They had taken the city. Bestial predators with a singular goal of consumption and reproduction. A gnawing ate through his stomach, threatening to loosen.

"No, they're in the street ahead, behind us as well." Fleur's words sent a shiver down Vincentas's spine. A coldness grew within no warmth could dispel.

"Flesh. People. New." The words filled an empty void of silence in Riemkeler. Fleur clicked her repeater, picking targets. Handbows clanged. Primals do not speak. The Inquisitor scanned the rooftops. Sharp, penetrative lights flared among shadowed faces. A putrid magenta of smouldering coals burned in distant sockets. Seeing.

"Stick close." Vincentas commanded.

"Feast… feast." A cackling, world trembling laugh ignited every muscle in his body to run.

"The Mystic." Arno's voice pulsed into his mind, clearing senses.

"They're Afflicted." He knew. Controlled by Mystics, lost souls, the walking possessed.

Animalistic roars chorused their charge. Scrambling off rooftop's tiles shattered on sleek cobbled stones. Shoulders jerked, bracing to fire. Violet moved with a militaristic precision, dropping foes quicker than they could leap. Vincentas ran down the darkened street, heart hammering in his ears. Vision shaking with each blistering stride. Thighs burned. Handbow held in a tight grasp, glued to his hand with sweat.

A bipedal shape dropped ahead. Antagonistic light drowned growling features in azure, salivating light, its white, slavering maw gaping wide. Handbow fired, the finger kept the trigger down while running. It flung back, whimpered like a wounded, starving dog, as it writhed in agony and crashed to the ground. Vincentas kept moving. Flight or fight.

Twang of a handbow, buzzing whistle of a repeater. Growling, roaring and mewling drowned out weapon fire. Vincentas skidded and fell back, blurring face screamed in his vision. Weightlessness washed over him, pinning aching body to uneven streets.

It was a woman, contorted with living rage. Hands shot up, keeping her at bay. Frothing jaws snapped. Rapid firing of a whistling repeater killed his foe. Cold blood and entails slapping on his clothing, punching his gut. She slumped into his arms. Kicking her off, he gasped for eager breaths.

A hand dragged him to shaking feet. Dehqan at his side, shoving him to run. Vincentas turned, watching Fleur unleash bolt after bolt, dropping assailants with lethal ferocity.

"I'm out, cover." Dehqan shouted.

Vincentas levelled the handbow. More shapes surged onto dark rooftops.

They leapt.

Then froze.

Figures floated in air, suspended in descension. Limb's flailing. Rocks levitated. Water parted around the handbow as it ascended. Gloves soaked from rising liquids. Vincentas's eyes widened. Exactly like the Konniak house.

The attacking shapes thrashed. Contorted. Their bodies turned like wool on a spindle. A blur of molten colour, limbs and screeching anguish. His stomach knotted, the handbow lowered. People twisted into shaking knots. Legs tied to hands. Heads suffocated. Backs bent to impossible angles.

"The Mystic." Arno wheezed. He looked at his old friend. Magenta glow flooded Faunish features.

"This is something else." The Inquisitor turned away from the people defying gravity. Their attire attributed to Cytheans of Riemkeler.

In shrieks that shook his vision, they tore apart. Ripped bodies emptied ribbons of inky blood. Burgundy entrails burst like a flower exploding in petals. Bruising an amalgamated world of colour.

Bodies scattered and clashed with other limbs. They merged, twirled and splattered together, time grounded to a near halt. He turned away, inescapable stench punched deep in his nostrils and threatened to empty his guts to block the stench. A taste of raw blood clogged drying throat.

Vincentas staggered off, catching up with Fleur. Despite smelling worse, and seeing the decaying bodies in the morgue, this overpowering, raw aroma caught him off guard. A stench as powerful as memories of burnt hair.

Two eyes stared up at him from a blood-soaked face.

She clutched a doll. Head lowered and eyes raised. The ruin of her chignon, smears of dirt and sewage lingering odour spoke of uncleanliness. No lavender, penetrative eyes. Whites of her eyes stark against the red, silent mask.

"What the…" Vincentas stopped. A survivor. He looked around, the only person they had encountered here. The only one. Even Athgeric there was no sign.

"Come with me." He grasped her hand and sprinted away, dragging the girl behind him. Streets narrowed and alleyways darkened. Footsteps echoed with a rushing hastiness that matched fleeting shadows on contorting lilac walls.

Vincentas bent over on catching up with the others. No wonder he was last being the oldest, frailest. Thighs burned, knees quivered as if they were about to drop into his boots.

"Who is the child?" Arno inquired. He sucked in metallic, hot air. Acidic sweat trickled down his brow, smell of salt replacing distant, silent massacre.

"Found her… found her." He replied, between wheezing breaths.

"Only person we found so far." Arno's voice added with a hint of curiosity.

"We'll take her into the Hall, hurry, before there's more Afflicted." Vincentas straightened his back and looked up. A dominant building lay head, bathed in a pink light with black, swirling smoke wafting around battered corners of the structure. His pace quickened, climbing dais steps, stretching wider than the building. The Hall. The Inquirer Hall of Riemkeler. Athgeric could be inside.

"Let's go." Vincentas croaked to the girl beside him. She backed away, her doll clutched at her chest, pressed against tattered clothing, like a religious totem of protection. "It's alright, we'll be safe." More for himself than the girl.

He caught up to Fleur, who pushed open the doors of the Inquirers Hall. Yellow light flooded into squinting eyes. Someone gasped. Fleur cursed. Vincentas blinked to adjust. Voices. Precise sounds filtered into his hearing. Footsteps in a stone room. People walked, robed, jacketed, men and women. He stepped forward.

The Hall remained immaculate.

Gaslamps burned in all corners, candles flickered on chandeliers. Arbiters stood holding a bruised man. An Interrogator walked past them. Two Chanters stood before a wooden, raised desk inspecting their smoking thuribles, sickly sweet incense a welcomed invasion than sweating iron or death.

Vincentas turned back to witness the outside world. The ruins of Riemkeler. Purple sky and city awash with wounding light. No people. The bustling, contrasting Inquirer Hall. Doors closed on the desolate, abandoned city.

Cass

Chapter VII

Hands holding her back were stronger than the barred doors, but nothing would stop her.

"Need to get a hold of yourself, Cassy." Jolam groaned in resistance, a tightness trapped around her shoulders, the Fauns' strength pressing against her body.

"Lilly was outside Jol, she was outside." She protested, jerking her body to break free. Her voice echoed in her mind, sounding shrill.

She spun round, redness blurred, facing the Fauns with wide brown eyes.

"There was not one there, Cassy. No one." Jolam's determined voice nulling strength, but he did not see what she saw. Her limbs softened, shoulders sagging in the warm grasp of secure hands.

"She was there, I saw it." She shrugged captive arms offnand stepped back, bracing into the wooden door.

"Listen to yourself, Cass." The Faun pleaded, eyes dwindled to rounded, watery pools. "She's in Cythea, waiting for her mom to come back. Why would she be here? In this dump?" His arms gestured around. She could not deny her waking vision and what she saw. She killed Karwen, but saw her alive.

"I saw it." Taze whispered. Cass looked at the murderer, who faced the closed giant door. Taze placed a gloved hand on the wooden frame. Angular features hardened under flickering lights.

"What… what did you see?" She closed their distance, words more a breath than a whisper, being careful not to make sudden, jolting movements. She stood beside Taze, who mumbled.

She turned and smiled; a sincere smile. Black eyes awash with moisture. A coldness crept down Cass, having never see Taze smile like that before.

"Wilmar." Stygian eyes looked up, sparkling under low lights inside the entombed building.

"Where was Wilmar?" Her reply more a breathy gasp. Cass fixated on Taze's eyes, daring not to look at the burnt brand of "WILMAR" scarred on her forehead.

Her head jerked towards the barred door. "Out there, where you saw Lilly, I saw Wilmar." Sighing, she pushed herself away and rolled her shoulders. Their eyes locked on each other.

"Our minds, Cass the convict, are the same." Taze pointed at her temple, where the long braid hung. Cass peered at the barred doors. Scratchings and markings flared a deep red, looked like writing, more angular, more shape than cursive. No writing she had seen before, but she was no scholar or academic. Faint, white outlines of people decorated the pine beams in various positions, ranging from kneeling to flying.

Narrowing her eyes, she stepped back. Braziers on walls burned with a smoky amber, casting orange flame across the face of the wide enclosure. She continued stepping back in small echoing steps until the door filled her vision.

The writing was a pattern; it moulded with angular postures of people to display an avian-faced creature, its broad wings unfolded, spanning hinge to hinge. Eyes flashed along the door, her breath tight in dried throat, stomach gurgled. Her hand grasped into a fist.

Stell flashed in her mind. Taken by a flying creature.

"What in the name of the Tree Father is this place." Jolam whispered under his breath.

Cass turned her back to the aggravating door and stared deep into an elongated, broad tunnel that led to a glowing dais of steps, where many robed people stood. The village folk lay under the shadows of the tunnel, panting, sobbing, mumbling in their throaty Sabanese voices. Her eyes found Grodol, the small face of the girl close to his chest.

"Stay with us." She pointed at Grodol. Her voice echoed. "Grodol, stay with us." Cass lifted her gaze to the ceiling, lost in shadow. Burning braziers flickered around the many pillars that formed the foundation of the tunnel.

Echoing shouts ignited her skin with goose-pimples. Her eyes narrowed, focusing on where the robed people stood in solitary stoicism. They parted from their group. The sight of wings brought Cass's repeater to aim. Clicks echoed with other repeaters. Lucijan shuffled to her side, locked his repeater to fire.

Shaking arms lowered her weapon. The wings did not beat, they could not. A statue stood where the robed people gathered. Obsidian in colour and rippled with red light cast by hanging, burning oil lamps around the perimeter of the ornate sculpture.

"What is it with these people?" Jolam gasped. Whimpers waved through the gathered villagers, who pointed at the statue and moved away. Mothers shielded children, men fell to the ground, covering their shaking heads with trembling hands. She gazed at the statue. Its shadowed face avian with the body of a human.

Cass held onto her repeater, finger on the trigger.

"No chance." Taze snapped. Her voice growing louder. Silence descended in the tunnel, even flames dimmed. She broke into a sprint, but slowed, walking with purpose towards the congregation near the statue. Cass followed. Boots echoed on the stone floor, her breath pulling at the cold air.

"No chance. No chance." The murderer laughed, then barked. Picking up her speed. Cass ran to reach the murderer. Her eyes caught the robed figure Taze headed towards. She shook her head at the raven faced woman, ironic how she stood near the avian statute.

"You're dead, dead." Taze grasped Karwen's robe and pulled her from the dais and pushed her away. Karwen collapsed onto the stone floor, dark robes spilling open, as she lay grumbled on the stonework. She looked like she was melting as the robes covered her crumbled form.

Cass raised her repeater on approaching, snapping the bolter between the robed, stationary crowd surrounding the elevated statue. Their faces, stoic, unmoving, they looked at her and no one else. Even under minimal candlelight, it was clear the robed ones were all female.

"I put enough bolts in you to stop a Primal, Karwen." She spoke. Taze crouched and picked up Karwen with ease, making no resistance. No complaints raised among the gathered women. They made no move, no protest. Standing with their hands in long sleeves, robes partially opened. She gritted her teeth. Nothing about this was right, they were not acting right.

"Cass, I made it out." Karwen pleaded. Lucijan and Jolam panted as they caught up. Stinging sweat trickled down her forehead.

"You couldn't have." She snapped, louder than she wanted. Echoing foot falls made her turn, Grodol approached, hand holding the girl. His eyes averted on the large avian statue. He shook, shadows flickered along his shivering form. Grodol crossed his face with his fingers, making symbols and patterns, rustic rituals of protection.

"I made it. You must have got someone else, Cass." Karwen remained calm in Taze's grip. The murderer restrained Karwen.

"I'll show you, no bolt has struck me. Men have only stabbed me." A known half-smile cut her face.

"Let her go." Cass matched Karwen's stare. Taze released her captive. Repeater clicked in her hands, drum set. If the supposed dead convict ran, she had enough bolts to see her dead a second and final time.

"Sorry to disappoint you." Karwen opened her robes. Light flickered across bare body. Skin prickled by unseen coldness, a body fed well but not excessively. Sharp frame remained as Cass remembered. No scar tissues from bolts, no surgical stitching. She shook her head, no faulting the unblemished body before her. Only branded lips on Karwen's right cheek marked her body.

"No disappointment here, raven." Jolam sighed in one long breath. Cass faced the robed woman around them, still unmoving. Faces indistinguishable under fading light. She turned, looking down the tunnel towards the door. The entire village lay in darkness further away.

"I saw the body." Taze held her repeater. Cass studied Karwen, as her robes came back together.

"So did I." Jolam chimed in.

Karwen's thin lips parted, curling up in a toothy grimace. Black, empty eyes rotated on each of them.

"A rapist and a murderer, what evidence we have here." Karwen fed arms into long sleeves, resuming her stoic appearance.

Taze growled. "She killed you. I saw the body."

"I've been here days, hiding." Karwen replied, her face dropping the calculating grimace.

"This is madness." Jolam's cracked voice added.

"You died. I saw you." Cass eyed the convict. She could not believe her own words.

"These people saved me, they save me still." Karwen gestured around, sweeping arms to the sides where the others stood.

"Stell got out," Cass lamented, "but some bird took her."

Harsh whispers broke out among the hooded, robed women. She stepped back, eyes snapping between the gathered crowd. Their cowls turning to talk to one another, hissing words spat between their number. She thought the word "heretic" was whispered. Lucijan stepped back from their sudden movements. Jolam and Taze closed to her sides. Her repeater lowered, the weapon growing too heavy to level at a target.

"And she was the lucky one." A measured, oozing voice pulsed into her mind. An echoing tap on stone turned Cass to face a figure approach from behind the avian statue. Faun hooves clacked, a taloned hand caressed stone wings of the birdman statue, twisted black leaves crinkled in tangled hair, crowned with curling, black horns.

"By the Tree Father." Jolam cursed.

Ruffled movement of fabric echoed. The gathered throng of women turned and bowed to the newly appeared Faun.

"How was she lucky?" Lucijan questioned.

A solitary, dismissive hand raised. She did not face Cass or Lucijan, looking at the statue with adoring eyes.

"I will not address those beneath my station." Her head turned. Red light flared, illuminating skin cracked like broken plaster cut into a thousand pieces.

"I will address a sister only." She brought her hands meticulously to her staff, curling long, talons around the mangled wooden shaft. Milk coloured eyes, round and stark against decaying skin, bore into Cass. She looked away under the stare, eyes flickered to the base of the birdman statue. An Orschallian coat lay trapped in stone talons. Ripped. Heart thudded.

She returned the Faun's stare. Lips cracked ear to ear, a smile that scythed her face in half.

"What is this place?" Her hands held the repeater in clammy, aching palms.

The Faun unfurled her arms, mimicking the birdman statue behind her. "Sanctuary." She pulsed each syllable with her croaking voice.

Cass jerked her head behind. "Sanctuary? What about them?"

"The uninitiated. Ignorance breeds fear." The Faun brought hands together around the shaft. Hoofed feet clicked, taking steps down from the statue.

"Fear. Fear of that." She pointed her repeater at the statue. Shouts and rebukes screeched from the robed women, even joined them Karwen, who slunk back to their rank, her hood down. The Faun's talon scything to the right. Silence followed her singular move.

"Yes." The Faun hissed. "Fear of the harpy. Fear of legacy. Fear of the stone."

"Fear of the harpy. Fear of legacy. Fear of the stone." The women chanted in unison. Together, the women removed their hoods. Black sable hair of the Sabanese, hard angular faces of Orschallians. Branded Cythean convicts. A dark-skinned Kheda Ishan.

"You think that." Cass pointed at the statue. "Will stop what's out there?"

"No." The Faun claimed. She stopped descending the dais. "We are to embrace it. To accept it. To be fearless." She came closer. Milky, blurring eyes focused solely on her.

"What's going on out there? She was dead. Things in the sky. Purple light." She stared at the lidless eyes of the Faun. An overriding stench of rot turned her face away.

"It is the Change." The Faun declared. Candles flickered, braziers dimmed. "The shadow. The end. The last dream. The Verge." She listed as she walked, using the staff to enunciate each word with a harsh wooden tap on the stone floor. Long, tattered robes of hairs, feathers and rags gave her a tall, slender appearance as she floated back up the smooth stairs.

"The Verge." Lucijan echoed under his breath.

"We're Cytheans, we don't understand." She tried to reason with the cult leader, who stood before the harpy.

"Nobody understands. It is not for the living. It is not for us." Her voice echoed in the tunnel.

"Break your chains of ignorance, Cass." Karwen stepped forward. Outstretched hands ready to embrace, like a mother would do to a child. Cass stepped back.

An explosive shout jolted her skin. Taze leapt forward. In a blinding blur, Karwen crashed to the ground, being pummelled with furious, wild blows.

"Show me. Show me." The murderer raged. Cass jumped forward, letting the repeater hang on its strap at her shoulder. Hands grasping to separate the two.

"No, Taze, they'll attack." She shouted, in vain to stop the berserk action.

"Show me. Show me." The murderer's voice cracked. Taze grappled with Karwen, who remained submissive beneath the strength of the murderer. Her attempt futile to subdue the assault.

The struggle stopped. Cass stood up, panting. Her eyes leered at Taze, looking at the exposed arm of Karwen. Taze's knuckles tightened and shook with the strength of holding the arm.

Cass narrowed her eyes. Block shaped tattoos, all black, lined the arm. Circular patterns, lines, squares and rectangles marked around her bicep, down to her wrist and up the shoulder. Her eyes found Karwen's smiling eyes.

"No." The murderer roared and latched her hands around Karwen's throat. Her demented face twisting in anguish. Cass wrapped her arms around Taze's neck and chest, trying to ply her off.

"Heck Taze, stop. Stop." She panted. Muscles burned and her back tensed. Taze remained fixed, unmoveable. Determined.

"No. No." she spat. Karwen's face reddened, one of her eyes bloodied and welled up.

"You. You." Taze growled. Karwen's eyes rolled in the back of her head, glossy white pooled.

Jolam came into the fray, arms wrapped around her. Gritting her teeth, Cass pulled at Taze and kicked at the ground, resistance give way.

"Calm down. Calm down." She barked. Crashed to the stone floor, she pushed herself away, Taze sprawled beside her, kicking like a trampled mare with a broken foot.

"Where is she? Where is the murderer?" Taze slathered, kicking herself to a crouch, and launched to a groggy stand.

"Not now, Taze. Not now." She stood before the raging woman overshadowing her. Cass held her by the wrist. Wild eyes stared back; manic desperation contorted face. This was not the calculating criminal in Ralake. It was a Primal in human clothes.

"She's the murderer, Cass." Hand gripped her shoulder and squeezed. Cass winced. "She's the murderer." Taze's teeth flashed like a Bulkett, baring fangs before the charge.

"Cassidy." The shout froze her thoughts. It could not be. It was a voice not heard for ten years. A voice from the Purifier Rebellion. A voice of her past. She turned to see a native of the Thousand Isles, olive skinned, shaven head, a black moustache harder than his eyebrows and fiercer than his ink-coloured eyes, ignited by burning braziers around him.

"Armande." Cass breathed.

"You've aged, Cassidy." Armande stood near the Faun, a gloved finger wagged. "If you stayed with the group, we'd have looked after you." Her heart sunk into her chest, burying within a shaking stomach.

"Not one for staying in one place for long." She replied, holding onto a calmer Taze.

"Liar, Cassidy." Armande pointed. His face hardened, as it usually did when he was pressed, but it was always a ruse. Cass snorted.

"Heard about Ralake, there sometime." The Thousand Islander smiled. "You didn't even send me a letter. I'm heartbroken." He feigned actions, placing a hand over his forehead, hand over his heart. If he had one.

"Cythean justice is a lengthy term." She backed away, keeping eye contact with the Captain of the Irregulars during the Purifier Rebellion, bald head reared back.

"Got to join us, Cassidy. Better than the rebellion, this one makes sense." Armande's voice echoed, his arms widened and outstretched, mimicking the statue.

"Got to get back to Cythea." Cass saluted and turned, heading for the door. Trouble followed him like a personal shadow, trouble she could do without. Battle and murder raced through her mind, what she was, what she turned into long gone and buried. Jolam caught up, Cass focused ahead, better out there, with him, the Faun and distance from the ominous statue.

"Cass? Outside?" Jolam piped in.

"Better to risk out there than in here." She turned back nearing the door. The stone harpy prominent under flickering fires, Armande stood with the Faun. The robed women flocked around the dais, standing as still as the statue. Cass nodded on seeing Lucijan and Taze joining her, Grodol and the girl followed. She braved a smile for the girl.

"It's a whole new world, Cassidy, and she won't let you go." Armande's laughing voice echoed through the tunnel.

A shout peeled through ears, jolting skin.

"Look." Lucijan yelled. Pointing at the door.

Solid wood leaked redness. A resin light and oozing. Her stomach threatened to shake from her body.

The door bled.

Cass backed away. Jolam cursed. The girl with Grodol whimpered and cried. Copper stench, thick and raw, clambered through flaring nostrils breathing heavier for cleaner air.

"What is this?" The Faun cursed. Her eyes rounded to the sides of the door. Along the walls, cracks oozed purple light. A thousand thoughts raced through Cass. None of them her own.

A blood-curdling scream ripped Cass's eyes from the wall to see a woman dragged into the air. She raised her repeater. The woman, arms flailing, her body contorted. Writhing in mid-air. Defying gravity. A snap echoed in the tunnel as her head turned completely around. She dropped, crashing into skulking villagers below.

A second scream erupted. Third. Fourth.

People swarmed and cried deafening Cass. She turned; the door blocked by a creature. Rippling sinewy flesh. Its chest opened with snapping teeth. Searching limbs pulled it along the floor, slapping off stone. It flooded towards them.

"What the…" Jolam squealed.

"Kill it!" Taze raged. Cass aimed and fired. The recoil hammered her shoulder. Bolts thundered into its fleshy, carcass exterior and lumbered back. Shrieking like a newborn.

"Back away." Lucijan shouted. She turned and jogged back, hand pressing into the back of the girl with Grodol. Echoing footsteps on iron rang in her ears. Villagers shouted. Purple flames discoloured braziers. Black and velvet drowned her vision. Screaming people vaulted to the ceiling, pulled apart, defiled.

A hand pulled her clothing. Cass looked at the Sabanese girl, tears flowing, pointing to the floor. An iron grate lay on the stone floor. A trap door, or a cellar door, either way it was an escape.

"Down. With me." She shouted.

Lucijan reacted first. He peered down the hole. Cass caught up, holding the girl by the hand.

"Where does it go?" Lucijan looked down.

"Anywhere but here." She shouted. More bulbous creatures merged from pink, oozing walls. People floated, writhing in mid-air. Grodol helped Jolam open the iron grate. Taze fired indiscriminately at the writhing, sinewy creatures surrounding them.

"Lead them." Cass shoved Lucijan. The boy slung the repeater over his back and climbed down the rattling steps of a rusting ladder. Grodol shouted at the girl in his guttural voice. She went next. Grodol followed.

"Don't be a hero and follow me. Make sure Taze is with us." Cass pulled Jolam's coat roughly in the ball of her fist.

"You know me, Cassy, I'm never a hero." Jolam smiled, lips trembled.

Cass descended the ringing ladder. She looked up, the Faun and Armande staring at her, standing like statues among turbulent chaos. Faces blank and expressionless. She descended into eternal darkness, the gurgling world above vanishing under her own rattling steps and echo filled panting.

Vincentas

Chapter VIII

It should have been a sight for welcoming eyes, a brief respite against the torrent of Riemkeler's bleak demise, but nothing brought warming comfort to weary bones. Stone pillars held up an invisible ceiling, lost in shadow. Yellow, thick Gaslamp light could not dispel lingering darkness. Emptiness gnawed at Vincentas's mind; an emptiness so vast it threatened to swallow him.

Only the golden "I" encircled by the obsidian "C" signalled to the Inquisitor as he stood in the building of his profession. Riemkeler's order always played down their own importance. No tapestries or banners hung, showing a continuous struggle against the Mystic. They did not mark pillars in heraldic duties or statues of heroes.

The occasional Inquisitor and Interrogator drew his glance, but it was the people reading, carrying tomes, unfolded scrolls of reed paper and papyrus that dragged his wandering vision to them. Silence deafened him.

"Dehqan check the door." He ordered, his voice resounding in the cathedral of Mystic struggles, snapping him into focus. A raised desk spanned the width of two pillars, plain glass window spilt light, promising a cloudless day. No lavender hue distorted the desk, hall, and pillars in a myriad of purple shades.

"It's locked." Dehqan hissed as he joined them, boots echoed on the tiled floor.

"Stick with me." Vincentas commanded, his voice drew Alleck to straighten his back. The Entrant focused. In feigned control, he held the handbow in a shaking hand. The weapon grew heavy within his grasp.

"They're ignoring us." Fleur whispered, her voice raised by an octave. People conversed in small groups, conversations unavailable to hear. Nobody looked at them, not even the woman carrying a tome under her arm, head high, walking past them so closely she could have bumped into his handbow.

"They cannot see us." Arno's words matched his thoughts. Lips curled back. He should not be thinking. The Mystic was at work here. Words gave strength to a chilling hand down his spine. Tilting his head upwards, sweat threatened to itch down a tight forehead.

"It can't be." He growled. His handbow clicked into life. Dehqan's own handbows echoed with a reverent beat. Fingers flexed around the obsidian hilt, pushing free the concealed scabbard beneath the thick, open greatcoat.

"It's the Verge." The aging Inquisitor realised. Merging of present and thought, a domain manufactured by Mystic power and weak minds. He looked around. It smelt real, but it could not be. How could the Inquirers Hall be immaculate, serene and clear of pain and bloodshed, but beyond the walls in the city of Riemkeler breathed horror. Burying the word Verge in his stomach, it replied with a growl of unknown that could not digest.

"Mystic is strong." Arno whispered, sounding complimentary. Vincentas moved forward. A sharp gasp forced him around. The girl from outside flinched, grasping her doll in protective hands. Two people, in conversation near the desk, turned and faced him. He moved away from the girl. Their eyes followed him.

"What day is this?" Vincentas's voice broke through eclipsing silence. The Inquisitor stopped a boy. The boy's eyes widened, mouth parted. Young one breathed, his own heartbeat thumping in his ears. He knew their eyes were on him. He had entered the Verge, communed with it.

"Twenty eighth day of LeafFall, sir." The boy stammered.

The Inquisitor made a gesture for the boy to go. Hasty footsteps echoed as he left. He gingerly carried the buckets, but water spilled, slapping stone floor.

"We're in SnowFall." Dehqan whispered.

"Market Feast Day of Riemkeler." Vincentas turned on hearing Violet. Athgeric's Combatant looked at him. Almost as if she read his mind. His dream.

"We must leave, please." The girl yanked at his sleeve. Tears welled in blue eyes. Streaks of cleanliness removing crimson stains.

"You are wanted upstairs, Inquisitor." A Chanter spoke to him. The girl did not relent, pulling and tugging in her attempt to lead him away. For a girl of nine, she was strong. White pupils burned with a ferocity as she leaned back, yanking with all her strength. A warmth grew in her grasp.

"We need to leave." Her teeth clenched, soft features contorted into feral rage. Vincentas stuttered. Never good at consoling children, he had no time for it, nor the patience. He shook his arm, trying in vain to break her hold.

"I like her, she's a feisty one." Fleur snorted.

"Must stay here, safer here." Vincentas rasped. Smoke kindled at the girl's grasp. He gritted his teeth, keeping much-needed outburst within himself. Heat smouldered his skin.

The girl let go of his arm. She staggered and collapsed on the stone floor. She breathed rapidly while looking around, her eyes flashed wide open. Chanters continued talking. The cacophony of noise picked up. Desperate hands slapped over her ears. Crouching down, she hid herself in her arms.

Laughter burst from everyone. Inquisitors, workers, tome carriers, Chanters. Vincentas flinched at the headache pounding noise of laughter thundering through the echoing Inquirer Hall.

Snapping back her head, teeth bare and snarling, the girl unleashed a scream.

Vincentas slammed hands over his ears, dropping the handbow. Nothing defended his senses from the shaking noise. Quivering eyes closed, guts heaved, rippling through tired, burning lungs. Light flashed in the darkness of closed eyes, glass rained in a thousand shards from empty windows. Coloured, mottled eyes winking at him, looking at him. Judging him. They stopped falling. Hanging in mid-air, like leaves caught in the breeze.

Immediately, the noise died. He collapsed to the ground, others fell panting beside him. Fleur cursed. He looked up to see people standing, frozen, locked in still motion. All of them looked his way.

Hurried steps clattered on stone, the sound of the fleeing girl dying off as she rounded a corner.

"It's her. It's her." Vincentas rasped, pushing himself up to stand, every limb in his body screaming to stop. The Entrant snatched a fallen repeater. He ran in the direction where the Mystic vanished through, a swinging door a signal of her escape.

"No, Alleck, she's too strong." He shouted. Sucking in cold air, calmness soothed muscles, he snatched his handbow and staggered after the Entrant. Eyes focused, narrowed to the corridor. He barraged through the swinging door, knocking it against the plaster with a thud.

Rattling feet on wooden stairs signalled her hasty ascension along with Alleck's mindless pursuit. He turned to the right. The staircase echoed her escape. He vaulted up the stairs. Well carved, simple brown wooden bannisters. Long, wide steps. Nothing decorative lay on the unblemished walls. He took the stairs two at a time. Alleck's hasty steps grew closer, his retinues shouts more distant.

Vincentas plunged into nothingness and lashed out.

Legs kicked vacant air. Arms scrambled for anything for stability. Handbow clattered on the stairs before him, crashing on wood. He clawed helplessly at the stairs, fingers biting into brittle wood, breaking in flailing grasp. Strained throat departed panting breath.

Splinters ate into his fingers, pain jabbing Vincentas's flesh. Nothing but air at his feet. He cried out on digging bleeding hands at the wood to keep him safe. His face punched the steps, careening off the wood. Grogginess clouding his battered mind. Blurring hands fought to hold on. Heavy footfalls ricochet up the stairs. Vibrations rippling down grappling arms, burning with agony, yearning for release.

"Careful. Careful." He muffled a vain warning to his ascending retinue. Heavy trotting footsteps ceased. Creaking wood echoed behind.

"Careful, hole in the stairs." Fleur's voice broke through the numbness.

"Damn, how this happen?" Dehqan gasped.

"Jump the gap, Fleur, and help him up." Arno instructed.

"Stay still, Vin, and don't move." Fleur commanded. Her firm voice echoed, but not calming thunder of his heart. A heavy thud crashed beside as air whipped his balding head. Fleur obscured his vision; relief grew in his legs. Her unseen hand grasped his coat, a powerful tug yanked at his neck.

"You look down my coat like a good boy and help yourself up, don't think about the climb. On three." Fleur laughed. She was as close as lovers. His eyes looked deep into her tight fitted bodice; his mind focused on the Mystic.

"Three." Fleur snapped. Vincentas pulled himself forward, head swirling in nausea. She groaned and leaned back, Fleur's taunt neck bulging. He climbed on her. Grappling on broken stairs, hoping to feel solid ground. Legs kicked out at nothingness; thighs collided with demolished, torn wood. Heavy boots scraped as he swung up, latching onto solid reassurance.

"That's it, roll Vin, roll the leg." Fleur encouraged through gritted teeth. A hand clawed his back, pulling him up. Welcomed steadiness of solid stairs greeted his easing body. His heartbeat grew steadier, slower.

He vaulted up on sturdy ground and sat on the stairs three up from the gaping black maw where the staircase had disappeared, a mouth that nearly swallowed him. His singular pursuit of the Mystic clouded vision. It must have been.

"Be a gentleman and help her ladyship up." Fleur winked, extending her arm to him as she lay on her back.

"I'm an old man. You can do it yourself. But since you asked nicely." Vincentas's bitter tone echoed on the staircase while helping Fleur to her feet. He climbed the staircase, keeping sight of the others. Dehqan jumped first. The Inquisitor picked up his fallen handbow.

Vincentas surveyed the surroundings. Fragmented shadows crossed flaking, plastered walls. Stale stench of dust and unused dampness seeped into flaring nostrils. A constant drip filtered into his ears, like the house in Konniak.

He gulped, eyes catching words carved into the walls, scarred with crude lethality. Capital letters. Cythean script. "HELP ME" "WHY US?" "HOW COULD YOU?"

"Any sign of the Entrant?" Arno climbed towards him. He looked away, the aged Chanter wrinkled in frowns.

"No, he was up before anyone of us and headed after her. I suspect he went after her to prove his innocence, an innocence I suspect lacks with him." The Inquisitor declared. His voice travelled further than he expected. The word "innocence" recoiling around him, whispered from the walls, sneered at him from behind, beside and in his mind.

Vincentas's eyes narrowed. Sounded like several voices echoed. Mockingly, the word innocence muttered again. He looked up, nothing but darkened stairs and dust fogged his vision.

"Implausible. He is as innocent as a child." Arno replied. The Chanter's words consumed his mind. Vincentas lowered his gaze on the Faun. Purple light grew on Arno's old face, cold eyes looked up, blurring pink in the ambience.

"Innocent as a child. Like the child that ran off?" He stepped forward, moving towards Arno. Something hung in the air, thick and moist, shoulders sagged. Patience drained.

"Let's find the girl and find the truth." Arno gestured to the ascending stairs. Vincentas ascended, shadows retreated leaving the hibernation of ruined walls. More scribbles, more carvings. The wall a memorial, flaking skin, the remnants of plaster cut to make scratchy, stark words.

Childish giggling reverberated down the staircase. A door slammed above.

"Ascend. Fleur on point, Dehqan at the rear." Vincentas locked the handbow and peered up the winding staircase.

Fleur vaulted up the stairs. He followed on, behind the Combatants vanished trail. Arno's mumbles signalled the Chanter's preparations. He could not hear it but guessed the prayers or litanies ready to face the Mystic. Humidity grew. Dampness melted on itchy skin. Stench of neglect rapidly removed for decay and rot. A meaty rot, leaving a gagging taste in the throat.

A fly buzzed close. A second and a third itched nearby. Murmuring wind picked up. Low moans of a forlorn wind creaked the bannisters, and the ruined stairs. He halted on Fleur, stopping, her right hand clenched into a steady fist. Her voice broke through the itching whine.

"Keep your eyes off the walls. Touch nothing. Touch nothing." Her warning tightened the grip on his handbow. He swatted a fly on his hand but missed. The echoing thud of hand on leather rippled through stale air.

"Whatever you see on these stairs, it is not real. It is the Mystic. Stop thinking." Vincentas commanded, the Verge lived here, devastating to witness, revealing the innermost worries, hates and fears. The retinue would be fine, but the Entrant had to be found. Violet would remain steady. Looking back, she took up the rear, dual handbows raised.

Creaking wood echoed their ascension. His throat threatened to cough from the stench. The diseased smell like a carcass. A rotten one. Buzzing flies flew, Vincentas kept his head down. The murmuring of wind picked up, festering with voices, harsh and pleading. Crawling insects itched dry skin. Hairs on neck stood. Every sweat drop rolling down his flesh tortured him to move his hand and wipe it away.

Eyes flashed to the walls. They were people.

Eyes open, mouths agape, arms nailed to walls pointing up the stairs. Not the wind making the murmuring, it was people. Throats rippled. Eyes, big, bright and pleading. Stark whites followed him. Eyes where eyes should not be mouths were mouths could not be.

He kept his trembling head down. It could not be real. Mystic trickery only. Eyes closed. Murmuring grew. Moans bled into ears, hearing blurred, fogging his mind.

Creaking boards groaned underfoot, eyes snapped open expecting to see people's faces, but only chipped wood, dilapidated stairs and his shaking boots climbing the staircase. He spat contempt onto the dusty floor.

His shaking hand snatched at the banister for support.

Something wriggled.

Vincentas froze. He turned to look at his hand moving under rippling, sinewy texture of the pink banister. Fleshy, pale, and naked. Hands tied to feet. Head bound. Eyes looking at him expectedly. A woman.

"We need to keep moving. Can hear the Mystic." Arno's cool voice interjected.

Vincentas blinked. The woman vanished.

The mangled corpse banister replaced with growing darkness and yawning shadows. Looking up the staircase, amber light pushed into darkness by Dehqan's Gaslamp. Purple's sick colour oozed through long, thin windows. Fleur's lavender silhouette quivered. Reaching the top of the staircase, it rounded to a long, narrow corridor, enough for two to walk side by side. He could smell himself.

Vincentas stopped. A little girl-shaped silhouette doused in lavender stood in the distance.

"You… you… charged with Mysticism." A broken voice shouted, not Alleck, or anyone he knew, or any of his group. He gripped the handle of his sword. The same voice in the distance cracked, spitting their mumbled words. Babbled in fear.

"Looks like an Inquisitor." Fleur whispered, her repeater scything into his peripheral vision.

"No. Back away." Vincentas's arm flashed to the side. Fleur moved alongside him as her sweat filtered into his nostrils, purple ambience gleaming off her mask.

He stole a look over his shoulder at Dehqan, whose eyes enlarged. Wizened mouth opened.

Vincentas faced the corridor's depths.

In the mouth of darkness, a man floated in the air. Arms flailed; legs kicked wildly. He jerked and blurred with an inhuman speed. No sound accompanied the cavorting man.

The Mystic stood further down the corridor. The girl from outside. Streaked in blood. Her black hair hanging past wet, crimson shoulders. In silence, the levitating man reached the ceiling, twisting in impossible actions.

A scream pulsed down the corridor, rippling walls and punched Vincentas in the gut. The man rendered in a red shower flashing under lavender light. Walls of purple splattered black. A boot hung in the air. Sinews dripped down low ceilings. Raw stench of blood assaulted flaring nostrils, Vincentas gagged on the stench, turning his head aside.

"Like the people outside." Fleur whispered.

"She's powerful. Need to back away." Vincentas hissed.

His trembling feet moved back, inch by inch. Luckily, the floorboards did not creak. The girl lay still ahead. Sinewy, pink glowing tendrils entrapped the girl like a fist clutching her body. Hanging parts of the man that were pulled apart threatened to drown her.

Something solid hit his foot, preventing him moving back.

Vincentas's eyes widened. He took a deep breath, sliding back until he pressed into solid, unmoveable matter. The corridor lay ahead. Arno should have been behind. His old friend was not there. No wind brushed his nek. His breathing matched with an increased heartbeat. Flickering silhouette of the girl turned to face them.

"What the…" The Inquisitor breathed. His foot grazing against the solid object behind, a barrier preventing his escape. His back pushing against the immoveable object. Nothing budged, nothing gave way. Fleur turned beside him and backed away. Her solitary eye huge beneath blonde hair, then narrowed in scepticism.

"We need another plan." Her head shook.

Vincentas turned. No corridor extended to the staircase. There was only a wall. Solid, grey with crumpling mortar. No markings, no decorations. A solid wall. No Reticence, no Arno, no Violet. No Dehqan.

"No, don't." Fleur shouted. Vincentas turned to see the corridor extend under patched moonlight caste through long slit windows. A silent corridor. A solitary Gaslamp lay on the ground, its ebbing light threatened to fade.

No stench of blood. No Mystic girl. No bloody pulp of a man pulled apart in mid-air. Nothing. A barren corridor, silent. It stretched as far as he dared to see. Gaslamp yellow rays died. Darkness and thick purple light engulfed his vision, drowning him, pushing deep within.

"Fleur? Dehqan? Reticence? Violet? Arno?" Vincentas gasped. His voice travelled down the empty corridor, barren walls echoed forlorn words. No reply but the sound of silence and his solitary breathing.

Cass

Chapter VIII

Cass's shaking feet touched solid ground. Trembling hands let go of the rusting, iron ladder, rattling in perpetual darkness as others descended its rickety frame. She sank to her knees. Sprawling on the rock face of the uneven, jagged floor, and dragged herself away. Gasping echoes reverberated within her mind and the pitch-black of her imposing surroundings.

She crawled, unable to comprehend where she was. Hands swallowed in liquid; warm, sloshing water reeked with an overbearing nostril-filling stench of copper. She closed her eyes, sucking in moist air between ragged breaths. Thumping heart clogged ears, panting broke through laboured inhales threatening to break into solitary crying.

"Where in the name of beer are we?" Jolam panted. He sounded close. The ladder stopped chattering.

"Are we all here?" Cass tried to say aloud, her voice grated in rawness.

"Sound call. Lucijan." The conscript's reply echoed.

"Glad you're with us, Lucky J. Taze reporting for duty." The murderers strained call shadowed by sloshing water. A rippling, shallow tide bobbed around Cass's submerged wrist.

"Jolam. Tired, hungry and definitely fed up." The Faun spat.

"Grodol." A Sabanese guttural tone voiced nearby.

Fumbling echoed in the darkness. She lost her haversack, Cass shook her head.

"It's pitch-black down here wherever here is." Jolam's voice cut through steadying calmness of easing breaths.

"It maybe dark, Faun, but don't get any ideas." Taze threatened.

Periphery glowed orange. Grodol's wrinkled face illuminated along with his torso, bathed in flickering amber light. His unseen hands soon became visible, a hand-held Gaslamp flared. Cass sighed, noticing the girl shaking by his side. Lucijan came to the light along with Jolam.

"That's weird. Why is the water red?" Lucijan asked. She looked down. The limited light revealed her hands swilled in lapping liquids, red and opaque.

"It's not water." Taze's deep voice warned. A reflective object bobbed before her eyes, in causing small ripples. It rotated. Empty sockets stared at her. The skull drifted on the visible current.

"It's blood." Cass shouted, scrambling from the pool's edge, slapping palms on trousers to dry them in vain to remove stickiness plastered to her skin.

Jolam peeled back from the water's edge. She tried not to think about her soiled socks through the damp valenki boots. She rubbed her hands with a vigour to clean them. Sweat itched at her neck, crowning face and ignited under irritating clothes.

"So where are we then?" Looked around to distract herself and see if anything caught her eyes. Echoing drips resonated in the distance. Boots trudged on wet rocks clipped nearby.

"Cave, I think." Lucijan replied. She followed the meagre light the Gaslamp shared. Flickering shadow talons lashed across the rocky surface of black, jagged walls.

"What kind of cave has blood in it?" Jolam murmured.

A belly rumbling growl rushed through the cave. Whipping through her short hair.

The girl screamed. Cass snatched her repeater. Grodol's guttural voice mumbled in repetitive tones. Nothing but a red-blood pool, rippling with a shallow tide, and glistening rock faces.

"Tell me that was your hunger calling out, Jolam?" Cass asked.

"There must be another way out of here." Hissed the Faun.

"The ladder it's gone." Lucijan remarked. The light spun round. Cass stared at the bare rock wall of the enclosed cave. The rusting ladder of their escape had disappeared.

"Grodol." Cass faced the Sabanese elder. "See if there's anything around here to burn, more lights the better." Keeping them occupied would stop her mind from racing. She turned to survey the humid area. A red glow illuminated rocky, uneven ground. The floor looked like thousands of hands reaching up, clawing to escape.

Roughness of the rock drank crimson light, laughing shadows occupied her sight.

The pool swelled in scarlet light. Pointed stalagmites, barring its glistening, crimson stone fangs throughout her vision. No ceiling lay visible, no stars or lights, veins of the earth or glowing minerals. Grodol set fire to a blackened brazier. He handed it to Lucijan.

Taze stood on the precipice of the darkness. A repeater hung in a loose hand, her body sagged, head low. Cass stiffened her back and walked towards Taze, knowing that she could hear her approaching footfalls, valenki boots stamping on echoing, moist cavern floor.

"Stop." Taze hushed. Her striking portrait came into view as she turned her head.

"Wanted to see how you were." Cass asked, knowing how weak that sounded. Taze's features softened.

"Wanted to know if I was safe to be around." The murderer rasped, taking a deep exhale at the end.

"You're wrong." She stepped forward. The murderer turned her head, her braid whiplashing, then swinging by her temple.

"Then why speak to me, Cass the convict?" Taze's face narrowed as she tilted her head down. The branded "Wilmar" lost in frowning. Taze's scent more powerful than sticky blood across palms. Muscles flexed in repetitive gulps. She stood closer to her than anytime at Ralake.

"We've both seen our pasts today. I hated seeing mine." Cass looked down, breaking the stare. "We're both in this together." Growing conscious of the surrounding silence, even the footfalls on the rock had ceased in tempo and urgency.

More lights flared in the cave, Taze's legs and boots illuminated in colour, the murderers' muscles deep with crimson. Eyes dropped; corners of scarred mouth twitched.

"All." Taze spoke. Her iron voice grating. She coughed and spat to the side. "All in this together."

Cass's smile grew, the light reprieve invaluable. Exhaling a large, heavy sigh, she straightened her back and braced herself, knowing it had to be asked.

"The marks on Karwen." Words chosen careful, Taze's light in her black eyes leaving. "You recognised them. Never knew she had them." Cass had never seen the marks on Karwen's arms before, four years in Ralake, a Bit the inmates call it, but a lifetime ago.

"She didn't have them in prison, if she did…" she replied through clenched teeth.

"I will not stop you, the next time you see her." Cass knew what she was saying, no stopping a predator from their prey, nothing but foolishness would stop her holding back Taze if they saw Karwen again.

"The murderer had them." Taze fixed her gaze. "The one who killed Wilmar."

"It means you're innocent." Cass blurted out.

"Course I'm bloody innocent." She snapped. Cass stepped back. "Why would I kill…" Words trailed off, the fire in the murderer's eyes died off.

Under crimson murky light, the brooding matriarch of Ralake Prison did not stand before her, or the cold-blooded murderer wearing conviction as armour. Light could distort any feature, create any new angle of intensity. Her daughter, Lilly, nearing ten. Everyone wore a mask, even children.

She turned to join the others. Taze folded her arms and faced the darkness. Enough braziers illuminated several feet around. Sloshing scarlet blood-pool echoed. Shadows of a constant cloud that shrouded everything beyond. Nobody else was coming, a slight relief, but alternative escape now inevitable and had to be found.

"What's going on?" She asked, joining the others. Lucijan, Jolam, Grodol and girl came close. Bathed in murky red, blackness rimmed eyes, no light could push back. Jolam's naturally curly hair lay in a tangled mat on his face, sticking to his features.

"I don't know, nobody can know." The Faun shrugged.

"The battlefield." Lucijan spoke out. Cass looked at the conscript. His head lowered, shoulders dipped.

"Want to hear it, Lucijan. Less voices I hear, the more agitated I get." She tried to laugh, easing the tension in the unnatural cave, dwarfing them. Air thinner, precious breaths could not still a rapid heart.

"Fewer." Taze's voice exclaimed behind Cass. She shrugged it off.

"Purple light. Here and the battlefield. The fog. People attacking, acting like Primals. Both times." Lucijan noted, looking between her and Jolam. Taze approached and stood beside, muscled arms linked around the repeater. Eyes flared red under many fires.

"Boy's right. More than a coincidence." The murderer added.

"Each time hearing voices." Jolam interjected. Cass looked at the renowned Faun of jovial practise, his shoulder slouched.

"Me too." Lucijan admitted.

"Always." Taze rasped, darkly.

"Lilly." Cass whispered.

"Mom." A clear voice broke through the darkness.

Cass spun, holding her breath, straining to hear. Instincts guided her way. Stopping herself at dark boundaries where light died, she knew Lilly could not be down here. Impossible. Her voice, undeniable. A single word built on anguish.

"You hear that? Tell me you did?" She called back to the others. Within the red dome of light, the others stood separated. On the precipice of their own blackness, ready to be engulfed. Mirroring her, facing each other.

"Yes, I heard the voice. Did you?" Lucijan inquired, voice cracking.

"She couldn't be here." Jolam shook his head. "Cave, it's not her thing."

"What did you hear?" Cass walked to the others, flickering flames of brazier's lashing light against black canvas, shadowed talons whipping back and forth.

"Wilmar." Taze's voice sent a shiver down Cass's neck.

A heavy splash tore her around to face the blood pool. Skin jolted.

The girl screamed. Silent whispers and muffled crying echoed in her skull. Quivering light fell on the pool, rocking in crimson waves. A small tide crashed and bubbled at its rocky edge. Blood splashed on her valenki boots, dampening toes. Stickiness saturated her feet.

"By the Tree Father, what's going on?" Jolam cried.

"There's something in the water." Lucijan shrieked. A click of a repeater echoed. Her own repeater, strapped across her shoulder, shaking in tired hands. Hunger held body in uncontrolled shakes and tremors.

A bloodcurdling scream ripped from the girl. Cass spun, repeater raised. Light followed. Kicking valenki boots dangled. In gurgles, Grodol vaulted up the wall. A ushanka hat lay upside down beside the girl.

"Where the hell is the caravan guy?" Jolam shouted. She froze. The girl wrapped her arms around herself and sank to the cave floor. Aching limbs lowered the repeater. Lilly curled on the rocks, not Grodol's girl.

A rush of heated wind followed heavy spraying of blood out of the pool, showering Cass in hot liquids and foul stenches, threatening to empty her bowels. Taze erupted in a guttural cry, flailing and dragging to the pool. The murderer's legs pulled beneath rippling crimson waters. Lucijan dived for the scrambling convict, locking arms around her. Both submerged into swilling, bubbling redness.

"Cass, we got to go." Jolam cried. Her vision blurred as the Faun fired his repeater. Elongated shadows whipped at brazier's light. Fleshy, pale and slick ropes snapped on rock. The girl cradled on the ground.

Cass burst forward, slinging the repeater onto her back. Burning knees took her to the girl. Scooping her up, Cass ran into the darkness. Heavy footfalls led the way. Heart pounding quicker than fleeing steps. She did not look back, she could not look back. Shouts and something slapping wetly trailed in her departure. The girl's matted hair, thick and dark, tickled her cheek. Rapid breaths of emotions ignited limbs to move, only to move.

"It'll be fine, Lilly, it'll be alright. I promise." She smothered the girl in her body. Cass stumbled, tripped and fought against gravity and hit the unseen, hard ground. Picking herself up, and the girl, she gritted her teeth and powered on. Limping. Left followed right. Left followed right. The dead weight of the right leg scraped the cave floor.

A hand grasped her ankle.

"No." Cass erupted in blind panic. She looked down. Nothing but darkness, not even ungainly moist valenki boots.

Fingers caressed her thigh. She darted away. Her left leg dangled over a drop, free air swallowed around the swinging leg hanging in unseen depths. She gritted her teeth and pulled herself to the right, falling with the girl in her grasp.

Cass lay still, holding the sobbing girl.

The girl ripped away from her.

"NO." Cass screamed. Her scream echoed with the girls as it faded away.

She scrambled. Fought with air. Fighting nothing but darkness. She swiped stale underground air. Kicked. Lunged. Clutched. Grasped. Her hands full of air. Cold, isolated, unseen air.

Burying her face with her hands, she sobbed. How could she let the girl down, like she did with Lilly?

Unseen hands snatched her shoulder.

Cass jerked, and a scream clogged her throat. Heart leaping into her chest. Damp, clammy hands latched a leg, then another. She kicked; stomach quivered threatening to liquify. Shaking mind swam with a thousand thoughts, blurring strained vision, nausea curdled her stomach.

"Let her go. Let her go." A voice broke through fumbling murmurs, penetrating her mind.

Penetrative light blinded her, bringing the colour of a face, goatee and a thick jacket. Cass fell onto the rock floor, knocking warm wind out of her. She lay down, doe skin boots filled her vision, dirtied fur and hooves of a Faun. She tilted her head, using steady hands to sit up.

"Cassy, you're good. We're alright." Jolam breathed, his hand grasped her shoulder. She shrugged it off, a knee-jerk reaction. Faunish wide eyes peered back, unblinking, diluted and steady.

"The girl. Taze. Everyone." She panted.

"Here." A girl's voice piped up. The girl knelt beside Cass. A wane smile broke across dirtied face of the Sabanese child. Grodol stood behind her.

"Thanks for mentioning me, Cass." Taze's rasping voice added. Her hand found the girl's own hand and held it, giving the chilly hand a squeeze.

"What happened? Where are we?" She looked around. Fires flickered.

"There." Jolam pointed behind, his eyes looking up. Water hit her chin. She rubbed her hand and looked down. A small inky rock pool rippled. A reflective droplet of water rose before her eyes, hovered close enough to kiss. It split, rolling and colliding together. The droplet floated up. Cass followed it until it vanished into blackness. A liquid star in the void.

She held her breath. Unnatural occurrences were nothing new, and she hoped to hide it against judgmental eyes.

"Where are we?" Cass whispered. Another droplet of water floated upwards. Her outstretched palm blocking its ascension, dampening her hand.

"Look, see." Lucijan pointed. He threw the burning torch. It clattered on stone. Shadows darted, red illuminations leapt up rock-faced walls. She ventured over to where the torch lay, coming to the edge of the natural ledge.

She peered down, glistening pale ornaments lay piled together, strewn throughout the shallow pit. Her nose wrinkled. Eyes could not turn away. Empty skull sockets peered up.

Bones. Human bones.

"The pool of blood." She whispered, her voice echoing in the cave. Burning fires cackled. Drips of water collided together. A shiver itched down her spine. Looked like rain vaulting upwards. The ground raining.

"So, what's going on here? I'm losing my mind or something?" Jolam barked.

"It's a Mystic." Cass threw her arms to the side and turned her back to the bone pit, facing the Faun.

"Can't be." Jolam's eyes darted around. He posed to speak but remained silent.

"I've seen it." She pointed at the droplets of water floating upwards. Murky water rolling and splitting in mid-air, glistening like ice on a window.

"Purifier Rebellion. Mystics can do things." Facing Lucijan, who winced as Taze applied a makeshift bandage around his left hand.

"Lucijan." Cass called out, her voice hardening. He faced her, mouth open.

"Yes?" He answered.

"The woman, in the robes, near the statue up there." Cass pointed up. "She mentioned the Verge, and you whispered it, like you heard it before. Where have you heard it? What do you know?" She stepped forward.

Lucijan looked around. Cass balled her hands into fists. Shoulders heaved with breathing, her chest tightened. Taze smiled, easing the bandage wrap around his hand.

"It's nothing." He started, he looked a shade darker in the cave light, perspiration speckled his brow. "I heard about it, well, read about it in books."

"Where were these books?" Cass closed the distance between them.

"In the libraries." His voice cracked. Straightened his neck, he gulped under the reddening light.

"Lucijan, tell me what you know?" Her words more measured than before. "It will help us, anything."

"It's mentioned in myths and legends. Stories." He looked around and lowered his head. "It's all made up."

"I've heard of it too." Jolam stepped forward. Cass looked away as Taze finished the bandage with a tight knot, the conscript gritted and winced.

"Now is not the time for jokes, Jolam." She folded her arms.

"No joke, Cassy." The Faun replied, arms waving before him. "When young Faunlings grow up, we are told of the Father Tree. I don't believe it myself, I believe more in what you make of it than something controlling it."

The Faun bent down, rubbing his legs and stretching them out. Her own legs throbbed with standing aches, tiredness burning thighs. Muscles cried out for rest. Her stomach chorused a sympathetic reply.

"The Tree Father protects, from the voice of thousands." Big brown eyes caught Cass. "From the Verge. The Periphery. The End."

She turned to see the girl with Grodol. He held her like a father would a child. Too old to be her father. Her own arms empty, only wishing to hold Lilly in this darkness.

"What else is there? Anybody." Cass held her gloved hands together, shakes ran down her left hand. She flexed her fingers, hoping to hide the visible movements.

"I saw Wilmar." Taze's rough voice sent a shiver down her back. "He was trying to say something. It was outside the building where that demented woman was with the birdman statue."

"I saw my daughter there, too." She caught the murderer's eyes. The thousand-yard stare vanished. Black eyes reflective, not opaque or devoid of life. It pooled and rippled.

"A Mystic." Lucijan's voice whispered, echoing in the cave. "Making us see things that are not there."

"Mystic, birdman, Primal. It's all against us. They have Stell. I saw her clothes in the Birdman's talons." Cass faced each person. "We need to leave, get out of here, head to the surface and put everything between us and them…"

"The walls. Look." Lucijan called. Her skin jumped at the screech.

"It's changing." Jolam backed away.

"To me." Cass shouted.

She levelled her repeater, Jolam, and Taze flanked her. Grodol and the girl in the middle, that much Cass knew. Chain-linked fencing grew between red, shining rock, moulding over the cave. A metallic rasp echoed their creation. Torches extinguished. Gaslamps morphed into existence. Meshed fence knitted an iron canopy that extended over them, trapping them. Caging them.

She shuffled on her feet, the ground ungainly. Rattling and shaking of iron echoed. Fences of steel descended from the roof of the ironworks, forming cube cages. The group backed closer together. A tightness knotted in her stomach, breathing picked up. Hands shaking.

Gaslamps sickening yellow glow illuminated cages as far as Cass could see. Segments of missing link casting shadows on wooden walls. The cave vanished. Drips of water ceased. Iron, sweat and heat stench lingered. Sweat dampened short hair, every pulse of perspiration on her scalp itched her skin.

"I don't believe it." Jolam gasped. Cass watched as he rubbed a thumb over a dusty block of slate before the closest padlocked door. She stepped back. Cass's heart sank into her gut.

Cassidy R. Theft. 8 years. Release 1876.

Carved into the slate, the starkness of white on slate scarred into her memory.

"It's Ralake Island." She looked at the surrounding prison. "We're on Ralake Island."

Vincentas

Chapter IX

Time crawled. Vincentas stood alone, his back against an empty corridor. Purple light oozed through narrow-slit windows, without moving, without changing direction. There was no night. Only sickly, thick light of dark lilac.

He had to move. Light would dispel darkness.

Gloved fingers curled around rusting handle of his Gaslamp, the contraption scraped off his metallic scabbard, reverberating as it ascended in his tight grasp. He shook the Gaslamp, oil swilled within bronze bowels.

"V.R." lay inscribed along its base. An inscription drew his gaze, barely legible. *"When times are at their darkest. Athgeric."* His missing friend. A thousand thoughts raced through an unguarded mind.

He had to find his retinue, along with the Entrant. Vincentas walked down the corridor, each step straightening his back. But the Mystic, she could be here. No sign of the Mystic, not even the brutality she accomplished before. No blood of the rendered man, no girl, no retinue.

Oily, violet light followed like a diseased shadow, his only unwanted companion. A reverberating click echoed the handbows' catch. A tired fatigue-ridden arm bore the ungainly weapon.

He turned, a cold sweat moistened brow etched with increased wrinkles. The corridor stretched beyond comprehension, lost in blackness. Magenta, nauseating rays spilled through narrow-slit windows. Looking outside, blackened structures of Riemkeler covered the lavender horizon. A swirling pink fog bathed the world in murky tinted rose. An uncontrollable shiver coursed throughout his skin.

A bastion of excellence, pinnacle of Riemkeler and architectural marvel, the academy stood dominant, crowned by the flesh-coloured horizon. It appeared closer. The longer he watched, the closer it grew. Moving on its own. Moving closer. He had to turn away.

Shaking his head, Vincentas continued down the echoing corridor. He stopped. A door lay ahead. He dared not blink, the visage could disappear. Gritting his teeth, a slow, steady hand moved to the door and pushed with his handbow. He blinked. The door stayed closed. Not a mirage. It must be real. It had to be real. He hoped it was real.

Holstering his weapon, Vincentas outstretched a hand and clasped the heavy door handle. It turned with a multitude of metallic clicks. Footsteps approached on the unseen side. He braced himself and stepped back.

They barraged in and slammed the door behind them in a brown blur of a tattered duster.

Slumping against the door, heavy breathing sucked cold air as they crumbled to the stone floor. Their eyes peered beneath dirtied bangs fixated on him. He returned the look, the female features mired in grease. She had a plain look to her, thin lips parted to ingest more air. Brown eyes that never missed a movement. Brunette hair, in a messy chignon.

"Violet?" Vincentas gasped, coiled tension left heavy shoulders. Before he could speak, a handbow filled his vision. Two shaking hands on the lethal weapon, locked and loaded. Her eyes narrowed, then widened. Unwashed odour invaded his nostrils, dirt highlighted lines of her skin.

Violet sniped a gaze down the empty, silent corridor they inhabited and stepped back. Swinging the knapsack in her other hand to her shoulder, she walked off muttering and keeping low, bending to bypass the windows. Her loose duster weathered and slashed.

"Wait there, Combatant." Vincentas instructed and followed her, mimicking her movements. She hid her presence. The aged Inquisitor picked up his pace.

"You stop. You stop." Violet mouthed. Grime-stained face, flakes of blood stuck under black-rimmed, tired, bloodshot eyes intently peered back.

"Drawing a handbow on an Inquisitor carries an executional sentence." He returned a fixed gaze on the alert Combatant.

"Go on then, kill me, it'll end the misery in here." Violet rolled brown eyes to the lavender surroundings.

"You look… different." His rasping voice cracked.

"Seriously?" Head tilted, eyebrows raised, forming multiple wrinkles across her forehead.

"They separated us, less than a mark ago." Vincentas eyed Violet, who shook her head.

"Must have fallen, Inquisitor. It's been a week, maybe more." The Combatant chuckled, throat caught in a sob. A clear tear broke free of tired eyes.

"I thought you were…" He started.

"Down." She pulled him to the ground, laying side by side. Her unblinking eyes darted above, clutching his hand in a tight grip. Nails dug deep. Vincentas peered at Violet. Purple light glazed over alert features, darkness shrouded quivering eyes. Coldness expunged like a steamed vent.

"Quiet." Violet hissed. Purple light lanced through thin windows. The same inky lilac, like spilt oil. Light fanned down the hallway, bathing the corridor in an ambient bruise of swirling pinks.

Coloured forms swarm before Vincentas narrowed vision. Eyes. Mouths. Teeth. Faces. He shook his head. They were in the light. They made the light. The Verge.

Magentas strong glow vanished. Swirling flesh-coloured light and distorted features faded.

"Let's go. It comes back, sometimes worse." Violet crouched low and scuttled down the echoing corridor. He followed, hoping a wall would not appear between them, keeping close to her. Distant shouts blurted, Vincentas froze, pinning body underneath the windowsill. Inaudible shouts rose, one after another, in different distances. Screams shivered down his spine, screams for help.

"Can't stop here." Violet's hushed voice filtered in his ears. The Inquisitor crawled, laying as flat as possible under the windows. Dust clogged nostrils with a stale stench. His throat grew dry, limbs burned with eagerness to move.

"In here." Violet issued. She opened the door with abrasive confidence. The door to the staircase. Vincentas covered his mouth for the onslaught of flies and decaying rot, trying in desperation to conceal gut-churning death.

Hinges groaned as the door swung open. No gagging smell of a carcass, or murmuring of the maimed. No irritating flies with their skin-crawling buzz. A sigh of wind greeted him on the opened door. Vincentas stood up and merged into the darkness of the staircase. She closed the door behind.

Shrouded in shadow, weary eyes not adjusting to darkness, he stood within the void of nothingness. Only Violet breathed beside, reassured by working senses. Scratching stone clicked nearby, repetitive scrapes ticked and clicked together. A tinder box, or flint striking. Sparks flashed.

"Gotcha." Violet explained, as light burned on the candle. Orange glow illuminated her grinning face, the amber glow pushed back flickering ebony talons. Vincentas squinted and looked around the room. Plaster chipped walls, words scratched into them carved along walls skin. Dust hung, a dampness clogged nose. A singular, recurring drip echoed in the distance. But no staircase, no banister. It was a room, ruined in abandonment.

"I'm starving. Want to join me on an exotic tinned-food date?" Violet shrugged off her haversack and let it drop. The impact kicked up dust. She knelt and opened her haversack and retrieved a tin holding it up. Vincentas did not need the invitation and took the tin. Removing his gloves, he ripped open the seal, digging hands into the cold vegetables. Bright orange carrots. He filled his mouth, barely chewing, and consumed the carrots. Growling stomach surrendering to the desire of remembered hunger.

"You're hungrier than I am." Violet spoke as she ate. Looking at Vincentas through the Gaslamp's light.

"Age can do that to people. You're lucky, but you'll find out one year." He replied as she scooped through the tin and licking her fingers clean.

"Here, have a meat one." Vincentas raked through his own haversack and tossed a shining tin. She caught it without looking, Combatant reflexes. He knew Fleur would be safe. She could handle herself in any situation.

"If you weren't an Inquisitor you'd receive more than a handbow in the face." Violet laughed to herself. Her voice small in the room they shared. Light did not dance or flicker, but cast its orange glow in a sphere of welcoming light.

"Age would separate us. Along with appetite." Unfamiliar muscles along his face pulled, a smile formed. She dug the meat contents out of the tin.

"Have you seen anyone else?" He dared to hope, while peeling open a tin for himself. Beef, always beef, punching his nostrils with freshness. Salted for taste, chewy and filling. Meat sticking between the gap in his teeth.

"No, not even Alleck." Violet's words were sharp. He looked at her, gulping contents of an army official water canteen.

"There must be something, anything." He watched her lower the canteen. Moisture glistened pale thin lips.

"Saw crew of The Sojourn, they were taken." She shoved the rattling canteen back into her haversack.

"Who took them?" Vincentas asked.

"They were taken. Alright?" Violet snapped, she leaned forward. Flame in the Gaslamp flickered, darkening her features.

"Need to understand the situation. To find the retinue, Athgeric, kill the Mystic." He matched her gaze and softened the stare, which drew inconclusive with his wrinkled, age face.

"Bit eager you. You sure you're not the Mystic?" Violet's words left Vincentas with a coldness: his greatcoat could not give him warmth.

"I might be arrogant, brutish, stubborn and bigoted. But I'm no damn Mystic." Violet grinned at the end of his reply. She clapped her hands together.

"Well, I'm impressed. You sussed yourself out in what, sixty years? Guess we can head off home." Arms animated in their response. His cheeks hardened, lips smacking together.

"Arrogant, brutish, stubborn and bigoted. But not a Mystic." Hand ground the tin can within his palm, while watching Violet, who straightened her posture.

"And if you are not a Mystic, who is?" She looked around, shrugging. "Who caused this?"

"It's the girl." Vincentas placed down the empty tin. Violet snorted and shook her head.

"I've seen her, we've seen her, in the corridor just now, before I saw you. She killed a man by pulling him apart in mid-air. Did the same to some citizens before entering the Inquisitorial Hall. She screamed, it rippled the Hall, the Verge." Silence echoed after Vincentas spoke. He considered the empty tin, wishing it full of food again.

"Feels like a lifetime ago now." Violet pulled her knees to her chin. Her shadow smaller.

"Need to get to the catalogue of questions. See the recordings of recent Mystic activity in Riemkeler and the surrounding holdfasts." He groaned, while getting to his feet and shouldered his own haversack. He felt taller looking down on Violet, who remained closed within her own body.

"What is the catalogue of questions?" Violet asked, not looking up. Her voice echoing in the enclosed room, the diminutive voice reverberated back to him, quieter and quieter.

"Athgeric never took you inside an Inquirer Hall?" The secluded Inquisitor secretive till the end. His eyes narrowed, cursing himself for pessimism. Violet shook her head.

"Well, today's your lucky day." Vincentas crossed the gap between them and held out his hand. Large brown, glossy eyes peered back between dirtied bangs and muck-stained features.

"I need a Combatant, and if Athgeric picked you, you must be damn good. That means you're very damn good enough for me." She needed a purpose. He saw it in her posture. Felt it in the air. Hanging off the precipice of choices: surrender or pursuit.

"I'm your Combatant, Inquisitor." She took the hand with a firm grasp and vaulted up quicker than Vincentas expected. "Our first move, sir?"

"Catalogue of questions, in the Inquirer Hall, then go from there." He sounded more secure than he let on. Violet assembled her belongings, locked the handbow she carried and looked ready to take on a Deathwing.

Vincentas headed to the door and opened it. Violet reduced the glow of the Gaslamp and followed the Inquisitor. Darkness withdrew against chasing lances of putrid yellow light.

"I'll lead." The Combatant whispered, outstretched handbow guiding their way, his back straightened.

He walked down a staircase, like the one he chased Alleck and the Mystic through. Stench of abandonment filtered through his nostrils.

"You said people were taken. Where?" He inquired. The more he knew, the better.

"I don't stay around long enough to find out. But I avoid the academy." Violet replied, a harshness in her tone. Arno's words about the academy came to him as if the Chanter stood beside or entered his mind.

Implausible. People will head to the academy, as it is the centre of the city.

She stopped, jerking back to reality. Her Gaslamp lowered. A gap between the stairs yawned before his vision. Four stairs missing. Vincentas remembered where he dangled. Pursuing the Mystic. Chasing after Alleck.

"The stairs. When we were first here." She spoke, her voice quivered. Less than a candlemark for him, the Inquisitor heard of The Verge, read about it, but had never experienced it.

Violet jumped first, clearing the gap with precise ease. Vincentas joined her, knees shaking on reaching the other side. He steadied himself. Glad his age had not failed him. They continued their descent.

The Combatant stopped on the last stair. Cracked stone flooring signalled the end. She looked left. Vincentas knew it led to the main entrance of the Inquirer's Hall. No sound stirred. Nothing. A murky bruise colour shimmered underneath closed doors, smoking into blackness.

Violet crept in silence to the closed doors and nudged them open. Colour pushed back darkness, expelling the Gaslamp's yellow hues. He squinted. She beckoned with her hand. Vincentas joined her, knees burning with each shallow movement. He peered through the ajar door.

Several town's folk, their clothing tattered, stood between them and the raised desk. Magenta light flooded the room, dust circled, voices whispered, bickered and joked. Vincentas narrowed his eyes, not being able to see the rest of the speakers.

"Afflicted." Violet spoke, a reminiscence in her voice. The Inquisitor readied his handbow. Townsfolk, people he swore to defend: the innocent citizens of Riemkeler, his retinue could be one of them, or worse. "Afflicted are in a world of their own." He remembered the Mysticism Charter.

"These look different. They attacked us on entering the city." Vincentas flashed his eyes between those gathered in the hall. Sweat teemed on his forehead, irritating dried skin. His arms burned with holding the handbow in steady hands. Shakes reverberated through aching muscles.

"They act like they are stuck in the past. Watch out for red vines on the ground. That's… that's what is taking people." Violet spoke. He looked at her, eyes wide and searching. A brief relapse with haunting rims of tired irises. She had been through enough. He cursed his absence, but would make up for it.

Vincentas surveyed the possessed. The closest Afflicted, a woman, wearing a torn bodice and dishevelled hair covering her face. Arms weaved in front, as if mimicking a bird's wings or trying to ensnare a butterfly. Voices grew louder, cawing in his skull. He looked around. The Afflicted were not talking. They gargled and groaned, but none of them spoke. The voices of the Verge.

"Must leave. The main door will lead us somewhere else. Our only chance." Violet nodded to the main entrance. Shifting through notes would bring no respite to the dead, or Afflicted. Only duty would bring an end to this.

Violet slipped into the hall. The Afflicted had not noticed him. Chatter grew louder. Gibbering nothingness sharply pierced his hearing. He caught sight of one, shambling Afflicted, who swivelled and leered down at him five paces away.

Red light burned in place of purple, bruising eye-sockets. Vincentas raised his handbow, moving back from the female Afflicted and fired. The whistled shot pierced the Afflicted's face, it gargled and fell back.

"No." Violet shouted. He jumped at the sound, spinning round. A man grabbed Violet by the throat. Her handbow clattered to the ground. He aimed, they tussled. He gritted teeth as Violet and the man both came into vision. Vincentas turned, seeing the Afflicted woman he shot, head flung back, red pulsating eyes erupting in crimson light. The handbow shaft protruding from her broken forehead.

He squeezed the trigger. Whistling bolts blurred through the air. Three thuds punched into the Afflicted. She growled and collapsed backwards. Sweat bled on his forehead, he turned seeing a second Afflicted head for Violet. Others descended on him. They pulled, pushed, staggered against each other in Violet's grapple in their physical battle.

They stumbled towards the Combatant, red eyes glowing. Vincentas ran closer. Standing feet away from Violet and the man she fought, he fired. Bolts lanced into the man's chest and face, others spiralled over his body. Collapsing to his knees, red light diminished in glowing sockets.

He aimed at the onrushing Afflicted. Arms outstretched, head lopping back, they dragged themselves forward. The whistling of the discharged handbow coming quick and fast.

An empty click reverberated at the jammed trigger. Vincentas tore the spent cartridge from the handbow, send it clattering to the ground.

"Inquisitor." Violet commanded. He threw the handbow towards Violet. She caught it and loaded it with precision.

Handbow fire scythed around him, dropping multiple Afflicted with brutal efficiency. He looked behind him, the Afflicted Violet contended with dispatching. A broken neck the cause of death.

A nearby Afflicted's face contorted in agony. Features softened. Brown eyes emerged from the fading red glow. Vincentas's chest ready to explode. His stomach quivered.

"It's finished." Violet's soothing voice melted through the raging storm in his ears. Her face softer under red, pulsating light. Pink inked into the crimson, washing the world, cleansing the bruised atmosphere into a clearer, softer hue. The hall and Violet bathed in a colour that resembled tranquil plants of the Thousand Isles.

"Thank you. We must go, in case of others." She left him, shouldering her repeater and walking to the main closed doors. He loaded his handbow with fumbling, sweaty hands.

Vincentas glanced at the bodies of those he killed. They could have been his retinue. Catching glimpses of their still faces, he holstered the weapon and joined Violet, the dead stench followed as he passed them. He took in a depth breath to steady rocking stomach.

"Not sure what we're going to find out here. Could lead us outside, could lead us to another room." Violet unbolted the door and braced herself.

"Before we go, thank you Inquisitor." Vincentas stood beside Violet as she spoke, looking deep within his eyes.

"Let's move out, Combatant." He replied and stepped into the brightness of the ajar door, head held high with Violet beside him.

Cass

Chapter IX

Unsteady and shaking, Cass remembered the cages where she slept for the past four years. Four long, isolating years as a confined prisoner on Ralake Island. A living nightmare in the present; her past surging into waking vision. Quivering stomach sent a pulse of uncertainty through her mind. The repeater in shaking hands gained weight.

"Feels like we've been walking forever." Lucijan broke the deep silence. His voice cut through fence rattling and hissing steam.

Not the only thing that lasted forever, Cass observed the vast complex of chain-linked fences creating prison cages of Ralake. This was not the real Cythean prison complex. It could not be, senses told her otherwise. Ralake's musk of sweat, dead iron and trampled hope did not linger here. This place hung with an odour of rot, a feverish decay and nauseating vomit.

"We are where?" Grodol asked.

"Ralake," Jolam replied. "Island prison two hundred nautical miles from Cythea's eastern coast." She stopped and turned, looking at the shaking head of the trembling Faun.

"Why are we here, Cass?" Eyes glazed over in a shimmering ripple of emotion.

"Cythea." Lucijan lamented. "That's thousands of miles from Orschal continent. How did we get there so quickly?"

Cass looked at Taze, whose hand outstretched, touching the chain-link fence. Taze turned her back quickly and moved away. The convict's lips parted in a stream of soundless words. Eyes dragged to where the murderer had stood to find knitted barbed wire reading *"You killed Him"*.

"This isn't Ralake." Taze's jaw jutted out, spitting. "This is a mockery. A nightmare. Ralake was a bathhouse compared to this place."

It felt real. Smelt real. But could not be real. Beyond iron confinement, rolling blood clouds eclipsed any sense of direction, obscuring the horizon. Unseen mouths of industry bellowed crimson smog. Mists shifted and returned, breath on a cold, freezing day. It was breathing. The world breathed.

The girl beside Grodol whimpered. Black matted hair buried closer to him. Her outstretched, bony hand pointing up. Cass stepped back, skin crawling, as her eyes caught shapes hanging. They were small, child-like. Squinting, she looked closer. The things motley coloured, rich texture of varnished, rosy cheeks. A half smile came to her face on remembering Lilly playing with such dolls. These missed their eyes.

They turned. Clicking heads faced them, empty sockets peered at the group.

Jolam cried out. Cass jolted back, fence rattled underneath. A doll lay pinned to the fence beside the barbed wire message. It hung, not moving, defying gravity with its outstretched hand pointing down the endless caged corridor.

"We need to keep moving." Cass snapped, voice hardened. "Need to leave."

Daughters favourite dolls appearing, the prison surrounding them and talks of Mystics before in the cave. She shook her head to dispel growing thoughts to vacate her losing mind.

"Leave how?" Taze's demanded. Meshed fence rippled under each step. She stopped, opening the great coat lent to her by Grodol. Sweat forced her to unbutton the fur garment. Her body yearned for air. Gasping on being freed prickled with exposed humidity.

"This is the mountain. It doesn't look it, but it is." She faced the others. Thin burgundy vapours shrouded the group.

"It feels real to me." Taze grasped the fence and shook it. Hush of prison walls rattled through Cass's mind. "Looks real too."

"We are under the mountain." Cass walked forward, eyeing Taze. "You said it yourself, this is a mockery of Ralake."

"How can it be here?" Taze opened her arms wide, touching one side of the fence to the other, exactly how she could in Ralake. "Can't see the sky, must be under the mountain." The murderer pointed up, fingers poking through the chain-linked fence of the ceiling of their corridor, but the floor of the corridor above.

"It's a Mystic, Taze. Mocking us. Teasing us. Messing with our minds." Cass addressed Taze. Thick and musky stench hooking into her nostrils. A glistened forehead, branded with "Wilmar", creased in a deluge of sweat.

"Don't know where we're going." Black eyes lowered to stare at Cass.

"Can't go up." Cass jerked her head to the ceiling. "No ladder." Her hand slapped Taze's arm. Her arm grasped in the confines of a muscled, tight grip. Fingers held her in a fleshy constraint.

"I see a ladder." Taze lowered her angular features to Cass, taking up her world view with a dripping, tanned face. "I'll let you know, convict."

"Down the corridor. It's the only way so far." She turned without waiting for a reply and headed through the rattling fenced world. A sigh of relief escaped her, making sure nobody saw. Mesh fences continued downwards, enclosed on sides running parallel with the narrowed passage Cass walked through.

Dolls lay wired to caged walls. Flowers twisted, lining its floor. Resonating footfalls of boots on mesh reverberated through her feet, rising through aching legs. Sweat clogged nostrils, the intrusive stench of bodies hung around thick as her clothes, which she shed, layer by layer.

"Need to rest, Cass." Lucijan suggested with a tired voice.

"Find food as well." Jolam grumbled.

She turned, chain-linked floor buckled and whistled as she faced the group several paces behind. Her belly ached, churning for rest. Lucijan's eyes cast low. Taze looked around, not focusing on anyone. Jolam's shoulders slumped.

"There is no food here." Her voice travelled further than intended. She outstretched a hand, gesturing around. Heavy eyes looked to the wall of chain-linked fencing, the ceiling that extended with cages and corridors of iron works. Vapours of thick steam hissed through neatly cut holes of wrought metal. Their world a cage of iron, steam and a dull, hued red light that mimicked dying embers of a colossal earth breathing fire.

"Rest," Cass tapped her foot onto the rattling fence. "Can't rest on this, it could break."

You killed him. Shot into her ears. Her skin leapt. Heart screamed.

Harsh words crawled down her spine. Burning sweat bled down her forehead. The girl shrieked, Jolam cried out, Lucijan swore and raised his repeater.

Cass's eyes snapped around, searching for the figure who spoke. The group's rasping breaths hung around them. Her heartbeat trebled and battered her chest.

You abandoned your daughter. The words scythed into Cass, dropping heart into her rupturing stomach.

"Where are you?" Cass dropped her repeater and opened her arms out. "Coward. Where are you?" Vision blurred with stinging tears. Thin spittle dribbled down her chin.

You will kill them all for her. The deep, resonating voice hammered into Cass's skull as she clenched her teeth.

"What is this madness?" Jolam shouted. She tore a look at the Faun over her shoulder, covering one ear, his limp arm holding onto the repeater.

"It's some Mystic," Cass gritted her teeth. "It's not real." Shutting eyes.

Grating iron shivered down her spine. Eyes snapped open, looking up at the rattling fence for a ceiling, dividing another corridor above. The dolls danced on strings with the pounding.

"That was real." Jolam replied.

"There." Lucijan warned, his repeater pointing.

Cass watched a curve of chain-linked fence roll towards her. Pressure from above, something neared. Grating iron on iron, the rasp of steel echoed louder, sending shivers down her spine.

"Down." Shouted Taze. High-pitched whistle of something scythed through the air. Pointed steel broke above them. The girl screamed. Grodol shouted. Lucijan fired his repeater.

"Don't. You'll split the fence." Cass waved her hand. Shaking, unblinking eyes peered up. A pickaxe point swung above, dangling through the ceiling. Blood dripped from the handle.

Two, large jackboots crashed on the mesh above. She raised her repeater. He was massive, too big to be believed. Too big to move, but he crouched, thick fingers through the fence, hooded mask facing Cass. Black symbol of Arton etched on the hood. White hood of the Purifier, but tattered, peeling and stitched together. Standard tabard stretched over the hulking frame. He shone with a redness only blood could make.

"That's definitely real." Jolam stammered.

"Run." Cass screamed.

Burning muscles stabbed thighs. Ache of running. Pounding heartbeat. The chain-linked fence buckled underfoot, vision nothing but the corridor of iron. Shouts, chants, inaudible words punched through the monotonous hiss of steam and rattling off mesh fence dug by fleeing feet.

"Where are we heading?" Lucijan shouted.

Cass tunnelled vision lead her down corridors, through the iron maze of chain-linked fence, continuously running through the gauntlet of the caged world.

Another doll, pinned to the fence, arm outstretched, pointing onwards. Its dirtied porcelain head broken in shining pieces. She stopped, panting, the rush cooling as the others barged past her. Jolam snatched her arm by the bicep.

"Come on, Cass." He growled, "remember, no time to rest."

Her eyes only had sight for the painted word on the doll's chest, not part of its design. She gulped and nodded, reading the word *"mom"* on the chest. Her daughter's handwriting.

"Follow the dolls." Cass replied, eyes pinned open.

A loud clap of iron hammered the fencing. The group stopped.

Cass looked around, above her and below. Figures stood before the fences. Tattered clothes of inmates clad closing forms. Tools, pickaxes, welding gear. A mottled band of grease smelling shadows pressed against thin cell walls. Their faces hooded. Steam shrouded increasing numbers.

They hammered the fencing again in a hush of iron, in unison. Together. As one.

Again, the contained inmates hit the fences, together in their chorus. More here than in Ralake, as the crescendo picked up, matching her increased heartbeat. The iron chorus rattled and grating through skin, shaking down to her boots.

Cass startled back, flinching, when the inmates yelled. She broke into a sprint, sending her aching body sinking into her muscles for survival.

"Follow the dolls." She shouted; her words lost in the cacophony of violent shouting. Catching up to the group, Grodol carried the girl. Taze and Lucijan lead the way.

Her heart pounded, crashing into her chest. Coughing and spluttering while running, valenki boots weighing more than she moved. Burning thighs, aching ankles, she dragged herself in a half run along the corridor, panting with each stride.

Ruptures exploded above. She ducked and tripped, rolling her vision to the side as Cass clawed herself to stand. Inmates landed on the fence that made their enclosed cell. She lunged onwards, a manic smile formed on sticky skin, nearing the others with the panting, blurring Faun at her side.

Cass focused on the backs of Lucijan and Taze, the conscript held onto Taze as they made sharp, twisting turns. The girl buried her head in the shoulder of Grodol, black hair masking features. She will be okay. She would make sure of it. Cass gritted her teeth. Her hands tightened around the repeater. She would see Lilly again.

"They're breaking through." Cass heard through the cacophony of rattling steel, manic chanting and her own pounding heart blasting in her ears.

The fence narrowed, allowing only one at a time. Broken porcelain dolls lined the route. All pointing to a hopeful exit. All stitched against the fence. Her shaking vision caught words, daring not to stop, flashed on the dolls. "Mom". "Alive". "This". "Way".

Shredded iron sent Cass ducking. Ringing of boots on the chain-linked fence ceased. She looked up, heart stopping. Unblinking eyes watched as the cage separated, unjointed, unwound. Parted and split, she pushed herself up. Looking down, her throat rippled with an unending tremble. The floor unwinding beneath her feet.

"Hang on." Cass shouted in warning, clasping onto the unravelling chain-link. Cutting deep into her hands. Stinging fingers.

Weightlessness dragged her body down. Invisible clutches of gravity pulling her away. Screams echoed in numbing skull. Taze, Lucijan, Grodol, Jolam and the girl vanished below. Her eyes peeled open on hearing the innocent screams of the Sabanese girl, like her own daughter. She watched as the girl, black hair flocking above her head, arms spinning in helplessness, disappeared into the steam below.

"No!" Her throat erupted with a roar that shook her grip on the fence.

"Let go, mom." Cass vaulted her head up, eyes dared not close.

Lilly floated near, surrounded by levitating debris of the prison. Rendered iron danced, twirled, fluttered like leaves. A steel snow eased around her daughter. All in white, her hair tied back.

"Lilly, Lilly!" Cass gasped in disbelief. She struggled, fought, grappling with burning pain of fingers cutting on the chained fence.

"Let go mom." Her daughter pleaded. "Find me." Her voice cracked.

Black wings unfurled, engulfing a red horizon. A clawed hand wrapped round Lilly's head. Cass screamed and fell. Tumbling down, arms fighting to fly upwards.

The world bled fire and steam, swirled in collapsing mass of iron and steel of Ralake Prison.

Steady breathing pulsed on her face. She held her breath, eyes closed, not wanting to disturb what was ahead. Limbs lay on wood, fresh oak filtered into flaring nostrils. A stew boiled nearby, its aroma drawing gurgles of greed within aching stomach. Peeling sticky eyes open, opal coloured eyes stared back. Tiredness lined the woman's features. She sat up, the woman before her matched in unison. Brand marked her cheek. An open hand burned on the right cheek beneath the eye, marked her as a thief.

Cass vaulted up the chair she sat in, crashing to the floor. Her double doing the same. She looked up and down at the person who looked exactly like her, hair styled in the same short, convenient approach. She looked like her, but it was not her. Like a living mirror image.

"Don't know who you are, but you're not me." Cass spoke. The other her, standing like a flesh mirror one stride away, echoed her words. Black, angular markings ran down the right arm. The same tattoos as Karwen. She stepped backwards. The mockery of her double did the same, shadowing every movement.

"Mystic is doing this." Cass heard herself say, and the other echoed. She stopped. So did the twin. The imposter. She circled around the table. She snorted while the other copied.

"Don't know where this is. Still under the mountain." The two voices spoke in symmetry. Cass halted her movements. The mirror image ceased. Her eyes drifted around the room, keeping the other image of herself in sight. Cupboard nearby, an unvarnished table lay in the centre. The aroma of oak crinkled nose. Yellow, sickly light peeled through windows; a warmer Gaslamp flared in distant corners of the room. A range boiled, hissing water doused onto the range, a stew whistled for consumption.

Cass smiled, the opposite smiled back. A chill crawled down her back.

"This isn't Konniak." Shaking her head, eyeing the imposter. "Konniak is worse than this."

"You're right there, Cassidy." Armande's voice broke through her mind. His sharp accent tearing down her skull, forcing eyes to close. "But memories make it better."

Cass flinched. A cold, slithering hand ran down her back. Opening eyes, she saw nothing. No house, no table, no other mockery of herself. No hand. No Armande. Colour swirled. Oceans of colour ran with a current, tides of lavender rippled and rose with emerald. Sprays of crimson broke and fluttered into azure sparkles. She stood in an ocean of unfeeling colour.

"Bizarre." Mocked Armande. She turned, not seeing the Thousand Islander. The colour faded, sinking into nothingness. Mesh fencing grew from retreating waves of tangled spectrum. A steel forest enclosed Cass, a swelling grew deep within her chest. She tilted her head, clenched her fists and tried to steady her rapidly thumping heart. Sighing, she grasped her shirt, pulling it for air. Dried sweat broke, itching her neck and back.

"It never ceases to impress me." Armande commented. The former soldier she fought alongside stood before the cage's exit. A curling grin on his face pulled his moustache.

"Not with your Faun?" Cass asked, her eyes flashing for another way out. Nothing appeared.

Armande opened his arms wide. "Could say the same. You're minus some friends." He stepped forward. Cass held her ground.

Her arms folded. "Got no friends, you know me."

"I'm hurt, deeply. The blood we shed, the people we killed. Am I not a friend?" Armande clapped his hands together. It echoed a thousand times or more, grating through her mind. She focused on Armande, fists clenched. He must be the Mystic.

"Stop." Armande held his hand out and laughed. "Don't be foolish, because I am not the Mystic here."

"Then who is?" Her breath visible as she spoke.

A fierce smile sliced Armande's lip in two. "Told you." Head tilted up. "You should have joined us." He stepped to the side.

Slowly, a woman walked forward, her hands on the shoulders of a girl, no older than ten. They stopped. Cass looked at the woman. A black stained bandage obscured her eyes. She twitched with a nervousness; visible purple veins tensed along her pale neck.

Her breaths slowed. The girl swayed under the long-nailed grasp of the woman. Brown hair hung before her face, a length Cass would have if prison nits were not rife. Shaking worry swallowed down her throat, but not quelling her quivering gut.

"You knew. You tried to hide it. How foolish." Armande stood beside the girl and crouched down. She only looked at the girl. She needed to know, see the face, destroy her growing fears.

"Absent mother. An unknown father. What emotions can trigger the whispers of fear. The desires of stability." Armande's long fingers skirted through the girl's locks. Cass gritted her teeth. Loathing made her fists shake. A solitary tear blurred vision. She clawed at the weakness and slapped her hand away.

"Show me." Cass raged, spit flew.

"So be it." Armande whispered. She barely heard him through the heart pounding in her chest. His hand combing the girl's soft hair.

"Here's your Mystic." Cass did not hear Armande as the hair caressed back. Her jaw dropped. Lips trembled.

She had her mother's eyes, her father's nose. It could not be. She is in Konniak. She is in Konniak. Cass rapidly told herself. A barrage of thoughts, none of them her own, assaulted the mind.

"Lilly." She gasped. Stepping forward to reach her daughter. Iron hands snapped around aching wrists, kicking legs clenched by wires of steel. Cass vaulted upwards, pulled by mocking wire grated skin. She writhed, tensing, pulled at her limbs, metal ate skin, blood lined her flesh.

"Lilly. Lilly!" Cass screamed. Looking at the girl, her daughter. She shook her head, infuriated at the tears streaming from her eyes, blurring the vision of her sole purpose.

"Daralis was lazy. So, so lazy. Wasn't hard to not find her." Armande looked up.

"Lies. She's in Konniak." Her voice broke, straining as long and agonising as her burning limbs.

"No. This maybe her realm. But Konniak she is not in." He stepped backwards, standing beside the twitching, blindfolded woman and silent, still Lilly.

"I swear, I'll get her back. I'll get her back." Cass choked on her words. She pulled at her arms. Even if they tore from the wires, she would be free, free to pursue and take Lilly away.

"Your petty connection to this vessel is humbling, but there is a greater purpose for Lilly." A voice pulsed into Cass's mind, which echoed throughout her body. A multitude of accents gave life to words, in a monotone voice spoken through her aching skull.

Cass reared her head and screamed. She raged through scything iron, cutting into hands, fighting to be free.

"Do not pursue what is ours, do not come between an inevitable future and your suffering past." The voice spoke with a certainty that ignited her skin with heated fury.

"Mom." Lilly's peaceful voice stilled her.

Cass fell. Free of the wires, released from constraints biting into limbs. She tumbled into nothingness. The iron cages swooped above. Armande vanished, her daughter disappeared. She heard nothing but her hoarse screams.

Vincentas

Chapter X

Vincentas experienced nothing like it before in recent memory. The closest would-be times spent with his wife before her judgement and execution by his own hand. A warmth filled him with contempt and fulfilment. He forgot the Inquisition, Mystics and the decay and strangeness of Riemkeler. A firm grasp held his wrist. Violet glowed beside him. It all flooded back, tides of doubt washing away momentary tranquillity.

He was a burden. Confinement in the asylum, freed by Constance, blissful compared to harsh realities he witnessed. Safer in madness than spectating the rawness of the world. Violet smiled, her aura diminished. She turned her head, startled. Vincentas turned, expecting assailants and the Mystic. Shoulders tensed; his lungs eased a sigh when no immediate danger lay ahead.

A wealth of information formed before his vision. Bookshelf after bookshelf obscured walls. Unfamiliarity tugged at lips. Serenity grew, bliss doused aching limbs.

A smile engulfed him. They would have been incredible to read, to study, to learn. No time for books. He would have to make time for books in the future.

"Vincentas." Violet's hand tightened around his wrist. "Could be a trick. Mystic at work."

He hated to admit it. He could be an Afflicted: a mindless servant of falsehood and a wanton for desirable illusions. A small, self-established library would be ideal. A familiarity made it more unreal. Unsettling shiver prickled skin.

"The Verge and Mystics play on your weaknesses." The Inquisitor admitted.

Creaking leathers and swaying, heavy cloth rubbing together signalled Violet's motion. She stood in front of him, taking his hand. Her gloved hands grasped his upper arms, holding him at arm's length, her face unreadable.

"Look like you've seen a ghost, is everything alright?" Violet broke her hold.

"Nothing. I ran a bookstore before being an Inquisitor." Vincentas remembered. A lifetime ago, a different person. Easy to divulge information to someone he barely knew. Not like him to be an open book.

Violet laughed. "You a librarian?"

"I wasn't like this all my life." He shrugged, skin tensed, as coldness ran through it.

"If you've finished making me laugh, let's investigate." She turned. "Whoever lives here, they sure can cook." Sweet meats and boiled vegetables assaulted senses; a willing surrender nourished flaring nostrils.

"Careful, this could be an illusion." The Inquisitor watched as Violet walked towards the nearest bookshelf. Floorboards creaked; crackling meats spat on a stove.

Vincentas allowed himself to swallow air for the first time. Roasting aurochs, grilled parsnips. Leather-bound books, dead candle wax and fresh ink hit the back of his throat harder than any punch. It had to be real.

"Doesn't seem like it. It's as real as the Inquirer Hall." Violet examined the cooking pots on the small, steaming stove. Removing her gloves, she wrung her hands together.

Peeling off gloves, Vincentas traced fingers across cracked spines of several books. He turned, seeing the door they had entered had closed behind them. His retinue remained undiscovered out there, somewhere, along with Athgeric. The Mystic girl, too. Tiredness grew in his shoulders, he placed his Gaslamp down on the red rug.

"Hungry?" The Combatant raised her eyebrows, holding a black steel lid. Smoke wafted, cooked vegetables steamed with a relaxing hiss. Vapours curled alluring fingers towards Vincentas.

"I could definitely eat again." Violet chuckled. He headed towards her, who procured a plain plate. "Our absent dweller was expecting us." She waved the plate in her hand, presenting it to him.

The Inquisitor nodded and took the plate as Violet spooned freshly cooked food for him.

The door barraged open.

Vincentas snapped his head around, dropped the plate, which smashed on the floor. A well-weathered man slammed the door behind him and slid down, panting heavily.

Sitting on the floor, his black, worn hat fell before his gasping face. Vincentas's eyes widened on recognising the cockel design. A garb that would strike fear in those that came across a retinue of the militant order of the Continental Church. An Inquisitors hat.

He stepped forward. The Inquisitor removed his hat in a sweeping arc before his sweating face. A wrinkled forehead glistened while pitch coloured veins criss-crossed his gaunt face from black, streaking hair. His mouth dropped. Athgeric.

"For dinner, I'll have rump steak, stewed cabbage, sweet parsnips and side of Orschallian carrots. Ripe, tender and oh so fine." Athgeric clapped his hands and jumped to his feet. Bright eyes surveyed Vincentas, then moved to Violet.

"This. Is new." The newcomer whispered. His hands lowered.

"Inquisitor Athgeric it's me, Violet." She stepped forward.

"Intriguing, trying to gain my trust to hoodwink me, intruders in my domain. Who are you?" The Inquisitor placed his hands behind his back. Rain-streaked greatcoat dripping onto the red carpet. Torn, patched shirt clung to a wiry frame, several necklaces lay stringed on tattered fabric.

"Old friend, it's me Inquisitor Vincentas." Instinctively, his head tilted higher. He would make his old friend see they were no illusion. A way for the truth to be unveiled.

"Teaching of the voice is lacking, old one. Your tutor would certainly scold you for that tone." Athgeric walked over and placed a firm palm on his chest, grinding the hand against his ribs. Vincentas looked up to his friend's face, rough with stubble, nostrils clogged with bitter cheroot and unwashed odour. At least his habits have not changed.

"It comes from here, man, your voice. Here." The Inquisitor pressed and shook his palm entrenched into Vincentas's chest. Athgeric's stench grew unbearable, eyes squinted, and mouth closed, anything to subdue the smell. He realised why he always came away from Athgeric's meetings with a brewing headache.

"Enough. We know you, you must know us." Violet snapped.

"Now that's a voice." The Inquisitor nodded while backing away, raising his hands up in a surrendering fashion. "Now you're in the Inquisition. Not an Entrant, maybe a Combatant, or…"

"Enough. Geric. Enough!" Violet aimed the repeater at her Inquisitor, in shaking hands.

"You're pointing a Mark Two Model, Cythean variant, drum-cartridge loaded repeater bolter at Inquisitor Athgeric. That's a capital offence according to the Inquirer Council." He finished, while surveying, bright eyes fixed on Violet. This is the old Inquisitor Vincentas knew. A half-smile warmed his face.

"Hadramiel would be proud. Rebuking an individual carrying a repeater." He clapped, slowly, mockingly. Any chance his friend would recognise him, their tutor's name would be enough.

Athgeric turned while his arms lowered, a beady eye narrowed on studying Vincentas. A big, broad smile revealed yellow, forlorn teeth on Athgeric's dirtied face.

"You old dog." His old friend hooted.

"You're the oldest dog." They both said together. Finishing their sentences. They embraced, hugging, before the weathered Inquisitor stepped back.

"Yes. The Verge is strong." Sneered Athgeric, a sluggish smile wriggling across chapped lips. He moved away, removing a flask inside the weather-worn greatcoat, and uncorked the canteen. No mistaking the pungent aroma of whiskey malted the air, festering in Vincentas's nostrils. Nothing good ever came from whiskey. His alcoholism coping with loss testament of that.

"This is no trick, no Mystic illusion. This is friendship." He stepped forward.

"Friendship." Barked Athgeric, sitting down on a velvet lined seat. His feet raised and dropped leisurely on the nearest foot stool. Mud-caked boots smeared rich fabrics.

"Vincentas I knew never spoke of sentimentality. He was an Inquisitor, foremost. He'd do his duty, not care." Athgeric dabbed his face with a handkerchief and peeled off his greatcoat. Vincentas turned his head to avoid the overriding stench rising from his seated friend.

"Then if I'm in the Verge, get rid of us." Vincentas opened his arms wide, tilting his head back, calling bluff of his old comrade.

"Good call, but it would shatter my illusion. Spiralling me into depths that I could not surface." Athgeric drew his hands to his chin, joining them. Looking like a spearhead lancing up to his throat.

"Then oblige us, tell us of this Verge? I wish to know this answer." The Inquisitor took a swig of his canteen and leaned back, easing into relaxation. Both the same, he summarised, looking over the seated Inquisitor. No wonder they were close: blunt, crude and dismissive.

"What answer?" Laughed Athgeric, greasy hair hanging. Tranquillity followed as the drinking Inquisitor lost all strength and sank into the resting chair. He ground his feet against each other, removing thigh-high, mud-sleek boots oozed off his feet, falling onto soft carpets with a leather-bound slap.

"Answers. Answers lead to more questions. More questions lead to numbing questions." Athgeric spoke into his canteen. He corked the canteen and hammered it on a desk buried in papers. The drunk mumbled. Lost to the world. Lost in himself. Vincentas clenched his fists together. He would not travel down this route.

"Let's go, he's not… himself." Violet whispered, eyes portraying more than anguish. Her breath skirted his ear, close enough to mask Athgeric's stench with her own welcoming aromas. He only noticed her tight grip on his upper arm. She started walking away. He removed himself from her grasp.

"Read that. You wrote it." Vincentas threw the diary in front of the sitting Inquisitor. He stopped. A quivering finger underlined the threadbare lettering. Tentatively, it opened, with rustling, coarse papers.

"Your Combatant brought it to me. Why? I saw the bodies. The markings. What did you find? Why bring us here? I need answers." Head lifting as he spoke, fingers circled the obsidian hilt.

"Books everywhere. Read those. Books full of answers." Athgeric waved a pointed hand at the bookcases and deposited his diary onto the floor. He picked up a nearby book and read.

Snatching the book, Vincentas tossed it away. Slamming the door near Violet, pages ruffled and flapped before crumbling to the floor. Athgeric sat poised, eyebrows raised, considering the gap where the book had been. His hands caught in time, as if holding an absent object.

"You're foolish, just like Vincentas would be." A quiet voice broke the silence. A lethality poured out of his mouth through thin, parted lips. He smiled at hearing his friend's true voice return.

"We need answers." Violet said as she came behind him. Old, weary eyes lay on him.

"We all need answers." Athgeric agreed. Body inclined from the seat: torso sitting up; legs retracting from the footstool to rest on the carpet.

"I need answers. What's going on out there? I've encountered Mysticism, but this is different." He watched his old Inquisitorial friend.

Athgeric took a deep breath and shook his head. "You're not ready for the truth."

"Try me." Vincentas rasped. A lump grew in his throat. He gulped, trying to get rid of the taste of the unknown. His stomach gurgled.

"How did you arrive at Riemkeler?" Cracked knuckles echoed in the room.

"Airship. Did not use the tunnellers." Tunneller carts would have taken longer.

Athgeric smiled. A shiver coursed down Vincentas's spine. "Safe journey?"

A second, unconsumable lump grew in his throat. He must have known. "For the most part. Ship missed the airdock, crash landed outside the city."

The Inquisitor snorted, shaking his head but keeping eye contact with Vincentas. Those eyes, they hid something. He had seen that look before, a thousand times before, from so many people.

"No airship misses a dock. Unless the dock is covered." His friend mumbled. Covered the dock, he meant the fog. But airship pilots have always navigated through the worst of weathers. An experienced pilot could navigate through fog and outrun a Deathwing.

"Dock covered in fog. Thick fog. You're making fog sound as fearful as a Deathwing." Violet blurted out, tutting as she spoke.

The Inquisitor's hands cupped together. "Fear. Fear is the greatest truth." Athgeric tilted his head, looking at his bookshelves.

"Need answers. Not to discuss our ill-fated flight." Vincentas spoke, drawing a mocking salute from his old Inquisitor friend.

Athgeric smiled. "So, you're looking for answers. Then answer me this, would-be Vincentas, where are we?"

He tightened his grip on the obsidian hilt, smell of fresh wood lingered, the stench of dried paper, leather-bound books and melted wax of dying candles invaded welcoming nostrils. "A room. In Riemkeler."

Athgeric pointed at him and faced Violet. "That's what they want you to think." His sly face looked around the room. "You think you're in Riemkeler."

Vincentas folded his arms. Eyebrows knitting together. "Mystics have put us in the Verge, in Riemkeler."

"Mystics." Snorted Athgeric. "By themselves?" He cocked an eyebrow.

There was nothing worse than not knowing. "Is any of it real?" Vincentas whispered.

"It is real, but somewhere. It's difficult to explain." Athgeric rubbed his head and dabbed his forehead with a handkerchief.

"I can try to explain it." His friend leapt out of his chair before Vincentas realised. Backing away, he watched the Inquisitor mumble under his breath and headed to the nearest bookshelf.

"Aye, this might help." He ran his hands over the books, taking one and showing it to Vincentas. "This is you. A book. Pages are thoughts, dreams, passions, your past. It's you." Athgeric turned back to the bookcase, pulling more books off indiscriminately.

"That's what we all are. Books. People are books. Towns are books. Battlefields are books. Cities. Continents. Lakes. Anything and anywhere is a book." He trooped over to the desk, hands under the pile of books his chin rested on for support.

The book avalanche crashed onto the desk. "You." Athgeric announced, tearing out a page and taking a quill. The scratch of the quill grated over a torn page. Athgeric held it up, showing the scribbled "Vin".

"My alleged Combatant, Violet." Athgeric scratched again.

She straightened her back, repeater held in her hands.

Athgeric smiled. He tore another page out of the book and hastily scribbled onto it. "Violet." The Inquisitor picked up the individual torn pages and put them together.

"We are a book. But for now, a page. Shrunk down." He started tearing other pages, ripping books apart. "People. Friends. Neighbours. Lovers. Children."

He spun round, holding open a spine of a rendered book with loose pages piled together. He closed the cover of the makeshift book, pages crinkled, trapping the loose paper.

"See?" He whispered, holding the amalgamation within his hands. "This is us, right now."

Vincentas shook his head. "The Verge doesn't work like that. It's a bubble, something Hadramiel said. But let's go with your theory. Who is holding us together? Who is the spine and cover of the book?" Athgeric's smile grew wider and nodded the more Vincentas spoke, visibly shaking by the time he finished speaking.

"Mystics." Vincentas whispered. "Mystics are the cover."

"No." Athgeric's eyes shot open. He stepped back and placed the amalgamated self-made book on the desk. "They hold it together, bind it if you will, but they are not the cover, they are not the publisher, or the machine that makes it. They cause it to be together. Even this room." He halted.

"This room." Vincentas started withdrawing the malachite sword, never daring to blink as he watched Athgeric. His friend, the old Inquisitor, had his back to him, head lowered, shoulders slumped.

"Yes. Friend." His sympathetic reply matching his shrinking posture.

"Tell me, Inquisitor." His green sword, dull despite flaring lights around, held in shaking hands, faced his friend. "Where is the Mystic who made it happen?" Violet eased to the side, repeater raised in shaking hands.

The bookcase before Athgeric glowed purple. His head tilted back. Light ebbed and faded. Normalcy, or the closest to it, returned to the illusionary room.

"You are talking to him, friend." He turned, arms outstretched.

"How? Why?" Vincentas stepped forward, sword aimed at the one he sought after.

"Survival." He smiled. "You haven't seen what I've seen. The foes we are to face, they can't be beaten. Not with those. Not by you."

"There's always a way." Vincentas's mouth frothed, sword grew heavy in his hands. He would not hesitate before, has not hesitated, even on conviction of his wife. "How did you learn it?"

"From an old friend." Athgeric smiled, hidden knowledge rimmed his eyes.

"Tell me how to stop this and let me go, to fight it." He slammed the sword back into his scabbard.

"Academy is more than a pretty building. Look deep for its knowledge, delve deeper for its forbidden truth." Athgeric slurred. The academy, nothing special about it, famed for its knowledge in astrology, botany and philosophical arts.

"Leave this city, Mystic. I find you after I am done, no friendship will save you." Vincentas broke eye contact, severing the past, which he would cut with his malachite sword if it came to it.

"One more thing, Inquisitor." Athgeric's authentic voice resounded in the comforting room. Everything stopped. Vincentas did not turn.

"You bring true purpose to this more than I." His hands removed with dignified grace the cockel hat. He threw it, curling in the air, towards Vincentas, who caught it with delicate tenderness in fear of marking or breaking it.

"Leave this city." The Inquisitor dropped the cockel hat, shoulders further back, shadow crowning his forehead and eyes, chilling his skin. Violet stood near the only door. Opening it together, they stepped out into the unknown. He could not look back as the door closed on the Mystic. On his friend.

Cass

Chapter X

Cass crashed on solid rock. Lungs emptied. She rolled, unable to stop herself, skidding across rough stone, tears blurred eyes as the world tumbled. Stopping on her stomach, a ragged, beaten cough expunged from blood-tasting lips. Aching limbs pushed her to ascend, shakes racked her nimble, tender body.

"Lilly. Lilly." Singular word repeated through laborious cries. Uncontrolled breaths shook burning shoulders, trembling wrists gave way. Cass's chest caught her heavy fall. Arms closed around her sweating head, pulsating with crawling tears of perspiration.

"Cass, Cass." Jolam's voice broke through turbulent thoughts.

Stinging hands pushed on coarse, hardened stone. Eyes peeled open, fighting with sweat teaming down brows and sopping her itching face. Dried, cracked lips panted. On her knees, she wrapped her arms around Jolam, clinging onto him.

"Lilly. It's Lilly." Cass's voice broke. Words were nothing but ragged air escaping a parched throat.

"What? Lilly. She's in Konniak, Cass, Konniak." Jolam tried to laugh. Round face and curling beard filled her vision. Brown eyes sombre as a docile deer.

"No. She's a Mystic. She's a Mystic." She blurted between shaking sobs and gasps for air. Warm hands held her face. She looked at Jolam.

"Cassy, what… Lilly." The Faun stammered. She brushed off the inmate's hands. Shaking her head, biting pain lanced through wrists, her face twitched. Pain nothing but annoyance compared to crashing tides of turmoil rolling through her mind.

"She's doing this. Lilly is doing this." Cass rubbed watering emotion away with the back of her hand. Jolam stood up and moved back. She looked up at the Faun, mouth agape.

"She's a kid. Ten years old. You… knew." Jolam's cheeks twitched, eyes darted left and right, blinking. It pained more than her wrists, dug into her beating chest to see Jolam like this. Slowly, her heartbeat settled. Each long, cool breath brought realisation to her rocking thoughts.

"Armande has her. I saw her, Jol, she's here." Cass eased herself up to stand, relying on trembling knees than hands.

"Your daughter?" Taze's rasped. The convict stood by Lucijan, repeater in hands. Cass grew conscious, knowing she had no weapon. She shook her head, the singular braid hanging.

"No, little girl is making this. Mystics, it's a joke. There's something in the air. Our minds. Our guilt." Taze spat. Black, unwavering eyes bore into her own.

The assaulting eyes narrowed. Resistance braced her back, shaking muscles running along tired limbs.

"She is. Don't know how, but she is." Cass's words as concrete as her returning stare.

"Then what's this place? Your kid made this?" Taze waved the repeater. She broke her gaze and peered around. Dampness clogged her nose, smelt like an ordinary, moist cave network. A tunnel with a dark, gaping mouth at either end, which disappeared into the oesophagus of eternity. Glowing green veins ran along smooth, reflective walls.

A sturdy rock floor laid out in intricate squares, like a mosaic floor of an extravagant bathroom only found in the upper echelons of Konniak. No cave Cass had seen before. A cold, unsettled chill coursed down her spine. Pulsing veins of jade rock emitted an emerald shine that illuminated the area within staring eyesight.

"This place is crazy. One candlemark we're in the cells, now." Jolam spoke.

She could not care where this was. Finding Lilly was all that mattered. Her wrists stung, fingers curled inwards, making weakened fists. Blood wept into her palm. Tingles of sweat forced her clothes to stick to her back like a second skin.

"By the Tree Father, Cass." Jolam walked forward. "I've got the leaf, I do." He fumbled within a hide-skinned satchel. She watched as Faunish fingers wrapped around the wrist and palm with brown, dried Faunleaf. A soothing softness sunk into her blood, dousing the burning pulse.

"Always had my back." Cass sighed, looking up at the Faun. He stopped his apothecary work.

"Best back to look at is all." He winked, cheerful twinkle returning to doe-brown eyes. A ruddiness flaring at his cheeks beneath curling, matted bristles of an auburn beard.

"Even in this hell, you're still you." She patted Jolam on the shoulder, squeezing, and smiled. The pain faded from the wrist, wrapped in Faunleaf.

"That's twice now." Taze purred. "Twice you attempted to save me." The convict faced the conscript, repeaters in hands.

Taze placed a hand on Lucijan's shoulder. "I don't know why you did it, Lucky, but don't think I'm gonna repay you soon."

Lucijan turned a brighter shade of red and half smiled.

"You blushing, young-blood?" Taze nudged the soldier.

"No, it's boiling here is all." Lucijan spluttered. "Speaking of here, where is this?"

Stalactites illuminated under emerald glare, hanging with a lethality that made Cass step backwards. At least she could see the natural ceiling above, feel the hardness of stone beneath. Dampness hung around her nostrils, along with a stench that was hard to distinguish.

Grodol approached, holding the girl close to him. She braved a smile. The girl was so close to looking like Lilly, it unsettled her, heart dropping within her belly.

"You have repeaters? Loaded?" Cass turned, facing the others.

"Ready." Taze nodded. Straining to hide the pain of her fingers, which subsided with the Faunleaf working its wonders, she removed her bandolier and tossed it to the murderer.

"Make them count, no idea where mine is." She faced Lucijan, trying to make a softer face despite the heat and thousand direct thoughts on Lilly. Her daughter had to be close.

"Let's get out of here, don't want to be stuck here and have to use our repeaters." Cass looked around. Focusing on finding a way out, a way to find Lilly.

"So where do we go?" Jolam and Taze asked simultaneously.

Groaning wind raced out of the cave mouth. Warm breeze ruffled clothing, stifling air blasted down the cave. Green lights burned brighter, turning molten white as the sound flared louder. Falling silent, Cass peered where the noise erupted.

"Not there." She turned her back to the cave mouth and looked at the equally darker passage.

"Lucky and I will go first. We've got the repeaters. Goat…" Taze stopped herself. "Jolam. Stay at the back." The murderer stalked off, Lucijan shrugged and jogged to catch up with Taze, their footfalls echoing within the glowing jade cave.

"I'm beginning to like her." Jolam jovially announced, giving Cass a knowing look.

"Let's go." She smiled, heading off into the darkened cave tunnel.

Lilly occupied her mind. Kept her mobile as her body yearned for rest, much needed rest. Stomach growled in hungry protest. Her wrist had stopped bleeding due to the Faunleaf. There would be scars, nothing new. She carried scars her whole life, no reason to complain of another afflicted mark on a tiresome body.

Rock veins pulsed, providing faint light. A steady, meticulous glow continued to fade in and out of existence, highlighting obsidian, smooth rock face of the cave walls but not strong enough to reveal the natural tunnel floor. She swatted at the air, the odd fly buzzed irritating her ears.

"Stop." A resounding voice halted Cass in her steps. Green light blurred Taze and Lucijan into faint silhouettes. She smelt it now. Her hand slapping over a gagging mouth. Flies itched her scalp and neck, crawling on exposed skin.

The ground moved.

Peering down, she could see nothing below knees. Ground moved again. Squelches broke from raising her foot, an animalistic hiss spluttered as Cass lowered her foot on the uneven, rolling floor.

"Not liking this one bit." Jolam coughed.

She looked ahead and to the sides. Rock shone smooth, green veins turned into channels of emerald liquid oozing through intricate cracks along angular walls, twisting and circling above their heads, all running down the tunnel with the obsidian, reflective rock.

Taze lead the way, Cass watched as two green shadows picked their steps and casually ventured onwards, Lucijan being the shadow at the convict's back. The tunnel widened and sloped. She eased her way down, footing ungainly with the bubbling, unseen ground.

With every step taken, she winced. Taze and Lucijan silhouettes leading the way. Low moans muffled her hearing. Another step, cries and pleas for help. Sounding like the cave floors' hurtful reply by her footfalls.

"Help. Help." A whispering voice begged. Brow bled sweat. She dared not move, as it itched down her face. Something moved on the wall within her periphery. Greased hair, pale skin, startled eyes. More eyes, faces, mouths. Forms moved against shiny, black, reflective wall. People were on the wall. People were the wall.

"Grodol shield the girl." Cass called out. It could not real, it can not be. Her heart raced into her mouth. Stomach tumbled with tidal ferocity.

"Keep moving." She stalked ahead, groans from the floor echoed her steps. Orschallian, Cythean and Sabanese faces looked up at her. Picking up her pace, voices increased in pleas. She wanted to run, to drown out perpetual sobbing. Her hand clasped over her nose, defending in vain against gut-wrenching stench.

"Cass." An anguished cry echoed in the tunnel. She skidded looked at the walls.

"Keep moving." Jolam encouraged, snatching her arm, trying to pull her along. Green ebbing glow revealing faces contorted in speech. Blonde hair stood out, stark in the reflective sheen of where the body cemented to the wall. Darkness eclipsed Cass's vision.

"Come on, leave them, we could end up like them." Jolam rattled off, tugging her arm. Rooted to the spot. Head shook. She was here. She was here.

"Cass." A naïve voice gurgled. A shiver rippled down her back, sounded familiar. A sickly green light illuminated a face with branded lips on a pale cheek. Stell looked at her.

"Stell." She half screamed. Cass staggered to the convict. "No, Stell. No." She grappled at the thick, black resin bounding Stell to the wall, only looking at her hands.

"Kill me. Cass. Please." Gargled Stell. She looked down at the prisoner's body and backed away, her stomach twisted in knots. A black robe clothed Stell. It moved. There was no wind. Something other than Stell moved on the body of the convict stuck to the cave wall.

"Stell." She breathed. Skin stretched. A swollen abdomen, threatening to expand further. Only the bloated belly of flesh protruded from the convict's pinned state. Her pregnancy clear to Cass's doubtful eyes.

"Kill me." The pained shout startled Cass. She jerked at the outburst. Stell's head snapped back. Something moved under her drawn skin.

A face pressed against stretched flesh.

Stell's scream tore through Cass. Stuck, unmoving, paralysed. Her skin ignited with trembles.

A black claw crawled out of Stell's choking mouth. Blood dripping talons flexed. Yearning. Grabbing at the air.

Cass swung around, without realising, without thinking. She did not protest. Jolam's body moving her aside.

"Finish it Taze." Jolam's shout riddled throughout her mind. Whistling shots of a repeater filtered into her hearing. A bestial shriek followed.

Cass's face flushed with heat. Her legs finally moved, arms flexing with strength. Moving on her own will, she turned her back on silent Stell. The young woman would know no more pain. One less person to let down.

"Have to move." Her voice cracked, begging cries and moaning pleas broke under footfalls.

A scream tore Cass around to see Lucijan on his knees, holding his head. The conscripts back illuminated in green, shimmering light. Taze howled nearby. Jolam buckled and vomited, choked and gagged while he yelled, holding onto his head.

Blinding headaches ruptured her vision. The world spun and Cass knelt to steady herself. Air exhumed into sticking palms. Rock breathed into her skin. Shaking eyes closed, better to live in darkness than see the truth. The world pulsed like a heartbeat. Light flared in the corners of her closed eyes. Shaking pillars of energy flashed down her sockets.

Something sticky latched around her wrist. She yelled out. More grips clamped along her body, snatching legs and around her waist. Cass kicked. The others around shouted and pleaded.

"Get off! Get off!" Jolam yelped nearby.

She screamed while passed from unseen hand to unseen hand. Hard and entrapping in their vice, the tunnel mouth sloped down towards a crimson end. A blast of air ruffled Cass's short hair and flooded skin with a humidity that itched her skin.

The hands let go. Sliding down the cave throat towards the bowel of red light, vision blurred as she landed on crunching, brittle ground. She scrambled away, knowing the others would follow down the slope. Screams and shouts rushed closer as the others tumbled and crashed onto the snapping floor.

Cass launched to her feet, jerking to stand on seeing the bone strewn ground as she crawled over. Clean, pristine bones of people. Gasps and shouts echoed. Lucijan, Taze and Jolam stood, mouths open, peering at the foot-covering bones that lay discarded in white mounds. Nothing but high walls of cave rock and swirling clouds of crimson circled above, bathing bone floor in a murky redness.

"To me." She whispered. "To me." Finding her voice. A tone she had not used since the rebellion. Her stomach quivered. What she would not do for Merrick's back right now. Linen shirt became a second skin moulding to her back.

The ground convulsed, showering moist air in human remains. Eruption followed of rock. Dust exploded upwards, funnelled up the pit enclosure.

It crawled. Dragging itself clear of the self-made opening. A tangled blob of bare sinew, veins, and limbs. A raw, meat coloured body drenched the opposite side of the pit. It dwarfed them. Cass shivered under its immense shadow.

"It's not real. It's not real." Jolam chanted, backing away.

She recoiled under its stench. Bile boiled in her throat, forcing it back with a bitter grimace. It reared itself. Dust settled. A vertical slit parted down its bloated centre. Fangs flashed, slather swamped its bulbous body. A thousand eyes popped among the mass of skinned muscle, like wounds.

"It's not real!" Jolam shouted.

Taze stood forward, repeater raised. "Cover the girl and Grodol, me and Lucky have this."

Whistles of repeaters blitzed through Cass's hearing. Shafts lanced against fleshy, bloated body of the amalgamation. It defied the space it occupied, rolling into existence, extending to the walls in a web of skin, bubbling in its fluid mass. Waving feelers, mocking tendrils and slithering tentacles emerged from a multitude of open wounds. Her stomach turned in twisted knots.

"Back against the wall, move." She waved at Grodol, but looked at the girl, innocent, helpless. Just like Lilly, exactly like Lilly, but this time, she would not abandon her.

"Cass!" Jolam warned. Warmth rushed past her. She lurched forward, scrambling for something to steady herself. Crashing rock split, showering her head to foot in debris. Cass turned. The massive tendril of the beast slid back to its body. A second and third waved in unison, preparing to slap down.

With gritted teeth, she swallowed throbbing pain in her hands. Kicking herself to stand, she hunched her back ready to move, padding on aching legs, shifting weight on the balls of her feet. Bones crunched beneath hasty steps.

"Keep moving and aim for the limbs." Cass shouted. A pink tentacle launched her way.

"Which limbs?" Jolam screamed, firing his own repeater.

"This one." She jumped to the side, skidding, and fell as the second sinew hammered against the floor. She snatched it, flesh peeled off the appendage, like shredded meat off a bone. Nostrils flared with the stench of a raw carcass. Cass climbed onto the retreating limb, pushing down her weight.

"Sever the limbs. Sever them." She pinned herself against the slipping, bile smelling tendril of the beast.

Weightless rushed over her, as a hurling scream tossed her off the appendage. Wetness drenched hair and back, splattering her side and legs. She crumpled and lay winded, tucking legs together as she rolled. Her world nothing more than red sand that tasted of chalk and something else she dared not comprehend.

"It worked, Cass." Lucijan's voice filtered through the ringing in her skull. Pink mesh of flesh writhed and wobbled. It flailed, a pooling red liquid swelled before her.

"No Grodol." Jolam's defiant voice cleared her hearing.

She jerked her head, eyes wide, as Grodol waved, encouraging the creature. A limb swung to him, he ducked. Cass held her breath. The wall rumbled with the colliding strike. Pushing herself up, she staggered, seeing two of everything. Blinking a few times in eagerness to vanish the double vision, wiping her forehead with a stinging hand.

A rumbling crash sent her vision toppling. Cass dropped to her knees. Looking up, seeing Grodol on the floor near the beast. Its vertical set of teeth, chattering within its fleshy mass, snapped and slathered. It flowed upwards before slamming down, engulfing Grodol.

An unnatural scream erupted in Cass's ears. Her eyes, which recovered from its double vision, snapped to the source of the scream. The Sabanese girl.

"Jolam, to the girl." Cass heard herself shout, trying in vain to be louder than the despicable slobbering that erupted underneath the bloated mass of rolling meat flowed like a pink sinew tide back and forth beneath Grodol.

"Cass." Taze shouted. A repeater hurtled through the air. She snatched it and jumped into the blob. Her valenki boots sank into flesh, she fired while trudging on. Knees weighed deep into broken, squelching skin. She dry-heaved, gagging on the raw smell of open wounds.

Writhing mass moved under her, as Cass kicked herself up the beasts supposed back. Things moved under its skin, stretching it. Voices cried under her motion. Screams and shouts, but all of them pleas.

Woeful and pitying. A stretching outline pushed against the sinew. She dropped the repeater. A tortured face grew from the writhing flesh.

"MOM!" Lilly's voice bubbled under the surface of the beast's skin.

Cass hurled herself down, tearing at the flesh, ripping it apart with stinging fingers. Her world nothing more than blurred pink. No Lilly, Lilly. Cass fought, grappling with the beast's meaty skin and rolls of bulbous fat. She broke through the layers of copper smelling blubber. She vomited, showering her hands in bile. No Lilly. No faces. Blood boiled up the wound. A torn ushanka hat pushed up from the brewing, pulsating ichor.

The ground convulsed, she buckled and tried to stand on the shaking mass. The beast rolled backwards, Cass scrambled over it pulling at the fat and blubber for security. Steaming hot liquids drenching her body and gravity rushing underneath. She ran but could not move, stuck in the folds of the monster's mass.

"Jump, Cass, jump!" warned several voices. Lilly was one of them. It had to be.

Cass shouted as she dived forward, the beast sliding underneath. Hitting the rock, her boots dangled in weightlessness. Her own body ached; fingers clawed into cracking stone. She closed her eyes. *I failed you, Lilly.* She held on, not daring to open her eyes. The belching monster's groans disappeared beneath her, and emptiness yawned at her feet. Knees scraping rock. Fingers slipped.

"Got you." Lucijan declared. A firm hand snatched her own.

A second hand latched onto her right hand. "You got a death wish, Cass the convict." Taze's voice quipped in. "But today your wish is not coming true."

Her stomach threatened to cry, her mouth laughed hysterically. Her shoulders only sagged. She allowed Lucijan and Taze to lift her over the edge of the drop. She breathed a deep sigh on feeling solid rock beneath her crumpled state.

"Grodol." Cass whispered.

"Gone." Replied Lucijan. "Jolam is bringing the girl over. She's quiet. Not moving either."

Cass knew the feeling. Catatonic. Struck dumb with absolute hysteria, the stories from asylums, she dreaded if Lilly had to be detained in one for being a Mystic. She remembered the Purifier Rebellion: the madness that crept into people; separation of families and the torture of the unknown. She cursed Merrick for not being here, for not sticking by.

"It's changing." Taze warned. Groaning, Cass climbed up to stand, clothes stuck to her skin. Heavy eyes drifted upwards, preparing for the worst. Rocks knitted over the pit, forming a solid ceiling with dagger tipped stalactites threatening to drop. The last she saw before darkness swallowed them.

"Stay still." Lucijan's voice echoed in the darkness. His youthful voice resonated.

"It's only darkness, only darkness." Taze's voice whispered in a lonely prayer. The convicts heat and breath close. Cass turned but saw nothing.

"Light ahead." Lucijan called.

A swinging light approached, ebbing as it grew closer. Footfalls echoed. Humming shadowed the movements. Something clicked as it moved. Faun hooves clicking against rock.

Yellow, scattered light a flaring Gaslamp came first, bathing a warm glow on Cass. She raised a hand against its soothing rays, her eyes not ready to see. Hand lowered on hearing the humming, a soft, melancholic tune of a Cythean orchestral piece played by the lips of the woman carrying the Gaslamp.

"Hmm, new this is." Her distant voice sang around Cass's ears. The Faun tilted her head and looked among them with soft, round eyes, as the Gaslamp swung in her hand.

Vincentas

Chapter XI

Vincentas spared a moment to observe a lavender stained sky, magenta tainted clouds smudged across a bruised horizon. It looked like Riemkeler, but it could not be. Purple, nauseating glow bathed the world, a perpetual total eclipse fell across the city. Smelt of iron, rust, and decay. It did not smell of flower gardens, boiling yeast or brewing hops.

Distant thunder rumbled, not sounding like any normal thunder, more a dull, heavy cloth hammering inside a rusting bell. Flashes ignited between bruised magenta and lilac skies; pink clouds formed trenches between embattled skies blurring together. Not for the first time, Vincentas turned up his collar for expectant, threatening rain.

"I'm never going to get used to seeing that." Violet chimed in his ear. Sweat greased an already saturated forehead. How she looked more relaxed and not as flushed boggled his mind. A primary disadvantage of age.

"The Verge is a conundrum within an enigma. Getting used to anything here would weaken us." She referred to the floating, black buildings attached to visible landmasses. Hovering teeth. Singular houses lowered and raised, some specks in the distance, others close enough to climb onto from hanging roots dangling below.

"Nothing will weaken me." Violet stretched her legs out, looking around, hands on the repeater across her lap.

"Only time." Vincentas whispered. No sun illuminated, no moon risen and lowered to signal day's end. After leaving Athgeric's, they had slept once in an abandoned room within a house. Sleep interrupted with inhuman shrieks. Growls that shock them to the core. What little sleep they had taken its weary toll.

"We come across a Mystic. It's you that's leading the charge." She faced him.

"Agreed. And I'll be ready for it." He vowed, though they had not crossed a Mystic, or even his retinue, since leaving the Verge-made domain of his old friend.

"Not pleasant, is it?" Violet observed. Black, oily structures suspended in the distance, a stench of something decaying a constant irritation. Gaslamps flickered with an unnatural ability, flashing lightning blue, not the usual murky yellow.

A convulsion rocked their posture, wavering in unison with the shaking ground, Vincentas scrambled to his feet.

"There." Violet grasped his shoulder. Her voice hoarse, cracking with its low tone. A building levitated. Within a heartbeat, the world stopped shaking as the structure and foundational soil rose into the sky, breaking free of Riemkeler, forming its own haphazard city in the hazy sky along with the others.

"Before we realise it, the entire city will be floating." Vincentas eyed the house, which settled, suspended, like the others.

"Let's keep moving." Violet encouraged, leading the way.

They stalked through shadowed streets for many candlemarks, his resolve kept him going. Athgeric's madness playing within his mind. Many pages in a book, bound by Mystics, but made by something else.

Hardened taps on pebbled road forced Vincentas to stop. Violet merged beside him. Looking down the narrowed path led to more turns and houses missing light, music, and life. He pulled at his collar. Cloth itched at his throat, like thick, woollen fingers curling around him in suffocation.

"It is warm around here." She voiced his thoughts. The Combatant's forehead glistened. Her hand wiping at her mouth.

Searching between two houses which lay separated by a missing habitation, a fog bank clouded the missing road. Rolls of mist parted. Pink curtains drew back between horizon and sky. Curling fingers of mist drew Vincentas's eyes to the stark, obscured building, its captivating splendour as magnificent now as it was when he first saw it. The famed Academy of Riemkeler. Closer, but still far away.

An unsettling knot tightened within his gut. The academy lay in the centre of the city, not where it originally its foundations lay. Mysticism distorted the world; nothing logical could explain it. Forbidden knowledge and hidden truths, Athgeric's words echoed within his chilling mind.

A firm hand squeezed his shoulder. "Ahead." Violet breathed. Vincentas lowered. A click resonated in the pathway. Something chipped against unseen pebbles. Further clicks echoed like stone skimmed off rock. The sound travelled, reverberated closer. An icy shiver trickled down his spine.

Silver flash caught his eye. Warm, sticky breath sucked into dry mouth. The handbow raised. Leathers of Violet shuffled beside him, creaking as she moved. Metallic cracking grated behind.

It spun. Slowly. Twirling on an axis that changed by its own whim. The silver square caught his eye again, pale metal shimmering with a dimness not bathed by the oily sickness of purple light. The silver was a buckle.

The black shoe vaulted and twisted in the air during its floating travel.

Mystic.

Making sure nothing followed the inexplicable, floating shoe, Vincentas moved forward. He rounded the floating shoe, a girl's shoe made by skilled cobblers in Riemkeler. The distinctive patch work, the shine around the toes, the buckle with the flower etched around it. Every lady in Cythea wanted the famous Riemkeler shoes made at the renowned cobblers.

Even…

Something swiped his leg. His skin leapt from bones.

Force pulled him to the streets, crashing on hardened cobbles. His name called out, distant and ringing in his numb mind. Without thinking, back scrapped along Riemkeler's streets down the road away from pursuing footfalls and shouts of his name. Scabbard rasped over stone, body buckled and grated as it involuntarily yanked against his will.

Hands shot out, grasping at anything to slow him down. Gloves slipped off wet cobbles. Fingers itched for solid matter. Pulled around a corner, his arms shot out, grabbing a building's edge. Lifting in the air, he hung, not looking at what was pulling him away, taking him.

"Vincentas." Violet shouted, below him, by two feet. Repeater firing. An inhuman squeal echoed throughout his spine. The force let go. He tumbled to the ground, the crash knocking wind free of panting lungs.

"Should have been watching the ground, stupid me. Red vines. Could have taken you, like the others." Violet dived on Vincentas, eager to help him up.

High pitched shrill coursed down the road. It fed into beating chest with a coldness rippling through his body. Flickering flames wreathed ahead, red light curled around the corner where he was nearly dragged down. Violet came beside him, breathing deeply.

"Down." she warned, shielding him to the dark cobbles. A dark winged shape glided with ferocity overhead. It banked, circled and disappeared within the spires of the floating city.

"Deathwing?" His foreheads muscles knitted together. This far west of the Thousand Isles. Blinking to make sure he was seeing things, all in vain. The winged mass vanished.

"Too small for Deathwing. Even for a Roc. It's no bird I've ever seen." Violet pushed herself up, dusting down clothing. She extended a hand to Vincentas.

"The Verge has poisoned nature." His voice strained while standing up, taking her hand and climbing to his feet. A protective hand on the hilt of the sword during his movements.

"A Mystic can do anything they desire. But the price will always get them at the end." He spat, even Athgeric.

"Here. Inquisitor." Violet produced the cockel hat. He nodded and placing it on his head. She turned and walked on, keeping to the shadows of nearby houses. Stop thinking that will defeat them. Hadramiel's advice spoken to him in Athgeric's voice. Nothing so simple when confusion and illusion ate into him freely. Gloved hands wrapped around the obsidian hilt; his fingers settled.

"Any idea where we are?" Violet looked around.

Every house identical, awash in shadow and blackness. Street bunting hung between Gaslamp to dead Gaslamp, black webs trapping light. More life in the Undercity of Konniak than here. In the distance, ever elusive, the academy glowed like a welcoming beacon.

"Not in Konniak." Vincentas mused. Violet brushed her elbow into his ribs. He felt it through the thick layers.

"Any idea where we are, in Riemkeler?" She emphasised every word.

"I don't know. It's all different." He pointed at the academy, a golden pinnacle in the middle of a black void. "The academy in Riemkeler was never in the centre, but here it is. Everything else is off."

"Athgeric mentioned the academy." He nodded at Violet's hollow words. Look deep for its knowledge, delve deeper for its forbidden truth. No question about it. The academy possessed expert knowledge, but to look deeper for a forbidden truth. The academy had to be investigated.

"We have to go there. To the academy." He gripped the hilt of the Inquisitorial sword. He would need it there.

"You think he is right?" Her voice broke through growing silence. He did not want to admit it, but there was a cold, unsure hand on his spine filtering into his senses. A coldness no warmth could douse.

"There's only one way to be sure." Whatever Athgeric found or convinced of, it lay in the academy. Vincentas's eyes narrowed, gloved hands pained his fingers from gripping the hilt. He loosened the grip. The amount of times he has been to the academy and something could be within its depths, a Mystic.

"Soon we get to the academy, we'll find the truth." Whatever the truth may be.

"It's right in the centre. Big. Everything is pointing at it. Why not." Violet shrugged.

Muffled voices echoed off slick cobbles. Vincentas ducked and moved to the wall. Rounding the corner of the street, he peered down at it. Violet leaning over.

"Could be citizens. Or the retinue." He whispered.

"Chances are Afflicted." Whispered violet. Her voice could have been from his own mind.

"Don't want to stick around to find out. Let's go." She moved off. Vincentas followed, keeping close behind the scuttling, effective Combatant as they crossed cobbled, shadowed streets. Occasionally glancing down to see if any red vines lay waiting. A stench brought thoughts of the Inquirer Hall back to him. A distant voice chanted. Whips cracked. A shriek replied. Unseen flames cackled, their red shadows flickered.

Reeking stench of bile drowned his lungs. Vincentas closed his mouth, a stifled cough rumbled lips. He placed his handbow on the corner of the crumbling wall. Violet nodded to him to peer round. Holding his breath, he inched forward. Sweat bled between heated brows.

His skin leapt under a deranged howl. Bracing himself, he looked around the corner again, prepared for any noises. Fires littered the ground. Black, smouldering shadows gave fuel to twisting, vaulting red flames. The odour causing horrendous nausea.

Upside down, hung on a rope, a naked woman wriggled under a lashing whip. The thing that whipped the defenceless victim clad in loose Interrogator clothing. Standing taller than the hanging woman, standing impossibly tall for a human.

Two heads faced his shrieking victim every time the whip struck the bloodied back. Vincentas closed his eyes. The smoke caused hallucinations. The whip snapped again, another howl. His eyes opened. It scythed through his guts, like a piece of ice. Brutal mockery of the Interrogator with two heads, no illusion. It stood on limbs that were more insect than human, clacking on sleek stones.

"Come on." Violet shouted. He staggered forward, firing at the two-headed thing. Its heads revolved round facing him. It screamed. Vincentas's legs steadied as he moved, levelling the handbow at the monstrous Interrogator.

Shuffling, jittering townsfolk flanked the fires burning behind the abnormality. He turned his fury on the Afflicted. They crumbled to the ground. Thudding bolts shook their bodies, dropping like puppets after cutting string. Collapsing into limbs and ragged poses. Purple light fading from eyes.

A high-pitched squeal turned Vincentas. He held onto the cockel hat, thinking the force would knock it clean off. Fires writhing under the cry. The Interrogator moved forward, holding a guillotine blade. He dropped the handbow. Instinct led him to the hilt and withdrew the Inquisitor's sword. Green flashed in his eyes on unleashing the malachite blade, his teeth gritted.

Violet's voice a distant, inaudible muffle. A singular heartbeat pounded ears. The multi-limbed thing lumbered between isolated flames, towering over him. Taste of putrid stenches and spilt blood filled his throat. Sparks burst as the guillotine dragged across street cobbles, its metal ricocheting, shuddered his shaking shoulders. One slash should do it, it had to be a Mystic.

Movement jerked to his right. Violet tussled with an Afflicted. She pushed her assailant onto the fire, spitting flames on the deformed Interrogator. The beast engulfed in red, leaping flames. Its screech rippled the waters of Vincentas's bowels. It allowed him time to move back, ready to assault, malachite sword flaming in his eyes.

Fire consumed the deformed, living thing. It bloated red. Expunged in smoke. The guillotine fell with a metal ringing that clawed through Vincentas's ears, pushing his heartbeat down into his quivering chest.

Flames lowered. They died as one. Purple light fed into the world. Humidity returned with a sweating vengeance. Stench of burnt hair, charred flesh filtered into his nostrils.

Violet faced him. "Fire seems to work." A forced, hard smile crossed her lips.

Vincentas nodded toward the upside-down woman, moving, bending in suspension. He headed towards her, ignoring the dead Afflicted in case he knew any of them.

A crate lay near the suspended woman which held the captive's items: a folded black, tailored coat; a white Konniak blouse. His heart skipped a beat seeing a distinctive leather tied bodice. A satchel, a knapsack, and a rectangular metal quiver lay on the ground. An ivory composite bow lay on the woman's coat.

Fleur. Vincentas sheathed his sword, moving over to the upside-down woman. Whip marks lined her bleeding back, soft moans signalled her conscious state. He placed his hands on the woman's shoulders.

"Fleur. Fleur." The captive bolted under touch but calmed on hearing the name. He turned her around. A black eye swollen shut. Bleeding mouth. Hair matted with dry, cracking black stains, hanging limply. Smeared blood colluded around her left temple. Features contorted from the smell.

Black, distant eye opened as far as it could. "We'll cut you down." Vincentas stated. Withdrawing a dirk blade, single-edged and cut the ropes that bound Fleur's feet. A twang toppled the severed strands. Fleur fell into his waiting shoulders, heavier than she looked.

He carried Fleur to the crate near the Combatants' clothing. Violet helped ease the weight on the other side. The Combatant wheezed on being put down and spat on feeling free.

"I promise, I'm not into rope games." Fleur wheezed, her good eye closed.

Blonde, blood-soaked hair streaked over angular features, but no mistaking the brand of criminality on her cheek, or the name of a victim burnt onto her forehead.

"Damn, bastard animals cut my ear off." Fleur moved her hand over her left ear. Anger kept her going, it would only last so long. She needed rest, food, and time. Time they did not have.

Violet snorted. "A thank you would be nice." Vincentas looked at her. She shrugged.

"You got to see my gorgeous body, so that's thanks enough." Fleur leaned back and smiled a wicked crimson. She parted her free arm, exposing her whipped body for Violet.

"Let's get you clothed and bandage that ear." Vincentas whispered. He looked around, expecting assailants. Footsteps echoed on the cobbles. He turned to see Violet walking away.

"She's cute, too cute for you." Fleur purred and winced, sucking in air. Vincentas delved into Fleur's rucksack, finding gauze and pins, some Faunleaf in various states. Dried, wet and powdered. Always prepared.

"No damn need for this." Fleur picked up the bronze half-mask. It covered her criminal conviction, not scars. Vincentas rolled the bandage around Fleur's forehead, skirting down to the ruined remains of a black stump of an ear.

"It suits you, you should still wear it." His eyes caught hold of her forehead. Bruises merged with the branding of a name. Only one type of criminal received a branded name on their forehead: murderers. His interest piqued on the name, seeing "W" at the beginning, the rest obscured with bruises and hair.

Fleur eased her arms into the white blouse, covering black marked arms. They did not look like tattoos, but must have been. Angular marks, like rectangles and other shapes, lined her left and right arms. He thought immediately of the bodies in the morgues.

"Can you move on your own?" Vincentas asked, handing Fleur her bodice.

Fleur grimaced and placed the bodice around her torso. "If it's got a bar, I'll dance there." She fastened the bodice at the side.

"What can you remember after entering the Inquirer Hall?" She may have seen the others, or Alleck, or the Mystic.

Fleur groaned, putting the dovetail coat on, wincing as he fed her arms into the coat and stood up. "Chasing after the stupid Entrant." She placed her hands on her knees. "This is gonna get some getting used to."

"Come on, Combatant, on your feet." Vincentas helped her up. Ragged breath left her body.

"Found me naked, helped me get changed and now you put your hands on me." Fleur purred as best she could, trying to keep humour.

"It was too easy, got to make it hard for myself." He strained holding Fleur up. She leaned on his shoulder. She shook her head.

"Don't make me laugh, Vin." She grasped her bronze half-mask and fastened it around her face, covering the criminal branding. No wonder she was an efficient killer, already a killer before drafting into the Combatant role.

"Where to?" Violet inquired, holding her repeater across folded arms.

"The academy." He rasped through gritted teeth.

Fleur let out a low hiss. "Leave me behind, don't want to slow you lovebirds down."

Vincentas grasped Fleur. "Not leaving anyone behind." He caught Violet's gaze. She bit her lip and slung her repeater over her shoulder, taking Fleur roughly by the other arm.

Cass

Chapter XI

Cass held the girl close. She could have passed for Lilly. She was Lilly for now. Tightening her grip with a protective embrace, they moved as one. No stinging pain surfaced from wire inflicted wounds. Unseen wounds scarred the cruellest. They were deep, too deep.

Jackboots grated over rock. Someone coughed behind. Water dripped rhythmically, repetitive. Too tired to dwell on how far they walked, but she followed the female Faun wielding the Gaslamp with a melancholy hum to her casual stride.

Peering up, the light had ceased moving. Or maybe her eyes played tricks in the darkness. Metallic ringing resonated in the pitch-black cave. Moistness clung to Cass like an unwanted blanket. Soft inhales escaped the unresponsive girl. Soon they would sleep. She needed it, they all needed it.

She caught up with the female Faun, who raked through her tattered duster. Nose wrinkled at the stench of their underground guide, or maybe it was them. She had not washed since Ralake. The Faun retrieved a set of rattling keys from a stitched pocket. The Faun's face lit up with a smile before it disappeared. Bushy eyebrows raised, mouth agape as she looked at Cass.

"Hmm, did you get here? How?" The Faun pondered. Shrugging lithe shoulders, turning to face a wooden, plain door, illuminated by the Gaslamp. Loose, unreadable words carved into its frame.

"Once to the left, twice to the right, thrice back and click." The Faun chirped. With a clack, the door creaked outwards, pulled by the woman. The Gaslamp occupying her other hand swung casting yellow, lancing light into the cave darkness, tasting of thick, humid moistness.

"Enter, enter. Come on in, come on in." She gestured without turning. Her loud, welcoming voice echoed. Cass placed a hand over the girl's ear, smothered in her hair. The other ear placed on her chest.

Kindness a rarity in her world. A wounded past kept her feet still, unable to move forward. Her back tensed, readying to run and carry the child to safety. An illusive, distant safety. It entered her mind quicker than the glow leaking from the ajar door, spilling into black eclipse to roll back curtained shadows. It smelt real. Her stomach growled at the scenes of jasmine, mint, and snowberries.

Cass entered the shimmering shack, eyes darting, keeping the girl close. The Faun held the door open and kept bowing as she trudged inside, to stand on mottled carpet patched together with a multitude of colours. Gaudy but warm, she could not deny that. Colour ran riot within the room, oil paintings obscured walls. Gaslamps flared in various positions, washing the interior in a golden hue.

Her shoulders relaxed, for the first time since… she struggled to think the last time she relaxed. Before the Purifier Rebellion, she stole and lent services to petty crime lord Vansic Lo to feed her alcoholic mother. After the war, she had her joyous spell with Lilly, but also the most heart-breaking: not being able to provide for her.

Creaking hinges sent a grating shiver down Cass's spine, the door closed cocooning them against eternal darkness of the cave. The Faun mumbled to herself, while sliding many bolts, locking different coloured padlocks and linking chains to secure the door in place. Wooden beams lost under padlock and security. She kept her arm around the girl, keeping eyes on the female Faun who had them trapped.

With a sigh, the Faun turned, her oversized, tattered duster swished. Large, brown eyes peered behind two big lenses of bifocals, perched on her wide nose. Facing Cass, she rubbed her hands together. Broad, yellow-toothed smile dropped.

"Rough day?" She sighed, lowering her shoulders as she spoke. She bit her lip to stop a reply.

"Look all sweat," the Faun started, waving hands around spasmodically. Hooves muffled on motley, carpeted floor. "Towels I have for you." She finished, disappearing into an adjacent room with no door.

Cass looked at the others. Jolam swayed and rubbed his face, his Faun hair sleek with perspiration. Lucijan's features caked in grim and Taze looked as dishevelled as she felt. Her own skin drawn as she moved, sticky sweat and spilt drying blood webbed flesh. Relaxation doused her strength. She wanted nothing more than to lie on the soft carpet and sleep.

The Faun came back and handed a towel to each of them, ironic how clean, fluffy and white compared to the rest of the abode. Cass took the towel, too tired for pleasantries. She wanted to ask questions but crouched down facing the girl. She brushed her fingers through matted hair. Closed eyes greeted her, and soft, dreaming breath warmed her face.

"Need a bed." She whispered, her throat tight. "Need a bed, please." Turning to the female Faun.

"Hmm?" The female Faun stopped in mid-stride. She clicked her fingers and nodded. "Sleep, yes, tired definitely." She trotted over to a bookcase, festooned with parchments, books and tomes of various states and volume. Brushing books to the side of the cabinet, she pulled a brass lever.

A nearby wardrobe turned, revolving left to right. Springs and mesh replaced the wardrobe and fell outwards with a metallic cranking. Cass lifted the girl away before the makeshift bed fell to the ground and bounced, iron hinges vibrating in the air as it settled. A mattress, thick and inviting, lay on the stationary springs.

"Duvet, quilt. All necessities of a good rest." The Faun spoke while moving around, picking up items seemingly at random. Cass laid the girl on the soft mattress. The springs did not groan under pressure. The fallen bed had not woken the Sabanese girl.

She placed a soft towel around the wet hair of the girl and smiled, stroking the hair, thick like Lilly's. The girl even slept like Lilly; on her back and head turned to the right. She raised a finger to her eye, catching a cold tear as it broke.

"Promise, I'll look after you." Cass whispered.

Trying not to make a sound, she stood, seeing other beds available, too occupied by the girl and her thoughts to notice the furnishings. Lucijan mouthed he would take the first watch. She shook her head and motioned two palms together and placed them on her head. They needed rest; they all did.

Lucijan and Taze shared one bed. The conscript motioned to the congested floor, Taze shrugged and patted her mattress. Jolam had his own cot. Before long, the three slept.

Cass tip-toed out of the room. Every step she took made a noise that forced a wince out of her. She entered the other room where the Faun scuttled about, on hands and knees, looking around and mumbled inaudible words. Sounded Sabanese, because of the guttural tone.

"Thank you…" Cass started. The Faun vaulted towards her. She braced for a fight, fists clenched, left arm drawn closer to the body. One hairy, dirt-stained finger raised and hovered close to her lips. The Faun raised another finger, which shook to her own cracked lips.

"Shh." The Faun whispered. Unblinking eyes glued open. Opal eyes ringing in bloodshot. The Faun jerked her head to the right and left, keeping her intense gaze.

"It can hear you. It's out there." She breathed, her breath as harsh as raw garlic, compared to everything else she tasted and smelt recently, Cass did not mind.

"What can? What's out there?" She matched the quietness of the Faun. Anything she could learn was better than not knowing.

"The shadows." The Faun removed her mucky finger. Wide eyes still on Cass. "The Verge."

"What is the Verge?" She replied, stepping forward. "Tell me, please."

The Faun stepped back, "Hmm, no. No, that's not right at all." The Faun breathed, looking away, tilted her head.

"The Verge, what do you know?" She asked, stepping forward filling the gap between them. She could know about the Mystics, about her daughter. Information she lacked and needed more of to fight for Lilly.

"Can't fight it. Fight yourself." The Faun replied in her whispering voice. She returned to her manic scuttles. Cass folded her arms, tiredness ached limbs and shoulders. Felt like an aurochs sat on it.

The Faun stopped rummaging through the disarray, to turn around and hold up an elaborate cup.

"Tea?" she squeaked. Her smile broad and eyebrows raised.

"I'll get some sleep." Cass forced a smile. She vacated the room, the Faun mumbled, shifting papers, cutlery rattled in its resonating clatter. The odd "shh" broke through the hubbub of overexcited activities.

She eased herself down next to the girl, who had her back turned, legs pulled up to her chest. Curling against the girl comforted her. She paused. She would panic in the morning, if it's morning. Stretching her feet down on the bed, she fought with tiredness to remove her valenki boots. Eyes relaxed, darkness swam in her vision.

Jerking awake, her legs kicked and arms spasmed. Eyes snapped open but closed on brightness encompassing around the room. Gaslamp odour, decaying papers and humid sweat clogged flaring nostrils. Silently, the Sabanese girl slept, cradled in her human ball. A natural smile warmed Cass's lips, relaxing under the girl's quiet posture.

Springs on nearby beds twanged. Lucijan sat up, eyes alert. Taze crept up, rubbing her left eye. Deep, throaty inhales chorused with whistling, squeaky exhales brought a head shake of remembrance: Jolam's sleeping state. Ralake, in Sabinate after the battle and even now the Faun could sleep through anything.

Her eyes tracked for a sign of time: hunting for a burning candle with marks or anything that would show how long time had passed. Running fingers through short, greasy hair, she realised the stillness of tight air caressed her arms. Cass flexed her toes, the freedom unnerving. Toes visible, valenki boots removed.

Clattering of iron and metal work resonated from the second opening, leading into the other chamber. Swinging her legs round, she stood up. Dizziness swam in her waking vision. Sitting back down, feeling the tightness of the breeches clothing her legs. Her tattered clothing lay rolled on a nearby chair.

Standing up, she headed to the other room. Warmth cushioned bare toes, floor clear of debris. A woollen rug, thick and dyed, lay from the bed to the room entrance. Wooden flooring, not varnished and left uncovered, lay beneath the mismatched carpets.

"Thank you." Cass spoke as she looked round the second entrance.

The Faun stopped and braced herself against the wall. Opal eyes wide behind dirtied bifocals, her mouth fell agape. She relaxed, placing a hand on her chest, where she still wore her tatty duster and nothing else.

"Scared me you did. Hungry?" The Faun smiled. Her tone of voice more conversational and open than last night, or was it last night? Her stomach growled.

"Starving. Could eat anything." Cass smiled back.

"Excellent." Exclaimed the Faun. She clapped her hands together in rapid succession. Moving to a nearby cooking pot suspended over a dying fire, she tossed another chipped log on the spitting embers. "Give time, give time." She mumbled.

"Thank you for helping us." Cass piped up, trying to start a conversation with the stranger.

A hand waved from the crouched, humming Faun, who prodded the fire with an iron black poker, making it crackle and spark.

"How long have you been here?" She enquired, inching forward.

The Faun stopped. Humming ceased. Fire crackled. Thinly veiled smoke drifted up beyond her vision. She stood up and turned around, eyes holding a look Taze could handle: a thousand-yard stare.

"I'm sorry." Cass sighed, softening her own eyes. "I'm Cass. You have been too kind to us." Her shoulders sagged.

"An." The Faun squeaked. She worded something. "Anrech."

"Anrech? You are Anrech?" She stepped forward. A lightness lifted in Cass's chest.

"Anrech..el." The Faun sighed and wiped her forehead. "Anrechel." She announced, holding her hands aloft like in praise.

"Anrechel." Cass smiled. "Thank you for helping us, Anrechel."

"Hunger! Cass hungry." Anrechel beamed, her eyes wide as she turned back to the spitting fire.

"That was smooth." A groggy, deep voice interjected. She looked over her shoulder, seeing Taze, who fumbled with her braid, curling it around her finger. A tight shirt threatened to render under strain of her solid physique. Taze's other hand lay deep in her breeches, tucked into the depth of a pocket. The black "M" and "Wimar" lay subdued on her face.

"She has helped us." Cass replied, nodding to Taze's left leg, who leaned on the entrance wall, head tilted. Her dark eyes gazed down, stretching out her leg to find a bandage wrapped round the breeches, cut above the knee.

"Least she's a woman, anybody else would have taken advantage." She folded her arms, pushing herself off the wall.

"Always thinking the worst?" She shook her head.

"Keeps me alive, Cass the Convict." Taze smiled and half-winked. A softness lined angular features, for the first time in four years, on Taze's hard-boned face.

"I'll sleep on the floor tomorrow then." Lucijan quipped in. Cass could not help hide her smile. The conscript looked older. Black rings marked his eyes, still holding a young light. He stood on the other side of the entrance, hands behind his back.

"You most certainly will, Lucky J." The murderer turned her head to the conscript. "But then again, you have saved me twice now. So, you can sleep tonight on the bed."

"The girl." Cass thought out loud.

"Asleep. I checked on her when you came in here." Lucijan replied. "What's for breakfast. Or is it breakfast?" The man cupped his hands together and rubbed them.

She faced the cooking pot. Anrechel stood stirring the contents with a wooden ladle mumbling to herself as waves of steam drifted up out of the polished-bronze pot. A rich, meaty smell left the boiling cauldron. Smelt better than Ralake slops.

"Now that's room service." Jolam grumbled. The Faun stretched and rubbed his chest while entering the room.

"I thought I could smell ugly." Taze shook her head and moved closer to Cass.

"Words, only words, Taze." Jolam replied, standing next to Lucijan.

She turned as Anrechel spoke something inaudible and stepped back from the cooking pot, bowing, holding her hands out.

"Is that a Faun thing?" Taze spoke, not facing Jolam.

"No, it's a considerate 'let the guests serve themselves first' thing. No wonder you're so uptight." Jolam's hooves echoed in the enclosed room as he approached the pot. Gaslamps burned-out, sickly-sweet taste of lowering gas levels flooded out by cooking food.

"Cassy, you're first." The Faun picked up a wooden bowl and served out a thick serving of warm looking broth. She looked around for remains or a carcass. This is a cave. Cass forward and gave Anrechel a thin-lipped smile. She glanced over at their host. No shaking hands, not a cannibal. Least not a Faun cannibal could be different if she ate humans.

"Gentleman, are you? Maybe you should try the grub first." Taze insisted.

"Don't worry, I'll certainly have my fill." Jolam inspected the broth.

Cass took the warm wooden bowl in two hands and looked over at Anrechel, whose hands wrapped against each other while chewing her cheek. Yellowed broth steamed in the bowl, smelling good. Her stomach agreed. Good enough not to ignore. Good enough not to care. Looked like chicken soup she had during the Purifier Rebellion.

Smiling, she took the spoon and swallowed a mouthful. A resurgence of warmth filled her throat, running down her parched mouth and entered her rumbling stomach, quelling its gurgling murmur. Cass opened her eyes, only noticing it now that they were closed. Tasted of fresh parsley, onion, mushroom and something meaty that could pass for pork.

"That's good. That's very good." A grin came to her tired, drawn face. Anrechel's face lit up, and she clapped, making a little hoot.

She took her time with the soup; the others devoured their own. Jolam lay spread out across the floor. Lucijan and Taze ate together and traded little conversation. They all acknowledged Anrechel, who stood there, hopping one foot to the other.

Bedsprings squeaked in the other room. Cass heard it through the dim crackling of the fire and the slurping of food, courteous of Jolam. She refilled her bowl and grabbed an extra wooden spoon, this one smaller than the others.

Taking a deep breath, she entered the makeshift sleeping room. The girl sat on the bed, shoulders hunched, hair dangled before her face. Towels lay on the mattress.

"Got some food. It's good, taste like pork." She held out the bowl as she walked, taking her time to approach the girl. She reminded her of docile deer of Cythean plains, this deer she could not afford to pounce away.

"It's nice, really nice." Easing herself towards the girl whose eyes never blinked beneath tangled hair.

"I'll place it here, don't worry." Placing the bowl of soup nearby on a chair that housed a pile of clothes.

"Love your hair, by the way." Her hand reached up, stroking black locks with the back of her hand, grazing knuckles through tatted strands of wet hair. "Like my daughters." Whispered Cass.

"Can't have soup in your hair." She tried to laugh. No response. She did not expect one.

She smiled, blank, reflective eyes of the Sabanese girl stared ahead. "Oh, with this hair, we could have it in a braid. A Sabinate braid. Not Cythean, no no, don't want ringlets in your hair. Your hair is too good for it." She stopped combing the hair, thinking about what she said. They were the words she said to Lilly before being arrested. Before the Arbiters of the Law broke into her home and took her away, her crime: stealing bread for a starving family.

The world blurred. She rubbed coldness off her eye and grinned. "There, all back and long too. We'll dry it off after you've had something to eat." She took the filled, steaming wooden, warm bowl and cradled it in her lap.

"Now, where are my manners? I'm Cass." She raised the spoon to the girl's lips. She did not blink. Did not acknowledge the spoon. Even her breathing remained silent. She tilted the spoon, pouring the liquid broth into the girl's lips. With bated breath, the girl gulping the food. "Mm, warm yeah? It's lovely."

"I'm Cass, real name is Cassidy but don't tell anyone." She winked and brought another spoonful of broth to the girl's lips.

"I wish." She stopped. A thousand things she could say, and it would not be right. "You know when you watch a moonrise above the forest? When the entire world is at peace? Where a taluko chirps with a soft call? When the wind sighs and barely reaches a whisper? I wish I could give you that. Peace."

She continued to the feed the mute girl. "I'm sorry."

Cass shook her head. Only solid matters of the broth covered by the remaining, warm, glowing liquid. "You don't understand me, but I promise you on my daughter's life I will protect you, so long as I live."

Standing up, she placed the bowl on the chair, leaving the spoon behind. Crouching before the girl and looked up at the blank gaze painted on her face. Like one of her daughters' porcelain dolls, unmoving, emotionless.

"We'll be in the next room." She placed a hand over the girl's palms, linked in her lap.

"I'll always be next to you, I promise." Squeezing hands with each word spoken. Standing up, she turned around, a shake rippling through shoulders. Had to hold it together, for her sake.

Wooden spoon scraped the bowl. A diminutive slurp of food followed. She stopped, daring to turn around. She smiled on hearing the slurps of broth, the little squeaking noise of swallowing food by a child wanting to be quiet.

Sighing, her head lifted, and she walked towards the entrance to the next room.

"Nin." The girl's voice penetrated Cass's heart.

She turned, mouth open. The girl's eyes met her own. Bowl in hands.

"Ninsar." The girl stammered. Cass nodded, smiling. "Ninsar." The girl spoke in the accent of the Sabanese.

Vincentas

Chapter XII

Heat flickered in his face. Taste of raw, roasting flesh gagged his throat. A distorted, manic face contorted its wide mouth in slow, animated movements. White teeth shouted without sound, making no noise as they closed on each other between plea-ridden, petrified words. Same face that would nod, lose itself in a local paper or evaluate the surplus of materials.

Sound smashed his hearing, boiled around numb ears rising through quietness. Sobbing thundered with each gasping inhale and shaking breath.

If only he could escape now, with a soft kite shaped like a Roc or a bluebird of the Thousand Isles. His sister laughing at his failed attempts to make the kite soar. She always laughed while her kite flew so high they dared to skim white clouds. She could do nothing wrong and there was no jealousy about it. There was never jealousy.

Cries of sobbing a chorus, their macabre hymn the tune of mourning. He moved back. Vincentas observed himself: boiled anger; eyes wreathed in resentfulness; teeth consumed with bitterness. He struck himself, bruised, with closed fists and open stinging palms. Each connection beat a memory of his wife into his mind. Evalyn. Images of her crumpled and broke like a mirror, the fists of himself smashing them into shards.

A final strike sent him sprawling. The ground did not uppercut ribs, or flailing legs. He fell. No stopping, no end. No wind whipped through stale air. He tasted wood, the aroma of carpenters. The carpenters in Konniak always smelt of rotting wood.

He pushed himself up on tired limbs, staring down at a wooden board, varnished and smooth. Rain tickled his neck. He looked up at distant faces peering down. Shadowed figures stood above the hole he occupied. Standing up, he looked down. The holes end consumed by a carved box. Long enough for a person to lie in. Someone laid inside.

Rain picked up. Soiled clothing stuck to him. Hair peeled down his face. The hole filling with dirtied water. He grabbed at the earth that trapped him, squelching mud fell apart in his hands. Stench of soil clogged burning lungs, soggy dirt festooned through eager fingers built with escape and smudged his palms. Water rose, covering soaked thighs. Soon his waist. Then his pounding chest. His tilted, gasping lips submerged under freezing water.

A hand grasped his leg…

Vincentas bolted up right. Colour exploded, margining with a fadedness blurring into darkness and creeping shadows. Taste of leather threatened to gag him, rough coarseness of a gloved hand covered trembling lips. His back stiffened.

"Ssh. Going to remove my hand. Relax, relax." Violet's breath brushed his ear. She lay underneath him, holding him around the waist with her other hand. Glove moved free of his face. Vincentas fought to regain focus and cease trembling pulses, cursing weakened body.

Coldness clamped around aching legs. Pushing off the greatcoat acting like a makeshift cover, he peered at his legs. They were dry. At least he had not soiled himself – it would not be the first time from a nightmare.

"Who's Evalyn?" Violet questioned. His back tensed. Sweating, shaking hand brushed through thinning, greasy hair. A deluge of perspiration drenched a trembling palm from unwashed locks that grew a little too long for his liking. Tasted stale.

"My wife." He whispered. Violet angled her legs and sat beside him, half-cast in lilac shadow. Thick purple light bruised her features and exposed neckline.

"No. A librarian and married?" Her eyes that large he thought they would fall out of her head.

"Not implausible." His eyes meet hers. Reflective amber that held their own story but shone with a compassion he had not seen since his younger years. Pale skin glowed with a blue twinge where the loose blouse could not cover the neckline. He looked away.

"I rarely speak of her." Vincentas brought his legs up. Joints numbed with cramp. They needed a rest, begged for rest, ached for rest.

"If she means that much to you." Her hand gripped his shoulder. "You should talk about it."

"Nothing much to say." He looked around, avoiding Violet. They occupied a room within a terraced house. Sparsely furnished area, unless Violet had emptied it.

Floating specks of dust lifted under beams of magenta light lancing through barred square windows.

"I'm not much of a listener, but I can help." The hand on his shoulder squeezed.

"I judged her." He faced Violet. She straightened up, eyes narrowed on the Combatant's pale face.

"You condemned her to death?" Her words penetrated his chest worse than any blade cut he had endured in his professional life. Her eyes held condemnation that a judge would hold.

"Joined the Inquisition after the closure of the library. Ironic, how the Inquirer Council shut down libraries in Doctrine Article two hundred and eight. As an Entrant, condemned her for Mysticism. The signs were there, all there." He shook his head, finding it easier to talk now than ever before. It did not matter anymore. They were not leaving Riemkeler alive.

"Been on duty. Anything to report?" Vincentas found his voice. Violet moved away.

"Close to the academy. It keeps moving, today its closer." Floorboards creaked in her motion. He watched her stand before the barred window, casting shadows that covered him, her silhouette blocked light threatening to spill purple into the room.

"Moving? How?" She looked down at him, arms crossed, fingers gripping and tightening at her biceps, never holding on. She continued to search for a holding with agile, determined fingers.

"Mysticism. Strange sciences beyond me. My eyesight?" Violet offered, moving forward to kneel beside him.

"So long as it's not floating." Vincentas spat.

"I've been a Combatant for six years. I've killed Afflicted, saw Mystics die. But this." Violet caught Vincentas's eyes with her gaze. He could not look away. "But this. It's not real. How can you fight it?"

"By not thinking." Regurgitated words spoken by Hadramiel and Athgeric. He sat up, the obsidian hilt nearby. His mind straightened like the rapier in its sheath. The academy held something, and he would find it.

"Six years I've been hearing that damned saying. It never stops them. Nothing stops them. Inquisition has been fighting them for over three hundred years." The Combatant folded her arms. He looked at her. Unwavering eyes stared back.

"For three hundred years, we'll continue fighting." Vincentas declared. Violet leaned back, brows knitted together. Her mouth opened to speak, but she closed it.

"This won't end overnight. It's not a civil war, not a rebellion. Not a continental war." Hadramiel's words spilled out of his mouth.

"Then let's get fighting." Violet sighed. Her voice pulled places within Vincentas he did not know he possessed. Places the death of Evalyn had burned out of him. Silence grew, only calm breaths of Violet echoed in his hearing.

Finally, someone to hear him speak. She would listen, Violet would always listen, at least she looked like she was listening. She moved closer, keeping his voice lower and to themselves. They whispered like lovers would. He talked about everything and nothing and by the end, both of their gurgling stomachs told them to stop.

"Hadramiel found me in Konniak. I don't know what he saw, I don't see it, but he asked me to join him. A chance to start afresh, clean slate, so to speak." Vincentas rubbed his throat, raw to the touch. Could not believe he talked that long and freely.

Violet's face so close he could see every line of her features. "You've waited a long time for that." She breathed. He did not realise how many freckles she had across her face until now.

"Guess I was waiting for the right person to invite me to." It sounded stupid, but nothing could be closer to the truth.

"Eight years I've known you, Vin." Vincentas skin leapt. Fingers snatched his handbow. He turned, Fleur buried in black shadow, slumped against a wall. "Not once you mentioned anything of your past. Shame, shame, shame."

"Been awake long. You could have let us know." He holstered the handbow and headed over to Fleur. She smelt worse.

Fleur half-raised her hands. "Relax, Inquisitor. Relax. I'll keep your librarian past a secret." She wiped her forehead, bandaged, and stained crimson, with the back of a calloused hand. Fleur moved better now, but not her agile self. Swelling lessened across her face, bruising gave her a rotting complexion.

"Nice tattoos. Where did you get them?" Violet flanked him. Fleur rolled her head to face Vincentas. Her mask a burning sapphire in the room, a tight, sleeveless blouse clothed her body. She always looked at her best and knew what to wear for her figure.

"He's the Inquisitor, not you. Army, during the Purifier Rebellion." Fleur's eyes never left Vincentas, even the eye beneath the bronze mask fixed on him. She pushed herself to stand, groaning while doing so.

"We need to get going. Sooner we finish this, I can hit the bars. I need it." Fleur dressed as swift as she could, wincing when feeding arms through the dovetail black coat and lacing black boots.

"We should have something to eat and check your bandages." Vincentas instructed. Under the constant glare of lilac light, they ate in silence. Lavender bordering on blue, moist pink and a bruising purple which was more prominent than the others filtered through the room.

"Never thought I'd thank Fauns for easing pain." Fleur cracked a laugh on changing her bandages. Brown, dried brittle Faunleaf applied to cut skin leaked, wafting a sour stench.

"You can thank Arno when you see him next." Vincentas bandaged his Combatant's head, arms and left leg.

"Inquisitor." Violet hissed. The Combatant stood before the window. He crossed the room and peered down at where she pointed.

A white figure skipped down the cobbled road. Vincentas lowered and stared. Violet moved to his side. She caught her breath. Hands gripped the rough, marked windowsill.

"It's her." Violet gasped. He dared not believe it.

A convulsion rocked the house. Debris clattered to the ground. The world shook, blurring, like living in Konniak during one of its tremors.

Vincentas looked up. Cracked webs broke across plastered ceiling. Grasping Fleur, he ran for the staircase, shouting. "This building is about to collapse." Stairs creaked and buckled to his left. Reaching the door, he pulled it open and bundled Fleur outside.

Cobbles vibrated underfoot, spreading his arms out to steady himself. Stomach churned with shaking mobility. Closing eyes helped. Nothing stopped the rumbling of the streets, crushed timbers falling and tiles screeching as they crashed into alleys.

"We have to move." A voice shouted over the groaning world. Peeling his eyes open, Violet started moving through the pulsating street, helping Fleur.

Buildings collapsed, dust rose in triumph over fallen wreckage. Purple silhouetted structures lay on the horizon. The entire world shook and moved as one, like the quakes southern Cythea experienced on a weekly occurrence or the seasonal quakes in Konniak.

This was different.

Violet ran ahead, pulling Fleur down the road as she paced on, arm linked around the Combatant. Tripping over raised cobbles, Vincentas steadied himself while catching up. Metallic stench uppercut flaring nostrils, the quake hammered his ears rattling his rapid pounding heart.

Rounding a corner, they stopped and gathered their breaths. Hard, long, laborious breaths tore aching lungs, hot air sucked deep within. Vibrations vanished as quick as they started. Vincentas looked up, hot air compressed against his burning scalp, despite the cockel hat crowning him.

"The academy. It's not far. Let's go." Violet panted and walked on, leaving Fleur wheezing on the street corner.

Tall, spired and distant. The academy looked as far away as ever before, despite being uncharacteristically central in Riemkeler. More houses hung on the bruised horizon. His eyes searched the ground. No red vines at least. Circling an arm around Fleur, they walked behind Violet.

Countless dwellings, structures and shacks lay in blackness. Not even the brightest flame could give them colour, a void of perpetual darkness. Only the academy, a beacon of light, lay in any other spectrum. Lavender washed the world, pinks swirled in the thunderous, but silent, sky. A groan, metallic and harsh, reverberated down Vincentas's spine. It quivered through his teeth.

"Streets look deserted." Violet whispered, her loaded repeater leading the way. Eyes flashed down the vacant street, more like Fleur's captive may lurk in the depths.

Black iron wrought fences started at random and finished inexplicably on roofs, walls, and doorways. Spikes lanced through broken cobbled roads, metal weeds stabbing up smashed street tiles. Humidity grew, clenched around like a dry throat.

Entering another street, the same cobbled roads shadowed by two-tier houses formed a clear, barren road. Smashed windows shared no light. Standing Gaslamps shed no light. Nothing floated, but distant shouts, frantic pleas and wailings echoed around each corner. Fleur walked unaided, showing her strength and unbridled stubbornness.

A high-pitched laugh stopped Vincentas dead in his tracks. His skin ignited. The Mystic. Something else. A hand moved to his obsidian hilt.

Wind whipped above him. He looked up, swaying threads of black webs stretching across rooftop to rooftop filling his shaking vision. Bunting. Bunting of the festival of market day. Bunting from the nightmare on the airship. They waved again but returned to limply hang.

"Run." A piercing, accented shout warned around them. Vincentas ducked.

"Can't be." Fleur winced in pain.

"Move." Violet shouted, turning back. Something fell from the tangled shadow shrouded bunting. A wide-brimmed hat spun on its own weight, clapping with the cobbles. It twisted before lying flat.

"Dehqan. Dehqan." Fleur's pained voice cut deep into Vincentas's gut.

"Run." A Sabanese voice called out. More of a gargled plea. He strained his eyes to peer down the darkened street. A gaping maw of blackness that had no end stared back. Something broke through it.

In mid-air. Face. Jacket. Arms. Dangling arms. Upside down. Vincetnas's hands clenched into fists.

"No." Violet clutched Vincentas's arm as he started walking towards it.

Dehqan came into view. Upside down. Arms hanging. Face etched in strain. Legs in the maw of blackness.

He started shaking his head, unable to blink. Unable to move. Dehqan's waist lost within black, bristling hair. A tangled mass of thorns, legs, and tendrils slithered and crawled forward. It swarmed his vision. It had to be a wicked dream, a cruel hallucination. His mind clung on. He stared into the abyss that threatened to engulf him.

Fleur's raging scream yanked Vincentas from his frozen state. Multiple bone-breaking crunches snapped throughout the street. Dehqan fell to the cobbles, thudding on sleek stones. His body slapped, lifeless, and stayed still. Warm blood sprayed his face.

"More. More." laughed the shrilling voice, sounding as grotesque as nails down a blackboard. Unfurling, the creature spun itself across the width of the street, tendril and leg lost in shadows, hooking onto walls, high roofs and breaking through windows. Levelling where it ate Dehqan to face Vincentas, a rotating maw of crimson slush bloomed outward like a fly-trap readying to devour.

"We have to go." Violet's words stormed in his ears. She uprooted him and moved, breaking his uninvited gaze from something that should not exist. Something that no Mystic could make. Something no Mystic could ever become.

"On your feet. On your feet." Violet barked at Fleur. Half dragging her across the cobbles.

"I'll slow you down. Go." Fleur notched her bow, unleashing a quick arrow. Hollow twang whistled, followed by a fleshy thud. Deep, reverberating chuckle replied to Fleur's assault.

"Need you. Get to the academy." He shook Fleur, clawing at her clothing to pull her along.

"Three's a crowd. Besides, I don't want to share her with you, Vin." Fleur let loose three more arrows.

"More. My children. My children." A coldness clawed down Vincentas's spine.

Scuttling rattled on cobbles. He snapped around; blurred images trickled under the black void of the creature. Along the walls. Hanging from bunting and lowering themselves. They swarmed, they descended on them.

"Leave her." Violet shouted and ran. Vincentas gave Fleur one last look. He sped after Violet. Thundering heartbeat pounded within, threatening to burst a racked chest.

Same purple washed cobble stones rattled underfoot. Same enclosed city grew smaller and narrower with each step taken away from Fleur. Different tears blurred his eyes as he ran faster and faster away into the tangled, laughing, tormenting streets of Riemkeler.

Cass

Chapter XII

Crackling fire warmed Cass in comfort. Roasting meat spat on a sizzling spit; nose flared with hunger. Best part of being in the cave, in the presumed miners' lodge deep underground, was mealtime. She stood facing the bookshelf brimming with folded papyrus; rolled yellow papers; thick tomes of large, leather-bound books and scrolls unfurled. She lacked education to read, unlike Lucijan, who picked at the shelves time to time.

She slept four times in isolated tranquillity. Cass rubbed her fingers across her bare stomach. Rough, calloused tips fleeted over taunt muscle of her abdomen. Scars of child giving marked toned skin. Standing, unwashed mirror allowed eyes to study herself. Welcomed weight came back to her frame. Short edges of hair crowned temples and scalp. She combed her hair back, sleeking it away off a sticky, unwashed forehead. She preferred the slick-back look; easier to manage.

Hearing boots resonate in the caved walls, Cass buttoned up her linen shirt provided by Anrechel, since her army issued shirt was beyond repair; the smell matched its soiled nature, glad to be rid of it. At least now she tasted clean.

"Got to hand it to that Faun. She cooks a fine meal." Taze's dry voice announced her entrance. Taze walked into the room, hands deep in pockets of tight-fitting breeches. Her own shirt open. Gaslamps' glow and spitting fire added a healthy glow on her angular face, darkening her naturally tanned complexion. Despite the hardened features, they seemed soft, for now.

"You can say that again. Despite the food coming from cans." She nudged an opened tin near the fire-pit, scrape of her boot sending a metallic shiver through the air.

"Better than prison slops." The murderers' face cut a half-smile, creasing the burnt "M" and the other bruising lines of prison tattoos on her face, their purple tinge flared under warm light.

"Can't wait to have decent food again." Taze rasped, sounded like her voice had softened. Even throughout the past few days, the murderer sounded less like an angry version of herself.

"And what would you call decent food?" Cass smiled back, first time she had spoken about nothing in a while, different and better than dwelling on the past few days.

"Anything not from a can, or slops from prison." She ceased before the fire. Broad hands upon hips, linen sleeves rolled to elbows allowing taunt, defined muscles to flex freely. Good physique, and sculptured from eating canned food.

"Anything not from a can, or slops from prison." Cass toasted, raising a cup of steaming tea.

"Here, here." Taze raised a hand, "I reckon that meat's done."

Cass settled down and placed the spitting meat, brown in the flaring light, on a wooden plate and dished out boiling vegetables out of a cooking pot. She handed a plate to Taze, who nodded and took it with one hand.

"Can't beat a bit of aurochs." The murderer inhaled the wafting steam. Cass stared at her own wooden plate. Vegetables swimming with meat juices made her stomach grumble. She had not eaten this well since the ending of the Rebellion. She would eat together with Lilly, she promised.

"You've got that look in your eye." The murderer mumbled through a mouthful of food. She looked up. Taze sat cross-legged on the opposite side of the fire. A mirror image of each other, eating away.

"What look?" Cass remarked.

"This one." Taze made a frown and smiled, eyebrows lifting again, screwing up "Wilmar" on her tattooed forehead. "It's your thinking face. Seen no one frown when they think before."

"It's been four days, well, it's been four sleeps." Cass quietened her voice, dwelling on words of Anrechel, the fearful Faun's words of "they are listening" flooding back into her mind.

Taze ate slowly, not chomping her food anymore. Black, unblinking eyes peered through the fire onto Cass, the weight and focus of those eyes growing heavy within. She could not look away.

"Where's that thing that killed Grodol? Where did this Faun come from? Is this place real or like the other places we've seen? Are we laying down on the battlefield thinking before we die, eventually…" Cass rattled.

"Enough." Taze snapped, pointing her fork at her. "Enough." She swallowed.

"We have to face what's going on." She stared, eye to eye, with Taze. Her own voice hardening. Same naïve courage in the feeding halls on Ralake Island.

"We do." The murderer admitted, breaking the stare and continued eating. "But not when we're eating."

Cass sat in silence and ate. Fire crackled, rays of light flickered across walls. They shared another can of food, meat darker and brown in texture. Smelt raw, bloody. Tasted of copper, the same copper she smelt in Ralake, same coppery smell from the battlefield and the fleshy monster that killed Grodol.

Taze burped. "Sign of a good meal." She placed the plate down before the fire. Her eyes lifting.

"So, what's on your mind, Cass?" The murderer asked.

"Need to find Lilly." Her back straightened. "I'm going to thank Anrechel when she gets back and leave afterwards." The Faun was not in the cave when she awoke.

Taze nodded, her shoulders sloped. Dark eyes gleaming before rising steam off the boiling vegetables, cooking in grease and fat of the previous tin contents.

"It's been a nightmare these past days. What we've seen." She shook her head. "No wonder there's more people in the asylum than before." She fed her fingers through her hair, felt thicker than before.

"I have to find Lilly." Cass stared at Taze. Her stomach churned, mentioning her daughter's name out loud to someone she did not fully know. "It's the only thing right now that could stop it."

"That's one way to get a death sentence, Cass." Taze drew her fingers across shaved hair and skirted back to the slicked hair on her scalp. She rolled her head side-to-side, cracking a broad neck.

"However," the murderer sighed, tapping her cheek and then her forehead, at the brandishing of her conviction. "They have branded me for murder; my sentence isn't death."

Cass half smiled and nodded. "I understand that, Taze. The less people who come with me, the better."

"Fewer." Taze sighed, placing her hands behind her head, legs extended.

"What will you do?" Cass asked.

"Could settle down in Orschal. Find myself a decent man and grow old listening to grandkids bicker about wanting more than what I can give them." Taze's voice strained during the stretch but returned to normal afterwards.

Cass laughed. "You liar."

"How dare you, Cass, how dare you." She tutted and winked at her. "How did you know I was lying?" She punctuated every syllable. A wolfish grin carved across her angular, hard face.

"You're not the settling down type." She replied.

"In my past I was." Taze's features relaxed. Black eyes staring in the distance, or maybe the past. Silence grew between them, broken only by the interspersed crackles of coughing fire.

"That smells like some good grub." Jolam announced at the door. Cass flinched. Taze snapped her head to the right, peering over her shoulder. The braid flickered outwards like a whip before falling at her turned face.

"It is good grub and you better have some before we finish it." The murderer rasped.

"Back to being Taze the toughy, eh?" Jolam swanned into the room and flexed his muscles. "I'm Taze. Hear me roar."

Cass bit her lip and looked ahead. If looks would kill, Jolam would have died.

"I know what smells better than aurochs," Taze whispered. "Roasting Faun."

"Least you didn't say goat this time." Jolam shrugged. He trotted beside Cass and sat down, crossing his legs. Picking up a plate, he spooned food onto a plate.

"We've been through a lot now. Lakes of blood. An insane cult up there. Massive bloating monstery things. And the cold weather." The Faun started eating, munching succulent meat and vegetable soup together in his furry jaw. "Right now, all that matters is food."

"Lost my reputation because of a ravenous Faun." Taze shook her head and raised her arms up, showing the world her palms. "What am I to do?"

"Next, you'll be giving me hugs." Lucijan announced with a grin so vibrant nothing could swipe it from his youthful face. Cass smiled and lowered her head, hiding the brewing chuckle.

"Now don't you start, don't start." Taze's voice cracked with her own laugh. She looked up. Lucijan and Ninsar sat by the fire, Ninsar nearest to Cass, who sat with her legs stretched to the side. She smiled at the Sabanese girl, who helped herself to food.

"So, what's the conversation today? How to correctly plant hanging Carveli? How to grill a Roc egg? Or not to decorate a mining lodge?" Jolam chewed his food.

"Or how to learn manners while eating?" Taze tapped her chin with each word. The Faun held his hand up and continued eating. Ninsar smiled. Cass's heart lifted. Innocence deserved better.

"We've been here too long. I need to find Lilly." Silence grew between the eaters.

"Hmm." Jolam acknowledged and licked his plate clean. He dabbed his chin with his own handkerchief. "Well, I'm not up for going back to the country that put me in irons and Orschal is too cold. Besides, if I didn't go with you, you'd get lost." The Faun winked at Cass.

"We'll go together." She placed a hand on Ninsar's shoulder. The girl faced her as she ate, small cheeks swelling up with food like a chipmunk. Just like Lilly. Cass smiled.

"They conscripted me in the army and didn't want to fight. Don't want to fight. But reckon this is worth fighting for." Lucijan spoke up.

"Don't owe you anything, Cass the convict." Taze's voice cut through the crackling fire, who rocked, slowly, as her hands lay clasped on raised knees.

"Very true. You came this far, and we wouldn't have made it without you." She admitted.

"Noble of you." Taze ceased her rocking, keeping her gaze, not reading the angular features, despite every curve and line highlighted with Gaslamps and spitting fire.

"I'll say my goodbyes to Anrechel, then we'll go." Cass broke the brewing silence. The others pushed themselves to their feet, groaning and stretching themselves out. Only Taze remained, staring at the fire.

"I didn't say I'd leave you alone." Taze's voice raised up, as they filed away from the ebbing fire towards the other room. Cass turned, the murderer still sitting but peering up at her.

"You've got us this far, by accidental fortune or sheer luck, but you have. So, I can return the favour and get you to your daughter. Besides, Karwen is with those cult people, that Armande is with the cult, Armande has your daughter. So long as Karwen breathes, I'm with you." Taze finished.

Cass did not know whether to hug or laugh manically. The urge to embrace Taze swelled within her chest, but she returned a warm, genuine smile.

Venturing back into the shared area that lingered with a damp, humid smell of unwashed bodies compared to the bookish, mothball smell it had before. Her nose wrinkled, while she fumbled with the haversack that Jolam strapped to his back. Lucijan reloaded his repeater, checking the bandoliers available.

"How many rounds?" Cass enquired.

"Let's hope we don't encounter a Primal pack." The click and lock of the repeater echoed. Bolts snapped into place. "We have two bandoliers full. One half full. Close to two hundred and seventy rounds, at least."

"Make them count. If we have to." Her voice hardened.

Tying boot laces with steady hands, she threw on her half-cut duster jacket, borrowed from Anrechel. Stench of uncleanliness filled her but fit better than the Sabanese woollen coat she possessed. Cass glanced at herself in a dusty glass bowl. Not the picture of a Cythean convict, more like a rogue trader.

"What's that?" Jolam spat in panic. She held out her hand for silence and strained her ears, heart pounding in her chest.

"It's outside." Lucijan whispered. Muffled speech grew louder, high pitched and argumentative.

"Lucijan the door. Taze secure in here with Jolam." She cleared the distance between the bed and the door.

"It's outside." She warned, flashing an arm to her side and backed away. The soldier followed. Noise grew louder, clearer. It sounded like two or three people. They can hear. They're out there, she remembered, her brows knitted together.

The door swung open. It cracked on the wall and groaned on wheezing hinges. Two people, grappling, emerged from the darkness. Anrechel held a woman wearing a tattered Cythean uniform. They staggered into the room.

"I'm not going back, back, back. Not going back." The Faun shouted. Her voice trailing to a soft mewling. Large, brown, bloodshot eyes clogged in tears.

"I don't know what you're talking about, let me go." Pleaded a voice that Cass swore was… the Cythean soldier reared back. Black hair stuck on a pale face, cheeks welling with intakes of breath. A sharpened hawk nose protruded between lank hair.

"Karwen." Cass breathed. Her stomach sank deeper than she could think possible.

"What the." Jolam exclaimed.

"Easy," she snapped, easing out two hands, keeping her eyes fixed on Karwen. "Back down." She barked. Silence descended on the room. Ears flooded with a rapid heartbeat. Fire crackled. Karwen and Anrechel breathed rapidly. Cass swore she heard whimpering of a girl.

"Not going back. She's one of many, many, many. Not going back." Anrechel looked at Cass, her face resolute. Hard. Determined.

"Lucijan, close the door. Taze, Taze lower the repeater." Never breaking her gaze from Karwen. Karwen. *One of many. Not going back*. Her eyebrows creased in thought.

"She's got your daughter, Cassy. Let's talk to her, army style." Taze rasped.

"Where did you find her?" She looked at Anrechel, her voice steady.

"She's one of many. Many. Many." The Faun replied, voice quietening.

"LOOK!" The Faun screamed. Cass flinched, flexing her arms. Anrechel forced Karwen's arm out. "The marks. Like mine. Mine."

Black marks covered Karwen's pale skin. Writing, or something. Marks she could not understand. She hated her lack of education. Did not look like Cythean language tattooed in black along Karwen's exposed arm. It was angular, sharp, like math drawings Merrick would make when designing his ship.

Anrechel lurched forward, stumbling. Cass caught the yelping Faun and held her close. Snapping her vision on Karwen, who stood, head up, repeaters aimed at her neck.

The Faun buried her head into Cass, like a child frightened of strangers. "Mine. Mine." The Faun mumbled. She looked down to see Faunish arms unclothed. Black markings like Karwen's, shaped like Karwen's, alive as Karwen's etched over the Fauns arms.

"She's one of many." Cass whispered, mouthing each syllable. Eyes bore into Karwen, or whatever she looked at. "I killed you on the battlefield."

"She's crazy. You going to believe a crazed Faun over me?" The convict laughed. Her arms poised half raised, elbows at the hips, recoiling her fingers. She never did that before.

"Might be nutty as squirrel shit, but she's good in my books compared to you." Taze rasped, poking Karwen's angular cheek with the nuzzle of the repeater.

"Anrechel might be a recluse, but I'd trust her over you." Cass shot back. "You call her crazy, but you've got black marks on your arms. I don't. Neither does Taze, Jolam or Lucijan."

"She must have got them in the same place as me." Karwen answered, her voice strained, veins bulged at her throat.

"One of many, many. Not going back, back." Anrechel mewled into Cass's chest, the Faun's calming hands held onto her linen shirt. She half-hugged the distressed woman.

"Same place as you? You were in Ralake, nobody had those symbols there." Jolam enquired.

"Redemption." Karwen mouthed.

"Bah, it's a myth." Jolam laughed.

"Karwen." Cass threatened. The hawkish features stared back. "I've killed you once. I'll do it again. Don't lie to me."

"It's the truth, Cass. I was in Redemption before moving into Ralake." Karwen shook, visibly. Isolated tears traced down her cheek.

"Stop lying!" Cass screamed. Her skin threatened to leap off her body. Face vibrated. Words echoed. Resonating in ringing ears. "Stop lying." She growled, emphasising every syllable.

"It's the truth." Karwen's shoulders racked.

"It can't be." She whispered. "Because I captured Purifiers, and we didn't send them to Redemption. We killed them." Silence cut into her. She felt their eyes too, even though their repeaters aimed at Karwen.

"What's Redemption, Cass?" Taze asked.

"A myth." Taking a deep breath and rubbing sweat from her face. "The Purifiers made up a jail for the rebellion. It scared people. Turn people against the Cythean government and for moral support of the Purifiers. But it was a lie, a hoax." Her body relaxed. Taking several deep breaths, keeping her eyes on Karwen. Shaking had ceased through her legs. Quivering stopped in her stomach.

"How do you have these marks?" Cass looked at Karwen.

"All the same, the same. One of many, many. From the metal world." Anrechel breathed onto her body, she patted the Fauns back, she maybe crazed but there was something she knew that nobody else could explain.

"Metal world, see? Factories. In Redemption." Karwen argued.

"Shut up." Jolam stabbed Karwen's gut with the repeater.

"Metal world, tell me, what metal world?" Cass cooed Anrechel, rubbing the small of her back, easing her, soothing her. Whatever she knew, it would help them.

The Faun's head eased up, eyes closed. Quivering lips parted. Watery, reflective eyes opened, a flicker of light illuminating opal pupils.

"It's not here." The Faun whispered. Her hand retreated from the Faun's back, coming around and holding the head of the Faun, massaging the damp, greasy scalp.

"Where is the metal world?" Cass tried to mimic the quietness of Anrechel, to match her subdued, serene tone.

"It's not here." Anrechel spoke up, eyes opening further. "It's not anywhere." A slow shiver clawed down her back. Cass looked at Karwen, but kept her soothing hands on the Faun's face.

"The metal world. What is it?" She demanded.

"Factories. Redemption. It's all I know, I swear it." Karwen's watery eyes fixed on her.

"An image she sees, but does not live, live. Live." Anrechel's monotone voice echoed around the enclosed cave.

"A Mystic." Lucijan shouldered his repeater, the conviction in his voice damning. Scraping of feet peeled throughout the room. Wooden beams creaked. Shapes crept back from Karwen. She dared flick her eyes around, noticing Taze and Jolam had backed away. Ninsar leaned into Cass's side, brushing up against her leg and hip. The girl's arm circled around her lower back.

"I'm not a Mystic, you got to believe me." Karwen laughed.

"I don't know what to believe, but I don't believe you." Cass held onto Ninsar.

She took Jolam's repeater, Anrechel shuffled behind her. Ninsar's head turned, the girl looking behind, which was good. She did not have to see this. The repeater cocked. The echo thundered through Cass louder than her heartbeat.

"Where have you been? Since we saw you last?" Taze jabbed her repeater under the chin of Karwen, forcing the convict to stand on tiptoes, but still stood shorter than the murderer.

"In the cave. With the Stone Sisters." Her head jerked towards the door, keeping her eyes on Cass. "I remember the ladder that disappeared, which you all climbed down. Then chaos. I kept going in the darkness, looking for any sign of you, was wrong about going with them, but kept walking, it seemed for days. I came across the shaft that would lead me out, but they blocked it with debris and boarded up, so I came back into the mine to look for dynamite to blast my way out. Then she found me. Kidnapped me." Karwen nodded to Anrechel.

"Fine speech." Jolam muttered.

"Very much rehearsed." Added Taze.

"Believe what you want, but it's the truth." She sighed and tilted her head up. "You can't kill me Cass, I'm your friend."

"The only friend I have is my daughter." She levelled the repeater, growing heavy in her hands, at Karwen; it shook her biceps with its weight. She's one of many. Cass racked her mind to think through the riddles.

"She's not yours to kill, Cass." Taze stepped between them. She lowered her repeater. "The one who killed Wilmar had the same marks as Karwen, and that Faun. This, this is justice."

"It's changing." Karwen lamented.

Her skin leapt at Jolam's blurting out. Swiftly, she turned. Cave walls bled. Books leaked black, shiny goo.

Veins of the earth cracking into metal grids, wooden blanks ascended through the rock-face. A living pulse shook her vision. A hand reached out to steady her. Sickness welled in trembling stomach.

"On me." Cass shouted. Her voice bubbling in the pulsating world.

"She's gone." Taze shouted. She turned to see Karwen's back vanish behind concrete wall. As if she walked right through it.

Cass snatched onto murmuring Ninsar, hugging her with two hands and dropping the repeater. Keeping her safe would distract churning guts threatening sickness. Pulsating ebbed and died. The wall stood in silence, which crept away, replaced by hollow, distant ringing and crackles of unseen thunder.

"No, it can't be." Jolam gasped. Cass peered around.

Dim, dying Gaslamps hung on blackened posts. Concrete scorched walls. Corroded iron works formed fence-like pathways. Steam vapours poured into the world, hazing vision with a thick, grey gas. A street of a city where no sunlight could reach.

"Konniak." Cass breathed, tightening her hold on Ninsar, burying her into her body. Shielding the girl. The city she grew up in, the city where Lilly was born. A city thousand miles away appeared around her from nothing.

Vincentas

Chapter XIII

The world could not stop shaking. Blinking did not help, closing tired eyes did not lessen the struggles of blurred reality. Gloved hands gripped a steady, resilient handbow. Its contraption more lethal than sense, locked bolt ready to answer.

Metallic ringing circled numbness, punctuating an already fleeting mind drifted to pleading rest. Repetitive tremors, a chorus of alloy crying, Dunright Hospital sounded better with its hysteria and manic preaching.

"No chance of rest here." Violet voiced plain thoughts. Eyes peeled open, drawing back on sticky eyelids and aching skin. She looked how he felt.

"How did we." Vincentas faced Violet. Her eyes had changed, everyone changes when exposed to Mysticism. Lines grew where youth lived. The Combatant lurked beneath crossed, drawn flesh. Stoic unblinking eyes stared back, repeater between raised legs, a ready finger poised on the trigger. Unwavering eyes rounding onto him.

"Ran." She sighed, stretching her legs out in creaking fabrics, boots grated off rubble. "Ran as fast as we could, for as long as we could. Until those things stopped following us."

Vincentas had no recollection of what happened, how they got here. Dehqan's body. Leaving Fleur was all he remembered. An Inquisitor leaving their retinue behind haunted waking thoughts. A meal he could not digest: cowardice gurgled in empty pits, filling him more than any canned food.

"Been here for two sleeps. Well, I've slept twice. You've slept sparingly." Her fluid words broke through. Metallic ringing ceased giving Violet's words clarity. Or maybe he had grown used to it. He could block out the torture to pass as mundane.

"Anywhere near the academy?" Vincentas asked, not looking at Violet, who stood. Riemkeler's jewel housed what they needed. It had to. Athgeric would not dive into insanity over nothing.

"Closer than you think. Should look at the view." Her head lowered. Wind brushed untidied hair. She did not seem to mind. Pushing himself up, legs burning with pins and needles, price of sitting too long, age catching up. Breathing caught unawares, warm and thin, like the deserts of Kheda Ishan.

Standing beside Violet, the world opened before him in a Mystic dwelling, ready to devour any hope lurking within.

Riemkeler broke.

Structures lay suspended in air, defining gravity. Open, endless craters scattered across the circular city.

Houses and roads linked, chains of improbability joining them as one forming a web of concrete, buildings and floating flotilla of Riemkeler's ruins. At its centre, dominant and growing, the academy.

Winged creatures flew, banking and diving. They could not be Rocs, too streamline. Wings coated black as pitch, Rocs were brown and white. Sickly purple did not illuminate them. Wings of soulless shadow drank light, as they swam the thick, iron-tasting air, devoid of colour.

"Get to the academy. End this? Right?" He felt her gaze on him. A shudder reverberated through his arm, rattling the handbow. This must have been what the first Mystic occurrence looked like. Three hundred years ago, the twenty-fifth city state of Cythea obliterated under Mystic power. Now a crater, a ruin, a monastery to the Continental Church and an epitaph for Inquisitors to remember what they face, what they fight against.

"No." Vincentas replied. He turned; the Combatant's movements shifted in his periphery. "To make sure this doesn't happen to another city. Whatever the cost."

"Whatever the cost." She replied, nodding.

His hand stopped shaking. Vincentas found where he laid to rest and picked up the cockel hat and placed the identifiable mark of his trade on his head, a piece of fabric that instilled fear in most and bring terror to Mystics. Head straightened, shoulders leaned back, knowing he had to be that man, to be an instigator of fear, the bringer of justice and the executioner of the Mystic.

Violet ahead, being a Combatant and more experienced in finding a pathway. Raised repeater pointing, scanning darkened corners and blind spots. As thorough as Fleur and moved with a lethality only matched by the Combatant he left behind: he would leave no one else behind.

She led him through tendrils of the floating city, over rooftops threatening to collapse, stepping on cobblestones hanging close together, bobbing like leaves in a shallow pool. Riemkeler beneath them, never far from sight, but death instantaneously if they fell.

"Afflicted." Violet warned. Citizens of Riemkeler, eyes glowing purple like the horizon that bathed the world. Blood-streaked clothing. Men, women and children. Shuffling from doorways, leaping like Primals across decrepit rooftops.

"Keep an eye out for a Mystic." Vincentas's handbow guided his vision, each bolt finding a mark. Eyes flared. It saw. His weapon ending the light. Twice he reloaded, fifteen rounds in all. Never hesitating, one less to worry about, never stopping to see if they were Reticence or Fleur, or Arno. Where could his old friend be in this city?

"We haven't got time for a firefight." Violet's militaristic words made her sound like Fleur. Vincentas agreed, following the agile Combatant, moving before landing, jumping before looking, firing without sight and picking targets.

Agility not his strongest suit, age and tiredness fatigued aching bones. Burning lungs sucked metal air. At least they were heading down, leaving floating buildings and suspended streets. Heading towards the academy. All webs of mockery of wrought iron-tasting city led to its centre.

Violet skidded on a rooftop and stopped. The building they shared angled against another, part of it crushed. She turned back, pointing down. Before

Vincentas could signal, she jumped, disappearing into the collapsed structure, staying still without completing its fall by another equally poised building ready to give way.

Vincentas crossed the motley pathway. Looking below, Violet's shadow descended over the building's walls, disappearing into a smashed doorframe. He jumped down, allowing gravity to skid plastering wall, slowing his descent. Blurring signalled his speed. Luckily, not nauseating, but he would take an airship again before trying this.

Zipping by a doorframe, Vincentas feet churned up plaster, heels ricocheting off brick, wood and paper. Debris snagged fleeting face, muscle and sinew pulled against a force dragging him back. Quicker he moved.

Grinding to a definite halt, eyes blurred. Debris rattled down, flakes of paper and dust settled around. Pushing himself to his feet, Violet stood on the structure's wall, a cracked escape route their point of freedom.

"Least we're on solid ground." He mumbled, leaving the creaking structure. Patting off specks of plaster from the black cockel hat. Wet cobbles, sleek under flashing magenta light, formed a snaking pathway between toppled homes and vacant craters where dwelling should have been.

"Great. Now we have to watch the skies." Violet trained the repeater up, quick snaps to the left and right of her, scanning with her loaded weapon.

Metallic grating off wet stone sent shivers down his spine. Vincentas withdrew his malachite sword, holstering the handbow. Murmurs chorused the grating. Crying resonated through his skull, tightening his grip around the obsidian hilt.

Skin ignited with a quiver. Something dragged across the stone.

It came around the corner on a multitude of legs.

Naked as a newborn and just as bloody. Steel chains wrapped in two sinewy limbs. Sparks ignited its pulled weight on sleek cobbles. Screams erupted as the cage grinded into view. Arms, several of them, stuck out between bars. Pleading faces blurred, their cries a human echo of the steel reverberation of their pulled container.

Turning its bulbous head around, facing them without eyes, its maw opened to its fleshy, fattened chest. It saw and shrieked.

Vincentas raised the malachite sword, gripping it in two hands, and stalked forward. Violet unleashed fury, whistling of the repeater zipped by. Bolts thudded into the bloated body. No effect.

Breaking into a paced jog, feet slipped. The Mystic dropped the chain, clattering on ringing stone. Moving forward like a spider, legs weaving, body sagging on the moist ground, it wormed closer to Vincentas. Crawling, arm over arm, leg dragging leg, the thing screamed like an incoherent infant, distressed and hungry.

Fleshy, bloodied hand reached for the Inquisitor. Moving to the side, he hacked down as the putrid smelling fatty arm squelched on cobblestones, ichor flooded from the wound. The malachite sword scythed through skin like a glowing knife through warm butter. Meat fell. Unseen bone cracked. A gut filled scream rang in his ears.

Legs gave way.

His back ate pain, air knocked out of him, eyes staring at the beast looming over. Hearing muffled to blurring nothingness.

A wall emerged from nowhere. It grew like a forest, blocking the Mystic from finishing him. He searched around. Another Mystic, it had to be. Violet rushed over. Words left her mouth, but no sound emitted. Pulled to his feet, he peered at the makeshift wall, made with mortar and brick from nearby structures.

"Vincentas. Have to go, come on." His hearing popped and sound resumed, despite the metallic ringing which echoed in the depths of his mind.

Hammering struck the wall. Cries sounded distant and forgotten. Forlorn in their pleas.

"No idea where the wall came from but thank whatever is out there who helped us." Violet turned to head down the road. She stopped. Heels ceased clicking.

Vincentas inclined his head. A solitary figure stood, hands outstretched, as if to stop an object hitting their face. The Mystic. Hands lowered. Fiery red hair, youthful, pale innocent face etched in worry. He had not changed since chasing the Mystic in the Inquirer Hall.

"Alleck." Vincentas rasped. The word coughed out in surprise. Heat boiled in his lungs, lips curled, teeth barred in heat.

"Entrant." His voice filled the void.

Silence stilled a changing world. The hammering ceased, cries stopped. Breathing reduced to calmness. Every pore ignited, traces of sweat lingered on hands, back, neck, and chest.

Alleck bolted. Vincentas chased.

Violet's shouts did not matter. The abomination with the caged people not his concern. A breaking world on the cusp of oblivion shrunk to a hindrance. Eyes focused ahead, ducking and weaving through debris cluttered buildings and over streets cracked and ready to rise.

The Entrant's footsteps echoed his guilty fleeing. He was shouting behind him, but Vincentas ignored it. The malachite sword hung heavy in his hands.

Without thinking, he bundled into Alleck, standing still, hands up in front to stop a collision with the chasing Inquisitor. The Entrant's eyes peeled open.

"Why did you run? You ran after her in the Inquirer Hall. She was too powerful." Vincentas raged. Free hand grasping the collar of the Entrants duster, shaking it. Alleck's eyes watered, lip quivered. He was not ready to give a response. He was not ready at all.

"Why." Vincentas hissed. The fight left him as the malachite sword lowered. Stepping back, he did not turn on hearing Violet catch up. Chest hammered deep within clothes, threatening to explode with heavy breaths. Fresh, sticky perspiration poured onto congealed mottled sweat lingering on an already damp tasting skin.

"I had to prove." Alleck started rubbing moistness from a quivering face.

"You prove by following." Vincentas shook his head.

"Let the boy have his word. We were all young once." Violet suggested, moving to stand next to the Entrant. Her flushed cheeks crimson under bruising light.

Arno's words in the Inquirer Hall at Konniak. They were young, but a burden. Thought too much on missing Athgeric. Had no time to take others under his wing, an unwelcomed weight would slow down his private investigation into the disappearance of a true Inquisitor. Hadramiel the same. Ever distant. But Vincentas, young, naïve and out to prove himself, became reckless. Defied orders. He was Alleck. Alleck was him.

"It was reckless to pursue the Mystic by yourself." The Inquisitor started. Violet's unrepentant eyes caught his gaze. "But you are an Entrant, and what you did was brave."

Alleck's head raised up, mouth agape, gurgled sounds emitted. Vincentas raised a hand.

"We both need to keep our emotions in check. It fuels the Mystic. Fighting between each other will only embolden the heretics that have done this to Riemkeler." His hand rested on the Entrant's shoulder, who straightened his neck out.

"These heretics need punishing, Entrant. Are you with me?" He questioned Alleck.

"Yes, Inquisitor, I am with you." Quivers rippled through his grasp. He squeezed the Entrant's shoulder in a sign of reassurance, more to himself than the naïve boy.

"We're heading to the academy. You were once a citizen here. Tell me all you know about it." Vincentas moved back, Alleck bathed in a pink glow. Violet flanked him and whispered her thanks.

"The academy was my home after I left." Hands wrung together; wavering eyes locked.

"Anything unusual? Different. Even Mystical, like what's happening out there." Vincentas inquired.

The Entrant shook his head, lowering his gaze to the floor. Arms skirting up to thinning arms and stroked them, as if he was keeping warm.

"We're losing time. Anything comes to your mind tell us." He turned his back, had to be patient with Alleck, his patience wearing thin. Checking his handbow, he loaded it and holstered the weapon. He sheathed the malachite sword, its grating sound therapeutic, to return the weapon back to its scabbard. He would need it.

"Wait. There is." The Inquisitor looked over his shoulder, surveying Alleck with a half look. The Entrant's face screwed up, features flanked in wrinkles.

"Your Faun was there before I left for Konniak. He was speaking to Dargus Enote, the head scholar on Mysticism at the academy." Alleck sighed after speaking.

"Academy doesn't research or write lore on Mysticism." Vincentas replied. That was odd. Alleck associating Mysticism with the academy. And the Faun…

"You mean Arno, the Chanter?" The Inquisitor rounded quickly; the Entrant backed away, taking two strides back. He nodded.

Arno could not have been in Riemkeler. The Entrant must have confused him with another Faun. Fauns were similar at the same age. Nodding his thanks, Vincentas turned, knowing the academy's secrets would be revealed. Vincentas had a name: Dargus Enote.

"To the academy. As quick as we can." Leaving the security of the building, venturing back into dilapidated, bruising streets awash under magentas oozing rays. Metallic ringing continued throughout decrepit Riemkeler.

Alleck spoke little of his time spent in the academy. Vincentas guessed the Entrant held more secrets, the way he skirted past abandonment, how he grew up in a strict family home where the patriarchal dynasty of the household lay rooted in the Continental Church. Maybe Alleck was found with a girl or boy and cast out by his zealous father. The Inquisitor only speculated with the bare knowledge obtained but did not press the subject.

The path to the academy twisted and vanished. Levitated onto floating stones, climbing over rooftops and through cracked, floorless buildings. Shoes hung in suspension. Dolls twisted on invisible strings as they hung, lifeless, in mid-air. A pungent stench of iron, like a working forge, circled the Inquisitor's nostrils, but no smouldering ironworks functioned nearby.

Life rotted away. Blood stains, fresh and stinking of copper, lashed walls, ceilings dripped red. Hand marks smeared doors. Something marked a crimson smudge, like tracing of a dragged carcass. Attacker and the victim nowhere to be seen. Time vanished like preys lost under Mystic assault.

Pink misty curtains unveiled. Above a ring of stairs, the spires of the academy lay clear. Its working orrery, turning on metal teeth, signalled its mechanical brilliance. It covered one structural wing of the multitude of buildings that made Riemkeler's centre piece for learning.

Violet scouted the route, stepping on dry, smooth steps. They ascended to the grounds of the academy. Gaslamps flared, yellow glow smothering out tendrils of darkness, shadow and Mystic purples. LeafFall season smacked nostrils with a freshness that made Vincentas cough. Trees stood. Bushes bloomed in life. The academy untouched, like the Inquirer Hall.

Vincentas kept a cautious hand on the obsidian hilt.

"Too quiet." Violet's words pulsed into his mind, wording his thoughts.

"Academies ahead. We'll make for it." He encouraged. Eyes on the sky, circling around. The winged things had gone. No Afflicted. No beastly Mystic. The carnage of Riemkeler a distant memory of the immaculate domain of learning and knowledge.

Crossing through groomed gardens, they heard nothing. Not a sigh of wind. Bird in the sky. Even their footsteps gave no sound. Closer, closer. Large doors, too big for people, too extravagant for a place of learning, grew. Ajar and open, inviting them in.

Under the shadow of the academy, looming overhead like a tidal wave of structural marvel grandiose, they broke for the door, shrouding hidden truths. Stepping inside, a smell all too familiar assaulted the Inquisitor's senses.

He stood on something that squelched beneath his boot. Hotness flared beneath an uncomfortable neck. Alleck struck matches to light a Gaslamp he carried. At least he had something.

The Entrant gasped and stepped back.

Something red, snake like and bloated with muscle, slithered away under flaring light. Ashen shadows pushed back along marbled floor, oozing in reflective glossy redness.

"Move on." Vincentas's echoing voice filtered through the academy.

Doors closed behind them. A half-smile carved through his tight lips. He told Violet they would not be returning home. He had a feeling someone had been listening to him.

Cass

Chapter XIII

It tasted of rusting iron. Mechanised mouths belched hissing steam. Combustion engines whirred, ready to convulse. It was home; an unfamiliar habitation that shed no sun or stars, and even fewer hopes and dreams. The world pulsed, stomach trembled under blurring vision. Vomit brewed in unsettled guts. She closed her eyes. Let it stop, let it all stop.

"Can we do anything about that?" Jolam shouted. Crouched, shaking Faun twisted and doubled as Cass peered at her cellmate. Head spun like a spindle wheel. Rupturing sickness emptied over the convulsing ground. Acidic bile burned a stinging tongue. She spat on the ground. Damn the movement. Damn this world.

She buckled, legs bent and ached to the straining of world distorting. Throbbing ceased. Vibrations of the world died instantaneously. Her vision snapped to levelled normalcy. Straightening her back, she spat, hoping to remove the disgusting taste of vomit.

"That's the third time since the change. Why does it happen?" Groaned Jolam, staggering to his feet. Hooves clopped on stone in his eagerness to steady himself.

"Trying to disorient us. Make us vulnerable." Lucijan's shaking voice replied, both Taze and Lucijan aided each other to stand, the murderer more stable of the two.

"Need to find a way out of here while the world isn't rocking." Cass walked on, keeping Ninsar close, shielding the girl from emptied sickness, not holding her with the hand she wiped her mouth with.

"Careful back there, sick on the ground." She shot back, without turning around.

Invisible thunder rumbled above. Resonating sounds shivered down metallic spines of structures they walked through, journeying deeper into the bowels of Konniak.

This was Konniak, but not as she remembered.

Looking up in the real Konniak, Cass would find a world of elevated ironworks: a continuous horizon of overlapping black steel; hissing vents expunging grey smog; bricked dilapidated buildings, ebbing yellow lights cast by Gaslamps.

Instead, the world shrouded in darkness. Eclipsed in a sickly purple, luminous hue doused the world in ominous light. Shadows shifted. Morphed. Changed. Looked like Konniak, but not the real Konniak. Lilly could make this her only thought.

Cass stopped, pressing her back against a wall. Peering around, various shacks of iron and crude bolted roofs that doubled for walkways stretched ahead. Alleys lingered underneath, echoing footfalls pierced through dim, rolling thunder.

She turned around to see them lined up behind her, crouching, ready. Anrechel followed, but twitched at the slightest sound. "No more. No more. No more." The Faun mumbled. She mouthed to Lucijan to go on point. The conscript crept out and kept low as he scurried to the other side of the dishevelled, elevated street.

"Where are we? Mid-level, or near Bogside?" Jolam breathed at her back.

"Can't smell the Bog, could be Mid-level." Cass whispered, daring not to break lips with its sound. They could not smell Bogside because this was not real. Rust filtered into flaring nostrils. A stronger stench clawed into her itching nose.

Lucijan extended an arm. Horizontal and gripped his hand into a fist. Trouble. Cass's heart thumped faster. Sweat burned down her forehead. She wrinkled it in irritation and gritted her teeth. Cursing her breath, she wished for a repeater. Jolam, Taze and Lucijan were armed. Protection of herself would safeguard Ninsar.

Bestial roars and panicked screams erupted. Cass crouched lower; skin leapt against sticking clothes. Ache in her thighs throbbing, her back twitched. Ninsar mewled softly at her side. She placed a hand around her exposed ear, the other ear buried against her beating chest.

Inching around the corner, Cass spotted isolated fires dotted along the cobbled street. Stench of a butcher's abattoir masked the taste of rust. Something roasted, nothing like aurochs. A lumbering, colossal figure staggered toward the fire. A scream followed. The dragged woman lay flaying as her legs kicked for freedom. Cass gripped the side of the building. It wore a Purifier hood.

The thing threw the shrieking woman onto the fire; it engulfed her in ravenous flames. The screaming stopped. Crackling intensified. Her face warmed, despite being far away. Turning back, she closed her eyes and held onto Ninsar, taking deep breaths. Got to find Lilly. Got to stop this.

Cass's eyes bolted open. Lilly.

"No time for shut eye, Cassy." Taze rasped at her side. "Where to?" The words pulsed into her mind.

"Head up. Get out of here." She turned to face Taze. "Jolam, lead the way. Lucijan is in the rear. We need a different route to the one we're on."

"And keep an eye out for Karwen." The murderer nodded and turned to leave.

Anrechel picked her nails and hummed a soft tune. The Faun's eyebrows arched as she bobbed her head from side to side. Cass envied the Faun's docile nature.

Karwen had to be here. It consumed her thoughts as she followed Jolam through winding, contorting iron streets of Konniak's subterranean city complex. An unsettling ripple churned her guts. First the prison, now her birth city. She shook her head, focusing on keeping Ninsar close, always close. She gritted her teeth, the bile taste not as pungent as before.

Jolam stopped and raised a clenched fist. Her knees lowered with a crack. She growled at her body. She was not that old. The Faun turned, mouth open, he pointed at Ninsar with a shaking hand and mimicked covering his eyes. Cass curled Ninsar into her body, burying the child's head into her beating chest. Jolam nodded and continued. Her nose wrinkled under the lingering smell curling in flaring nostrils. An irritating buzz shimmered ahead, growing louder.

Cass followed the Faun as he rounded the corner. She straightened her back and took a deep breath. Light flickered and flashed, back and forth. Its yellow colour bright and welcoming, better than the purple hue that clouded the world above. Valenki boots could not grip on the rounded, slippery surface. Her grip on Ninsar tightened, taking quick breaths. The taste threatened to empty her twisting stomach.

A fog of flies buzzed, flickering on her face, itched in her hair. Irritation clawed and scuttled against a sweating neck. Her head lowered, fighting against the swarm of flies shaking her hearing.

Eyes looked up. Bleeding, unblinking eyes. Cass wrapped herself around Ninsar, who flinched under the constant, crawling buzzard of zipping flies.

"We're free of it." Jolam whispered in relief. A hand clinched her arm. She flexed. Tension vaulting nerves, sending tremors down her back.

"Don't turn around." Lucijan shook as he passed. "Don't look back." He was saying it more to himself than to anyone else.

"Doing well, Lucky. Doing well." Taze clasped Lucijan on the back and rubbed his shoulder, shaking it playfully.

"People. Down." Jolam urged. The group scattered. Cass pulled the girl to the right, following Jolam as she crouched low. The girl cradled into her body, breathing into her chest.

A man walked across her vision. His arms lay limp, wrists twisting. He looked upwards, head tilted backwards beyond possibility. Gurgling sounds shadowed slow, dragging movements. Weathered frock-coat speckled in blood hung loosely on his frame. Dirtied breeches fitted long legs, torn around the knees.

"He isn't alone." Jolam's words voiced her thoughts. Others milled aimlessly in the makeshift alley ahead. A maid. A leather-apron clad blacksmith. A boy no older than ten. All dragged their feet behind them, looking up, gargling as if drowning in their own fluids.

Cass tilted her head up, eyes following. Blackened soot walls pulsed like a heartbeat, rippling like broken still water. Eyes flashed where lightless Gaslamps hung. A paleness covered the sky. Cass's legs froze, thinking it moved like a blanket drying in the wind. The sky breathed.

"Cassidy." Armande's voice broke through rupturing thoughts. She turned away from the breathing sky. *Murderer. Rapist. Thief. Worthless. Unwanted.* Words flashed across pulsing structures, written in writhing ink slashed across brick, iron and steam. They overlapped, covered entire walls. Everywhere she looked, the words lay stark, sharp, and carved before her.

"My love." An anguished voice forced her to turn around. A figure stood cloaked in shadow. Bare, quivering legs stepped out. Red running liquid dribbled down pale thighs and calves.

"No. No." Taze staggered back.

The man stepped forward, naked. Blood running down his waist. His belly lined in deep, black gashes.

"Justice. My love." A pained voice broke out.

He left the shadows. Red, leaking blindfold tied around his face.

"Is blind." A slithering voice finished. The man's mouth opened. Two round, white orbs fell from the spluttering, saliva drenched jaw.

Taze's scream jolted Cass. She raised her repeater and fired till the cartridge emptied. Bolts stuck out of the man, lay imbedded in the stomach. The man gargled as his belly split open, a gaping wound emptied in a red tide, splashing sleek cobbles.

He stepped forward. Fangs split up the ribcage, opening a bloodied maw naval to neck.

"Join Wilmar, Taze." Frothing jaws snapped at the convict, who backed away from the beast.

"No." Lucijan roared, smashing a yellow Gaslamp into the snapping mouth. Fire combusted in the deformed human, flames engulfed in a burning hug around the man's flailing frame.

Cass carried Ninsar away from the shrieking man, turning towards a distant alley and running. Valenki boots rattled over corrugated iron. Heat flared on skin. Sweat bled from every pore.

"Cass, wait." Jolam's voice shouted behind.

"Mom." She froze on hearing Lilly's clear voice. Close enough to whisper. She skidded to a halt, turning around to find her daughter.

Violent vibrations shook the world. The others ran to her, Jolam dragging Anrechel, Lucijan's arm around Taze, who stared at the floor with wide, unblinking eyes. Cass snapped her head up. A cold shadow cast overhead. The sky moved. Paleness turning to webbed, spiked blackness lancing across a pink hue.

"What." Jolam breathed.

A red line split across the sky, dousing the world in crimson for a chilling moment. Redness widened along the pink sky, curling at horizon tipped edges. Whiteness grew from the cracking red sky, too white for clear clouds. They were angular, straight, sharp.

"It's a mouth." Lucijan gasped. She tightened her grip on Ninsar, the Sabanese girl moaned into her chest.

A long tendril extended between white mountains in the sky within the cracks of the bloodlines. Lancing down, aiming. It flexed like a bulging arm. A reflective, glassy surface crowned its end. Sharpness coating the sky. It pointed at them.

"Get them." A multitude of voices electrified the poisoned sky. Cass knelt under the verbal barrage into her body, pushing against tired shoulders.

"Them. Look." Lucijan warned. Denizens of the city amassed. Heads twisted at angles beyond measure. They faced the group, facing Cass. She felt their stares without seeing their eyes.

Faces. Bodies. Limbs. Things flickered and faded from view above the inhabitants of Konniak. Shambling forward, legs dragged on iron works, shivers rippled down her shaking spine. Arms vaulted up, levelling at her.

"Let's go." Lucijan ordered, he stepped forward blocking her view. Repeaters whirled in her ears. Bestial groans and choking gargles burst echoed after scything bolts. She pushed herself up, holding onto Ninsar, and ran.

Taze, Anrechel and Jolam were ahead, always ahead, but she kept them within blurring sight. Aiming for their backs with burning limbs powering tired legs. Needed to reach them, keep with them, keep Ninsar safe.

Cass blurred around corners, feet hammered corrugated ground. Walls narrowed. Slopes rose and fell. Jumping over walls, she landed on her back, having Ninsar within her grasp. She never let go of the Sabanese girl, holding her by the wrist.

"Need to run with me. Come on." Cass shouted. The girl kept pace, running side by side with each burning stride she took.

Taze, Anrechel and Jolam disappeared through steam, vaulted over walls. Dodging outstretched limbs at every angle. Cass screamed, ducked and powered on, yanking Ninsar close every time danger burst into her periphery.

"Lucijan, hurry." Cass shouted, not seeing the conscript behind her. Whistles of the repeater fading as distance grew between them.

Skidding to a halt, Jolam, Anrechel and Taze stood before a ladder. Cut off, a dead end within the concrete jungle of Konniak's city. The ladder an access point to another level. Cass looked up as the rusting structure penetrated through grey, hissing steam.

"Go, we'll be right behind you." Jolam held onto the ladder, moving to the side to allow Anrechel up first.

"Where's Lucijan?" Taze grasped her shoulder.

Heartbeat deafening, hearing clouded except her pounding chest, ragged breaths and hissing steam.

"He was behind." Cass panted, leading Ninsar to the ladder, bypassing Taze.

"He's saved me three times, Cass." Taze moved away, walking back the way she came.

"No, Taze, we stick together." She shouted, weary of the shallow, monotonous dragging of feet reverberating off corrugated iron growing closer.

"Save your daughter, Cass." Taze did not turn back. Grasping her repeater in two hands, she jogged on, away from the ladder, away from them all.

"Damn it. Jolam, climb up, you lead." She jerked her head to the ladder.

"Here." Jolam tossed the repeater to Cass and jumped onto the ladder. He climbed, the structure rattling with his hooves, hammering the steps as he ascended.

"We don't know what's up there." She tracked his ascent.

"Then don't shoot me, besides you get to see me climb." Jolam's voice descended as he scaled.

"Ninsar, you go. Come on." She cooed the Sabanese girl, who clung onto Cass' waist, curling diminutive arms around her body.

"I'll be right with you, I promise." She whispered into the girl's ear. Picking up the girl, she placed her as high as she could on the ladder. With a little squeak, the girl started her ascension, Jolam and Anrechel lost in the steam above.

A scream tore Cass around. Two bodies shambled forward. Arms outstretched. Heads flung back. Feet dragging behind them. She raised the heavy repeater in shaking hands. Placing the stock under her right arm, holding the weapon with her left.

Levelling the repeater at the nearest target, she squeezed the trigger. Tightness paused her finger. She tried again and again. They ambled forward. Two bolt shafts sticking from its neck. Not fired from her own repeater. Cass spat a curse and turned the weapon to its side, slamming the safety off. Two arms outstretched before her wide vision. Screaming, she hammered the trigger.

The stock kicked back into her side, elevating the weapon. Twitching like the man she killed in the warehouse, her attacker dropped backwards, kicking at the ground. She wheeled right, facing her second attacker. A woman. Torn bodice of a lady of pleasure. Powdered wig hanging off her pale, painted face. Cass gritted her teeth and squeezed the trigger, dropping the woman with inhumane screams and ruptured twitching.

Slinging the repeater over her shoulder, Cass jumped for the ladder and scaled upwards. Her feet hammering iron. Steps shaking at every touch. Rust cutting into eager fingers. Sweat blurring everything above. Ninsar's boots a few steps ahead, slowly but steadily climbing. She entered the steam and did not look back, or below, but faced only above.

"Keep going, Cass. The top of the ladder isn't far." Jolam's voice shouted through the mist. Strength fuelled her legs. Hastily, she scaled the steps of the rattling, rusty ladder. Ninsar always close by.

Black shadows of buildings swam around Cass. She dared not look down, gripping the coarse step with dry hands, knuckles burning white with tension. Heights never a strong suit, and she knew it now more than ever. Steam blanketed the ground, Ninsar's small steps echoed above. Nothing followed. No Taze. No Lucijan.

Lifting her head, the ladder neared its end. Anrechel and Jolam were off, but neither of them peered over the edge. Black iron legs held up the second part of the city, disappearing into unseen depths. She continued climbing, eyes fixed on the step as she ascended.

"Cass." Jolam's scream shook her. Looking up, shaking in her haste. The Faun stepped at the edge, he wavered. Time slowed as the Faun held his gut, looking down. Raven haired, hawkish face, she stood next to him holding a long knife coated in blood.

"Welcome home, Cass." Karwen's voice oozed into her hearing.

Karwen turned Jolam to face her, plunging the knife into the Faun's stomach.

Cass shouted with trembling rage. Knuckles pulling at the stair she held onto. Karwen discarded the Faun away from her.

Jolam fell.

He passed Cass quicker than she could look. Within a heartbeat, the second person she came to trust in her life disappeared. Tears burned her eyes in agony to look for Jolam. Seeing nothing through shrouding steam below.

Snapping her head to face up the ladder, she raged and spat, sounding more like a Primal than herself. She allowed the descension of her humanity in the singular pursuit of Karwen.

"Come on, Ninsar, hurry." Cass snapped, reaching for the Sabanese girl shaking in her cries.

"Ninsar, listen to me. She's gone, I'm here, I've got a repeater, we can do this. Move. Move."

She spat, Karwen's murder of Jolam fuelling her muscles to burn. The girl took small, quivering steps. Their ascension took time, too much time for Cass climbing two steps at a time behind Ninsar in her haste to find Karwen.

The girl cleared the ladder. Cass swooped up, dragging herself to stable ground. In sweating hands, she tore the repeater off the leather shoulder strap and aimed it in steady hands around her. One building lay ahead. A solitary two-tier shack made of brick and iron, soot coated the dwelling. Blue, decaying paint faded from the door. It could not be. She lowered the repeater.

Hooking an arm around Ninsar, the other hand grasped the repeater. Her forearm bulged with aching muscles. She jogged to the front door of her house, the house where Lilly grew up in, where they lived before her sentence. The house of Cass's birth and raising.

Nearing the front door, the stench of Konniak clogged nostrils, blocking her own odour. Keeping the girl tight by her side, Cass kicked the door. Swinging open, wood crashed against the wall. Peering wide-eyed into the darkened house, her repeater lowered in shaking grasp on seeing a girl sitting in the chair. Her chest tightened.

"Lilly." Cass whispered. Stepping over the threshold, she walked towards her daughter, bound, unmoving and asleep on the chair, the same type of contraption used in the asylum.

"Not a step closer. Or she'll be gone for good." Armande's voice broke through the shadows. Stepping forward, placing hands on Lilly's sagged shoulders.

"Dare touch her." Cass spluttered, Ninsar scuttled away. Eyes only on Armande. The repeater raised and fired. Bolts left the mechanised weapon straight for the manic officer of her past.

Tilting his head back, arms stretched to the sides, embracing a death that did not arrive. Bolts hung in the air. Suspended. Silent. Unmoving. Lined together facing Armande's face with their deadly points but losing their lethality with stopped motion.

"You know what your daughter is. And she isn't alone." His thick accented voice drawled; head lowered. Eyes ignited in something worse than passion, focused on Cass. It bore deeper now than anytime during the Purifier Rebellion.

"She is needed. And this. This is the catalyst." A wind tore through the house as he spoke, ripping words from

Cass's throat. Falling to the floor, she crawled to Lilly, bound and stationary, amongst the maelstrom. Wood spat, nicking skin. A raging torrent deafened thought to a single consciousness: get Lilly.

"Give up, Cassidy. A living world is against you." Armande's voice, blurred with Karwen's, whispered in her ear. She lashed out with a right hook, blinded by whipping debris scything across her dry face. They should have been right beside her. They spoke so clearly.

Cass flipped on her back. The world shook, blurring walls as they melted. Cracked ceiling broke apart, showering upwards to an endless sky filled with grinning mouths. Her head dropped below the current of thought, consumed in tides of doubt and confusion. Lilly on her lips, Lilly seen in closed eyes.

Vincentas

Chapter XIV

Vincentas' memories of walking through the city sized domain of Riemkeler's pinnacle flooded back; the vast academy contained a wealth of knowledge obtained from thousands of years of recorded wisdom. Now, unrecognisable to the Inquisitors' waking eyes. Books flipped open, pages flicked front to back. Torrent of irritating papers ruffled by invisible fingers sent shivers down his back. A phenomenon most would blame the poor, unchecked drafts, but this was Mysticism at its sensory-shredding start.

"Wish it would stop." Alleck's chattering voice broke through the continuous ruffle. Scrolls unfolded and wrapped back and forth, rippling in motion. The hush switched to repeated, shorter bursts of waving: it was laughing. The library laughed without a sound of the living.

"If only it were plants, it would be a lot more tolerable." Violet interjected. Repeater raised, guiding her sight.

"It's what it wants. Stop thinking." Vincentas fired back without turning. They walked for the best part of a day and feared not to sleep in case of change in the world. The Inquisitor knew they could ill afford to be separated when Mysticism reached these heights. Surprised once in the corridor, the wall separation a horrid reality that amplified here.

Forgotten smells of incense, full inkwells and freshly weaved papyrus filtered his mind how the academy's aroma should be. Mockery hung in tired nostrils, rotten death, forgotten and discarded, lingered in an inescapable stench that no amount of nose rubbing could remove.

"Close to the alchemy ward." Alleck spoke. Vincentas faced his raw recruit. The boy who knew Riemkeler more than himself. Coincidence of how the roles reversed. Yellow shafts of dying light could not push back vaulting darkness from ceiling arches. They could have been in a cavern for all the light achieved. Braziers stood dead. Windows boarded up. Unseen chandeliers creaked.

"Must go down." The Inquisitor theorised. Athgeric must have been onto something. He knew. The bowels of the academy held the truth of their knowledge.

Vincentas stopped. Lowering the Gaslamp and braced himself against a bookshelf that cloaked him in shadow. Alleck copied. Their breaths rustled in wheezing throats.

A hand shot out, placing it over Alleck's mouth. He knew the youngling would speak and ask questions. The

Entrant's eye wavered and blinked, before returning to stare ahead. Pupils stark in minimal light.

"Listen. Don't think. Listen." The Inquisitor breathed, removing hand from the stuttered mouth of the Entrant. Innocent eyes looked, searching for answers in unquestioned surroundings. The old Inquisitor recognised realisation in bright, wide eyes of the Entrant. He gulped. Alleck seemed to shrink under darkness, pressing himself further into the security of the solid bookshelf.

"It's quiet now." Vincentas nodded. Nothing stirred. No wind or flapping books. Creaks of chandeliers or distant footfalls.

The Inquisitor searched. Books lay half opened in motion. Scrolls hung in the air from their chained locks. Ladders used for scaling shelves pivoted to fall but caught in the invisible hand of still-time. The world ceased moving. Frozen in motion.

"It's unreal. Like my dream of the festival." Alleck summarised. A cold sweat crept down his spine, like his own dream on The Sojourn. You were not the only one screaming this night, Arno's words. Instinct curled fingers around an all too familiar hilt. The Entrant shook his head and turned, facing his mentor.

"It's unreal. How many things I'm seeing. My mind is too open." Slumped shoulders and hanging head told more than his hollow words. He could not be the Mystic, too weak to play along, too naïve to lie.

Vincentas freed a steady hand off his obsidian hilt and placed it on the shoulder of Alleck. Gloved hand gripped a lithe frame.

"We need to find a way down. Into something. Something worse than this." No reason to lie now. They had entered the endgame. Alleck's shining eyes peered between strands of unwashed, greasy hair.

"I don't need a boy from Riemkeler. I need an Entrant I found in Konniak." He squeezed the shoulder. Clothing fabrics crackled. "Are you with me?"

The Entrant expelled a long sigh, foul breath pungent, but worse than an unclean body. Worse than charred flesh from Inquisitor fires.

"I'm your Entrant." He nodded, but the eyes held the boy's unspoken truth.

A low squeal echoed down the spine of Vincentas. He launched into the shadows, snapping off the Gaslamp and withdrawing the handbow. Teeth gritted, cursing tired limbs and old bones.

"Combatant, on point." The Inquisitor instructed, head leering from protective shadows. Violet responded with agility and whispered, lethal movements. Within a heartbeat she was ahead, several paces or more, repeater inching forward.

"To the alchemy ward." He mouthed to Alleck, who shivered like iron vibrating under forges heated hammer.

Flanking Violet, they moved towards closed, barred doors. Under dim light, a green hue encompassed brass door handles in a figure of eight, locking the door in writhing bonds. His eyes flashed along the handle, snaking outwards to hinges. An emerald web sprung across their entrance.

Wrapped vines bound rusting hinges and forgotten locks. Murmurs escaped narrow gaps of the closed chamber. Anguish tore in streams of squeals. Female voices echoed in his mind.

Green vines, pulsing in azure, uncurled its shielding state. Creaking doors of the antechamber opened.

Pungent stench of wildflowers and bodily fluids hissed from the yawning, emerald maw.

"Alchemy ward has a way down?" Vincentas half turned.

"Yes. Off limits to students. Only scholars have admittance." Alleck spoke through hand covering his coughing face.

Vincentas eased the door open, stepping into the room. Greenery grew everywhere. Nature reclaimed a room built for study. Plants broke through tables, weeds consumed bookshelves, roots devoured windows. No flowers. No petals. No colour other than shades of sprouting plants.

"Help." A squeal dragged his vision to the floor. Lying on her side, a woman, naked and with a swollen belly. Others begged. Strained voices filling his racing mind. They were everywhere, women, pregnant, pleading.

"It'll be alright." Vincentas moved to the closest. She quivered, sweat glistened off her body. Haggard breaths. Blood-shot eyes fixed on him, penetrating and needful.

"Kill… kill me." She gasped. Fleshy hand reached out, shaking.

"Please." She screamed. Veins bulged across her neck. Face flared in heated redness.

Stepping back, the Inquisitor looked down at the bloated belly. He thought it was the pale light, or her squirming desire to move away, to reach him with clawing, eager hands of his held handbow. Uncontrolled coldness crept down his chilling spine. Moving back further, distancing himself from the woman, screaming an inhuman piercing shriek.

Something moved beneath her skin.

"Violet. Alleck to me." Vincentas kept his eyes on the woman, screaming, fixed his legs to the unnatural ground. Rolling onto her back, the woman's hands quivered in clear, teal coloured air, writhing shadows mocked her movements.

Tearing. Rendered flesh. Cutting ripped through hearing. Blood fanned from the woman's quiet body. Taste of death entered his unguarded throat.

The repeater levelled beside him. Alleck shrieked. Stench of death and faeces knocked aside nature's aroma. Red vines snaked from opened wombs. Easing side to side, pivoting like weeds in a solstice wind. Vincentas stole an unblinking glance around the room. All the women, dead, laying still, their faces trapped in unbridled, silent agony. Wriggling redness emerged.

"This happened to them. Those taken." Violet whispered, her words darker than the brewing gulf descending from the vaulted ceiling.

"Move back." Vincentas warned, feet slipping, tangled in roots as he kept his eyes looking up. Captivated.

It lowered.

Mass of tendrils and feelers, multi-coloured petals crowned its bulbous, incomprehensible shape. Protruding, spherical black orbs, glossy and dripping, rotated and moved, lunged from within the uncoordinated flower-shaped monstrosity, moving as a spider would descend on a web wriggling towards its caught foe. Throughout his decades as an Inquisitor, nothing could prepare for the gut shaking, inescapable quiver rattling his trapped stomach.

Vincentas dived to the right. Feelers lashed ahead, whipping in redness. Slurping noises sucked warm, pungent air. Something slapped behind, sounding like tenderised meat. Snapping his head up, gargantuan fingers lowered. Could not count them in haste. Attached and groaning, dangled men and women, children and elderly. Naked, streaked in moist redness. Blood vines latched to shaking heads, linking to its suspended master.

"Destroy the beast. Avoid the people." The Inquisitor shouted, hoping Violet heard and would fight on her own, capable and resourceful. A scream tore eyes onto Alleck, scrambled back in flustering confusion.

"Entrant." The Inquisitor snapped, he threw his handbow to him in vain desperation. He was not armed. How he survived in Riemkeler till now was beyond luck.

Withdrawing the malachite sword, he swung against one feeler launched at him. It scythed through fleshy tentacle, slicing it in two. More sinewy appendages snaked his way, vines wriggled on the creaking ground, rearing, poised to strike.

He hacked. Swung. Diced. Slashed. The rapier a blur, stabbing and lunging. Vines slapped to the ground, writhing. He had to move, feet tangled in overgrown roots, glass crunched under feet, paper ruffled as he jumped clear of outreaching tendrils.

Violet swerved behind a bookcase, roots tore it apart, splinters shattered before her. Whistling repeater, the Combatants reply. She ducked, tumbled and rolled in a black and white wind. Repeater fire covering constant dodges. The thing ate her bolts.

It had to be a Mystic. Its vessel would be inside, the human conduit manifesting incomprehensible mayhem. Vincentas gritted his teeth and ran forward, limbs begged to stop moving. Malachite sword dipped low, held in one tired hand, dragged behind.

"Look out." Violet's voice broke through his mind. Orange burned above, like a distant sun. It could not be. Slipping on the sleek surface, he ground to a halt. Wreathed flames plummeted down. Vincentas turned back, head lowered, legs powering him to move.

"Make clear." The Combatant screamed, her voice breaking. Vincentas lifted to his feet, pushed forward, and crashed into a broken bookshelf. Breath knocked out of him, he scrambled, hand latching onto anything stable. His other hand clutched the malachite sword for all its worth. Crashing to the floor, his legs gave out, slumping down the crooked bookshelf.

Fire consumed his vision. Familiar heat burned along neck and chest. Fabric of the air scorched aching lungs. The thing squealed. Tendrils whipped. Stench of burnt wood filtered through tired, gasping nostrils and open, gagging mouth, inhaled thick acidic air.

"Vincentas." Violet crouched beside him. The world shook, pulsating weary eyes. Wood broke apart amid a convulsion that rocked his slumped posture, shaking legs and jarring him to move. Tremors rippled through his core, threatening to rip apart his spine.

Within a heartbeat, the fiery inferno of the massed feelers and red vines collapsed through the antechambers floor. Roots ripped from solid flooring, splinters showered the air. A cacophony of crashes, smashed bark, tearing weeds, inhuman shrieks and soaring flames burst through Vincentas's hearing.

Flames descended with the monster, whipping roots followed it, deep into the bowels of the academy. Flooring, walls, pillars, bodies. All attached were pulled into the blazing inferno. Fires crackled in isolated areas.

Wood groaned. Items fluttered among the collapsed cacophony.

A dim hush followed. Ears ringing as if submerged under water. A heartbeat faster than a chasing Bulkett thundered within pained ribs.

He looked up. A thick rope dangled from the unseen ceiling, lost in shadow and vague purple lights. A figure, hooded, scaled down the rope. Wincing, Vincentas pushed himself to his feet, almost laughing, but coughed under acidic-tasting black smoke filtering through the wrecked alchemy ward.

"Reticence. Reticence is that you?" He shouted, voice distant in muffled hearing. He spat, looking where the abomination vanished. A wooden maw left behind, darkness dwelling within. No sound emitted in endless depths. No fires leapt up; the sound of silence echoed within the breech.

He watched the descending Interrogator, who swung the rope to the side while lowering. Over stable ground, the retinue member jumped, landing on creaking wooden beams. Vincentas circled the room, staying on stability outside the cracked room's centre built on emptiness.

"I never thought to see you again." The Inquisitor smiled, looking at the wicker-mask. The Interrogator nodded, silent now and silent always.

"What you drop on it?" Vincentas looked up the rope, swinging above the gaping maw. Creaked boards signalled Violets and Alleck's approach. Reticence outstretched a gloved hand and rotated it, keeping fingers elongated and separate. He joined his other hand together, his fingers rotating back and forth, interlocking but not clasped together.

"A cog." He waved away the acidic tasting smoke wafting before him. Ash coated his throat, lungs smouldered on breathing.

"Have an Interrogator, chances of us surviving have increased tenfold." Violet's voice pulsed behind. Vincentas turned, looking at the Combatant reload the Mark II repeater, without observing what she was doing.

"Not only an Interrogator, but one of us." The Inquisitor's skin prickled at his words.

"Great." The repeater clicked into position. "He can torture the Mystics to stop." She looked up, brown eyes darker than before.

"Found stairs. Leading down." Alleck panted, rubbing a handkerchief over his face.

"Well done. Entrant, lead the way." Vincentas made to move. A firm grasp held him still. He turned. The towering torturer held his arm by the bicep, one gloved hand covering his upper arm. Fingers locked despite him wearing layers and a duster over his body.

"They didn't make it." All he could say. No need to delve into details about Dehqan and Fleur. All that mattered was finding the Mystics and ending this. Reticence let go, arm returning to his tattered, robed side.

"We'll avenge them." Vincentas turned, heading towards Alleck, waiting near a collapsed door entering a torn up, broken side-room off the antechamber. Books lined walls, more open pages lay crumpled on the floor carpeting it in strung books and piles of papers.

"Looks sturdy." Alleck pointed. Black stairs, wrought iron, lay in spiral fashion, corkscrewing into the depths beyond the opened door. Paper crunched under heavy boots, sounding like leaves kicked through LeafFall season.

"Good find, Entrant. Down we go." Into the hidden depths for forbidden truths. Darkness obscured ten feet, all stairs and nothing else. An empty void that could be any length, height, or width. Vincentas descended first, echoing with footfalls. A smell of forgotten food and forge, smelted iron filtered through his nostrils. Better than acidic smoke and burning nature.

Gaslamp ignited, yellow rays lanced ahead and below, illuminating the way, pushing back stronger shadows and black claws of empty light tried to hold on, but the Gaslamp too powerful to be subdued by eager darkness. Growing heavy in his hand, Vincentas lowered it to his side. The spiral staircase brought on spinning headaches and drifting eyes. He had to stop occasionally.

Resounded hard step reverberated up his leg. Vincentas turned around, staring into a decorated room.

Red bricked walls, fine Kheda Ishan carpets, rugs from the Thousand Isles. A long, three-seated chair against one wall. Books in piles, stacked higher than a child. Towers of books stood in no order at all on the woven multicoloured fabrics.

Lowering the Gaslamp, he killed the light, no need for it with candles and standing Gaslamps, with softer, clean glass emitting a radiant warm glow. Nobody else was here. Violet, Reticence and Alleck. Not a soul. A wooden door eased open. He started shaking his head as a lady, who smiled, entered the room.

"No, no, this isn't right." Skin frowned, the hand holding the Gaslamp quivered.

"Course it's not right. I haven't changed yet." The woman laughed, the same laugh she had since their first encounter. The laugh that died in Inquisitorial fires never to be heard again.

"This, this isn't right. This isn't real." Vincentas started shouting. The woman stopped in her tracks, fingering the earring delicately. She faced him. Soft opal eyes narrowed.

"Vin, I know the library isn't working. Least the Inquisition hasn't taken it." She turned back from him, auburn hair, veined in flame, formed in a chignon perfectly balanced behind her.

"I know you hate meeting new people. I know you, Vinny." Brushing down her immaculate dress, as if removing stains or crumbs off the form-fitting outfit. Rounding through stacks of books, eyes clasped on his, half-smile curled on unblemished skin.

"Am I some ghost? Maybe a Primal." She laughed, raising a white-gloved hand to hide her outburst, stepping back from her approach.

"Evalyn." Vincentas whispered. He had not spoken about her until Violet, and before that, buried within his mind, locked away his greatest weakness. The greatest strength for Mystics.

"Ooh. I've done something wrong, not Eva. Eve. Trouble. Beautiful." She moved forward, a warm, smouldering glint in her eye. Gloved hands patted his chest when she listed the words he adorned her with. Her caressing touch warm, skin ignited under her touch beneath heavy layers.

"This can't be real." Vincentas shook his head, looking straight into Evalyn's eyes, sparks flaring within brown hues of her reflective, bright eyes. Lavender perfumes and aromatic fragrances did not assault his nerves, her aroma like a dying forge, coal embers crackling before extinguished.

"This one of your books? We aren't really here sort of thing." She rolled her head, shoulders raised. Her vision consumed him. He did not want to let go. How could he?

"Real is what we make it." Her voice stoked inside his weakening mind, making his knees quiver. Impossible thoughts raced through him. Stirring emotion boiled his guts.

"Real is real, not what we make it." Vincentas placed his hand on Evalyn. She held firm stronger than his push. Smoke filtered through walls. He faced her.

She smelt of fire. Burnt hair.

"For once, can you relax and give in?" Evalyn, what looked like Evalyn, moved forward and pressed her lips against his. She tasted of charred meat. He pulled back, eyes daring not to blink. Air caught within threatened to explode with mind numbing aches.

"I am real." Her face cracked, and broke. Flesh peeled for burnt blackness. Fire raged around them. Vincentas shouted, his voice lost within a torrent of flames waving between them, caught within. Something wetted his head. He looked up, eyes filled with a bleeding roof break, split, and collapse.

Cass

Chapter XIV

"Wake up." Lilly's distant voice encouraged. "Wake up." She pleaded, whispering.
Cass swam to the surface of blurring light and mumbling noises. Breaking into pain and numbness, eyes snapped shut under penetrative green glow haunting the humid world. Tight, chilling iron clasped around wrist and foot. She lay suspended with a gut churning motion of weightlessness surrounding her body. Unseen, restrictive chains rattled under movements, constricting arms and legs. Chest heaved. Shakes rippled tense muscles.

"That you awake, Cass?" Taze coughed. She turned to look for the distinctive rasp echoing from all different directions. A nauseating ringing, nothing metallic or constructed, but a deep-set sound within her ears chimed within an aching skull.

"Taze? Taze." Her throat cracked in response. Emerald light doused her vision, an itching coldness crawled up her skin. Black gleaming walls rippled like a river, appearing solid in one blink, before morphing and swirled as ink in water. She blinked, fighting off the treble vision of the shifting wall, but failed to capture surroundings in one clear distinction.

Cass turned her head to find Taze. Muscles burned in her neck and back. Shoulders strained with motion to find her convict-in-arms. Taze hung in chains, arms pulled up. Restraints could not allow shoulders to sag, a torturous hold that kept her consistent and upright.

"Sorry Taze, sorry." She mumbled. Blood smeared the woman's face. Her clothing torn and shredded. Lowering her head not able to keep eye contact. Could not keep eye contact with those she let down.

"Got you too, yeah? The bastards." Taze spat.

"Didn't mean for this to happen, didn't mean for any of this to happen." Cass replied. Muscles stung along her back, spanning her shoulders. She only meant to find Lilly, to be free with her daughter.

"So is life." Taze mumbled. "Least we're going out in some glory. Got some of the… the things before they got me." She coughed.

"What they did, Cass. What they did." Her voice broke off in panting sobs. Chains clinked under shaking movements; Cass could not bring her eyes to look.

"Wish it was more." Cass vowed. "There will be more, more will pay." Hands curled into fists.

"That's the spirit." Taze half-laughed. "Hurts, but damn, that was worth it."

"Lucijan? You find him?" A swelling pulsed in her cheek, near the brand. Groaning, she closed her eyes to push away the pain. Jaw throbbed, skirting back to her ear. A dull pulse ebbed around her eyes, a discoloured bruise would form, the only makeup she had worn in years.

"Oh, yeah." Taze spoke, brashness gone. "He got some too. Saw the bodies. Didn't see him." Her voice dwindled. Head lowered under jade light; ashen shadows crossed her angular face.

"That's a good sign. He could be free. He *is* free." Cass fought through blurring senses and sharp stinging around delicate features. They had to be strong. This was not over. Lilly remained out there, and she would find her.

"Saved me three times, Cass." Taze lifted her head. Blood-stained face gave her a doubt to whether or not she was lived, only her eyes, black and unforgiving, watered with emotion, signalled her being alive.

"He'll save you a fourth time. You watch." She struggled to laugh.

"If he does, I'll never let him go." Taze's teeth flared stark white, highlighted in red with a wide grin, her eyes narrowed with a sharpness attributed to pain.

Cass leaned forward, trying to relieve aching pain of stretched limbs and pulled muscles. Her nostrils clogged with dampness; a metallic taste lined her throat. Tight, iron air sucked into her mouth. She wanted to close her eyes, but again, she did not listen to her body.

"I envy you, Cass." Taze breathed. Emerald light faded, it glowed a deep jade within the moving walls, even on the sleek, inky floor that swirled with a liquid texture. She faced the innocent murderer, who returned her gaze. Green light flared, making blood-stained features glistened with a thick, inky sickness.

"We're in the same place, Taze, can't envy that." Cass spat, blood welled in her mouth.

"Not about this." Laughed a reply. "You have Jolam, you have your daughter."

She did not have her daughter, not yet. Anrechel and Ninsar, both under her charge now gone.

"Nothing to be envious about, definitely not now." She mumbled. Weight of her head growing.

"Nothing is worth grieving for, but everything is worth living for." Taze spoke. "You lived Cass, you lived more than me."

"What are you talking about, you damn cut-throat convict?" Cass growled, raising her voice. Her throat shook as she strained to face Taze. "You heard me, the fearful matriarch of Cell Block Eight."

Taze looked up, matching the stare, returning the dead-eyes. The thousand-yard stare. Cass welled inside, her heart strengthened muscles in her taunt, stretched body. She had to escape. She needed the murderer back.

"What would your crew say now? The Sweet Sisters, their leader turn sweeter? Talking about the past and not the future?" She tried to shout, dry throat caught words in gurgled tones.

"You looking for a scrap you can't win, Cass the convict?" A sneer scarred the face. The bloodied eye winked.

"What kind of name is Taze, anyway?" She asked. "Since you think we will not make it, I can't tell anyone, can I?"

"It's short for Metazea." Hands signalled their movements in rattled chains, fingers pointed at Cass. "Don't you dare say anything."

A half-smile ignited her jaw with lingering pain. She could not help but think of Taze before her conviction, the sort of person she became. Her eyebrows sank lower. Metazea was dead and reborn as the renowned convict.

"Mei." Cass breathed. "I'm gonna call you Mei from now on. It's better than Taze."

"You bitch." Metazea coughed.

Unseen iron grated on metal, locks turned and chains rattled. Brighter lights drowned the room, forcing Cass to close her eyes. Putrid green faded to blurred colours within shut eyes.

Pained eyes opened, black walls glowed with a radiated green hue. Its watery texture now a solid, opaque mass enclosing her in the room. Footsteps clunked on metallic flooring, echoing as someone approached. One was a Faun.

"You people better not have heard our conversation or you'll not live to breathe it." Taze growled, returning to normal.

Cass faced forward, easier than to turn. A cloaked figure emerged from her left. She stood with arms folded. Her cracked, featureless face tilted up. Small curling horns protruded between thick, knotted black hair crowning a Faunish head. The Faun leader in the Sabanese temple, in front of the stone bird creature. The temple where she saw Armande for the first time in ten years.

"Where is my daughter?" Cass rattled in her chains. Silence growing more painful to hear. Her breathing increased. Nothing, not a shimmer of light in vacant pools of sight.

"Answer her, you goathole." Taze rasped and spat. A gob of blood splat on the woman's robe. It shivered under minimal light and threatened to swill towards her gaping chest.

The Faun inclined her head, only noticeable by the horn shadows criss-crossing her peeling, cracked face. A taloned finger scooped the tracing blood and raised it to her lips. She licked the finger clean.

Cass heard the strike. She turned to face Taze, leaning to the right, her bruised, tattooed face contorted. Features shrank as she exhaled winded breaths. A second smack landed on her ribs from a club wielding woman.

"Stop, just stop. Where's my daughter? Where's my daughter?" Her wheezing words failed to rise above strained taunts of Taze. Metallic ringing of bound chains jangled with each twisted turn.

The Faun raised a hand. Silence descended. Cass's erratic breathing tightened in her throat. She stared at the robed woman, who shrugged.

"Safe." The Faun smiled. "But you will bear another." Safe. Lilly would never be safe unless within her own arms. Her heart thumped harder, ears threatened to burst from its lurching rhythm.

"Now my question." Cass heard; a shiver crawled down her suspended body. "What were you doing in the Sabanese village? Defiling our sacred temples with your sacrilegious self." Each syllable ground into her ears. Clopping hooves resonated as the Faun paced, stopping in her periphery, constraining chains limiting view.

"We're lost, you crazed, religious hag." Taze wheezed.

"No." Cass hushed as she turned to catch Metazea's face.

Shadowed cat-o'-nine-tails raised before Taze and lashed down.

Cass screamed, but it did not match the bestial yell Mei erupted, shaking her vision. A metallic rattle followed. A hooded woman yanked the two-handed weapon away. Taze's scream forced Cass to close her eyes and look away. Hot wetness splashed her cheek.

"Leave her alone. Leave her alone." She shouted. "Please. Please stop."

"Not the womb, or the chest." Commanded the Faun. Her voice thundered. "Aim for her face next time, or arms." Ice slithered down Cass's spine at the passive tone returning to the calming Faun.

"We're lost." Cold tears tracing down her cheek.

"Lost." Mouthed the Faun. "Or searching?"

Taze moaned. A hooded woman stepped back, the cat-o'-nine-tails hung by her side, dull and limp. Blood slashed white robes. Serenity cloaked her, moving with a smoothness of tranquillity.

"Lost in the mountain. After fleeing from you and him." Cass faced their leader. She had to keep her mind straight, playing their game.

"In the mountain, you killed a child. Was that part of being lost?" The Faun spoke with a thin voice, she strained to hear over Taze's sobbing.

"What child? We killed no child in the mountain." She retorted, eyeing the Faun's blank expression of her broken-skinned face and the dead, milky eyes occupying cracked sockets.

"Child of many. Child of stone. Child of the Great Ones." Several voices chorused together. Stell. Cass remembered. Stell bound to the cave wall, pregnant with that thing inside her. The black arm crawling out of Stell's screaming mouth.

"Stell. No." she blurted out.

"The human host. Unwilling and vibrant…" The Faun leader declared.

"Her name was Stell." Cass snapped, chains shook in her jerked movements. "And you… you did that to her."

"She was unlucky not to birth a child of the stone. But others will." The Faun tilted back her head, light pooling over her splitting face. Grey lips parted in a crimson smile.

"After murdering the child of the stone, where did you go?" The Faun moved again, clothes sighing as she circled behind Cass.

"Where's my daughter? You said she was safe? Give her to me. I'll answer any question you want." She tried to turn, wrists chafing under iron grasp.

"Give her." Taze gargled. "Give her an answer." The pained voice broke through Cass.

"A Faun, a female Faun found us. She took care of us in the mines." She played their game, hoping to reveal answers about Lilly.

Hooves stopped clicking. "Ah, my sister." Movement blurred in her periphery. Someone sat in a chair, head low. Matted, dirtied dreadlocks hung before her face, dangling on her seated knees. Her torn duster ripped and worse for wear.

"Anrechel." Cass gasped.

"I was wondering when she would crawl out of darkness and into true light." The Faun walked to Anrechel, talons brushed through thick hair, stroking her like a pet. Anrechel's head reared back, enormous eyes peering behind bifocals making them huge, unblinking orbs of opal in the light.

"My dear sister, you know too much for your little mind." The Faun patted her sister's face, while combing matted, dirtied hair.

"Your sister? How could you leave her in that state? How could you leave her in the mines?" Cass spat; her jaw numbed.

"On the contrary, she left us." Taloned hand gripped her sister's shoulder. Pale, soulless eyes looked up at Cass from the peeling face.

"I'd leave you too." Snarled Taze. "With that face, not even the blind would be near you." A rasping laugh turned into a gurgled cough.

"Physicality of oneself a minor hinderance and does not deter the purpose of the one." The Faun shook her head. A hooded woman, who carried the cat-o'-nine-tails, walked forward.

"No." The word resonated through the metallic room. "We need her for breeding. She's had enough physical punishment for one day."

"Any man who touches me won't be a man afterwards." Taze threatened.

"It won't be a human who will bless you with a child." The Faun replied, while looking at Cass. A thin, blood-red smile widened. Stell. Cass's eyes shook, kept them open, hoping to see beyond the Faun's lack of words, to witness between the lines.

"I've told you everything, now my daughter. Where is she?" An uncontrollable tremor bubbled in her tight throat.

"Anguish has followed you all your life." The Faun's head tilted, surveying her with a curiosity. "I guess you can manage one more."

Her heart stopped. *Anguish in all my life can manage one more.* She did not need one more. Iron grated on metal. Teal light bled into the room, washing the Faun and sitting Anrechel in its ambient glow. Footsteps followed.

Cass turned in vain. Emotions breaking in quivering eyes, she blinked to clear her vision.

Cass only saw her daughter.

Lilly stood in silence, head down. She did not know whether to scream or cry. Tightness welled in her womb, a yearning for complete surrender to be with her child. At any cost.

A hand stroked her thick hair away from her sleeping face. Cass's muscles exploded along her neck. Thick beating of hate pounded at her temples. Armande stood behind Lilly, his gloved hand ruffling her daughter's hair. Blue light dampened his face, darkening thick brows and a groomed moustache curling into a sneering smile.

"Relax, Cassidy. Relax. Harm will not come to precious Lilly, needed she is after all. Bring out truth in all things." Armande's voice fuelling strength and brewing depths within her quivering gut.

Combusting in a tirade, Cass unleashed every emotional thought in her mind that raced through it quicker than a repeater bolt, wishing it were just as deadly, accurate, and swift. She pulled and kicked at the chains for exotic freedom, but they held firm. Digging into flesh with each robust turn and twist. Pleas and shouts, mocking laughter and cries muffled in Cass's ears. Only her own voice broke louder above other noises.

"Mom." It broke through the descending fog and focused on her hearing. Ceasing her struggle for freedom, she looked at her daughter, who stared back.

"Lilly." Cass gasped.

"Mom, it's fine." Lilly spoke too wise for her age. She had grown up. Her head shook, admiring the spirit of her ten-year-old daughter, a picture of calm in a sea of chaos within her mind.

"We'll be together. We will." She promised, nodding to herself.

A single, clear tear broke down her daughter's vibrant, lighter eyes verging on blue, so much like her fathers. Cass wanted to catch it, remove the tear from her daughter's cheek. Remove the cause of the tear.

"See?" Croaked the Faun. "Anguish. Why put yourself through that?"

"She's my daughter. She's my world." Cass's heart warmed as Lilly smiled.

"Take her away." The Faun waved her hand. Armande turned her around, turning to leave. She dared not blink, wanting to see her daughter and remember every line, every hair, every feature.

"I failed you." Cass admitted.

"You never have." The youthful voice scythed through Cass. Breaking eye contact with her daughter. Strong and forgiving, nothing like her mother. She shook in her restraints. Metal, unseen doors groaned to a close, blue light snuffed out, returning the room into a shade darker than jade, with its emerald hue phasing in corners of the black-walled domain.

"We can learn so much from innocence. They see things differently." The Faun stood where her daughter had been, folding her arms together into long, shimmering sleeves of vestments, garbing an exposed body.

"Prepare them both. We will breed the violent one next morrow. The Voices mother." The Faun turned, looking at Cass. "Will be used today."

She remained silent as the Faun vacated. Taze's vile retorts followed as their captors left the room, even continuing afterwards. Hanging in silence, only her daughter consumed her mind. Nothing else mattered. She was alive. *I could reach her.* Time not on her side. A candlemark or more could have passed, when she surfaced in the waking world. She had to escape.

Clanking of chains echoed above, Cass crumpled on the hard, cold floor. Hands unbound them, freeing tight iron teeth around wrists and feet. Though free, swift bonds were lashed around their limbs, locking them together. She sat with her back to Taze, both propping each other up.

"Wilmar was my husband." Metazea's dry voice echoed. "He was a surveyor. Architect. Spent more time in the Thousand Isles than in his home. We joked he was married to the past than to me."

"We always wanted a child." Taze's head moved to her right. Cass turned hers to the left in acknowledgement.

Metallic screeching forced her to face the door, pouring teal light into the room. She lowered her head, the brunt of the light burning her iris.

"You bastards always spoil the one-to-one, don't you?" Taze rasped.

"Your time has come." A monotone voice called out. Two women entered, robed like the Faun.

Whistling scythed through the air. Cass flinched, wiggling in her bonds for cover. Repeater bolts. Dull thuds filled their cell. Gasps rocked from the women as they jerked. Collapsing to the ground, dead at her feet. She looked up, a black silhouette of a repeater carrying man stood blocking teal light.

"Sorry, didn't know where you were." Lucijan's innocent voice filled her ears.

"Lucky. Lucky." Taze gasped out. "That's four times you save my ass. When I get better."

Cass and Lucijan shushed together. The conscript entered the room, closing it behind. He trotted to her, lowering the repeater. Pulling out a knife, he sawed at the bonds.

"Good seeing you, Lucijan." Cass thanked, he blushed while hacking at the ropes.

"Keep your damn eyes to yourself." Taze rasped.

"How did you… where are we?" She asked, tripping over her tongue. So many questions, not a lot of time.

"One candle mark I was in Konniak. Next." She brushed off the ropes and stood up, rubbing her legs and wrung her hands together, gathering motion back into her limbs. "Next. In the mountain, but doesn't look like the mountain, or the inside of one." He started cutting Taze free.

Cass noticed Lucijan had a repeater strapped to his back, and one by her feet.

"Any sign of Jolam? Or Ninsar?" She picked up the repeater, feeling its weight in her tired arms, but knowledge of Lilly nearby fuelled her muscles.

"There're other areas. The locks in this place are strange, th…" Lucijan finished cutting Taze free when she lurched at him, grasped his hair with blood-soaked hands and smothered Lucijan in wet, deep kisses. Cass watched as Lucijan's face turned to shock. Taze yanked away.

"When I get better, you are mine." She swore as she grasped the collar of Lucijan's duster around his neck.

Lucijan looked between Cass and Taze, lost for words, mouthing words with no sound.

"When you're free, he's yours." She chuckled. Lucijan aided the murderer to stand, who stood a good foot taller and wider than the conscript, but he held her up.

"How do we get out?" She looked around.

"Follow the red lights. This isn't like the mountain. This is something else." The conscript spoke. Sweat glistened across his forehead under the green glow.

"You found a way out?" Cass asked.

Lucijan nodded, shifting Taze up, and shuffled to the door.

"After Konniak turned back to this. I walked around the tunnels, eventually I saw light. I thought it was light from rocks, being so dark, it was the side of the mountain." Lucijan spoke while she headed to the closed iron door.

"You were free. Why come back?" Cass looked at the conscript.

"Had a reason to come back." Lucijan moved to the right-hand side of the barred exit.

"Oh, this man. I'm not having him for a week, I'm having him for life." Taze croaked. She sounded drunk and looked it with her head lolling back and forth, feet dragged on the floor.

"Place your entire hand on the orb. The door opens." Lucijan instructed. Reaching over, he placed his hand over a black, glassy orb. The door opened horizontally, separating in two parts. Fingers tightened around the repeater.

"Follow the red lights, I'll see you outside." Cass turned and nodded to Lucijan.

"You're not coming with us?" Lucijan gasped.

"Got to find my daughter." Cass squeezed Taze's arm.

"Cass." Lucijan unhooked himself from Taze and removed his bandolier, handing it to her. "Good luck."

She took the bandolier from Lucijan's shaking arm.

"I'll see you outside." She vowed, slinging the bandolier over her shoulder.

Vincentas

Chapter XV

Fangs of night closed around the Inquirer's Hall. Tainted windows bled faint, diminished light onto the filled courtyard of justice. Acidic smoke clogged tired throats, murmured prayers caused a human breeze to infiltrate alert senses.

She struggled against her bonds, as they all did, tied to the erect, blackened pole penetrating through stacks of kindling. An Acolyte, ready to dispense sentence, held the burning torch ready to ignite her fate. Flames doused faces in fiery tongues.

"You could do so much more than this." Her eyes of molten gold reflected his unblinking gaze. A different time, a different year.

"Being summoned by an Inquisitor is a high honour." Vincentas heard his reply, but it held no weight. Sounded like someone else speaking for him than his own words. Words from the mind, not the heart.

"You and honour. No wonder you married me before taking your prize." She teased, propping herself up on the soft, inviting bed, sun-drenched, thick hair falling onto azure, crumpled sheets. Lavender a stronger aroma than the musky, natural scent of his wife. No denying they were opposites. It added to their mutual attraction.

"Stop changing the subject. And no one can deny an Inquisitor." He could have lost himself in time at what he saw, never wanting to change this moment.

"Could you deny a wife, Vinny?" A soft hand caressed his chin. She smiled, her eyes did not.

Those same eyes looked ahead. Hair sawn to bare scalp, tuffs of auburn hair flaked in black blood.

"Evalyn Haldis Raivo. You have been charged with Mysticism. Abetting the Mystic ways. And being a Mystic. How do you plead?" Grand Justice Inquisitor Irieth Garryk announced. Might as well have condemned her here.

He saw the heretical books, bizarre tapestries she hid in their shared lives. From the same person he married, the woman who promised the world and gave him hope. There it was, unbridled hope, a caring facet only a Mystic could conjure onto the weak.

She looked his way. A wife of eight years. A constant supporter of what he did and how he achieved it. Swelling tears ignited her eyes, bruised lips promised to break. Colour drained from flawless features. She died the moment of her discovery, her wailing, pleading discovery when the truth availed. Pleading for their marriage, praying to a faith she had no time for. Condemnation settling in with steely resolution.

"Guilty." Her word ice within his stomach and sharper than any blade.

"Guilty. Guilty." A singular, unknown voice pulled him from darkness to blurring emerald light ebbing into existence. Hands gnawed into ropes. Sweat traced down itching skin. A pulsing glow, malachite coloured, faded and grew around him.

Vincentas turned his head, powerless below the waist unable to move. Fleur hung beside. Head tilted in the shadows, twitches jerked taut shoulders. Inaudible mumbles broke from the suspended Combatant. Taste of copper lingered in his dry throat, the familiar odour of blood.

"Fleur. Fleur." He whispered, words cracked in dried lips.

Blurring light pulsed again, illuminating Fleur's condition. Whites of her eyes occupied open sockets. Scarlet tears ran down open-mouthed face. Features displaying unwavering shock.

"Let her go. Mystic, let her go." Vincentas shouted. Sounding weak even to his ears, from his strained, tried voice.

"Let her go? Look at her, only she can free herself. How much she enjoys illusions of grandeur. Let her go? From pleasure. From excess. From an eternal high? What kind of friend would do that?" A multitude of voices replied. Vincentas searched, hearing three or four voices say each part in thick, enunciated accents of Cythean, Orschal and Kheda Ishan. His teeth gritted. Forehead creased in wrinkles.

"Reveal yourself. Or are you a coward?" He snapped. Green veins of light bled throughout obsidian walls of his occupation, illuminating a cube shaped room. Nothing else lay present, not even a guard or their captor.

"And you are no coward?" Coyly, a woman's voice pulsated in his ear. Soft hands stroked through thin hair, igniting a tingle filtering down his exposed neck. He could not escape the touch. Perfumed knuckles traced his scalp. He tried to turn. Bonds restricted him. Shaking to form rudimentary movement, Vincentas tilted his neck to see the would-be torturer.

"Let me go, and I'll show you my cowardice." His own voice quivered. Pulsating light illuminated more of the room. A swimming conscious caught sight of Arno, bound and hanging, suspended above the metal grated floor. Reticence, hooded and cloaked in the torturer's attire, held in black bonds. Alleck, innocent and mumbling the loudest, hung beside Fleur.

His stomach filled with heaviness. No waters could douse or deflate.

"Idol threats do nothing here, Inquisitor." The voice echoed throughout the room. The speaker had to be here. Coldness blew against him, a shiver he could not shake coursed unwillingly down his spine. Perfumed hands left their lingering scent on his scalp.

"Vincentas. That you?" Fleur's strained voice coughed.

"Fleur? Keep awake, keep your eyes open. Stop thinking, above all else, stop thinking." Instinct kicked in. Free minds working together would overpower the Mystic, no matter the odds.

"Will do. Will do." Her voice quietening.

"Combatant." Vincentas shot. Fleur fixed her eyes on him. She stiffened despite being held in bonds. "Remember. The Mystic will use your mind against you.

Even the strongest of wills, the mightiest of minds. A mind is no fortress and all can be breeched."

"Yes, Inquisitor." Fleur replied. Her eyes as dead as her half-mask. She gave a half smile.

"Very true, Inquisitor. I apologise for the rudimentary predicament I find myself in." Arno added. Vincentas's strength surged through his captured arms, straining his neck. He turned to witness Arno trying to rotate in his captive state to face him.

"Glad you're free too, Chanter." The Inquisitor proclaimed. A warmth crept along his body, welcomed compared to the coldness of the cell and brighter than the emerald glare of flaring veins of light ebbing throughout their black, metallic cell.

"Awake Faun? See, you're into rope games too. Guess we've got two things in common." Fleur chuckled.

"I shall not rise to your vulgar tastes, Combatant." Arno replied without breaking his usual stoic tone.

"Where are we?" Alleck's pained plea caught Vincentas's hearing.

"Arno's dungeon." Fleur quipped.

"Combatant, enough. Entrant, keep your mind focused. Do not think. Clear your mind and focus on staying conscious." Instructions came to him from decades of training, they always did. Same rules did not work in Riemkeler, they would work here. Alleck remained clouded in suspicion. He was weak, vulnerable and now a key for Mystics to unlock the door of those minds around him.

"Yes, Inquisitor. I'll not fail you." Alleck replied, the need to impress on his naïve tongue, but sensed the tiredness and, above all, the uncertainty.

"Awake at last." A stern voice broke Vincentas's concentration to look straight ahead. Bright white light flared behind a shadowed figure. He squinted. A top-hat wearing man stood before him. Vincentas could identify no other features or clothing.

"You have our attention now, Mystic." He replied. The shadowed man made no sound as he stepped forward. A black vertical line descended, closing off the white glow. Trapped in the black room, ebbing green ambience continued its pulsating beat.

"So, how do you feel? Are you ready?" The newcomer spoke, a hint of Cythean to his voice with an edge of academy trained. Their features coming into focus, Vincentas dared not break his stare.

"Ready for what?" The Inquisitor watched as the individual glided closer. Pulsing greens flared behind, casting him in an ominous emerald glow. Robes clothed him in the lecturer variety. A black cape-coat hung from lithe shoulders. An unblemished face, waxy and pale, gazed at Arno with surveying blue, lightening eyes within taut, smooth features. Not a wrinkle in sight.

Black lines weaved across his face, stretching beneath the rim of the top-hat, forming a dark, shining web trapping the male's features. Lines not caused from sleek dampness on hair, it was something else entirely. Vincentas's guts twisted into knots.

"Arno. Are you ready?" A hand outstretched. Long, pale fingers raised towards the hanging Faun. Its voice not his own, lips not moving, but every word crystal clear. Vincentas steeled himself, tensing his muscles. He fought against his mind to think, to show weakness, to leave a gap that could be exploited.

"I am not ready." Arno lowered his head. Defeat lined his voice. He shuffled to move his body, legs bound, the obsidian hilt clasped around his belted waist.

"Chanter. Chanter, you know this man?" Best to be professional, to snap Arno out of submission, but the Faun remained unresponsive, head lowered.

"You are ready. You do not want to submit yourself to the path you will transcend." The figure circled Arno, hands contorting to enunciate his words. Metallic echoing signalled footfalls. The man bypassed Vincentas and stood before Alleck.

"Are you ready? The doubter. The abandoned. Are you ready for a new life?" Its long fingers reached up to embrace Alleck's face. The Entrant burst into tears, shaking in his constraints.

"Leave the boy alone. Come, Mystic, try a mind to rival your nonsense." The Inquisitor snapped. He twisted in his bonds, shaking in suspended captivity, and spat at the pale man.

Smooth features turned to observe Vincentas. Hand cradled Alleck's face in long, sinewy fingers. He never stopped holding the Entrant's face. An odour of steel mixed with bruised skin flared in his nostrils. Leaving the Entrant alone, the figure stepped forward, gliding towards him.

"How peculiar. A mere blood vessel in the arteries of the living world concerning himself with beings beyond comprehension that could render continents obsolete." The words filtered into Vincentas's mind as sharp as the elongated fingers circumnavigated his face.

Ice eyes, unblinking and shifting, observed him from lidless sockets. A stench of oil, not for a Gaslamp, but the putrid black blood of the earth, clouded the unwanted visitor. He turned against the slippery grasp, unnaturally long fingers held his face to avoid bowel rupturing odour.

"You are nothing. Vinny." A woman's voice. A voice Vincentas had not heard since Inquisitor fires claimed her life by his judgement pulsed into his mind.

Pushing thoughts into his gut, dissolving in guilt, he stared at the would-be torturer. Black lines snaked beneath the top hat down his face. One stabbed into a collar. Dried crimson blood lay on the cape-coat, where the blackness sank under tight-fitted clothing.

"What's your name? Let me guess, you have many." The Inquisitor smiled. Hot air burned his lungs under suspended motion with each word he spoke.

"Those you have encountered before give you rudimentary reference, this is different. Significantly different." Cythean words poured through transparent lips lost within pale skin. He knew the Mystic could twist and deform, its sight alone killing their foes before a fatal strike. This was no different.

"You're wrong." A curling snarl tugged his cheeks. The bony, strong fingers left his face, but not before leaving a chill on the skin. "You're exactly like them. Every single one of them. All can die. All will die."

"You say that to yourself before killing your wife? Or to justify a punishment you regret?" Its head turned. Tension clenched his teeth. Fingers tug into bound palms. Vincentas's snarl disappeared as his eyes narrowed on the Mystic. Legs shook with inevitable uncontrolled anger.

"You're good. But I've killed better." The Inquisitor fought to keep surfacing thoughts silent. He knew one or two had slipped. An open mind a fortress unguarded; pointless and perilous.

"Was it you who killed them? Did he claim them as his own?" The pale man turned, facing Arno. The familiarity of the Mystic used grew heavy in Vincentas's foggy mind. Mystic, using divide and conquer upon them, sow suspicion that was not there. An icy chill descended his posture, unable to shake off. The first time a Mystic attempted this.

"Implausible. We are merchants, lost scurrying in the expanse of Riemkeler." Arno stated. Fleur cracked a laugh. Alleck's loud cries of woe drifted to sobs in quietening solitude and inaudible mumbles.

"Don't lower to their standards, Ferde." He sighed. Disappointment lined every word, a genuine hurt. Their captor shook his head.

Ferde, Arno's surname, the Mystic must have read his mind. Vincentas gritted his teeth. The Mystic's smile scythed his face in two. He glided towards the suspended Chanter. Eyes never leaving Vincentas. Smile never changing.

"Reading minds is child's play. My knowledge of Arno's name is horrendously simplistic. Why not ask him, Inquisitor? Is that not what you do, ask questions?" The torturer's hand circled the Faun's head, turning him in suspension to view Vincentas. The Chanter did not raise his eyes.

"Clever. Trying to sow paranoia in our ranks. Fight amongst ourselves." Making suspicion grow between them, try to think, searching for another chink in the armour of weakness. Vincentas tried to steel his rapid heartbeat, pounding within his chest and ears. He could not remove the sliding tendrils of suggestion probing the inner sanctum of his mind.

"You have been fighting amongst yourselves since the ones you brand Mystic walked this world." The torturer shook his head. Nothing revealed his motives. Unblemished features never showing a crack of feeling, or a twitch of a hidden agenda.

"Perhaps you're right. So, I apologise. You know his name, you know mine. I don't know yours." Knowing the enemy was half the battle, their thoughts, feelings and desires manifesting for their defence and twist on the world. Vincentas cursed himself for not looking for the answer sooner.

"True, Vin. Present me, Arno. My fellow warrior. Compatriot. Struggler. Tell your 'old friend' my name." The torturer transfixed his gaze on the Faun. It had to be a trick, a vain attempt to goad the Chanter or himself, to cause an emotional response. Green light ebbed and returned with a sickening emerald colour, losing to a hint of violet.

"Nobody." Arno uttered, his stoicism returning.

"Spoken like a true chosen." The pale, slender man patted the hanging Faun on the shoulder. It floated over to Alleck, who had stopped sobbing. Silently, the man crossed the iron grated floor. Long fingers cupped the Entrant's wet face, and he coddled it like a doctor would hold a child for a new mother.

"Who am I?" The torturer spoke, his face as close to Alleck's quivering features held within slender digits.

"Dargus Enote." The Entrant spat, as if the words were poison and he wanted them vacated from his throat.

"What is Dargus Enote?" The pale man continued stroking the trapped face of Alleck.

"Lecturer in the Academy of Riemkeler." The Entrant gasped between words, pulling air into heaving lungs, tired and tight.

Dargus Enote, the Lecturer. Vincentas studied Dargus, remembering his brief and realistic encounter with Athgeric. Details of the academy, trying to get underground. Built from the foundations of a city before recorded time.

"So, we meet, Dargus." The Inquisitor fixed his gaze on the lecturer, their kidnapper, an attempted torturer. Pale man, shining under flaring green lights imbued in the walls, nothing like an esteemed lecturer in a major city of learning. Mysticism had altered him, warped his very being; what remained of Dargus may not be alive at all.

"We heard a lot about you, from a reliable source." The lecturer faced Arno on saying reliable. A poignant look lanced at the suspended Faun. Another method to bury secrecy, a tool to seek havoc where there was none. A shiver ate into the Inquisitor at Dargus's methodical words.

"You keep referencing the Chanter as if you know him. You do not know him." Vincentas voiced, but an unknown feeling pulled at his skin, hairs stood on end. An Inquisitor could never ignore a gut feeling.

"If your unbelieving, self-doubting Entrant knows of me, then your illustrious, ever-faithful 'Old Friend' should certainly know me." The way Dargus spoke awakened his inner mind. He struggled to contain them, push aside and refute as nonsense. Mysticism could not be allowed to win against reality.

"I forgot in all this pitiful misdirection. Arno, are you ready?" The lecturer spoke, gliding towards the Faun.

"No." Struggled the Chanter. Vincentas looked at Arno, hanging there like a prized boar. As limp as his voice, unsure and defeated. He looked up again, black bonds lost in darkness of the unseen ceiling. Fleur moved, Alleck remained useless. Reticence remained in solitary silence. He could do with Violet, the Combatant would help.

"Stop. It is useless." Dargus's hand snapped to the side, lancing towards Vincentas with a steady, pointing finger of judgement.

"Arno, our brother. Embrace your path. Welcome to your destiny." The Inquisitor watched as Arno lowered, hooved feet hitting metallic floor making a soft hollow echo. Black ropes, shiny and sleek, retracted off the Chanter's wrists and slid upwards, disappearing into nothingness. Dargus dwarfed the crumpled Faun.

"Arno. You can not deny this, you can not run from this. You sought us out, remember?" They conversed like old friends; as lovers would. Everything was wrong. An unspeakable closeness between them beyond Mystic illusions.

The Chanter turned, head lowered. Green glows, bathing his simple robed form. Wisps of smoke skittered across the metallic floor. Jade shafts of light blurred between the cracks of Arno's unmovable form; he lay caught within the web of Dargus's shadow strings.

"Tell him. Tell your old friend who you really are." Pale, elongated fingers slid over the lithe shoulders crowned in black robes. Like bird talons ensnaring prey.

"Arno." Vincentas whispered. He was losing. His mind raced beyond waking limits of thinking. He opened the gates of defence. A thousand thoughts bled and twisted together. Arno's head lifted. Tears cleaned his Faunish face. Coldness crept down Vincentas's back, his breath caught and hung within him, tight and secure. He feared to let it go.

"Plausible." Arno's eyes drifted up, settling on his old friend.

Reality sunk into his mind, plying it open in cold, iron fingers. Athgeric a Mystic altered his own realm. Taught by an "old friend." Alleck seeing Dargus Enote rushed into his mind, the Inquisitor stood before the scholar and the Chanter, watching them beneath the academy, flanked by naked Mystics. A coven, within the bowels of philosophy and intellect. Underneath the Inquisition all this time.

"End this Arno. Why." Vincentas shouted, teeth gritted.

"Do you accept?" Dargus drew a paled finger around Arno's face.

The Faun's lips manoeuvred into a smile, both wicked and pleasant, before Vincentas's waking eyes. His hearing hammered as surging air rage emptied his tired throat. Arno disappeared as he descended, suspended in black wires. Thrashing to escape. Twisting and writhing in would-be vengeance.

Watery, irritating eyes flashed around him as redness washed over his sight. A horizon crowned in crying voices of men, women and children descending from the blackened maw of an iron sky, lowered to the bleeding, waiting dawn.

Cass

Chapter XV

During six of the ten years of the Purifier Rebellion, Cass fought with the Cythean Irregulars. Understanding and maintaining the Mark IV Repeater, reading layouts of land, living off food an aurochs would not touch and how to evade lurking Primals part and parcel of the ragtag Irregulars created for enemy disposal with insufficient resources. Only twice were orders given to venture underground, or within the womb of a mountain. This looked nothing like the inside of a mountain.

Cass grew conscious of valenki boots reverberating off reflective, smooth floor, which looked like glass but harder than steel. Other footsteps alerted her to hostiles, they echoed down passages lost in blackness. Green veins flared along curving, smooth walls, flowing left to right. Ahead of her illuminated, before the emerald pulse debilitated, only for it to beat again and illuminate dark tunnels in a burst of jade.

Time vanished. No candles with its rudimentary marks to highlight passed time, or mechanisations to show what remained of the day. No natural light to show when to sleep or eat. Time as distant as the sun. No alarms raised since Cass left the confinement of the prison room. She hoped Lucijan and Taze had made it. She smiled. It would not be Taze after this, it would be Mei.

Rounding a corner, two robed women guarded a door. Raising her repeater, with the leather strap eating into her shoulder, she squeezed the trigger. Twitching in shock and snuffed air from their lungs, the women dropped, clunking on the sleek surface. Blood pooled under black robes, spreading as liquid does to fill up volume. Cass did not look at their faces. She had killed during the war for survival, and that ate into her mind. This was different, this was for Lilly, and their dead, pleading faces of stillness would not breed gut-consuming guilt.

Stepping over the bodies, she pressed her hand over the orb. Pacing backwards and keeping her eyes on the door, the heavy repeater tucked under her arm, freeing a heavy left hand to wipe brewing sweat off her forehead, which threatened to trickle and merge into her eyes.

Steam hissed, air sucked back while the door vaulted upwards. Cass braced herself, tilting to the side to make herself narrow, less of a target. Greying mist faded, highlighted green from the continuous pulse. Two black tunnels extended. One beating with a teal headache-brewing light, the other a violent red. Red is the way out, Cass remembered Lucijan's useful words. Turning to the blue lit corridor, she trekked on.

"What do you hope to achieve?" A deep, resonating voice rocked in her skull. Vision twisted, pulled, and elongated. She stopped walking, gritting her teeth not to shout out.

"Believing yourself free to continue a life of ignorance. What purpose is that to us?" continued the barrage in her breaking mind.

Walls steadied her staking balance, as an eager hand raced out to steady her world. Metal tasting air filled her throat. Lungs burned. Sickness swelled in rippled stomach. Ringing strained ears. Shouts not of her own making pulled Cass's senses to the brink.

"I want my daughter." She spat. Breaking free of the turbulent, shaking vision to clarity and steadiness.

Beating heart threatened to explode, rasping breath fogged hearing. The tunnel sloped upwards, no stairs clear on the black incline. Turning round, repeater clasped in shaking hands, searching for the speaker of the deep voice. Nobody. Only the endless shadows accompanied her. Pulsing sick, teal light revealed the emptiness of the tunnel. An unshakable coldness held onto her gut.

Hurried, chasing footfalls spun Cass around. Distant shouts pricked her ears. Secrecy died the moment she escaped, but the dead guards would be found, eventually. Blackened shadows, more definitive than the ones cast by the walls, raced towards the sloped tunnel, followed by hammering steps growing louder and louder. Cass turned and ran, having the initiative and the head start. Now it was gaining a larger gap between herself and the pursuers.

Feet ran quicker than her pounding heart, but all that mattered was finding Lilly before being caught. Turning round one corridor, banked around another. Skidded on slippery, metallic surface of the reflective floor and gritted her teeth against burning muscles. No matter how fast she ran, her pursuers grew closer.

Voices ahead shouted in rough, guttural Sabanese tones. Cass looked up. Four robed women stood ahead, holding nets to ensnare her. Shouts rang in the corridor. She answered with whistles of the repeater. Bolts thudded into the pack, dropping two, scattering the others. She turned and ran down another tunnel. Teal veins flashing with a quickness matching her quivering stomach.

Three doors lay ahead at the neck of the corridor. Cass bolted for the middle door, slamming her hand over the orb. She wheezed as the door swished open, darted for the other orbs, igniting them to slow down her pursuers. Entering the middle ajar door, Cass's breath beat out of her. She jumped into a bright white room. With a hiss, the metallic door closed behind her.

People clouded her vision.

She raised the repeater. The motion echoed in the room ten times or more. Calming her nerves, the people in the room were stationary, unmoving. She tried to swallow the shaking in her throat, quivering muscles held the heavy repeater. Her gulp echoed in the room as she stepped away from the door.

A Faun hung in the air. Black wires, thick as robe, fed into exposed arms, legs, chest and face. A Cythean woman, pale skinned with brunette hair. Dark, coal skinned Kheda Ishan man. Two Sabanese. Three from the Enclave. Their eyes open. Unblinking. Not following Cass as she neared them. A coldness steamed from exposed skin. Her eyes dared not blink.

Cass stopped. A girl with black matted hair, delicate features and the tone of the Sabanese.

"Ninsar." She gasped. Her voice stuttered around the room, echoing in unfamiliar tones, intonations, and accents.

The girl did not move. Unblinking, glassy eyes continued to stare ahead. Chill coursed down her spine. She closed the distance between the suspended girl and herself, letting the repeater hang from the strap.

"I'll get you free. I'll get you free." Cass repeated, looking at the black, shiny wires holding Ninsar in place. Her coarse fingers curled around the softness of the imbedded, smooth wire. Eyebrows came together, frowning. This was not metal. It was not anything she had felt between her fingers before. Suppressing a shudder, she tried pulling the wire snaking into Ninsar's left arm above the wrist.

Ninsar swung at the motion, bare, freezing legs brushing against Cass. Gritting her teeth, she yanked at the wires, determined to break Ninsar free at any cost. The Sabanese girl continued to stare down, glassy, reflective eyes unresponsive to her strain and labour at pulling the bonds inserted into Ninsar's flesh. She stopped, warm blood trickled between the penetrative wires, dampening her grasp.

"Stop." An annoyed shout echoed in the dome room. Cass broke free and spun, holding up the repeater in two hands. Eyes fixed on a man wearing black, which fitted his body like a second skin, standing before an opened, circular door, which shrank behind him.

"My work. My research. How dare you?" He stammered, fists shaking before him. His black clothes, nothing Cass had seen before, broke apart, revealing tweed waistcoat, white shirt and trousers of Cythean design.

"You talk." She snapped. The man ceased moving. "You breathe too much for my liking. You walk too much for my liking. I'll snatch the life right out of you." She closed the distance between them, repeater raised, until the repeater muzzle jabbed the man in the face.

"Cut her loose and I'll think about sparing you." She tilted her head to the right, did not break her gaze from the unreadable, unblinking eyes of the man.

"I can't." The man exclaimed. She locked the trigger. Its echoing metallic click jolted the newcomer. He looked Cythean. Smelt of money. Dressed in bureaucracy. Everything that made Cass bristle in anger. Even his arrogant skin crawled with lauded prestige.

"Last chance." Cass snarled with as much fake calmness she could muster.

"You'll kill her, setting her free. Ther-" The man talked too much for Cass's liking. Squeezing the trigger was as natural as breathing. She did not turn away, but watched his face disintegrate. Bolts carved through his skull. Blood fanned from the back of his split head. Red petals floated from collapsing body, which coated white walls behind him.

He did not smell of richness; he stunk of death. Cythean trousers already soiling. She turned back to face Ninsar, still hanging with the black wires, unmoving.

"I'll find Lilly, then come back." She spoke to the silent girl. Her shaking hand reached out and grasped the girl's thin, stiff arm, squeezing it.

"I swear I'd never let you go, remember?" Looking up at the unblinking eyes, her thumb stroked over cold, damp skin. Blinking back tears, ready to break down her face.

Letting go of Ninsar, Cass walked to the door where the Cythean man had entered. The door increased in size as she came nearer and fully opened on her approach. She stopped; repeater raised in steady hands.

Muzzle aimed at targets, flashing between different bodies, all unmoving.

Keeping her finger on the trigger, Cass inched forward. Within the black tunnel that extended as far as light covered, hanging from a singular black wire, were people. Swinging in motion, head down, feet dangling above grated iron floor. Bodies dripped with perspiration, constant drip of water prickled her hearing, like a light rain patting on corrugated iron. Her eyes fleeted from body to body. They were all from Kheda Ishan. All men.

Walking down the pathway, she dared not blink. She glanced at the bodies. She looked at the arms, her heart sank. Black angular markings, rectangles and shapes unknown to Cass. Half circles eaten by triangles, all black markings covered the skin like tattoos.

Searching their faces, she held her breath, switching her glance to the ones behind, beside each other and in front. A gulp she could not swallow rippled down her throat, into a stomach that would not settle. Arms quivered on their hold of the repeater.

They all had the same face. They were the same person.

Cass picked up her pace, jogging to the end of the grated pathway. Bypassing many of the same Kheda Ishan man, many of the same Faun, many of the Cythean woman with brunette hair. Grinding to a halt, her valenki boots hammered the grated floor. Cass shook her head at the last two suspended bodies. Shorter than the rest. Female. Sabanese. Both looked identical to Ninsar.

Humid bodies brought sweat to Cass's forehead. She reached out, taking Ninsar's arm and squeezing her hand. This was not Ninsar. It was someone who looked like her. Real Ninsar was hanging in the white room. She could not take her eyes off the black markings running the length of the girl's bare, stiff arms. Exactly like Karwen.

Stepping back, she grasped the repeater in two hands. A black metallic door lay ahead at the end of the pathway, past the hanging bodies. Her shaking hand placed over the orb, doors slid up engulfing her in blue, warm, penetrative light. She strode into the opening.

Cass took four echoing steps into the light before collapsing to the ground, screaming.

She held her head, her brain punching her skull. Closing her eyes, she fought against the splitting force that threatened to tear everything apart.

"Breathe." A voice, collective as it was serene, filled the torrent of her hearing. She focused on the singularity of the voice, could smell nothing, could not feel the surrounding air. Muscles contracted. Throat closed. Lungs drowned. Warmness flooded from her flickering, uncontrollable eyes.

"Breathe." The same calm voice pulsed again. Cass opened her eyes. A pair of Cythean boots, dirtied with usage, stood on a pool of rippling light. She looked up, hands grasping at the legs, hoping they would help her. She struggled to breathe, to talk, to make sense.

"Breathe."

A hand, feminine in its delicate nature but marked with callouses and wear, a hand scarred in toiled labour. Cass grasped it. They linked as one. Same shaped hand, same fingers, same grasp. With effortless ease, she raised to stand before herself.

"Breathe." Her mirror image spoke. Cass shook her head to the impossibility.

"No. No." Eyes rippled, coldness caressed flaring cheeks.

"Your mind gives us vision. Here." It changed, phasing from herself to the father of Lilly. Stubble beard, kind eyes, lines etching over smooth skin. Merrick.

"Could be worse." She rubbed her eyes, clearing them, in vain hope of seeing clarity through fakery. The soldier, part of her militia unit, a cornerstone of her past. He stood close to her.

"Let your daughter go." Meaningless words fed into her mind from Merrick's lips.

"Coming from him, don't know me." Cass could have laughed, her chest welling with air, calmness ceased the shakes quivering in her stomach.

"She is more to us than she is to you." The man shimmered, rippling, like broken still water in a shallow pool.

"You're wrong." Cass let go of the hand holding her and kept her hands on the repeater. "She's my everything."

"She is what you call a Mystic. She is more to us than she is to you." More voices spoke. Figures, black and shapeless, merged around, circling her. Shaking arms held the repeater, the weapon's stock under her arm, supported by the elbow.

"I can help her, let her go, let me have my daughter." Cass shouted.

"No." She shivered at the reply. A hundred voices in defiance.

"She's my child. She's everything." Shapeless beings stood, unmoving.

"How can you protect her from them? When we can protect her forever." Merrick spoke.

"Protect her? From them?"

Images flooded, vast and insurmountable, in Cass's mind. Merrick disappeared, the shadows ringing her vanished. Stone statues stood, praised by the horned Faun, face cracked and peeling, as a thousand arms waved up, elevating the Faun and statues, to a metal sky wreathed in a thousand eyes.

Cass collapsed to metal floor and vomited.

"Let her go. Only we can stop them." Multitude of voices spoke, ringing inside her brain.

She spat, pushing herself to stand, and held the repeater in two steady hands. Her dry throat pained to speak and breathe. Eyeing Merrick, she shook her head.

"I will protect her by killing them all."

The repeater in steady hands raised to face Merrick. "Where is she?"

"See for yourself." Lilly's father pointed. A triangular door opened. Nature's coldness and snow light blitzed into the black, ringing room. Cass turned, standing alone. She headed for the opening.

Assaulting, icy winds pushed against her, dipping her head as she powered through nature's turbulent force. Lavender glazed her vision, mountain dew battered nostrils sucking in cold air with the tendrils of natural, unwashed stench. Head raised, two people stood on the precipice. A light more unnatural than what she encountered on the mountain, their destination.

Focused on two people in the haze, Cass knew one was Karwen. She was pulling a girl with her, who fought the prisoner every step of the way. Distinctive, unforgettable hair, thick as carpet. Cass's voice choked in her throat. Unable to shout, she powered her legs to run faster, fighting the onslaught of wind that proved her equal.

"Karwen, Lilly." Cass screamed, nearing the two. Karwen turned, holding Lilly, pulling her daughter against the convict. Lilly moved forward, hand outstretched to her mother. The convict yanked her back.

"Mom." Her daughter pleaded, her shout unrivalled by the wind, deafening nature's call. She fuelled herself in her daughter's plight.

"It's too late, Cass. Accept it." Karwen's strained shout punctuated the air. She moved forward, legs burning. Nearing her daughter. The repeater would be useless against the gale. She had to be quick.

The light was quicker.

A roving beam of light, impenetrable with the waking eye, obscured Lilly. Only her daughter's scream emitted through the vertical glow. Karwen's silhouette blurred beyond, her image a more twisted shadow. The light lanced towards the sky.

Karwen stood alone.

Cass collapsed. The repeater crashed to the ground, hands outstretched. Ten strides or fewer from Lilly, now missing. Gone. Taken. Cass unloaded her emotions against the approaching wind. The air snatching desperation. Screaming till her body failed her. Pulling at the burning lungs in her body, raked in a fire, she fought through the ache to rasp a hollow cry. She fell to the ground, shaking arms, ceased her hitting the rock face of the weathered mountainside.

Nothing but a trick, nothing but a cheap trick. Her throat drying. Lilly was taken somewhere. She could still be found.

She must be safe. Safe. Cass swam through turbulent thoughts raging in her mind. Nothing made sense. Everything pulled her below the surface of sanity. She felt like sinking.

"Accept it. It would be easier if you did." Karwen spoke.

Cass tilted her head up. The convict stood crowned in lavender, murky light. Smiling.

Clenching fists, she lunged for Karwen. Grappling with each other, she kicked, they both buckled.

Breaking free of the equal tussle, she swiped Karwen with her left leg, sending her opponent tumbling to the ground. She pounced, her nemesis blurred in frantic haste to regain a standing position.

Cass's fists ate Karwen's tough, angled face. Repeatedly, her fists hammered to relieve the pain of witnessing Lilly gone, failing her daughter again. But it was never enough.

Over and over again. Dull pain numbed Cass's knuckles. Warm liquid splashed her face underneath the broken features staring up at her.

"This is for my daughter, my daughter." She slathered, hammering Karwen's broken face, coated in blood and black hair streaking down, looking like grease of an oiled machine.

Karwen laughed. Pearly white teeth shone, a stark contrast to the blood mask ruptured with a maniacal laugh.

"This. This is it. Embracing yourself." The convict laughed. "Your daughter will fuel you."

Black eyes stared from the ruined face and she saw herself within the wild pools.

"We are winning. You are letting go, Cassidy." Her words stopped Cass. Not even the barrage of nature's breath could sway her steadiness.

"Fine. You win." She climbed off Karwen and dragged her by the scruff of the neck and walked to the precipice. The body dragged on the ground, boots scraping, Cass's rage fuelling her ability to carry her assailant. There was no resistance.

Swinging Karwen over the edge, feet dangled off the mountain. Muscles burned holding the convict in the vastness of air. She stared into the ruined, bloodied face. She knew it was not the real Karwen, a crude mockery like the two of Ninsar she saw.

"You're right. I need to let go." She brought Karwen's face to her own, close enough to see herself in reflective black eyes. "But before I let you go. Know this: I'm going to find my daughter. And kill every one of you."

Cass let go.

She watched as Karwen fell, silently, down the mountainside. Lost among the purple hazed rocky surface, her body grew smaller and smaller, until lost in the vastness of nature's expanse. Cass stumbled back, the wind dying down. Violet light faded to red. She looked up as horizons brisk yawn broke over the shimmering snow tops of Sabanese mountains.

Aches of numbed joints and tiredness drowned beating muscles. Burning limbs sagged and forgot, unwilling, to work. Head lowered, eyes closed. She welcomed a darkness of comfort, the wind her only companion.

Vincentas

Chapter XVI

Violent tremors broke Vincentas's solitary moment. Waves of sound, a cacophony of deafening noise, battered his skull. Gloved, rough hands slapped over ears, hoping in meagre vainness to defend weakened senses to the onslaught of over amplified motions. Aging eyes closing could do nothing to steady turbulent awakening.

Panicked shouts. Cries of desperation. Fear gurgled in maniacs' laughter. Their teasing hands, Mystics barbed fingers, stroked inner sanctum of worn, shielded mind, besieging decades of training to cower as a cradled newborn.

Easier to surrender. Arno's betrayal. Alleck's infiltration. Athgeric's capitulation. Riemkeler lost to madness and subterfuge. A winged species no biologist had seen before but found in myth and legends. Against these odds, there was no fighting. Against an ever-changing world, could resistance truly make a difference.

Vincentas sunk. Body melded into a softness that resembled flesh. A child like state of cowardice. Mystic was strong, they had always been too strong. He swam in self-made darkness, engulfed in eclipsing weight of reality.

Eyes snapped open. Limbs pushed him up, away from sinking, endless void of desperation. Racked sobs, uncontrolled wails continued to blur Vincentas's hearing. People stood, clustered together, a sea of lives catching him in a tidal wave of isolation and inescapable emotion.

These were no Mystics. They were the populace of Riemkeler, judging by their torn garb, dishevelled attire and an unclean smell. With steady hands, he drew a whistle to his lips and let out a long, shrill call.

Silence deafened him. Short, gasping, smoky breaths lingered before eyes lost in shrunken faces. If these are Mystics, let them see true colours. He retrieved the malachite sword and lanced the jade weapon into the air. Aching arm shook, knowing eyes traced up the sword of his profession.

"Inquisitorial Retinue." His voice should have been louder, but it could not fill the space he occupied. "To me!" Vincentas's throat expanded with the yell.

Rippling mutters broke through the ranks. Families huddled close together and pulled children away. Inaudible whispers and hushed prayers of absolution surrounded him. He searched for Fleur, Reticence, Violet, even Alleck. A flurry of movements parted the throng of people in haste. His shoulders softened.

"Combatant Fleur, reporting in." Fleur half saluted. She looked rough, but ready. Her composite longbow held in two blood-streaked hands. Her mask gone; the murder conviction laid bare for the world to see along with her victim. "W" it began with, but greased hair and matted locks obscured the full name.

"Look like hell, Fleur, but glad you're here." Vincentas nodded.

"Looking like a statue with that sword held high, never took you for a poser." Fleur folded her arms, cocking her head to the side.

"Fall in, Combatant." Laughed the Inquisitor and sheathed the sword.

Distant shouts, a singular brief scream and another group of people parted like lambs before a Bulkett. Towering head and shoulder above those around him, clothed in robes of the Interrogator, but smeared in grime and blood, Reticence stepped forward, holding his flail.

"Welcome, Interrogator." Vincentas made the Inquisitorial salute. Reticence remained silent.

"The three of us must work together, for the people of Riemkeler, to escape this. And bring justice to the Mystics." Increasing his voice as he spoke, so it could spread among the people. An Inquisitor's authority could sway the masses. He knew the tattooed "I" would stir fear as much as devotion. He needed every weapon.

"I can help, too." Vincentas's hairs prickled on the back of his neck. He turned, Alleck stood before him. The Entrant, head held high, calm with a tremor to his chin and smoky, frequent breaths.

"You stand there ready to help whom? Your kind, or the rest of the world?" Vincentas levelled his malachite sword. Alleck raised his head higher, quivering chin levelled at the approaching Inquisitor.

"Dargus Enote could be wrong. I do not know. There… could be some truths to it." The Entrant remained unflinching, even as the sword pressed into his chest. A gasp escaped him.

"No." a woman pleaded. Her shawl-covered, wrinkled face pleaded with Vincentas while her hands attempted to shield Alleck.

"You have not answered my question." The Inquisitor breathed. Aware of the uneven ground, first time he felt it since standing. It felt like he was sinking, like a swamp.

"I want to help everyone." The Entrant replied. Vincentas pressed the rapier closer. He knew the point would break the skin soon. Arno had been alongside him for decades. He could have been the reason so many Mystics were slain. Not the Inquisitor's rapier, but the secret Mystic. He gritted his teeth, knowing the sword would kill him, no matter what.

"Nobody can help everyone. Stop being naïve. Choose your side or be damned." Vincentas spat. Gloved, shaking hand gripped the obsidian hilt tighter.

"Inquisitor. Please, my son." The elderly woman left Alleck, wrapping her bandaged hands around the malachite sword. Wrinkled fingers circled the blade, red tears trickled down her frail arms, tracing down to her body where she lowered herself to kneel, shivering.

"Mother, no. Vincentas please, I want to help." The young boy knelt, hands raised.

The Inquisitor swiped his sword away in a green arc, while moving back. A stifled breeze flustered his greatcoat. Eyes opened wider. Faces appeared behind Alleck's shoulder. Mystic power, and he was using it.

"Enough, scourge." Vincentas growled.

"No, Vincentas look." Fleur pointed up, blocking his vision. "Be angry at him. The one putting thoughts in our heads. The real Mystic."

His squinting eyes followed Fleur's arm. A criss-cross of black beams, wide enough for an airship to descend through, spanned the dark skies above gigantic webs across the world. Swirling purples and bleeding reds blurred between darkened strands. Webs of black shadow, too high to climb and reach, kept them down on the soft ground, which shielded the eldritch sky above.

He looked around, people huddled in crowds. Looking up again, the caged horizon could be as wide as Riemkeler itself. He searched in vain to find anything to compare the size too, his gritted cursing aged eyes.

"Get a light going. Gaslamp. Torch. Burn clothing if you have to." Vincentas ordered. Sweat itched down his brow.

"Now, together." A voice split the sky. Vincentas crouched under the booming voice. A cacophony of squeals crashed around him.

"Father and son, scholar and student. Past and present. How quaint. Life leading us to a point of unilateral direction. Awaken Riemkeler, breathe blood of logic. Arise Azrankar." The deep voice thundered from the lightening racked sky contorting and bruising, shifting between morbid colour to a fresh, decaying ruin. Vincentas's free fist clenched, knowing only one who sounded like that.

"Your words are meaningless, Mystic." He shouted. "They are your last."

Daring not to blink, he snapped free his telescope, without breaking sight of the descension and trained the glass onto a form lowering into the pit. Levitating down, basking in vein-coloured tendrils acting like wings, the Faun he knew for twenty-eight plus years.

"Track that heretic." The Inquisitor lowered his telescope.

"You got it." Fleur's composite longbow whirred, as tension grew in taunt strings. She could meld into crowds, lost, a poacher concealed by the bodies of Riemkeler's shrieking populace.

"Nothing can stop us. You think malachite, steel, iron, wood will hurt me?" Arno's voice clawed into his mind. People shouted, arms pointing up at the descending Faun. It looked like fingers cradled him, like a newborn, red and careful.

"Malachite sword is the bane of the Mystic." Vincentas never broke his gaze on his old friend. He should have known him. Blinded to the truth for so many decades. He spat on the ground, hoping the taste of failure would leave his parched throat.

"Who taught you this? Who was there when you fought so many? When you fumbled in darkness, ignorant and blind, who saved you?" The Chanters assured voice, never breaking stoic tone, continued within Vincentas's mind. Not even the citizens of Riemkeler, panic-stricken and hysteric, could break through the Faun's voice. The Mystic's voice. It was not Arno, Arno was dead.

"You are trying to influence me, using your mind. It's clever, but it won't work." Vincentas stepped forward, heading to the location where Arno lowered. Despite the distance, he knew it was Arno, though a speck among swirling redness and shadowed webs allowing him to hang down into the opened maw of his deformed world.

"Should I not warn you, friend? Of your useless sensibilities? Your illogical fallacies built on manipulated lies? I extend my hand, old friend, this one, final time." Five shadows lanced across the sky, blotting reds and bruising purples, landing short of Vincentas, shrieking people dodged the shadows huddling as confused, crying children.

"Friend? You dare call me friend." He spat on one tendril of shadow, reaching from the suspended Faun above the pink, uneven ground.

"So be it." The shadow retreated at Arno's sighing words. "There will be no escape. Awakened must be fed. Knowledge must be returned. Ascension must come from offering." The thunderous voice rang in Vincentas's ears, forcing him to fall to aching, quivering knees on soft, squelching surface, that oozed as he landed on it. That sinking motion returned to trembling hands and numb joints.

"Arno talking crap again. Next time, I'll put one right through his Goathole mouth." Fleur spat, her approaching footfalls squelched as she neared.

Vincentas stood up, looking around the crater they inhabited. *No escape. Awakened must be fed. Ascension from offering.* The same undigested feelings in his gurgling stomach lay etched on people's faces. The survivors of this madness.

Raised mounds lay in the distance, too dark to make out in colour. He looked down. The ground was not pink as he first thought. Parts were yellow, a bile yellow. Red snakes wound together, not interlocking. They slithered side by side without a sound. Following one tendril, it disappeared in loops and twirls, snaking side by side with other worming, sleek veins.

Pointing the malachite sword down, the blade lowered, slipping into the ground, obscured by bulbous, sleek masses snaking one way and the other. A moan replied to the penetrating weapon. His flesh crinkled. Retrieving the blade, magenta, thick liquid pooled from the sword wound.

Awakened must be fed. An unwavering coldness coursed down Vincentas's back. Every hair, every muscle tensed. Red, pink and yellow tendrils snaked the ground, covering it. It was the ground. It was the pit.

"Not the time to say I have nineteen shafts for my bow, is it?" Fleur's voice mumbled through the tsunami of thoughts cascading through his mind.

A minor rumble convulsed throughout the unsteady, slimy ground. Others followed, each echoed by screams and cries of desperation. Chanting for salvation, to the Continental Church, old religions and redemption. Foul smelling odours punched Vincentas's nostrils, igniting throat to cough and splutter. Many retched beside him. Fleur held her own.

"The mounds are moving." He heard Fleur over one tremor, her hand grasping his greatcoat by the collar. His teeth gritted, stamping feet against the moist, slippery ground to find steadiness, a pitiful murmur responded to his aggressive footfalls. With a bubbling, liquid suction, like a drain being cleared, convulsions ceased. A taste of metallic blood clogged his gasping throat.

He followed Fleur's gaze. On the horizon, crested by eternal blackness, shadowed mounds moved. He shook his head, absence of light playing tricks on the mind, aging eyes, tired from insight in Riemkeler's reality causing him to see unlikely illusions.

"Ground. It's all..." The Inquisitor spoke, trying to form a rational thought.

Screams erupted. Vincentas could not turn quick enough.

He was stuck. Rooted. Held in place. Snapping his head down, a tendril wrapped around his leg. He swung the sword, hacking into the fleshy rope. A second strike. A third cut him free. Purple fluid boiled from the severed limb, pungent, sickening stench like an open cadaver expunged left the bleeding wound.

Kicking himself free, everyone around him clawed at the snaking vines around limbs, torsos and necks. They waved like dead trees in dusks horizon. Stuck. Rooted to one singular space, their howls a cacophony of captivity.

"Come on, we got to run." Fleur surged past, unleashing arrows at vaulting, bulbous veins intent on ensnaring.

Vincentas ran, not looking at the people needing his help, those he should help in their hour of need. Prayers and curses, pleas and damnation for the Inquisitor falling on deaf ears. A sinew lanced in front, hovering before an inevitable strike. An eye, lidless and wreathed in wanton, kept its gaze on him. Slipping on the ground, the eye snaked at him.

Metal flashed before his vision, pulsating red liquids burst from the eyeball, its ropey body falling dead. Reticence strode forward, flail in hand, standing tall. The silent Interrogator pointed toward Fleur, leaping and manoeuvring over the sleek, putrid ground.

"Let's go." He shouted, straining his voice over the boiling panic sweeping the pit.

Others broke free inside his fleeting periphery vision. They struggled to help loved ones. Sliding to a halt, a boy of eight lay waist deep in the ground. Watery eyes looking up. Shaking, small hands outstretched. Blonde hair alive in writhing feelers.

"He doesn't have a chance." The assuredness made him angry. The certainty caused Vincentas to turn to face the speaker: Reticence. It was his turn to be silent, nothing he could say. The first time the Interrogator spoke, and he had nothing to say to him.

In their own silence, they abandoned the child, submerged under the ground's writhing form. Footfalls squelched in quivering tendrils. Strained cries diminished. Shouts of order and help faded. The ending never came. It continued in Vincentas's mind, a cavern, a realm with no candlemark or light to show their passing. Only the rising feelers. Lunging palps of eagerness. Searching, snaking eyes haunting their journey.

Convulsing ground forced him to collapse, hitting the wet surface. Writhing tendrils ascended. He blinked, heart stopping momentarily. Faces grew within them, smiling. He slipped and fell, rolling down the slanted elevation.

Reticence clutched on top of the mound, white garb shrinking, Fleur's gasps and curses high-pitched compared to the rustling of the rising mound, as he continued tumbling downwards.

Grasping onto anything stable, digging fist into bloodied sinew of the earth, filing his nostrils with a sickening stench of decay, he clung on slowing down his descent. Fleur caught her own holding. He looked down. The mound had grown in rapid succession as the beginning lay in shadow.

Around him, the pit contained its own throbbing pink mounds, red hillocks and purple hills. Beating. Like a heartbeat. Only the mound murmured when he dug his hands in globs of meaty pulp filled the void of silence. His own heartbeat pounding in rapid succession, crushing his strained ears. No sound emitted below. The pleas had diminished. Even at this elevation, he should have heard their cries. Their woes. A quiver rippled through his spine. He fled, abandoned them.

"Fighting against an unmovable tide. What do you wish to succeed from this? Look around you, old friend. Alone. Forgotten. Hanging on to decrees of morality, not of your choosing." Arno's voice tangled within his mind. Vincentas clawed his way up the mound, drawing out moans and gasps with each fist ploughing through slippery tendrils. Not his own voice or gasps, but the earth he dug into.

"Your words mean nothing." Vincentas spat. Fleur at his side. A stench rivalled by an open cadaver flooded his world. Fingers sticky with red residue and pulping blood.

"Continue. Hold out. Keep fighting. It will allow the ascension of the Azrankar to be glorious." The Faun's voice oozed into his mind. Azrankar.

His legs vaulted up. The mound collapsed. Fleur's rough scream ringing his world. He remembered The Sojourn. Its descension, sinking to the world below. Arms grasped tighter onto fleshy, slippery tendrils, pulling himself closer to the fluidity of the solid matter.

"Hold on." He warned. Ichor slapped his cheeks and slithered into his mouth. Bile erupted leaving his heaving stomach. Vomit more pleasant than the faeces-smelling sticky-substance streaking across his face.

Sizzling of cooking meats replaced the rush of air whistling through his ears. The descension ceased. Untangling himself free of sinewed ground, felt like muscle, the muscle of a body, the body of…

He reached over for Fleur, pulling her up. Dark eyes bright and open, face lost in a sliding mask of ichor oozing down her features. Vincentas, aches ignited his face, stood up straight on trembling limbs and looked around, withdrawing his sword.

It looked like reeds.

Thin, lanky and moving. A grass that reached head height. Crimson against the shadowed eternal horizon. Cobras ready to strike. Holding things, making a bulbous lesion around their middle, or head.

Tendrils incomprehensible to Vincentas's counting stood before him. Eyes flickered between each one. A hand. A foot. An eight-year-old's torso. Eyes that were not watering stared back. Fleur's trembling hand grasped into his own.

"I never said this before. But thank you, Vin." Fleur's sincerity boiled his guts.

"Take that back, Combatant, we're going to get out of this." Spittle broke between sticking lips. Foam building, bowels on the verge of turning to water within quivering stomach.

A snap like a whip turned Vincentas to the right. Fleur screamed. He lunged forward in desperation; fingertips too short. His Combatant screamed.

Dragged across slippery ground, too quick to be caught. One, two, three. A fourth tendril. Fifth feeler. A snapping palp drowned Fleur. She kicked and squirmed. Her scream defiant as she struggled.

Fleur grew silent.

He could not move. No bonds or sinewy hands held him. He was not sinking into the depths of murky, flesh-made ground. His own will lost, a mind hanging precariously close to the precipice looking into the void and the void stared back. Vincentas blinked first.

Strengthened grasp forced him down. A heavy, unrivalled weight pushed down on his back. Hitting the meat smelling ground face-first, wind knocked out of him. Blurry eyes caught sight of shadows writhing, and two unblemished Faun hooves approached.

"See? Even her immoral one fell into ruin." Arno's voice haunted his hearing. Sounding closer than he had ever been. Strong, taloned grasp yanked his head back. A spluttering gasp escaped cold lungs. Something leathery encompassed his head, pressing thin hair onto sweating scalp with a warm, oozing residue.

It moved with a fluidity. Twisting and twirling, snaking and binding. A sea of red knots. One distinctive black boot lay on the ground. A pale foot hung limply, trapped in the throng of sinew and tightening muscle.

"She always gloated on pleasures. Now, she barely utters a simple thank you." Arno shielded The Inquisitors view. An inhuman scream tore from Vincentas. His vision shaking under the exploding emotion deep within his core.

"Now for you. My old friend." Vincentas yanked upwards. Hanging before Arno. The Chanter did not look like Arno anymore. He was twisted, different. A sickness had settled inside that split his skin. Black mucus leaked free of broken pores. Flies clotted greasy fur. A gagging stench surrounding his old friend. He was a corpse. He was a Mystic.

"Awaken from ignorance. And fill the Azrankar." Arno declared, placing a mangled hand over Vincentas's vision.

A baying mob shouted and heckled, tied on a stake mounted on a pyre…

No. He was there, staring at the naked, bound Mystic crying at her innocence.

"Vin. It's me. It's me." She pleaded. Sawn hair, bruised eyes, bloodied knees. "Vin, I'm your wife."

The burning torch crackled in his hands.

"It must be done. You are an Entrant. Do this to become the Inquisitor." He heard the Chanter's voice. A voice he trusted for years during his initiation into the Inquisitorial Order.

Arno stood smoking thurible in hands.

He had seen the evidence. The idols. The books. Had seen her mysterious works. The illusions.

The torch left his hand. Pyre caught alight, passing its dancing flames one stacked log to another.

She screamed. The woman he loved. The woman convicted of Mysticism.

Her cries faded through the roar of flames.

Leaping reds, dancing yellows blurred in watered eyes. It was the smoke. The acrid, choking smoke that caused his eyes to water, wetting his cheeks with acidic doubt.

"All an illusion. All lead here. All our Mystics doing." Arno's hand slid back from his waking, blurred eyes.

"Never a Mystic. Innocent to the end. A death needed for your life in Inquisitorial practice. To help us." The Faun's word slipped into his mind, pulling back the curtain of lies he lived behind. Arno was there, weaving fate for decades.

The ground parted, a maw of tendrils separating. Vincentas stared into living blackness and something incomprehensible stared back.

He screamed into eternity, and the voice of the world awakened.

Acknowledgements

Thank you to a supportive and loving family, who allowed fantasy, science fiction and horror to be part of their son's life, I am eternally grateful.

To the Brothers-in-Books, who started reading and sharing ideas in a dark, decrepit pub in 2004. You kept the spark alive when the embers were nearly snuffed out, thank you Joe and Craig.

To editors and beta-readers, proofreaders and the gears behind the machine which allowed this project to run.

To Alex, who visualised the front cover.

To Alice, to help create and manifest a man's dreams into digital reality and for going beyond the pale on so many occasions.

And, to you, avid reader. You are about to partake on a journey into a world and meet characters that were hard to share and even harder to put into form, but they are here at long last and the author has awoken to share his dream with you. Thank you, I do genuinely mean that.

www.ingramcontent.com/pod-product-compliance
Lightning Source LLC
La Vergne TN
LVHW091137150826
845672LV00005B/958

* 9 7 8 1 7 3 9 1 5 5 7 4 2 *